Robert Diemer '81

THE WIDOW'S SON

BY

ROBERT DIEMER

Publisher: Golden Gate Publishing
www.GoldenGatePublish.com

Cover Design: Ramon Abad
Author Photograph: Siovonne Smith Diemer

For information regarding permission, write to:
Golden Gate Publishing, Attention: Permissions Department,
P.O. Box 27478, San Francisco, CA 94127 U.S.A.

Golden Gate Publishing authors are available for select speaking events. To contact us please email GoldenGatePublishing@gmail.com.

Printed in the U.S.A.

ISBN 978-0-9856631-0-0
Library of Congress Control Number: 2012941145

For Siovonne and Jean-Pierre

And in memory of the Honorable Marv

Acknowledgment:

The phrase "Poor Innocent Victim" is by Nigerian novelist Chinua Achebe

PROLOGUE

Mario Perez, M.D., Chief of Staff at the Pohnpei Island Hospital, heaved open the heavy door to the windowless morgue. The room - big enough for two only if you stacked the bodies - was colder than the economy cabin on an Air Mike flight, just enough to keep remains from going, which corpses tend to do quickly within a few hundred miles of the equator. Micronesian custom is to bury within a day of death, a tradition, I suspect, stemming from a lack of embalming fluid, a substance apparently unknown in the islands between Guam and Hawaii.

Mario shivered the door shut behind me. The body lay beneath a sheet on a gurney on one side of the narrow room. The sheet wasn't long enough to cover the feet, which were not typically Micronesian. Locals' feet tend to be cut and scarred, spread wide from a lifetime of wearing zoris. These feet were clean and unmarked, as if he had worn shoes for years. A scarlet John Doe toe tag, curled by the humidity, dangled from the right foot.

"John Doe Number One?" I asked.

"First unidentified body this year. First in five years as a matter of fact."

"I know who he is Mario. He's a client."

"You mean a former client. Not only is he dead, he's as dead as the likelihood of another Marcos presidency."

A piece of paper was wedged between the first two toes.

I pulled it gingerly, just enough to see a bench warrant, signed by Justice Maximinus T. Coleman.

Mario pulled back the sheet and folded it neatly at the neck to reveal the familiar face, handsome, even in repose. It was Jangle Elwell, my client, my adversary. I lifted the sheet and checked Jangle's right hand, the middle and ring fingers deformed just like I remembered.

"One possible cause of death is here on this side." Doctor Perez pulled the gurney from the wall and pointed to the left side of Jangle's head. The glossy, black hair above the ear was matted with dried blood, and the skull beneath was indented.

Bile began to rise in my belly. I spoke to stem the tide. "Someone smashed in his skull."

"When I cleaned the wound I found bits of heavy plastic casing." Mario pushed the gurney back to the wall, turned to a cabinet and pulled a ziplock evidence bag from a drawer. Inside were bits and hunks of gray black plastic, along with clumps of hair and clotted blood. "Looks like someone bashed him with some sort of electrical equipment, like a keyboard, maybe a tape deck."

"He was struck with a blunt instrument."

"Say, can I use that in my post-mortem?"

"The cause of death looks straightforward to me." I turned to grab the door and sprint for the men's room.

"Sorry, counsel. There's more. We have to consider lead poisoning, too."

"I don't get it."

"How about acute and traumatically induced lead poisoning?"

Perez doubled the sheet back again. A couple of bullet wounds, like bleeding ulcers, punctured Jangle's rib cage on the left side. Beneath the rib cage on the right side was another wound the size of a guava. My stomach started to flip like a Russian gymnast.

"This big one on the right is a through-and-through. There's an exit wound about this size on John Doe's back." Mario made a ring with his thumb and finger. "But I might be able to fish out slugs to match the wounds on the left. There's also a scoring flesh wound here on the right torso, as if John Doe was turning as the assailant, or assailants fired."

"More than one person?"

"More than one weapon. The through-and-through was probably from a higher caliber weapon, judging by the exit wound. I don't think the same weapon caused the smaller wounds. It could have been two people firing, or one person with a different gun in each hand."

"So two potential causes of death," I said. "The head wound and these."

"These are just the obvious ones. I also drew a blood sample and sent it to a crime lab in Honolulu on today's flight. I expect to find alcohol, but I requested a full range of tests. I'm actually interested in what else turns up, maybe methamphetamine."

"*Shabu?* Why test for that?"

"The reporting police officer suggested it. He said John Doe was a well-known drug smuggler."

"All I ever heard about was marijuana."

"The lab will test for cannabis, too. Full range of tests as I said."

"So rule out cannabis poisoning, that still leaves three possible causes of death. Jesus. This guy was like Rasputin."

"Closer than you think, Drake. Public Safety fished the body out of the Green River near Daosokele. His clothes were soaking wet, and when I turned him on the gurney to examine the exit wound he discharged at least a liter of brackish water. I suspect his lungs still retain a good deal of water."

"So he might have drowned?"

"If John Doe expired before hitting the drink there wouldn't be that much water in his lungs."

"Got a time of death yet?"

"Sometime before four a.m. We had a slack tide last night. Any later than four and the body would be swept right out to the reef."

"Have you started a post-mortem?"

"Just notes for a preliminary, and it's not because people like you keep interrupting me. State law, you know, requires us to obtain permission to autopsy from the next of kin."

"And when will you get the family's okay?"

"We don't know who he is. John Doe, remember?"

"Catch 22, huh. Well I can ID him."

"So did my other visitors. You're not a relative; you don't count."

"No family yet?"

"None. No sobbing mothers, silent fathers, weeping sisters, angry brothers. That's why he's still a John Doe."

"So no girlfriends or drinking buddies either."

"No one like that. You say you knew him, Drake. Did John Doe have any enemies?"

"More than the average bear." I paused for a moment, then asked. "Say Mario, would you let me see your post-mortem report when you send it to Public Safety?"

4

"That's illegal counselor."

"Maybe. Maybe not if I saw a draft of your report."

"I'm shocked, shocked, that you would suggest such a thing. But were someone to assist me to identify the next of kin of a John Doe." Mario let the thought trail off, then said, "What do you know about him?"

"As I said, he's a client."

"A former client," said Mario.

"Former client, then. I knew him mostly by reputation when I lived on Kosrae, though I talked with him once or twice. I think his parents still live there. His mother is supposedly from Chuuk."

"Half-half, huh. Can you contact the family?"

"I'll make a few calls. I still have local friends on Kosrae."

"That's more than you can say here." Mario smiled. "DSI said that John Doe's name is 'Ewell.' That doesn't sound Kosraen to me."

"It's 'Elwell.' The prosecutor misspelled the name on the application for the arrest warrant."

"Jangle Elwell? Of the Taro Patch Kids? I've sewn up a few of their victims. I take it he was a client in a criminal case?"

"Bank robbery."

"Bank robbery in Micronesia? I could see it in Manila, but not here. What happened? Did the thieves fight it out over the loot?"

"I just defend them, Mario. I don't solve them."

"Yeah? But sometimes you have to solve them in order to defend them."

5

CHAPTER ONE

"*H*aole. Oh *haole*."

The voice was young, loud, local, and very drunk. My eyes snapped open at the shout, but I wasn't sure if it was a nightmare until a second voice joined the first.

"Hey *haole*. Come on, white boy. Wake up."

The neighborhood dogs began a ruckus of howls, warning of trespassers. I heard my dog, Buster, barking with the rest. Aroused by the canine chorus, a rooster crowed.

"*Haole*. Come out your place."

I rolled from the sweaty spot on the sheets and glanced at the pale green glow of my wristwatch on the nightstand. 2:40 a.m. Damn. Another night's sleep lost to a drive-by shouting. I'd had a hard enough time sleeping since the trade winds died. Now this, the second drive-by in a week.

"Hey *haole*. We want to talk to you."

Yeah, but I ain't listening, I thought while waiting for the other *zori* to drop. A drive-by shouting rarely stopped at just that. Unless a police patrol happened by, the disturbance was likely to escalate. The dogs continued to bark, if anything louder than at first. Another rooster answered the first, adding to the din.

"Oh *haole*."

Rocks would be next, bouncing off the corrugated steel roof, banging on the front door, nicking the window screens. Good thing the rat screens were up. I didn't want to sweep up broken glass while barefoot, and finding custom-fit replacement louvers is a fool's errand.

The first stone banged heavily on the roof, bounced once, and rattled off the eaves. Rocks on the roof; that's a tested method to send outsiders an ancient island message – Leave! You are not welcome here! Two more bangs clapped in quick succession. The intruders were finding their range.

All they want to do is wake me, I thought. Two more stones hit the roof. None were thrown at the windows, none yet. But I know from painful experience how accurate locals can be with their throws. Childhoods spent trying to knock guavas from trees have honed the locals' aim. If they wanted to shatter a glass louver they certainly could. But what if they wanted more?

I rolled from bed and groped beneath the frame for the heavy dive flashlight, good for throwing a tight beam fifty yards, better as a club in a melee in close quarters. I grabbed the handle and snapped the elastic strap around my wrist, then held the lamp to a pillow to test the batteries. Good. Plenty of juice. An unexpected, high-watt light in the face can be as effective as an uppercut. But the last thing I wanted to do was mix it up with a couple of locals, drunk and half my age. Those guys don't hold back punches. Just in case, I reached further beneath the bed frame and grasped the hilt of the machete I stashed next to the flashlight. Only if they get inside the house, I reminded myself.

I snuck from the bedroom, head down, avoiding the windows, flashlight in one hand, machete in the other. I padded first to the kitchen to slide the dead bolt from the back door, leaving only the lock on the door handle in place. If necessary, I could slip out the back door and run to hide in the jungle. Then to keep the upper hand with surprise, I crept into the front room and quietly unlatched the lock to the too-thin plywood front door. If the stone throwers were so bold, or so drunk, to come to the door, they wouldn't expect it to be unlocked. I tiptoed to a window and crouched to one side.

The dogs continued to howl, sometimes louder, but so far from the same spot. That was good. If the sound from the dogs moved, it meant my visitors were moving, too. From the barking it seemed the stone tossers were still on the road. I turned a corner of a window shade and peaked out. The thin glow of a neighbor's kerosene lamp outlined two figures standing behind a shiny black pickup truck sixty feet from the house. The driver's door was ajar; the engine growled low in neutral, the twin taillights glowed smoky red like a demon's eyes. I recognized neither the truck, obviously new to the island, nor the stone throwers, though I had a pretty good idea of who sent them. One figure bent to pry up another stone from the chip seal at the edge of the road; the other took a long pull from a bottle. Hot stuff. They were drunk all right.

As I awaited the next stone, a beam of light suddenly illuminated the rock throwers at the rear of the truck. Sotaro Fritz, my neighbor, was awake. The trespassers must have been really loud, for Sotaro is blessed with the sleep of the dead. He shouted to the stone-tossers in Chuukese. An avalanche of angry words came in reply, "rrr's" trilling, even as the driver's door slammed shut and the rock throwers climbed onto the deck of the truck. I was about to step outside myself, now that I had an ally; ready to confront those who disturbed another night's sleep, those who awoke my neighbor and friend, whose only sin

8

was to live next door to an American. I wondered if Sotaro thought himself in danger.

The dogs – shorthaired curs and mangy three-legged cripples – emboldened by Sotaro's presence howled louder and crept paces closer to the truck. A stone whipped from the deck caught a canine flank, eliciting a pained yelp and scattering for a moment the would-be wolfpack. But the dogs soon closed ranks, bolder in each other's growls.

The truck engine rumbled louder.

"Hey *haole*," a voice in English was flung from the deck followed by a stone smacking the front door dead center. "This time we stone your place. Next time we stone you."

I peeked out the window again. The two locals had scrambled to stand on the deck of the truck, gesturing with the ring and middle fingers held together, gang sign of the Taro Patch Kids. Then the engine roared and the back tires spewed gravel as the truck accelerated from a standing start and fishtailed down the road. The dogs gave chase for a moment, spreading their alarm to other dogs nearby.

Inside the house, I slumped against the wall, suddenly aware of how tired I was. I walked to the bedroom and slipped the machete back beneath the bed. I grabbed a towel and wrapped it around my waist as a makeshift *lava-lava*, walked to the front door and slid into my *zoris*."

Sotaro was dressed in the same fashion, Micronesia nocturne, a beach towel wrapped around his beer tumor gut, dive flashlight in hand.

"Drake," he said as I approached. "I'm really sorry about that."

It was just like Sotaro to apologize for something over which he had no control. Sotaro apologized if it rained for too many days straight, or if the PM&O freighter was late, or if I had little luck fishing. I was actually a little tired of Sotaro's apologies.

"I should say sorry to you, Sotaro." I slipped into the pace and precise enunciation of Special English, like the radio announcers on Voice of America. "I think maybe if I did not live next door then you would get more sleep."

"No, Drake. What those boys are doing is not local style. I am sorry because those boys are rude."

"Do you know any of them?"

"No. But I think maybe that one who shouted at me is from Faichuuk, island of hooligans and rascals. Do you know why they came to our place?"

"I don't know, Sotaro. Maybe they just wanted to scare me."

"Why does anyone want to scare the Defender?"

"I'm not the Defender any more."

We stood side-by-side for a moment, glancing up the road, saying nothing. The night chorus of insects and toads, muffled by the drive-by, resumed. Sotaro hissed at the dogs – yipping playfully, tails erect – as they returned from their brief pursuit. I slapped at a mosquito.

"Do you know who did that?"

"No." I lied. I knew damn well that Jangle Elwell had sent his Taro Patch Kids, even if I didn't know the individuals. But I didn't want to worry Sotaro, a good neighbor who helped with some of my ham-handed home improvement schemes; who always shared whatever he had – fresh fish, bananas, breadfruit. Sotaro didn't deserve to get winged by a ricochet of anger directed at me.

"Did you call the police?" Sotaro has no telephone. He and his family frequently use mine.

"I'll report it in the morning." That too was a lie. I know that calling Pohnpei Public Safety about the Taro Patch Kids is not productive. There's a leak in that office the size of Keripohi Falls.

"Do you think they will come back?"

"Not tonight. But I'll stay up for a while just to be sure."

"Drake. Go have a rest. Those boys are finish."

"Finnish? You said they were Chuukese, not Scandinavian."

"That one who shouted at me is from Chuuk." Sotaro missed the pun. "I don't know about the others."

Sotaro shook his head and walked back to his door. He stopped and looked back. "That one makes me very angry. He knows that is not our way. This is Micronesia, not 'West Side Story.'"

Sotaro turned and hissed to scatter the dogs from his doorstep. The rooster, finding no one else would play, clucked into silence.

"Hey, Sotaro. Thanks for scaring those guys off."

"Scare? I wish I knew their fathers. That would scare them. Have a nice sleep, Drake."

Sotaro turned and walked inside. In a moment I heard voices, Sotaro's wife and a couple of children, then silence. I considered crawling back into bed myself, but figured it would be a while before jangling nerves let me. I walked instead between our houses to the *nahs*, the cookshed I share with Sotaro's family. I shined the flashlight up beneath the steeply pitched eaves to find the box of mosquito coils and a cigarette lighter tucked between the roof beam and the thatch. I opened the box and extracted two green coils, nesting like tree snakes on a freighter bound for Guam. I pulled the coils apart and set one on the metal stand, fingers still twitching with adrenaline, then held the lighter to the end until a wisp of smoke appeared. I set the coil on the ground

11

beneath the *nahs*, and returned the mosquito coils and lighter to their place. I stepped from beneath the thatch to stretch, noticing the few constellations visible between gathering clouds. Gemini had just arisen in the northeast. A Polynesian man from Porakiet Village once told me that in the South Pacific, too, Castor and Pollux are twins, named "Hui Tarara." Finally, I returned to the *nahs* to sit on the split bamboo platform, within the ring of noxious, comforting smoke. Before long, I heard the noxious, comforting sound of Sotaro snoring. At least someone would sleep tonight.

CHAPTER TWO

"K*aselehlia*, sleepy eyes." Jasmina was already at her desk when I arrived at the office, her gold-plated smile as warm as a Kosrae sunrise. "Were you out night-crawling? Or is it too much *sakau*?"

"No, Jazz. I had some unwelcome visitors last night."

I was used to Jasmina's morning cross-examinations any time she got to the office before me. Rarely pleasant were mornings that followed visits to a *sakau* bar, or a real tavern, or those nights out bottom fishing with handlines and a bottle of vodka to keep warm. This was not one of those mornings. Troubled thoughts kept me up the rest of the night, not all of them due to my visitors. But I had reached a sort-of island Zen state sitting cross-legged in the curl of smoke from the mosquito coil, and had stayed up long enough to watch a late moonrise, the half-orb backlighting the billowing clouds as if in a Rembrandt painting.

Jasmina's morning smile pushed her cheekbones higher than usual. She looked terrific; and I knew I did not. Lack of sleep left my eyes bloodshot, and I'm sure dark bags drooped beneath them like the udders of a boonie dog. I held my head in not-so-mock agony – it throbbed in anticipation of caffeine – and shuffled past Jasmina's desk.

I switched on the ancient air-conditioner in the small back office. It sounded like an overloaded Ting Hong fish flight struggling airborne from the airport on Taketik. By noon the coils of the air-conditioner would be encrusted with rime and I would have to turn the damn thing off and let the ice melt into a bucket.

"I did not know when you come in today so I did not 'on' the air-conditioner." Jasmina, like many locals, uses "off" and "on" as verbs.

"Did you at least make some coffee?" I called over the freon roar.

Jasmina slipped into the back office holding yesterday's mail and a few other papers against her chest. She smiled as she placed the papers on my desk. "Sorry, Drake. We have no coffee for one week now."

"Oh, I know. Don't forget we didn't buy office supplies last time in order to pay you."

"I'm always smiling for that."

I reached for my wallet and pulled out a five-dollar bill soiled with the grime of a thousand island hands. "Can you run downstairs and get me an espresso? And get something for yourself, too."

"Sorry, Boss. You know there's no expresso on Pohnpei."

"How about a caffé latté, then?"

"The only lattes in Micronesia are the latte stones on Guam. How about a nice hot coffee with creamer, the way you like it."

"And two sugars to make it sweet, please, just like you."

Jasmina ignored the compliment, pivoted on the heel of her *zori*, and left the office, her hips swinging beneath her muumuu. I sighed. Jasmina is a damn good secretary, but without a paying case and soon, I didn't know how long I could hold onto her.

I riffled through the mail, flyers and catalogs mostly, ship mail. A PM&O freighter had berthed earlier in the week, meaning bulk mail and fresh produce, if potatoes, cabbages, and onions loaded on the West

Coast three weeks ago could be considered fresh. No letters, though. No checks, but then no bills either.

Office supplies and coffee lay heavy on my mind, as did Jasmina's salary and rent and license fees and the other costs of keeping the office open. Without a paying case and soon, I would have to give up all this: linoleum peeling dusty floors and gecko eggs in jammed desk drawers, sagging bookshelves crammed with hopelessly outdated casebooks, their guts eaten out by termites, spider nests in file cabinets, even the view out the back window to somebody's breadfruit tree, framed by lengths of rebar sticking up from the roof next door. I'd have to take down my shingle, remove the firm name "Frost & Burnham" from the front door. And unless I married a local (perish the thought), I'd have to move back stateside and mine misery as a metal-desk lawyer at an insurance defense firm, or a p.i. mill, or worse, a collections practice. An uncertain future hung in the balance, and I didn't have a decent case to level the scales.

I had inherited the practice from the late, great Algonquin H. Frost, Attorney at Law, Proctor in Admiralty, and Barrister in Chancery. Al was that rarest of birds, an attorney who took nothing but his clients and their troubles very seriously.

Al Frost was the one who brought me to the islands in the first place. In one of his last official acts as Chief Public Defender, Al hired me as staff attorney for the Kosrae office, an act for which I remained consistently ambiguous – affectionate one day, aggravated the next – for most of my stint on that peaceful island. Three years later, Al hired me again, after the new Chief Public Defender, under pressure from the President's office, managed to get me fired from my cushy Kosrae posting as "insubordinate," a resume enhancer I note with some pride.

15

Soon enough, I hopped west from Kosrae to Pohnpei, where my name joined Al's on the office door and letterhead. Shortly after we became law partners, though, I realized what Frost had been denying himself for months. Al was dying. Convinced finally that stateside medicine might in the end do better than local doctors, Al sold me his half of the partnership for the price of a round trip ticket to the States. He never used the return ticket, passing within two weeks of his homecoming.

When I replaced my business cards for Al's on Jasmina's desk, I knew I had purchased half of a less-than-thriving practice. Frost's philosophy was to champion any person beset by grasping merchants, avaricious banks, or meddlesome government. The philosophy is fine in theory, in heartfelt discussions over beers, in Friday afternoon bull sessions, but it is a philosophy that I have found increasingly difficult to practice.

Frost & Burnham takes on cases of which I have scant hope of ever collecting a decent fee. We defend the guy who had defaulted on the $200 balance on his bank loan, or who lost his job and can't pay a penny on his open accounts with the big merchants on island. Inevitably, these poor suckers came to us only after a default judgment has been entered against them, unwilling or unable to read the legal papers served on them months earlier. We represent Filipino workers injured on construction sites, or who face deportation because their boss – who has a friend at Immigration – decides he can't afford their wages. Just a few months back, I finished up a suit against Ting Hong Oceanic Enterprises, what Al used to call "Ting Hong Satanic Enterprises." We had filed suit for better working conditions on behalf of a dozen workers from Indonesia who cleaned fish guts all day. The workers won an injunction and the princely total of $1,000 to be split evenly twelve ways.

16

For a Filipina wrongfully terminated from her bookkeeping job at a hotel, Frost & Burnham collected the grand sum of $551.27 in back pay, which we dutifully posted off to the Philippines with scant hope of receiving anything more than our $100 retainer, and perhaps her prayers for time off in purgatory.

Frost & Burnham subscribes to the cab rank rule, turning down no reasonable case, and very few unreasonable ones. We'll travel, too, and take land tenure cases on Kosrae and collection defenses on Chuuk. On principle, Frost & Burnham refuses case assignments from banks or the American, Japanese or Hong Kong exporters seeking to collect from locals. Al reasoned that companies with money could always hire lawyers; the folks who didn't have money had us.

As a result, Frost & Burnham has an enormous store of goodwill, but non-existent receivables. Fresh fish and produce is frequently a fee, so at least I won't starve. The form of payment often depends on the home island of the client: branches of betel nut from Yap, baskets of *sakau* brought by Pohnpeians, and from Kosrae, fresh tangerines and limes. At times I imagine myself countering war stories at a law school reunion by numbering the cases where I've gotten fresh spiny lobster for a fee. Al swore he had a Marshallese client who proposed to pay him with the names and addresses of graduates of Helicopter U., the local school of love on Arno Atoll.

So far as I could see, two items would make or break the bottom line. First was the Compact, what the locals call the treaty by which the United States funds most of the government functions here. Its twenty-year run is nearly finished, and the steady supply of dollars that a few years back made private practice in the islands potentially lucrative, is now drying up. A few American lawyers have already folded their tents and moved west to Palau, carpetbaggers chasing the lucre of a more-recently signed treaty. But the biggest difference in the firm's fortunes is the absence of one Algonquin H. Frost. When Al departed, the quality of the firm's professional work did not suffer, if I may say so myself. Al was famous for recycling his briefs; 'old wine into new bottles,' he called it. But Frost was a rainmaker extraordinaire. He had a flair for the dramatic gesture that brought out business like a full moon draws land crabs from their boltholes. Whenever he'd wrung out a verdict on behalf of some poor soul, Al would run up a makeshift Jolly Roger from the flagstaff in front of the office.

In local eyes, Algonquin H. Frost was the image of success. He sported the high round belly of the long-term ex-pat, what they call in French Polynesia the "colonial egg," in Al's case a legacy of Budweiser and feasting, the equivalent of a local's beer tumor gut. He knew so many people - chiefs and commoners, ex-pats and locals - in so many places, that referrals walked in the door seemingly daily. Now those connections were drying up like the Compact funds, or an island stream in an El Niño drought.

Unfortunately, I inherited Al's antiquated bookkeeping methods, and have no experience in that regard myself. Jasmina keeps the firm's books - tallying strings of reef fish and coconuts against dollars and cents of receivables - but does so by default, not training. I was a public defender back in the States, and I still have the civil servant's focus on the task rather than the time to complete it. I know how stateside lawyers keep track of time, but the idea of parsing the workday into six-minute intervals, of constantly referring to the clock, is alien to me. Al was no help. He sent one-line bills, "For services rendered," when he sent bills at all. Frost figured since island society is built on obligation, the correct fee for the task would eventually be tendered. But we live in the twentieth century and fees for business licenses must be paid quarterly. Rent for the two-room suite in the Namiki Building – known once, due to the number of lawyer's offices in the fat, early Compact days, as the "Den of Thieves" – is a bargain, but it isn't free. I suppose I could barter legal services for rent, should my landlord be sued, or in need of a contract or lease. I keep a secretary, but can afford to hire an investigator only case-by-case. Jasmina deserves more than I can pay. As for swapping services for salary, well, Jasmina has no legal problems to speak of, and I represent members of her extended family out of fidelity, not on faint hope of payment. For the past few months, I've signed to Jasmina a bigger paycheck than I cut for myself.

Jasmina returned with my coffee and an institutional sized can of cheese balls for herself. "Don't forget. Today is Thursday. Arraignment day at the State Court."

Arraignment day. Maybe I could hook a conflict case assignment, one of the few ways left to find steady, paying work. Nearly every criminal case is brought in the State Court, and conflicts of interest arise regularly, no surprise on a small island where everyone seems to be related. But with the Compact winding down, the bean counters at the State government watch every penny, and pour over conflict case statements as if picking nits from the scalp of an Outer Islands schoolboy. Conflict cases pay a flat rate of twenty-five dollars per hour, thirty-five for time in court. But payment is not authorized until the case is completed, by conviction, plea-bargain, or that blessed word, acquittal. Even then the bean counters take their sweet time in cutting a check. Last year, the conflict case budget ran dry early. On one case, I had to wait payment for five months, until the start of the next fiscal year.

All told, I'm glad to get conflict case assignments. It's one of the few places that I can still keep my hand in criminal defense. Hardly any defendants approach the private bar for representation, mostly those ex-pats who have run afoul of the law on drinking permits. Locals all go to the Public Defender offices, where legal help is free, as required by the constitution. The conflict case rate is set low, mostly to scare off ex-pat lawyers and encourage local trial counselors. (I can't remember the last time a rich collections lawyer like Dick Harkness, shill for the banks and Telecom, ever took on a criminal case conflict assignment.) I figure that with enough conflict cases, I might pay rent, utilities, and Jasmina's salary. Paying myself would have to wait for the big payoff, a personal injury case against a deep pocket defendant with a lock on liability. Al used to say that cases like that walk in the door of a thriving stateside practice maybe three times a year. In three years at Frost & Burnham, I had yet to catch a whiff of one.

I had time enough to finish my coffee before heading to the State Court for the arraignment calendar. I'm on good terms with Roberta Ely, the excellent staff attorney for the Pohnpei Public Defender office, and I can count on her for a recommendation. But getting conflict cases means getting face time. I had to get on over and press the flesh, a calling at which my late partner excelled effortlessly, but which leaves my mouth dry.

Once more before leaving I glanced about the tiny, cluttered office. Wedging up case books on the shelves were handicrafts taken as fees, a bust carved from rust red mangrove wood, a stone taro pounder, a couple of betel nut baskets. I also had up a few family photos, and a happy picture with Al and a couple of local friends after a successful fishing expedition. When I inherited the practice, I took down Frost's

20

shingle and law school diploma, which Al had neglected to pack, thinking perhaps of his return ticket. Frost's nonagenarian mother appreciated my offer to ship back more of Al's personal effects, but told me to give away the rest, that his worldly goods would be of more use in the islands than they would be back home.

And I kept Frost's framed portrait of Clarence Darrow. Al used to talk to the picture when preparing for trial, or sometimes, late at night after finishing a bottle of bourbon; deep discussions, less about tactics or strategy than jurisprudence and philosophy. Jasmina always noticed it. Even today, if I'm lost in thought, she'll ask if I'm "talking to Clarence." I kidded my late partner about his late night conversations, but then Frost always fumed about a framed portrait on the shelf behind my desk, Jack Lord, as Steve McGarrett.

"How can you, a public defender, have hanging on your office wall a picture of a cop?"

"Give me a break," I'd reply. "If not for 'Hawaii 5-0' neither of us would even be here."

CHAPTER THREE

At ten minutes to ten I was at the State Courthouse, yellow legal pad in hand, a scavenged ballpoint pen in the pocket of my Aloha shirt, and the mug of instant joe burning in my belly. Roberta Ely waved as I entered the building. She stood in the lobby with the Public Defender office investigator, Utticus Uziah, and a handful of young locals, probably her clients. If all those guys were charged together, I might get a shot at a conflict assignment. Even with an assignment, I didn't have a snowball's chance in a Pohnpei power outage of cutting myself a bigger check than I did Jasmina.

I nodded to Kazuo Olopai, already seated at the prosecutor's table, when I walked into the courtroom. Olopai is a Trust Territory holdover, a rotund, late middle-aged trial counselor from a village in Kitti, on the far side of the island. Kazuo is also a Baptist minister who stayed true to his ministry even though his American pastor, the Reverend Melchisedech Caldwasser, had been chased from the island last year on allegations of buggery.

Kazuo has poor eyesight. His Coke bottle eyeglasses make his eyeballs look huge, as if the orbs physically filled the space behind the lenses. Hence I nicknamed Olopai for the big-eye tuna, "Skipjack," a moniker he endures with befuddled grace. I've tried several cases against Kazuo, and I have more than a grudging respect for his ability. I also admire his patience. A perennial candidate for the bench, Olopai may never become a judge, not as long as certain Americans hold the posts.

I sat behind Kazuo and leaned on the bar. He turned and looked back, typical for a local, nervous to have anyone directly behind him.

"*Kaselehlia*, Drake Burnham, good morning. You are very handsome today."

"No, Mr. Prosecutor. I am not, because I do not sleep enough. You though, are very handsome. Is that a new shirt?"

"*Menlau*, Drake. Thank you. It is a new shirt, from Hawaii."

"I don't know how you can afford such fine garb on a prosecutor's salary."

"I told you. My nephew works at a men's store at the Ala Moana Shopping Center in Honolulu."

"Kazuo, I have to ask. When will the Pohnpei prosecutors get serious about the growing gang problem on-island?"

"This is not 'West Side Story.' We have no gangs on Pohnpei."

"What about the Taro Patch Kids?"

"That is a social club."

"Yeah? So are the Hell's Angels."

"Are those boys making you any trouble?"

"A few came by my place last night and woke me up."

"What did they do?"

"Just shouted and threw some stones on my roof."

"Sound like a prank. Did you report it?"

"I'm reporting it now."

"Drake, you know you have to go through proper channels. You have to report anything like this to Public Safety."

"It isn't worth calling the police, Kazuo. Not for something insignificant. If the police had to investigate every time some locals threw rocks on a *menwhi's* roof, they wouldn't have time for coffee and donuts or afternoon naps at Palikir."

"Every offense must be reported.' That's what our Governor says."

"One problem with reporting is you have a serious leak at Public Safety, one that goes right back to the Taro Patch. The last time I tattled on the Taro Patch Kids, a couple of them came to my place and ripped up the report right in front of me."

"That's destruction of government property."

"Kazuo, I haven't had a decent night's sleep in a month. You have to do something about the Taro Patch Kids ... or ...."

"Or what?" Skipjack hit the bait.

"You ever hear about sleep-deprivation psychosis?"

Kazuo shook his head.

"It's an actual psychological condition, listed in the DSM. Legally, it's a form of diminished capacity. I got an acquittal on that one back in the States. My client was accused of assaulting a prosecutor who wouldn't listen to him."

"Really?"

"Swear to God." I crossed my fingers behind my back.

"Please don't take the Lord's name in vain."

"Oh, I don't, Kazuo. Can't afford to. Any multiple defendant felonies today?"

"Sorry, Drake, no. Misdemeanors only this morning, malicious mischief, drunken and disorderly, one cursing phone case. Even if there was a conflict case, you'd have to wait until October, for the next 'physical year,' to get paid."

"Any cursing phone cases by Taro Patch Kids?"

"No. I don't think they have a telephone in the Taro Patch. Maybe if they did they would just call instead of stoning your roof."

I crossed to the defense side of the aisle when the bailiff called the courtroom to order, and sat behind Roberta Ely, lately a major felony specialist with the Los Angeles County Public Defender, now the public defender of the somewhat smaller jurisdiction, Pohnpei Island, Micronesia.

Roberta turned to whisper, "Stick around, Drake. We need to talk when this is done."

The bailiff asked all to rise for the entrance of Judge Omishima, an ex-Trust Territory magistrate who got bumped upstairs when the State Court was certified for full operations shortly after independence. Old Man Omishima is a middling bench warmer, paced in his deliberations, short on the letter of the law, but long on common sense. Still spry at seventy, Omishima has the hard, scaly hide you often see on longtime *sakau* drinkers, what locals call "fish skin." I'm told Judge Omishima doesn't like cases involving American lawyers; says we're too crafty. What's more likely is that his Japanese is better than his English, and his Pohnpeian is better than his Japanese.

The arraignment calendar went smoothly. The drunk driving and one drunken and disorderly defendants copped pleas. Roberta asked for extra time for a pre-trial motion on the cursing phone case. She claimed if her client had in fact cursed someone over the telephone, then it could be protected free speech because Telecom was owned and operated by the national government. Judge Omishima sighed, but said

25

nothing, in Pohnpeian, Japanese, or English. The calendar, true to recent form, held no conflict assignment for me.

"An obscene phone call as protected free speech?" I said as I held open the gate to the bar for Roberta. "Quite a stretch, counselor."

"I just need time enough for my client to make a traditional apology. You know how much local judges like those dismissals. What about you? Do you have anything cooking these days?"

"Are you asking 'who's cooking my rice?'" Roberta, den mother to all past and present public defenders, was unflagging in her efforts to introduce me to a 'nice young girl,' with whom I would settle down and start making babies.

"It's not that kind of set-up, Drake. Strictly business."

"Come on Ms. Ely. You know I haven't had a steady paycheck since I left the PD office, and business hasn't been jumping since even before Al left. I'm so broke that if it took a buck to get off-island, I couldn't get across the street."

"But you always seem so busy."

"Come by my office some time when all I have is a three-month old Sunday crossword puzzle."

"Still, a hard-working lawyer like yourself deserves a referral now and then."

That perked me up. "Got a p.i. case for me?"

"No, nothing that contingent."

"You mean an actual, fee-paying client?"

"How would you like a conflict assignment in a criminal case before the Supreme Court?"

"Who do I have to kill?"

"It's 'whom,' and perhaps not the best way to express interest in a criminal case."

"I am interested. But what kind of criminal case comes before the Supreme Court these days? A fishing violation? Ting Hong would never hire me. I've sued them too many times. Besides, they've got 'Heartless' Harkness on retainer, don't they? And I won't even think of representing a company that crashes longliners onto reefs, and steals food from the mouths of Chuukese babies."

"Calm down, Drake. It's not a fishing case."

"What else is there? Extradition maybe?" I had handled a complex extradition to Guam sandwiched between two murders when I first joined the public defender's office. After that, Al Frost had taken to calling me his "Murders & Extraditions" expert.

Roberta smiled and shook her head.

"Immigration? Customs violation?" I was running out of categories in the national jurisdiction, and most of those cases were boring in addition to being lead pipe cinch losers. "You're not sending me a tax case. Taxes were too taxing in law school. I nearly flunked."

"One charge is bank robbery."

"Bank robbery? Who'd rob a bank in Micronesia? Where would you go with the money?"

"Your would-be client, for one. Mine, too, according to the Complaint."

"Well, I've never represented a bank robber before. Who'd they hit?"

"Micronesian National Bank."

"Hah. Didn't get any of my money. Who's the case before?"

"You won't like it."

"Judge Coleman?"

Roberta nodded.

"Oh well. One must learn to take the bad with the good. When's the bail hearing?"

"We've already had it. Both defendants are out on the usual conditions. They surrendered their driver's licenses and have to report to the Justice Ombudsman each Friday. Air Mike and the shipping companies have been alerted not to allow them to leave the island."

"No bail?"

"Not a penny."

"That doesn't sound like Maximum Max Coleman."

"It wasn't. Coleman was off-island when the pair was arrested. The bail hearing was before a justice pro tem, our good friend Judge Omishima. And Omishima doesn't like the Micronesian National Bank."

"All right, Roberta. If Coleman is the bad news, what's the good?"

"It's a Supreme Court conflict case, so your hourly rate is fifty dollars, sixty-five for time in court. That isn't much, but remember lawyers in Alabama get thirty bucks an hour to defend capital murder."

"Yeah, but Coleman will hone down my time. Tosses a dime like it's a discus."

"You'd be paid a monthly draw as the case goes on, at least in theory, subject to adjustment for hours reported. Monthly payment means monthly reporting, more paperwork than you're used to, especially for expenses. But I'm sure Jasmina can handle it. There may even be some travel involved, so you might get a travel advance."

"Travel? How come?"

"The bank they supposedly robbed is in Chuuk."

"So why bring the case here on Pohnpei?"

"You got me. Anyway, if you agree to take the case, I already have in my office a check for three hundred dollars, dated today, made out to Frost & Burnham."

"Okay, Roberta. This isn't the first of April. But if you're pulling my leg I won't talk to you for a month."

"It's no joke, Drake. 'Swear to God.'"

"Say that again and I'll sic Kazuo Olopai on you. But why doesn't someone else from the public defender office take the case?"

"I'm representing the co-defendant, so I have a conflict. It's a felony charge in the Supreme Court, so they need a lawyer, not a trial counselor."

"What about the staff attorney on Kosrae, or better yet, on Chuuk?"

"The court won't pay someone to fly in from off-island. Besides that, they know you work cheap."

"Do I need to hire an investigator?"

"Why don't we both agree to use Utticus?"

"Sounds good to me."

"Before I forget. The most important reason we want to hire you, is that the defendant asked for you personally."

"Somebody asked for me? Ex-pat?"

"No, a local. Come to the office and see. He's waiting for us."

Roberta led the way from the dark and relative cool of the courthouse. Even though I've lived in the islands for years, walking from air conditioning to the coke oven blast of late morning heat and humidity still socks me like a punch in the gut. My eyes went swimmy and I

29

remembered that I was working on three hours sleep, a mug of coffee, and no breakfast.

The Pohnpei Public Defender Office is maybe two hundred yards from the courthouse, at the crest of the hill above the Namiki Building, across the car-strangled width of the main road. Traffic is definitely heavier, with more and more cars each year so that it seems the island might sink from all the Detroit iron piled on it. Utticus had driven the truck back to the office, but Roberta and I, on foot, would likely beat him back.

Although I was never the staff attorney there, I had taken several conflict cases from the Pohnpei Public Defender, to Kosrae at first, and then down the street to Frost & Burnham. In many ways, all public defender offices are alike: understaffed, overworked (except for Kosrae), cursed with ancient Rust Territory office equipment. The usual collection of would-be clients waited in front of the office, crowding the narrow bench beneath the eaves or loitering in front of the door. They're young guys mostly, the same ones who get in trouble with the law everywhere else on the planet, young guys with too much time on their hands and not enough to occupy it, teenagers with raging hormones, convinced they are indestructible. They dress in jeans and muscle tanks or black tee shirts silk-screened with the logos of heavy metal bands or Jawaiian Strength, their eyes inscrutable behind improbably current sunglasses.

The boys went silent and gazed hard as we walked past. Then Roberta recognized one, called his name, and a shy smile crossed his face. Behind the sunglasses, beneath attitudes copped from too many lousy kung fu videos, they were still island boys, and friendly. It took a lot to get one of them angry, a lot of alcohol mostly.

Inside the office was as crowded as outside, and the number of bodies in the lobby made the air conditioner struggle. This inside crowd was different, though, older men and women, many with young children. Most were the fathers and mothers, the aunties and uncles and grandparents, and, yes, even the children of those waiting outside, more and more it seemed each year, a population boom undoubtedly linked to the relative, yet fast-dwindling Compact prosperity. Straight ahead, half hidden by a phalanx of filing cabinets is the office secretary's desk. Noriko had her head down on her elbows. To the right are Roberta's office and a non-functioning bathroom. To the left is the main room. Three local trial counselors and the office investigator share space divvied up into cubicles so small it would make a Silicon Valley startup proud. Confidential communications are a bit of a problem in the hot, noisy room, a lot like a big city PD office back in the States. No wonder Roberta feels at home.

"Any calls, Noriko?" Roberta said as we passed, as much to wake her secretary as in any real possibility of her remembering a message. Noriko raised her head long enough to shake no.

"You'd better keep paying Jasmina a living wage," Roberta said inside her office. "I'll hire her the minute you don't."

"I don't know about you, but I could use about forty winks myself. All right, Ms. Ely. What's the big secret?"

"Why don't you take my seat?"

Roberta's desk was spotless, the only tidy place in the office, perhaps on the whole island maybe. Roberta had a rule never to put a file on her desk unless she was going to work on it, then to put it away when she was done. The rest of Roberta's office, her refuge, no doubt, was neat as a schoolgirl heading to church on Easter morning, the floor neatly swept, her books arrayed on shelves.

"You're setting me up for a major favor, Roberta," I said as she pulled out her chair.

Utticus Uziah knocked on the open door and handed Roberta the keys to the office truck.

"Utticus? Please bring in Bachelor Number One."

Utticus grinned at me through betel nut stained teeth, then went to usher in his charge. He smiled again when he returned and stepped aside to let the stranger in.

I almost leaped from the chair when I saw my would-be client. One stateside colleague, when undergoing a particularly stressful time, had heart palpitations so severe that you could actually see his heart thumping beneath his shirt. I didn't look, but I'm sure my shirt was jumping, too, for my ticker went suddenly haywire. It took almost all my self-control to keep my face passive, although beneath the desk, my knee was bouncing like a just-hooked tuna on the deck of a bait boat. I didn't break into a cold sweat; Pohnpei's too hot and I don't have malaria. But I felt my shirt go damp.

Smiling as he entered the room, gliding as smooth as a tiger shark closing in on its prey, was Jangle Elwell.

CHAPTER FOUR

"Well, counsel. Who will save the widow's sons?" Jangle slid into Roberta's office smooth as a tiger shark, as if with the flick of a tail he'd be on top of me, eyes hooded, gnawing.

I stared at Jangle for a long moment, saying nothing, willing my knee to bob to a stop, my heart to slow.

"I take it you two have met?" Roberta fretted like a party host.

"Have a seat." I nodded to a pair of folding chairs in front of the desk. I turned to Roberta, "Ms. Ely, may we borrow your office for a private conference?"

"Take all the time you want," Roberta said over her shoulder as she slipped past Utticus and out of the office.

"Utticus, you can leave, too," I said to the office investigator.

"You sure you don't need a witness, Drake?"

"It's OK, Utticus." I turned to Jangle. "I believe that Mr. Elwell and I will call a truce."

"I will stay right outside." Utticus closed the door behind him.

Jangle nodded to the door. "No witness? You getting cocky, *ahset.*"

"You're the one who wanted to see me."

Jangle leaned back in the folding chair and put his hands behind his head. "You want to take my case?"

"A question first. Why me?"

"You the best. I always said that."

Jangle paying a compliment seemed dangerous. I felt like a spear fisher in a blue hole who, just after stuffing his catch in his swim trunks, spots the trailing shark.

"You saw right through that little game at Lelu Island Trading Company."

"I haven't figured out why anyone would do that. Especially to his friends."

"I think you know why," Jangle smiled. "You were the Number One Defender on Kosrae. Everybody liked you. I don't know why you left."

"Circumstances were beyond my control."

"Maybe you should be like me and control the circumstances."

"You think too much of me, Jangle. And so do your Taro Patch Kids." I leaned forward and gestured island-style, measuring an inch off my left hand with my right. "I came this close to reporting your boys last night."

"So do it. But I don't know what you talking about."

"Come off it, Jangle. Thanks to your boys, my house has been stoned more times than Saint Stephen."

"Sound like a prank to me."

"Not at three in the morning."

"You want it to stop? Then take my case." Jangle snapped the fingers on his left hand. It sounded like a gunshot in the small office.

It was my turn to lean back and smile. "You must be in real trouble to make an offer like that."

"Things could get harder for you."

"I don't threaten easily. You should know that by now."

"Then how about a mutually beneficial arrangement. You scratch my back; I'll scratch yours."

"I don't follow you."

"I hear business isn't so good. No new cases come in; payments slow. I know an organization that could send new business your way, and help you collect your fee."

"I'm not interested in being a gang lawyer, Jangle. That life is nasty, brutish, and short."

"Now, now counselor. The Taro Patch Kids? That's a social club."

"So is la Cosa Nostra."

"How about a show of good faith, then?"

"Good faith? I'll tell you about good faith. Tell your boys to lay off. No rocks on the roof. No late night drive-bys. No more harassing me, my neighbors, my dog. Do that for a week, one week, and I'll think, and think only, about taking your case."

"Is that all?"

"For starters. Second point. If I take your case - that's if - and you cross me on the smallest thing, I'll be gone before you can blink. Got it?"

"Done. You get a week's worth of sleep and I'll be at your office next Thursday." Jangle rose from the chair. "You look like you could use some shut eye, counsel."

"Don't start calling me that. Not yet."

"I know you. You will take the case."

Jangle turned and pointed his left index and middle fingers at me, an L.A. gang sign for a gun. Then he smiled and extended his open right hand. Island scuttlebutt had it that Jangle's right hand was deformed, and I could see that his middle and ring fingers appeared to be fused. I glanced at the digits for what seemed like thirty seconds, but was probably more like two. I stood, and began to lean over the desk to shake Jangle's offered hand – and count my fingers after – when he slipped his right hand back in his pocket. I leaned back, still unsure where to put my hands.

Jangle opened the office door and chuckled, as if he had come upon Roberta and Utticus peeking through the keyhole. I followed to the door and watched him leave the office. On the way out, Jangle leaned over and whispered something to Noriko, who hissed at him, then smiled as he walked away. In the lobby, the crowd parted as Jangle sauntered through. Outside the front door, a couple of guys with invisible eyes behind sunglasses peeled off to follow Jangle, triggerfish trailing the shark. A moment later, I heard a truck start then roar out of the parking lot next door, tires spinning out gravel to ping off the louvers on that side of the Public Defender building. The trial counselors ducked, and I flinched.

Roberta came up from behind and placed a hand on my shoulder. "Here's the case file, Drake."

"Ms. Ely? I do believe you're trying to get me killed."

"Take this one off my hands and I owe you, big time. A month's worth of homemade dinners."

"You still owe me for the last time I pulled your yams from the *uhm.*"

"This time I mean it. Jangle gives me the creeps. He's not like the rest of our clients here, more like some South Central gang bangers I saw stateside. I've never seen a local like him."

"Me either."

"What's he mean when he says 'Who will save the widow's son?'"

"You've got me."

"Jangle surely knows you, though. From Kosrae?"

"Buy me lunch, Ms. Ely, and I'll tell you the whole story."

We decided on Joyful Lunch, after stopping at my office to drop off the file and pick up messages. (There were none.) I ordered the double special lunch – tuna sashimi followed by grilled tuna – and was soon tucking into ahi so fresh that it must have been swimming happily off the reef that morning.

"My first run-in with Jangle Elwell was on Kosrae, a few months before the coup d'état usurped me from office. No one really knew what he was up to."

"Not that we know now," said Roberta.

"Back then Jangle was just the tall, handsome kid back on-island after a long spell stateside. He was probably twenty or twenty-one then, the summer between his high school graduation and starting college here on Pohnpei. I thought that was a little odd. He was this obviously bright guy, who spoke terrific English."

"His English doesn't sound that good now."

"That's just attitude you heard, Roberta, Jangle showing off his gang banger bona fides. Anyway, I thought it strange that this ambitious kid, who could have his pick of schools to attend stateside – University of Hawaii, Oregon, a small international school – but he chose the College of Micronesia."

"Maybe he was homesick. It's happened before, Drake."

"But that's not Jangle. For every homesick local there's one chomping at the bit to get off-island and never look back. So Jangle's on Kosrae, ready to go to college, and people were falling all over him. He dressed like he stepped from a mainland mall right onto the plane, and that says a lot on an island where most laundry is still beaten against rocks in a stream. Jangle probably had a half-dozen girls fighting over him, you know, one in every village."

"I've heard a rumor here that Jangle had gotten a Peace Corps volunteer pregnant," Roberta said. "That he's the father of twins he won't even acknowledge."

"It wouldn't surprise me."

"Utticus calls Jangle 'Half-Half,' Kosrae father, Chuukese mother. Says it in that tone of voice like he just stepped in some dog poop."

"Calling someone a 'Half-Half' is an invitation to fisticuffs in some quarters, Ms. Ely. I've never met Jangle's family on Kosrae, but they're not in the Congregational Church. Supposedly they were among the first Kosraens converted by Mormon missionaries. The LDS helped Jangle go to Salt Lake City for high school. Now Jangle fit in about as well in Utah as an Eskimo in sealskin gloves and mukluks would here in Kolonia. "

"Utticus told me that Jangle joined the 'Sons of Samoa.'"

"So I've heard. He probably ran a little small for the Samoans, but he's quick, smart, and ruthless. Once back on Kosrae, with an education provided gratis by the Latter Day Saints, as well as the Sons of Samoa, Jangle made a big show of attending services at the Lelu Congregational Church, much to the Kosrae Mormons' dismay."

"That's just consistent with ambition, if what you've told me about Kosrae is true. So Jangle is going to church. So what?"

"So were I a missionary, I'd point to the deadly sin of hypocrisy. Even though he goes to church, Jangle is drinking, smoking, fooling around, all the things the Kosrae Congregational Church abhors. But everyone, even the pastors, cut him slack."

"High spirits? One last fling before he settles down?" said Roberta.

"Some fling. Jangle hangs out with a bunch of guys his age that summer. Of course he's the leader, the smartest of the crew, the only one to finish high school. The rest of the bunch are pretty sorry. You know the type, Ms. Ely. They're the ones who come to the Public Defender office for help, or are dragged to us by their families. One day, three of Jangle's 'boys' – I don't want to call them a gang just yet – came to the Kosrae Public Defender office. All three were charged with felonies. I split up the assignments in the office, with the local trial counselors Zebedee James and Hudson Henry each taking one defendant, and me the third. I had nineteen-year-old Carterson Micah, charged with burglary and grand theft. Zebedee represented Carterson's cousin, Wesley Klavan, also nineteen, and up for burglary and grand theft, too. Hudson had my client's older brother, Micah Micah, who was up for receiving stolen property."

"All in the family, huh?"

"You got it. All three are high school dropouts, had no real jobs other than fishing or farming, and no prospects, except maybe slinging gravel for Public Works. The victim was LITC, Lelu Island Trading Company, biggest store on-island, right in the middle of Lelu.

Carterson said he and Wesley were drinking yeast on a Saturday night. You know, drop a packet of baking yeast into a bucket of coconut milk."

"Micro home brew," said Roberta. "But you risk peritonitis if you drink it too soon."

"No such luck for these two. When they were bold enough, or drunk enough, they snuck around the back of the store, climbed a chain link fence, and pulled out the louvers from the only window on that side of the building. It's a ventilation window, so high up that you have to stand on top of the fence just to reach it."

"Doesn't anybody live on that side of the store?"

"No. The building backs onto the Lelu Ruins, which, all locals agree, are haunted. No one lives there. Of course, the locals all conclude the ruins are haunted because no one lives there."

"Which came first? The chicken or the egg?"

"Very perceptive, Ms. Ely. The back window used to hold an air-con unit, but once that was removed, someone had the bright idea of pushing a box from the inside, back up against the window, wedging it in so that no one could open the louvers from the outside. But if someone were to remove the louvers, then the only thing keeping you from going in is this cardboard box. And the box is empty. My client, Carterson, in an impressive display of dental strength, chews a hole in the box."

"Hmmm. High craft fiber diet."

"Carterson and Wesley then tunnel through the box and into the store. Once inside, they roam about the main shopping area, looking for anything interesting. Although there's a lot of stuff, very little of it catches their eyes. The owner, Yoshiwo Kanka, is a church-going *etawi*, so he doesn't sell alcohol or tobacco. Our boys swipe some costume jewelry from a stand near the check out counter, and two cans of Great Wall corned beef, which they open and eat at the foot of the fence outside the back window. The police found the empty cans."

"I'd guess the cardboard box wasn't very filling."

"It was neither nutritious nor delicious. Carterson and Wesley then meet Micah, who swaps them half a bottle of hot stuff for the costume jewelry. Maybe Micah figured he would get more money for vodka by selling the jewelry."

"After scaling the fence, your boys visit a fence."

"Micah starts selling the jewelry at, shall we say, a deep discount? A couple of days later, one of Micah's customers walks into Lelu Island Trading Company wearing some stolen jewelry. A clerk asks where she got it and she names Micah. The clerk calls the police, who arrest Micah. Micah coughs up the rest of the loot and spills the beans on his brother and cousin, Carterson and Wesley."

"Fifth Amendment problem?"

"No. The police didn't question Micah first; the clerk did. And Micah signed a statement with the police after he was arrested and Mirandized, so it was airtight. Public confession is ingrained on the Kosrae psyche. They confess their sins in church on Sunday in front of the entire congregation."

"Sounds like a pretty tough nut to defend."

"Open and shut."

"I suppose the holder-in-due-course defense wouldn't work. But how did the prosecutor come up with grand theft on those facts? Costume jewelry? Corned beef?"

"We asked ourselves that, too, figuring it was typical overcharging. So we thought we had a little wiggle room to cop out."

"If I were in your zoris, I'd ask the state to agree to let my clients plead down to the lesser-included offense. That would save the State the time and the prosecutor the aggravation of trying these guys. The State is happy. The clients get less time. The store is happy because the costume jewelry goes back on the shelf instead of gathering dust in the evidence room. Everybody wins."

"Even my loser client. We offer a global to cop out all three. Wesley and Carterson will cop a plea to breaking and entry and petty theft; Micah to receiving stolen property. It would be a first offense for all three, so we offer three weeks jail time to teach them a lesson, a few months on probation, and promise to fix the louvers. Maybe they'll be scared enough not to stray from the straight and narrow."

"Sounds reasonable."

"But the prosecutor won't bite. The state would accept B&E for burglary, but he wanted Carterson and Wesley to plead guilty to grand theft. He'd accept the promise to fix the louvers, but wanted sentencing to include hard time and restitution. Well I said the State can't prove grand theft; the value of the stolen goods was less than fifty dollars. As for restitution, well, restitution for what? The State recovered all the jewelry from Micah and his customers, which leaves the two cans of corned beef they ate. What's that? Three bucks?"

"Three fifty here on Pohnpei."

"And that's when it got really interesting. The prosecutor said, 'What about the five thousand dollars in cash taken from a desk in the office?' That water buffaloed me. The complaint and information said nothing about cash, but the prosecutor promised to amend. Carterson and Wesley swore they stayed in the main shopping area. They didn't go near the office. The police report said zilch about the office or cash. But

Kanka, the store owner, was willing to testify that someone broke into the office, pried open his desk drawer, rifled the cash box and took off with more than five grand, the weekend's cash receipts. Now there are some holes in that story. No one touched the register, the first place someone would look for money. Besides that five grand is a lot of cash for any business between the bank's closing on Friday and the close of business on Saturday."

"Especially on an island where most people sign IOUs in lieu of cash."

"Plus there's no indication that Carterson and Wesley got that kind of windfall. They haven't bought a pick-up or a boat, or started to buy rounds for the house at the Beach Pond Bar. They're still drinking yeast, not Johnny Walker. On top of that, why didn't anyone at the store tell the police about the missing cash? Supposedly, Kanka was off-island at the time of the break-in. No one told the police because no one went into his office. As for the amount of cash, maybe Kanka didn't go to the bank that week. Maybe he likes to have a wad of mad money. Who knows? But it looked to me like Carterson and Wesley were facing hard time and big money for something they say they didn't do. Neither had that kind of money, nor do their families. They'd probably have to sell some land to make restitution."

"What did you do?" said Roberta.

"I know what Steve McGarrett would do. Settle things with his fists, then swing that big black Mercury up to the Pali lookout for a windblown close-up. Then again McGarrett would be on the cops' side on this one. What could we do? Someone was lying. I sent our investigator to interview Kanka. But he corroborated everything the prosecutor said. He showed the jimmied desk drawer and the broken lock on an empty cash box. He even showed the books, which were scrupulously kept by an AVA, an Australian Volunteer Associate, accounting for more than five grand cash in the box."

"Did you share this with your clients?"

"You bet. We brought in Wesley and Carterson and leaned on them. Frankly, no one on Kosrae can lean quite as hard as our friend Zebedee James. He used to be a police sergeant, so we tried the good-cop-bad-cop routine. First I came in and said how sad I was that they had not told us the truth, then Zebedee came in, yelled at them, threatened to tell their fathers, shouted all the usual Kosraen insults. Then I came in and said, 'I can't control him. You'd better tell me.' But no go. We even left them together in the room alone, hoping they would convince each other to tell the truth and not concoct another story. But Wesley and Carterson said nothing. They just sat there with their arms folded. You know how locals are, Roberta. Basically honest; they'll confess at the drop of a hat, but they won't rat on their buddies to cut a deal because they are so loyal. And it seemed to me more and more that they are trying to protect someone."

"Jangle."

"Exactly. I think Jangle put them up to breaking into Lelu Island Trading. Maybe he even cased the joint before. He waited until they were out of the building and finished with their post-burglary prandial. Then Jangle climbed the fence, went through the cardboard tunnel, broke into the office and took the cash."

"So if the burglary is solved, Jangle has two guys in front of him ready to take the fall. But why would your clients protect him?"

"Plenty of reasons. Maybe, like good Kosraen boys, they knew they done wrong and deserved to be punished. Maybe there is honor among thieves on that island. Maybe Jangle promised them something, a bigger piece of the banana pie once everything settled down."

"Or maybe they were afraid."

"Right. When I first talked with Carterson, I asked if anyone else was involved. I saw fear in his eyes. Everybody knows Jangle is a Son of Samoa, and a' Half-Half.' His mother is supposed to be from Chuuk, and Zebedee mentioned something about Carterson and Wesley being afraid of Chuukese magic. Pretty powerful stuff."

"Any chance of proving another conspirator at trial?"

"On an alibi like that? 'Gee, Judge, we only committed half of the burglary.' They'd be laughed out of court and right into the hoosegow. Remember who Carterson and Wesley would accuse. Jangle was the golden boy that summer, back from the States and back in the church."

"So what did you do?"

"I went to the prosecutor and told him that something stunk bad about the whole thing. Then we went to Judge Abraham and said that Carterson and Wesley were going to enter Alford pleas. You know, plead guilty and accept the maximum sentence on the lesser-included offense to escape the maximum possible penalty on the offense charged. Our clients would plead to B&E and petty theft, but they wouldn't take the rap for grand theft and leave themselves open to a restitution sentence they couldn't possibly pay."

"You've got guts, Burnham. I've never heard of an Alford plea to anything other than murder two to avoid the death penalty on murder one. Did the judge buy it?"

"Give him credit. Judge Abraham didn't go to law school, but he's country shrewd and a good judge of character. Even though he could take a lot of heat for it, the Judge accepted both pleas. It probably helped that the prosecutor was still looking up the Alford decision when the judge made up his mind. Carterson and Wesley were sentenced to two years in jail, with probation for another two. That's a lot for first-time offenders, but no restitution was ordered. Yoshiwo squawked about his money, but Abraham told him to talk to his insurance agent, who happened to be the Judge's brother-in-law. I heard later the insurance company paid."

"I can't imagine Judge Coleman accepting a plea like that."

"We were lucky. I'm the first to admit it."

"Did you do anything about Jangle?"

"Yeah. Right before he left for college, I was so pissed off that I buttonholed him. My client had gotten a lot more time than he should have had coming, but because he was stupid, not venal. In the meantime, Jangle's running around like he's the frigging Gingerbread Man, shouting 'You can't catch me, you can't catch me.' When I cornered Jangle, I told him he was dirty and if I ever got the chance, I'd prove it."

"What did he say to that?"

"That's the weird part. Jangle laughed and said the same thing he said to me in the office today. 'Who will save the widow's sons?'"

"Did he say 'son' or 'sons?'"

"I didn't even think about it until today."

"What does it mean?"

"I don't know. Some nonsense he picked up along the way."

"He sounds sociopathic."

"More asocial, Roberta. Like he doesn't have a conscience. He's crazy like a fox, though. Ever since I confronted him, Jangle's been on my case. Harmless stuff, mostly, hassling me when he's bored. Like last night he sent over some boys to throw rocks on my roof. Then he'll stop, and it will be cool for months. Then, boom, it starts again, totally random. Or maybe there is a method to it. Keep me at the point of being rattled, but no further. He'll go far enough to let me know he's there, but not enough for me to do something."

"The 'Gaslight' treatment."

"Exactly."

"Nice client you have there, Drake."

"Client? Not yet."

CHAPTER FIVE

The harassment stopped. For a week, no more drive-bys, no midnight stones flung on the roof and fewer unexplained disappearances from the clothesline. Although I couldn't quite believe it, it even seemed less traffic passed at night, fewer cars or trucks rattling by to alarm neighborhood dogs. Sotaro and family were in good spirits, too. One day, he brought over several strings of reef fish. We smoked a mess over a coconut husk fire, and sliced up a few for sashimi chasers while Sotaro's wife fried the rest for a gut-busting Micronesian feast. Sotaro even produced some freshly-tapped *tuba* – palm wine – at meals' end, and we sat in the *nahs* to contemplate the sunset and emerging stars.

There was more to a growing sense of satisfaction. An old case, left over from Frost's days, settled for a fee of more than fish or produce, and a couple of new cases strolled into the office. Jasmina said that two Filipinos brought in, of all things, a real estate matter. The other was a pretty good liability case with the potential for some real money. Charlie Warheit, a young guy from Ngatik Atoll employed by Public Works, had several fingers smashed in a cement mixer when his crew boss hurried him to clear out a jam. The injury was gruesome; it looked as if he would not regain full use of his hand, and Charlie was evacuated to Manila for treatment. His brother, Daniel Warheit, a student at College of Micronesia, brought his case to the office. With potential new business,

I felt confident enough to have Jasmina deposit the retainer on Jangle's case, then make the quarterly payment, past due, on the Frost & Burnham foreign investment permit.

Jasmina seemed happy, too. She suspended all morning cross-examinations, and took a three-hour lunch one afternoon. I thought, but didn't ask, whether she had herself a new fellow. Of course, Jasmina could have her pick of young men. Her list of suitors was as long as a rainy Sunday on Kosrae.

Until she gets married, Jasmina seems content to be a career girl, local style. We both ignore inevitable island gossip that she and I are an item. Locals nodded and chuckled when Al had hired Jasmina, there being some basis for speculation. Algonquin H. Frost wooed a long line of local women, and was rumored to have a girl stashed on each of Micronesia's several thousand islands. I'll vouch for his lack of reputation. When I had just arrived on Pohnpei, Al asked if I wanted to go angling that evening. I expected a nautical expedition, but all Al meant was to drag chairs onto the building verandah to launch catcalls at passing local girls.

Once deep into a bottle of bourbon, Al confessed that he and Jasmina had a brief and tempestuous fling, that ended when Al discovered just why Jasmina's family nicknamed her "Typhoon." When she learned Al was catting around on the side, Jasmina took the office scissors and cut out the crotch from every pair of trousers Al owned, then threatened to complete the task on the pair he was wearing. I must confess I, too, had succumbed to imagined charms, and once asked a cousin if Jasmina would go out with me. This, of course, was long before I became her employer. I was told Jasmina no longer dates Americans.

Roberta Ely called one afternoon to remind me of the Bench & Bar Banquet at the Coral Reef Hotel. Roberta is president of the Pohnpei Bar Association, and the Banquet is the renewal of a somewhat hoary tradition of a cordial meeting of attorneys and judges in a setting less formal than the courtroom. In the past, the Bench & Bar Banquet was an excuse to get drunk with one's professional colleagues, and I had little doubt that this year's banquet would be more of the same. The only thing more tiresome than a lawyer telling war stories is a drunken lawyer telling war stories, and I had long ago resolved to never again attend another such function. But Roberta insisted and cinched the deal with a promise of live music, having hired a Filipino band called "The Operator." I had not heard of them, but had hopes. Decent live music is something of an island rarity. When Mobil sponsored a tour of a popular Hawaiian band a few years back, their concerts were packed at every stop. Truth be told, were the music good enough, I might be tempted to dance that old sailor's jig, the hornpipe.

The Coral Reef Hotel – about twenty minutes drive from town – is an eco-tourism resort, where tourists from the States and Japan pay top dollar to sleep in traditional-looking thatch huts with all the modern amenities such as hot water and flush toilets, plus expensive distractions like daily dive trips, deep sea fishing, and expeditions to island landmarks. The Coral Reef has a great setting, high on a ridge on the northeast corner of the island, from which the sunsets over Sokehs Rock are "enchanting," to quote the hotel's own promotional literature. The hotel has a real chef, and its bartender is a trained mixologist who can pour everything from an absinthe to a Zombie, on an island where most bartenders know only how to pop the top on a can of Budweiser. The

Reef is where to go for a splurge. And with Frost & Burnham fortunes lately so dismal, it had been many a moon since my last visit.

I arrived at the Banquet sociably late, thanks in part to my balking truck. A former client had rebuilt the engine in exchange for my waiving a fee, but I suspected that a few nuts and bolts were missing, if not from the engine then maybe from my skull for agreeing to let him work on it. The Banquet was a no-host function. Had the bar been buying, I would have taken a taxi. On the way in, I passed Judge Coleman's pickup truck, a late model, four-wheel drive Toyota, with the silver gray metallic flake finish and the front vanity plate that read "JUSTICE." By the time I walked into the open-air restaurant, Roberta was at the rostrum. After a benediction and obligatory acknowledgement of assorted big shots, she began her opening remarks.

"Good evening, and welcome to this year's, long-awaited renewal of the Pohnpei Bar Association's Bench and Bar Banquet. I am quite pleased to see so many members of the Bar in attendance. I extend a special welcome to the various court staffs - from the Supreme Court, the State Court, the Land and Municipal courts - all of whom are probably under orders to attend, as well as to those state and national prosecutors present who probably can't resist a little ex parte contact."

That got a chuckle from members of the Public Defender office.

"I'm sorry to say that the Chief Justice cannot be with us this evening, although he sends his profound regrets. In the meantime, Associate Justice Max Coleman will ably represent the Supreme Court. I see we have several justices from the state courts in attendance as well."

I glanced about the room for a table to join. Back in a corner, Judge Omishima sat with a pair of equally ancient Land Court judges, and a somewhat younger (in his mid- 60's) municipal court judge. At a stateside Bench & Bar banquet, attending judges would be spread out, one or two per table. In the islands, though, jurists cluster together like swifts huddling from the rain. I decided against joining the unhappy hour at their table. Conversation would be in strictly local argot on strictly local subjects.

Kazuo Olopai smiled from a table near the rostrum. Apparently the only one attending for the state prosecutors office, Kazuo sat outnumbered by trial counselors from the Public Defender and Legal Services offices. The only open chair there I suspected was Roberta's. No room at that inn. At a boisterous table front and center, the Clerk of the Supreme Court presided over members of both state and Supreme Court staffs. But Probation Officer Wartsilla Diesel was there, and I needed a break from her endless needling about what former clients had or had not done since release.

Next to that was a table claimed by a large contingent from the Attorney General's office, attorneys, investigators, and staff. Three Americans sat at one end; Lovey Wentworth and Natalie Schaeffer huddled with Ed Bundy, a mild international law specialist who had the misfortune of sharing his name with a serial killer. At the other end of the table, flanked by DSI agents – investigative muscle for the AG's office – sat the beautiful and imperious Marielle Hargraves, of the Litigation Department. Although I like Lovey and Nattie, I cannot stand Hargraves, and I made a mental note to avoid her for the rest of the evening, if not for the rest of my life.

A half-dozen attorneys in private practice, who, attached to no office had no assigned seats, sat at adjoining tables, Americans at one, locals at the other, from which adversaries could undoubtedly snipe at each other. I was probably expected to sit there. Rather than face the other members of the Bar, I removed myself to the bar. On the way out, I passed Dick Harkness.

"Burnham, stop for a minute. I'd like you to meet my clients."

"Heartless" Harkness enjoys his assumed role as a major player in the Bar. He fancies himself as the "go-to" guy for outsiders who need a mouth in Micronesia. His outsiders are the banks, stateside exporters, and on occasion, the U.S. government. The best indication of the size of the Pohnpei Bar is that Dick Harkness – a neckbone collections lawyer with a penchant for instantaneously appraising potentially valuable personal property – thinks he's the equivalent of a U.S. Attorney.

Harkness introduced Misters Cho, Lai, and Aang. Aang, the eldest, handed me his business card, the Macau-Micronesia Cooperation Association. Cho and Lai were younger toughs, who looked more like boxers than businessmen.

"These gentlemen are here from Macau," said Harkness, "to discuss with municipal and state leaders the possibility of operating a casino in Madolinimh, near Nan Madol. I'm sure you've heard of it, the 'Stone City Resort and Casino.'"

"I have heard of your scheme. Gentlemen, I wish you the very worst of luck; snake eyes, if you will. I think whatever minimal monetary benefit might come to Madolinimh from a casino will be more than offset by societal costs in increased crime, addiction to gambling, abandoned families and the like."

"What did I tell you, Mr. Aang? No one here can phrase a rhetorical flourish like Mr. Burnham. Drake, I was just telling my friends that you are the best advocate on-island, and that they would do well to hire you if they ever needed to go to court."

"I'll stick with crooks and debtors for now. Excuse me, gentlemen. But I'm needed down at the bar."

"Thanks for stopping, Drake," said Harkness and he glanced at my wrist as we shook hands. "Say, that's a nice watch. Is it new?"

"This old thing? I've had it for years."

I wasn't surprised to find Judge Coleman at the bar instead of sitting with the Supreme Court staff. But then Coleman's ruddy face would have looked more at home pulling a Guinness in an Irish pub than on the bench in Micronesia. Judge Maximinus T. Coleman is an expatriate, a *menwhi*, an American holdover from the Trust Territory High Court, who managed after independence to snag a spot on the Supreme Court bench through carefully cultivated connections with certain traditional leaders and movers and shakers of the national Congress. Coleman's family name is fitting, since he has a taste for Milwaukee's finest, and is generally known to have a case of cold ones stashed in an eponymous cooler in the deck of his pick-up truck. Around the corner to Coleman's left was the Pohnpei Justice Ombudsman, Valentin Onan, a high caste Pohnpeian whose main duty seems to be judicial drinking buddy, but whose real influence runs much deeper.

"Burnham, you're late. We've been here a couple of hours already." Coleman was bent so far over his beer that I wondered if he was going to fall in. I hoped he wasn't driving that night, or diving the next morning.

"Judge Coleman, Mr. Onan." I nodded and walked to the far end of the bar.

"What are you too damn good to drink with us? Sit down." Coleman smacked the bar stool to his right. "Barkeep? Get Burnham whatever he wants, on me."

"Thank you, Judge." I knew better than to decline. The bartender brought a stubby of Victoria Bitter, the bottle sweating with condensation. Though a marginally better beer, VB is cheaper than Budweiser. Supply and demand.

"Tell me, Burnham. How's that gorgeous secretary of yours? You ready to let me hire her for the Supreme Court staff?" Coleman paused and leaned toward Onan for emphasis. "Or better yet, have her meet me at the Blue Magic Night Club."

Onan and Coleman shared a chuckle.

"Jasmina's doing fine, Judge. I think she's dating someone new."

"That's no surprise. Good idea to revive these Bench and Bar dinners, don't you think?"

"You certainly seem to be enjoying yourself, Your Honor."

"Damn straight. You know, your partner always liked these events, Burnham."

I knew Al had shared my opinion of Bench & Bar functions, but had attended out of ugly necessity.

"You know what else, Burnham? Al Frost and I didn't always get along. I don't know if you knew that."

"I was aware of some friction."

"I hope you and I can get along better."

"Judge Coleman, nothing would please me more."

Actually, the Coleman-Frost bouts were the stuff of legend. When he first took the Supreme Court bench, Coleman had railed so loud and long against my late partner that in one three-month stretch, Al

55

resorted to motions to recuse for personal bias every time he had a case assigned to Judge Coleman. Now on a small island, a situation where the then-presiding judge won't hear cases involving the chief public defender cannot last very long, and the Chief Justice, a solemn clan elder from the outer islands of Chuuk, mediated the dispute before it took on the tone of say, Clarence Darrow versus William Jennings Bryant. Frost and Coleman had duked it out for years, starting in Trust Territory times, mostly in court, but outside as well. Coleman accused Frost of trying to run a speedboat over him as he surfaced from a scuba dive. Frost said that Coleman deliberately swerved his truck to whack one of Al's already three-legged dogs. But their most titanic tussle was about fifteen years ago over a local "wanted" woman. The object of their mutual desire has since ballooned into a buxom mother of six, none of whom resembles either Coleman or Frost in the least degree.

Up in the restaurant, the band started their first set. Once he got in the neighborhood of the key, Coleman began to sing the chorus. "Yellow bird, high in the mango tree."

If this was to be a night of off-key Coleman karaoke, I might as well get out the sharp knives to commit *seppuku* right away. I tried to distract him by asking a question.

"Judge Coleman?"

Coleman held up his hand, but barely raised his head from his beer. I couldn't tell, but it seemed as if he wanted to continue singing or say something profound. He lurched to his feet and turned to the men's room. "I've got to visit the Governor."

Visit the Governor? That was one of Al Frost's favorite sayings. Where had Coleman picked it up?

I smiled at the Justice Ombudsman. "I think I'll go back to the Banquet."

Valentin smiled, then belched. He was sloshed, too, and I thought of the societal good of demanding his car keys.

The band had segued into "Never On Sunday" with all the grace of a runaway gravel truck. I grabbed a chair at Roberta's table, and sat next to Kazuo.

"Hello, Mr. Drake Burnham. You are very handsome tonight." Olopai raised his voice over the din.

"Thank you, Kazuo. Is that a new shirt?"

"Yes. My nephew sent it this week from Honolulu."

"Do you have any conflict cases this week?" Speaking louder than a clumsy arpeggio from a Casio keyboard proved difficult.

"None so far, but come to court tomorrow to be sure."

"Another liquid meal, Drake?" Roberta leaned over and shook my beer. "Or will you join us for dinner?"

"I don't think so. Prices here are a little too dear for present circumstances."

"The local trial counselors said the same thing, so the Banquet's pot luck this year." Roberta pointed to the other tables, where people were already eating from paper plates piled high with chicken, fish, breadfruit, and rice.

"Damn, Roberta. You should have reminded me. I could have brought that honey-baked Spam."

"Join us, Drake," Roberta laughed. "You can celebrate getting the Elwell case."

"I haven't decided whether to take it."

"I know you'll take it, because it's a challenge. And when you take it I won't have to deal with it. As for tonight, I'm buying. You won't have to cash your retainer check or even sing for your supper."

"I don't know, Ms. Ely. It sounds like the band could use some help."

Two Filipinos – one on electric guitar, the other at a keyboard – made up the band. Neither should quit their day jobs; they were dreadful, tone deaf apparently. Not to make vast generalizations, but most Filipinos I know can at least carry a tune; many are fine musicians, in fact. Not these guys. Plus they had absolutely no stage presence. They simply stood there scowling and playing their instruments, badly. And even though it was hours after sunset, both wore sunglasses. In fact, "The Operator" was the scariest-looking act this side of a seventies punk rock band.

"Where did you find these guys, Roberta?"

"'The Operator?' I was told they were touring the islands, like that Hawaiian band, Kapena, did on the Mobil tour. Their fee was so low that I couldn't pass it up."

"I wonder if they plan to make up the difference in cassette sales."

The Operator wasn't awful enough to scare me away from a free supper, and I made my way to the makeshift buffet table, pieces of plywood perched on sawhorses, the tables bowing beneath the weight of food still piled on it. Women on the court staffs stood behind the tables waving paper plates and banana leaves to shoo flies from the feast, while the men lined up to take the choicest morsels.

I turned from the table with my plate piled high and nearly ran into Mr. Aang, the older gentleman from the Hong Kong delegation, who backed away from the near collision with fists up, like a boxer dodging a jab.

"Mr. Burnham, may I have a word with you in private." Aang dropped his guard.

We retreated from the Operator's sonic assault downstairs to the bar, where I was glad to see that Judge Coleman and Valentin Onan had left.

"After you left us earlier, Mr. Harkness mentioned your business looks a little slow at present. Would you be interested in handling some collections work for us on a case where our esteemed counsel has a conflict of interest?"

"Mr. Aang, I don't mean to sound ungrateful. In fact, I'm flattered that you would ask. But have you asked Dick why he is claiming a conflict? Maybe he just doesn't want to handle the matter. What's the case about?"

"It arises from a gambling debt."

"Want a little free legal advice then? Something Harkness won't tell you? You can't bring suit here to collect an illegal debt, like from gaming. Gambling, as you probably know, is illegal here on Pohnpei."

"The debt arose in Chuuk, where there is no law on gambling. Besides, the debt itself is legitimate, a contract case. We have signed promissory notes, so the issue of how the debt came about is not pertinent."

"I don't handle collections cases against locals."

"Oh, that is regrettable. But the case I'm thinking of involves one of yours, an American, living in Chuuk, as well as from a gentleman from Chuuk. If you were successful, I can assure you that we can send several more such cases your way."

"I am going to have to pass, Mr. Aang."

"Very well. It was a pleasure to meet you, Mr. Burnham. My colleagues and I will be on the island for several weeks. Perhaps we will meet again."

Thursday morning proved unusually busy. Jasmina had scheduled a meeting with new clients on the real estate case at 9:00, and I planned to check at the state court for conflict case assignments at the arraignment calendar at 10:00. The land case turned out to be the Operator, who at least took off their sunglasses when they stepped inside. They said I had come recommended and asked to help them buy some land on the island.

"Not only can't I help you buy some land here. No one can."

"Why not?" The keyboard player spoke.

"You're not citizens. Only citizens can own land in Micronesia. I can't own land and I've lived here for five years. My old partner lived here more than twenty years and he couldn't buy any land."

"Is that your partner?" The keyboard player pointed to the portrait of Clarence Darrow.

"Yeah. As a matter of fact it is. Now what you might be able to do is lease some land, and I can help you out with that."

"I guess that would work. We need an isolated place. A place with good water."

"You're going to set up a business? You'll need a business license, a foreign investment permit. I can help you with those, too."

"We're thinking maybe an import-export business," said the keyboard player.

At that, the guitar player nudged the keyboard player slightly, and the keyboard player changed his tune. "Well, not yet. We're musicians first. We need a place to practice where we won't bother anyone, and where no one will bother us."

"Far away, huh. The further the better?"

"The further the better, yeah." The guitar player finally spoke.

"So what do you need water for?" Neither member of the Operator answered me, so I moved on. "Do you have a place in mind?"

"We thought you could help us."

"My card says 'attorney-at-law,' not 'realtor;' not that you'd find one on-island. Ask around among your local friends. Somebody will know somebody who might be willing to lease you some land for a sufficient amount of money."

True to Kazuo's prediction, there were no new conflict assignments. Maybe my lucky streak was coming to a close. When I returned from the state court, Jasmina was giggling. I was about to ask her the joke when I glanced back into my office. I could see someone's boots – a pair of black, patent leather, stacked heel Elvis boots – up on my desk, pushing undoubtedly confidential papers aside. Leaning back in my chair, blowing smoke rings and using the floor as an ashtray, was Jangle.

"Morning, counselor. Back from begging crumbs at the state court?"

I didn't care for the tone, or the comment. "May I have my chair?"

Jangle swung his feet down and stood, taking his sweet time, and mine. He moved around the desk to one of the gunmetal gray

61

folding chairs with "U.S. Navy" stenciled on the back. "Maybe if you got some decent cases, you could get some decent furniture."

"It serves its purpose." I straightened stacks of paper and brushed dirt from the desktop. "What do you want?"

"I just wanted to see how you are sleeping."

"Very well, thank you."

"Maybe you should thank me."

"For not throwing stones on my roof?"

"Throw stones? Don't know what you're talking about. Maybe you should be thanking me for turning away traffic from going by your place. You looking good, counselor. I also want to see if business is picking up."

"We're doing fine."

"So you took the case on the guy from Ngatik?"

"How do you know about that?"

"Small island. Smaller than you think."

"Charlie Warheit. He wouldn't happen to be one of your boys?"

"My boys don't work at Public Works."

"Then what about Daniel, the one who brought the case in?"

"So what if he is?"

"So what? I've already told you. I'm not going to be a gang lawyer."

"And I told you that the Taro Patch Kids are a social organization. Besides, you don't have to take Charlie's case."

"And I don't have to take yours."

"You already deposit the retainer."

"What makes you so sure?"

"Small island. Smaller than you think." Jangle leaned forward and plucked a business card from the holder on the front of my desk. "Do you mind? Maybe you could use another referral."

"I haven't made up my mind to take your case."

"Yes you have. You just have to admit it to yourself."

"If I take the case, will you tell me the meaning of 'who will save the widow's sons?'"

"All in good time, counsel, all in good time. I left the papers for my case with your secretary. Me and her are getting to be good friends. Got a problem with that?"

Jasmina giggled again from the outer office.

"I'm not her father. Jasmina will do as she wishes. She always does."

Jangle stood and smiled, then left the room quickly, as if with a flick of a tail. Jasmina followed him outside, returned a moment later, and handed me a creased criminal complaint and arrest warrant.

"You be careful with him, Jazz." I tried to think of something more profound, but ended up by saying something entirely different. "Everything we do here is confidential. It cannot be discussed with anyone outside. You know that."

"He hasn't asked me anything, Mr. Burnham."

Jasmina hadn't called me Mr. Burnham in years.

CHAPTER SIX

Jangle's arraignment was set for nine o'clock on Monday morning. I was served with the notice of hearing at four on Friday afternoon. I was about to leave the office for a cold one at the Ox & Palm, before the Palikir ex-pat crowd, frequently including Judge Coleman, descended from Olympus to take over the bar as they did every Friday that wasn't a Payday Friday. Few *menwhi* dare brave the Ox & Palm on Payday Fridays, when locals have money to drink and occasion to rumble.

It was just like Judge Coleman to issue last minute notices, but then Maximum Max and I rarely see eye-to-eye. While Al Frost's dislike of Coleman centered at the crotch, my disagreement with the Judge is more cerebral, though not to say less visceral. On rights of the accused, Coleman wanders somewhere to the right of Rehnquist. He sets unattainable bail and impossible pretrial conditions, and refuses to even consider parole. Coleman used to be a D.A. somewhere in the States, and is so openly one-sided that he stops just short of sitting at the prosecutor's table. In sentencing, Maximum Max lives up to his name. A couple of my clients, Secman James and Daniel Mongospam, are waiting on Coleman to even set hearings on petitions for work release.

As for Jangle's arraignment, I had nothing else on that day, or for the rest of the week for that matter, so I didn't sweat a no-work appearance the first thing Monday morning. Stapled to the notice was a copy of a signed summons showing that a bailiff had already served Jangle. I didn't bother to confirm with him. Since the court went to the trouble of serving Jangle, it would be up to Jangle to get himself to court. Thanks to Kazuo, I know the Taro Patch Kids have no telephone. I could have sent someone to tell Jangle, but Utticus was likely to take off early from work on Friday afternoon, and no way would I send Jasmina alone down to La Brea. Besides, unless I agree to do so, I don't have to guarantee the presence of my client at any proceeding. Rarely would I offer that without wrangling some concession from the prosecutor.

Despite a warm Bud hangover (thank you, Sotaro), I was on the road early Monday morning. Coleman had once held me in contempt for being three minutes late, and Al Frost was tardy so many times that I barely acknowledge my late law partner's name in Coleman's courtroom. So I wheeled my ancient Sunny pick-up truck – its four speeds divided by three functioning cylinders – up to Palikir, all the while sifting through the static No-Amp Lester's morning radio show. Better a bogus missionary than the drivel on Voice of America. I arrived a good twenty minutes before nine, with time enough to gulp down a cup of scalding instant coffee at the Palikir canteen – served as always by Dysentery Mary – and sat at a table with a bunch of local workers, most of whom maintained *sakau* hangovers of varying degrees.

But for the fact that it often involves Judge Coleman, I like trying cases at the Supreme Court out in Palikir. The acoustics are nearly perfect and the furnishings are comfortable and relatively new, not like the state court's Rust Territory hand-me-downs. A big drawback when appearing before Coleman is that the Judge likes it hot. Coleman's chambers have no air-conditioning, and he orders the clerk to turn it off when he has a case in the courtroom.

Although ceiling fans and an occasional breeze can keep temperatures at merely torrid, the courtroom lacks the white noise of a cranked air-con unit. Proceedings are frequently interrupted when heavy trucks or cars with busted mufflers cruise by. The court staff dubbed one such malefactor on the Palikir maintenance crew "Three O'Clock Charlie." Every day at blue collar quitting time, Charlie, behind the wheel of an ancient Mazda truck, rolled past the courthouse with the paced dignity of a Kosraen pastor on the way to church, so timely that those inside the courthouse checked their watches, so slowly that Charlie delayed any hearing then taking place. Maximum Max finally issued a bench warrant for the arrest of Three O'Clock Charlie, and then held him in contempt. Then Chief Public Defender Al Frost managed to have the conviction reversed on appeal.

I slurped the dregs of my coffee before entering the courthouse. No eating, drinking, or chewing betel nut is permitted inside. At the defense table, I paged through my case file, which consisted of the criminal complaint signed by the Attorney General, the notice of hearing, and the summons. A misdemeanor may be charged on a criminal complaint alone. But Jangle was charged with felonies; the charging paper has to be an Information. (There is no grand jury in Micronesia; in fact, no juries at all.) It's a common and irritating practice of the AG's office to wait until the last minute to serve an Information. I assumed that one had been filed the week before – setting in motion the arraignment and summons – but decided against going into the Clerk's office to examine the official case file. Coleman probably had the file on his desk, and I wanted to preserve what slim argument I might have for prejudicial delay.

At ten minutes to nine, Pietro Joram, Coleman's bailiff, and Susanna Hilkiah, a court reporter, walked in to test the microphones and recording equipment. In Micronesia, court reporters tape proceedings, rather than produce a typed Q&A record. I stood to shake hands with both. I had helped Susanna's brother in a collections case and Pietro has a soft spot in his heart for Al Frost, who had saved his father from a yam-load of trouble in an official misconduct investigation back in Trust Territory times. As we chatted, Roberta Ely and her client, Entis Robert, a scared-looking kid with his arm in a sling, came into the courtroom and sat at the defense table.

"Easy on the handshake, Drake. Entis has a dislocated shoulder."

"How'd that happen?"

"He won't say," Roberta leaned to whisper. "In fact, he won't tell me a thing."

She said Entis was from Pingelap Atoll, a flyspeck of coral and palm trees about halfway between Pohnpei and Kosrae. In the meantime, a few spectators had wandered into the gallery, maybe looking for some free entertainment. Some may have been early arrivals for the 9:30 civil calendar. Jangle, however, was nowhere to be seen.

At five minutes to nine, a waft of orange blossom perfume and talcum powder heralded the entrance of Assistant Attorney General Marielle Hargraves. I turned to Roberta and groaned.

Roberta just shrugged her shoulders.

Trying a case before Coleman was bad enough, but trying it against Hargraves would test the patience of Job. Marielle, by then six months on-island, was supposed to be the hot-stuff prosecutor/trial attorney who would finally turn the fortunes of the Litigation

Department at the Attorney General's office. She had all the right credentials: Phi Beta Kappa at SMU, Texas law, certified by the National Institute for Trial Advocacy, plus she had worked for one of the biggest firms in Houston, Texas. Hargraves claimed boatloads of courtroom experience, and expectations ran high. Her press clippings arrived a week before she did, including a cushy piece in the Houston Chronicle – apparently one in a series on the debutante turned law student turned lawyer. In the piece, Marielle gushed about going to where she wouldn't have to where hose and heels, where she could hang out on beaches and learn to surf. It was obvious that no one had clued in Hargraves to the difficulty of surfing a mangrove swamp. Sokehs Rock might be the Diamond Head of Micronesia, but mucky Taketik is not its Waikiki.

Complaints started within, oh say twenty minutes of Marielle's arrival on-island, most of which were in the starts with "b" rhymes with "itch" category. Her living quarters were inadequate of course, because the air conditioning did not stay on during island-wide power outages. Marielle couldn't understand why she wasn't provided a staff car. After all, she lived in Kolonia and had to drive to work in Palikir every day. The fact that everyone else in her office had to do the same thing was somehow lost on Ms. Hargraves. And when shipment of her household goods was delayed, the PM&O agent fielded her daily telephone harangues and weekly threat of litigation like a clumsy third baseman fending off a bad hop grounder. Marielle even tried to subpoena all the shipping company's records, a subpoena quickly quashed.

Office life was little better. Marielle is far too aggressive for laid back Pohnpei. And it wasn't only the public defender and legal services offices that complained. Hargraves is whispered to be imperious with her own office staff, unforgiving of inevitable ESL typos and garbled or undelivered messages. Marielle quickly alienated the Supreme Court staff, too, and when she stalks the halls even her fellow assistant attorneys general scurry like roaches when a light is flicked on. The vaunted newspaper clipping was torn from the bulletin board once it was explained. Marielle Hargraves has a press agent. In fact, she has a book contract – with movie rights optioned – on her "unique" struggle as an American lawyer in Micronesia.

It turned out that Marielle's much-vaunted stateside courtroom experience was as spear-carrier, toting briefs for the big time litigators at her white-shoe firm. She turned heads with a flash of cleavage – and a much-rumored hidden tattoo – rather than an elegant argument. True, Ms. Hargraves had appeared in court stateside, although it was probably only arguing discovery before a commissioner, maybe a little law and motion. She had zero criminal cases and her only trials were in moot court. Marielle even put off Judge Coleman, who has an eye for a shapely calf, local or *menwhi.*

For Jangle's arraignment, Marielle was dressed conservatively, for her, in a pleated skirt that came to mid-calf, and a blouse unbuttoned to mid-chest. It looked as if she had brought half the law library with her – Rules of Evidence, Rules of Criminal Procedure, Volume i of the annotated Code – and her case file was already a half-inch thick. She shuffled some papers, then approached the defense table to hand Roberta and me copies of the two-page Information. As she did, she whispered in a husky Lauren Bacall, "I'd like to discuss this case after the hearing."

"Nice to let us know the charges so soon before arraignment," said Roberta.

I nodded, and glanced again at the clock. Three minutes to nine and the chair beside me was empty. My client was nowhere in sight.

The three-count Information was shorter than the criminal complaint. It charged Jangle Elwell and Entis Robert with Grand Theft, in violation of II FSMC section 931, to wit, theft from the Micronesian National Bank, Chuuk State Branch; with Conspiracy, in violation of II FSMC section 1145, to wit, conspiring to commit the offense of Grand Theft; and with Receiving stolen property, in violation of II FSMC section 937, to wit, receiving property stolen from the Micronesian National Bank, Chuuk State Branch. It was a lean Information, without much to attack or give a clue as to the actual facts.

At nine o'clock, Jangle had yet to appear.

At one minute past nine, all rose for the entrance Judge Coleman, a smile brightening his sunburned face. Coleman hosts Sunday afternoon softball scrums at the Spanish Wall ballfield, and while sunburns are a common post-game ailment, so too are twisted ankles and wrenched knees. Maximum Max does not like to lose.

"Oyez, oyez, oyez," Pietro called. "The Supreme Court is now in session, the Honorable Maximinus T. Coleman presiding. God bless the island of Pohnpei and this Honorable Court."

The other Supreme Court justices had long since dispensed with the formal invocation when entering the courtroom. But Maximum Max insists on pomp. The other justices had also dispensed with gavels as "un-Micronesian." Judge Coleman, who is used to having something to pound on the bench, substitutes a basalt taro pounder for his gavel. The piece is an antiquity, something Coleman claimed he dug up in his backyard. Even though it is an antiquity, Judge Coleman doesn't yet have to turn it over to anyone. The state antiquities law is a variation on "finders-keepers," in that anyone who unearths an antiquity can use it as he or she sees fit, so long as the finder doesn't sell it, lend it, give it away, or try to take it off-island, in which case title reverts to the state. The law, I'm told, is modeled on Yap's, where one can own stone money, a Spanish cannon, or a (non-functioning) German rifle. Just don't take them off-island.

Coleman asked the bailiff to call the morning's calendar as he settled into his chair. I know that Judge Coleman will often rush the preliminaries, but without Jangle in the courtroom, I would just as soon have him dawdle.

"There is only one case on the criminal calendar this morning, Your Honor. The People versus Jangle Elwell and Entis Robert, Criminal Case number 176." Pietro squinted at the clock on the wall. "This case is called for arraignment at 9:02 a.m."

"Thank you, Bailiff Joram," Coleman said. "I see Marielle Hargraves from the Attorney General's office is here for the prosecution. Good morning, Miss Hargraves."

"Good morning, Your Honor. And it's Ms. Hargraves."

"For the defense, I note Mrs. Roberta Ely, and her former confederate from the Public Defenders office, Mr. Drake Burnham, are both here. Whose client is that?"

"Mine, Your Honor. His name is Entis Robert." Roberta stood at the table to answer.

"Please stand at the podium when addressing the Court, Mrs. Ely."

"Good morning, Your Honor." I decided to take the initiative and stood. "Drake Burnham appearing on behalf of defendant Jangle Elwell. As you may see..."

Coleman clicked his pen a couple of times and pointed with it toward the podium. I took my time getting to the podium.

"As I was saying, Your Honor. It appears that Mr. Elwell is not yet in court."

"Not yet in court. Well, I see some things have not changed at Frost & Burnham. What's your excuse for being unable to proceed at the time noticed?"

"I'm ready. But it may be that my client was confused about where to come. As you know, bail was set by a justice pro tem in the state court, not here in Palikir. With the Court's indulgence, I could telephone my office to check the state court. If Mr. Elwell is there, I'll have him here quicker than you can say 'Kapingamarangi.'"

"Are you just trying to buy time, counsel? Because I'm not selling. I noticed this hearing for nine o'clock and you should have your client here."

"To the contrary, Your Honor, and with all due respect. As defense counsel, I am under no obligation to assure the presence of my client at any proceeding. In fact, it would be an error of constitutional dimensions if ..."

"Mr. Burnham." Coleman smacked the taro pounder on the bench to cut me off. "I'm in no mood to discuss anyone's constitutional rights at an arraignment. It is now four minutes past nine. I have a full civil calendar starting in less than half an hour, and I'm inches away from issuing a bench warrant for the arrest of your client."

"Before you do that, sir, perhaps the Court should recess. It may be that Mr. Elwell was not served with the notice of hearing. I myself did not receive a copy until the close of business on Friday."

"I have little patience ..." Coleman stopped. Squealing tires of a fast turning vehicle gusted into the courtroom, as if Three O'Clock Charlie had returned to do doughnuts in the gravel parking lot. Everyone in the gallery turned to look outside. Coleman waved Pietro to the bench, probably to have him arrest whoever made the racket. Before Pietro could hurry past the bar, the wide double doors to the courtroom swung open.

"Is that your client?"

I was relieved, and more than a little annoyed to see Jangle Elwell striding into court, sporting mirrored sunglasses as if he were an Alabama state trooper approaching the car of a speeding Yankee.

"Mr. Jangle Elwell?" Coleman asked.

Jangle nodded as he came to the defense table.

"Did you receive this summons?" Coleman held up the paper.

Jangle nodded again.

"You should have been here at nine o'clock."

"Why? What happened?"

The courtroom slithered into nervous laughter. Coleman glared through the chuckles until order returned.

"Another comment like that, Mr. Elwell, and I will hold you in contempt. Let's proceed."

Coleman read the Information aloud, word-for-word, and asked both defendants if they understood what he had read. Then he informed both of their constitutional rights. Maximum Max had done the routine countless times and ripped through the rights of the accused so quickly that you might think he thought the Bill of Rights was written on the back of a cocktail napkin. "Now I will inquire of each defendant how he intends to plead."

"Your Honor," I stood and gestured to Jangle, slouched in his chair. "I was served with the Information only this morning, just a few minutes before nine. I have had no time to discuss the charges with my client. I request that the Court schedule a separate arraignment to take the defendants' pleas."

"Request denied. Counsel, please approach the bench."

I frowned as I glanced at Roberta. I look forward to a Coleman sidebar about as much as a root canal. Coleman told the reporter not to tape the sidebar. What was said would not be part of the official record. Maximum Max leaned over the bench and wagged a finger in my face.

"Burnham, I know as conflict counsel you are paid a premium for time in court. But with the Compact past the second drawdown, I am not about to enter an order to underwrite any unnecessary inflation of your bill to this Court."

I was about to protest. Coleman cut me off with a karate chop that would do Bruce Lee proud and told us to return to our tables. "Susanna, back on the record, please. Mr. Burnham, how does your client plead?"

"He is not ready to plead, Your Honor." I stuck to my guns.

"Very well. Mr. Elwell, the Court will enter a plea of Not Guilty to all three counts, because your attorney is not ready."

I took the hit and kept my mouth shut.

"Now, Mrs. Ely, what about your client?"

Roberta, clever girl, knew better than to repeat my mistake. "Not Guilty."

"Very well. Let's set up a trial schedule. Does anyone anticipate a pre-trial motion?"

I stood again; although you'd think by then I'd know better. "Your Honor, the defendants are charged with robbing a bank in Chuuk State. The defendants may move for a change of venue."

"Your Honor, if I may be heard?" Marielle, seated at the prosecutor's table, spoke on the record for the first time. Arraignments are no-brainers for prosecutors, fitting if you think about it.

"Certainly, Miss Hargraves."

"Both defendants are charged with receiving money here on Pohnpei. It may also be that the plan and initial acts in furtherance of the conspiracy took place here as well. Venue over the conspiracy and receiving charges is therefore proper here on Pohnpei."

Coleman turned back to me. "Still want to make your motion, counsel?"

"I reserve the right."

"Very well. I will set the following dates: The discovery cut-off is July 16. The last day to file all pretrial motions is July 30, and let's have no corny canned briefs ala Al Frost, okay Mr. Burnham? Hearings on evidentiary motions, August 7. Trial is to begin at nine a.m. on August 8. That's nine o'clock, Mr. Elwell. Not five minutes past nine. If there are no questions, the Court will recess for fifteen minutes before calling today's civil calendar."

As Coleman left the courtroom, Roberta and I turned to our clients.

"I don't care why you were late," I said to Jangle. "Next time leave earlier. Don't gamble twenty years because you didn't leave twenty minutes earlier."

"Hey, I don't gamble."

"I don't care what you call it."

"Don't be waving twenty years at me, neither."

"Look, Jangle. Your next twenty years are in that man's hands. It doesn't pay to piss him off."

"Hey counsel, take it easy. It looked like Max Max was more mad at you."

"Precisely. If he turns his anger lose on the lawyer he's less likely to take it out on the client. Now wise up, or you'll be getting yourself a new lawyer."

"I didn't hire you to be my lawyer so you could be in my face. You're making this personal, and there's no accounting for what I might do if it's personal."

"I don't care what you're going to do, personal or not. I don't care what you think I'm here to do. What I am here to do is defend you and I can't do that if you tie my hands behind my back, by your being late, or your being in my face, or whatever."

Jangle chuckled, stood, and put on those damned mirrored shades. "See you later, Drake Burnham, attorney at law."

Jangle held out one of my business cards, maybe one he had grabbed from Jasmina's desk the week before. He snapped it, like a Vegas blackjack dealer, so the reverse side was up, slapped it on the defense counsel table, and left the courtroom. I counted to ten and took two deep, cleansing breaths before I even glanced at the card. I was angry, angry with Coleman for ripping me, pissed at my client for being late. When I heard Jangle's truck engine roar out in the lot, I picked up the business card. On the reverse side he had written, "Better win, motherfucker." Actually, the last word was in Kosraen, a phrase that on that island is an instant invitation to fight.

I stuffed the business card in my shirt pocket; Exhibit A to my motion to withdraw as counsel of record, if it came to that.

My sister-in-law had been a big city public defender right out of law school. She left that job after a couple of years following an incident with a client in a holding cell. She had advised her client to accept the offered plea bargain. Her client took exception to her advice, physical exception. He slugged her. Of course, she withdrew as the creep's counsel, and rather quickly got out of the public defender business altogether. Now she is in a prosperous civil practice. I wondered if that was in the cards for me.

Then I thought of another hand. I'd heard about lawyers retained by the Bloods in South Central L.A., guys who had gotten rich representing the gang. Some handled criminal cases; others were tax lawyers who helped launder dirty money and hide the gang's take. But the tax lawyers learned too much. After one of them was indicted by the feds for tax fraud, but before he could turn state's evidence, he disappeared. They found his body, or pieces of it anyway, hacked up and stuffed into a 55-gallon drum out in the desert somewhere. When they opened the barrel, the lawyer's hand was on top, twisted into a crude gang sign before rigor mortis set in.

Roberta turned to me once Entis had left the courtroom. "Looks like you have a bit of a client control problem."

"Yeah? But what I was really wondering was whether I could find some corny canned briefs on the meat aisle at Palm Terrace."

Roberta was about to reply, when Marielle Hargraves walked over.

"I have an offer to resolve this case before you all dedicate too much time and effort to it." Marielle gave me a half smirk, half smile, then bent forward and placed her hands on the table. I gazed in turn down her décolletage, trying to catch a glimpse of the much-rumored tattoo.

"Care to hear my modest proposal?" said Marielle.

"Okay. But be swift about it."

"Should one of us leave?" Roberta squeaked like a third wheel.

"No. The offer goes for both of your clients." Marielle turned to Ms. Ely, then stood back and folded her arms across her chest. Show over.

"I've only just begun to go through the evidence, there's just so much." Marielle sighed. "The government considers this case to be very serious, and my office is authorized to prosecute your clients to the fullest extent of the law."

"Cut the crap, Marielle," I said. "You're not on Court TV."

"Ms. Ely. Mr. Burnham. I want to make sure you realize what your clients are facing. When they are convicted ..."

"If they are convicted. Proof beyond a reasonable doubt, remember?"

"When they are convicted, I'll push for twenty-five years: ten for grand theft, ten for conspiracy, five for receiving stolen property, sentences to run consecutively, not concurrently."

Roberta said, "No reasonable judge would sentence a defendant to the statutory maximum for a non-violent first offense."

"Not even Judge Coleman?" said Marielle. "I've heard that some trial counselors in the Public Defenders office call Judge Coleman 'The Time Machine.'"

"We actually call him Maximum Max," I said. "But whatever Coleman's nickname is, I don't think you've thought your case through. How can anyone be charged with both robbing a bank and receiving property supposedly stolen from it?"

"We do not charge what we cannot prove."

"The prosecutor's ever-ready response," I said.

"What's your offer?" said Roberta.

"To save the government the expense in time and dollars of pursuing this prosecution," Marielle prattled on like a rookie trying to drown inexperience in a flood of rhetoric. "I propose that if your clients plead guilty to grand theft and conspiracy, we will drop the charge of receiving."

I waited for the other *zori* to drop.

"Sentencing recommendation?" Roberta finally prompted.

"Twenty years, plus full restitution, of course."

"Let me get this straight," I said. "You agree to drop the charge you cannot prove and in exchange Jangle pleads guilty and agrees to max out on the sentence? Gee, that's great. I'd like to tell him right now."

"Marielle, my client isn't even twenty years old," Roberta said. "You expect me to recommend that he spend the equivalent of his entire life in jail? Without a fight?"

"That's my proposal."

"Of course, we will inform our clients of your generous offer, won't we Drake? But without seeing any of your evidence, I can tell you that neither of us is likely to recommend your kind offer."

"As I said, this offer is made in the interest of efficiency. My proposal remains open until I have to respond to a discovery request or a pretrial motion. And this is a one-time offer."

"More like a one-time extortion," I said.

"Let's not make this personal." Marielle leveled what I'm sure she hoped was a 'killer' stare, then pivoted quickly and walked back to the prosecutor's table and scooped up her case file with the grace of a Manitowoc steam shovel dredging coral along the Causeway. That was twice in one morning that someone accused me of getting 'personal,' a new, personal best for me.

I turned to Roberta. "I think she digs me."

Ms. Ely, bless her soul, just laughed.

CHAPTER SEVEN

Unreasonable plea-bargain offers aside, fortunes at Frost & Burnham looked decidedly positive. For the first time in recent memory, I drew a check to myself for a sum more than Jasmina's paycheck. I ordered paper, toner for the printer, coffee, all on credit, of course, so long as most of the firm's assets were cached in the client trust account. The personal injury case looked straightforward, a low-effort file with a shot at a big payoff. Our client, Charlie Warheit, stopped in the office his first day back on-island from medical treatment in Manila. He scrawled the contingency fee contract left-handed while holding the paper steady with a right hand so heavily bandaged that it looked like the claw of a coconut crab. Charlie was pathetic; I knew any judge would be sympathetic, except maybe Maximum Max. Kazuo Olopai had called to say he was representing the State on Charlie's claim. He nearly admitted liability and sounded anxious to come to an agreement about the extent of Charlie's damages.

In the meantime, other business picked up, too. One of "The Operator" guys mentioned they had found a parcel in Kitti that met their needs, and that they had started to clear the land to lay a foundation. They asked me to review a lease. One difficulty they mentioned was that the owner had found some stone carvings on his land. I advised the musicians-turned-builders that they could not keep for themselves any antiquities they found, and that it would be best to turn over to me anything they unearthed.

All that work left me so busy that I actually spent an evening in the office preparing a pretrial motion to change the venue in Jangle's case from Pohnpei, where the case was filed, to Chuuk, where the bank was robbed. I knew the odds were stacked against Coleman's granting the motion, stacked like the basalt stone walls at Nan Madol, the pre-contact stone city on the far side of the island. Even if he granted the motion, Maximum Max could follow the case to Chuuk. A change in venue may not result in a change of jurists. But with Marielle so confident in her case, I had to make the most of any potential for error.

I agreed to a division of labor with Roberta. I took care of the venue motion while Ms. Ely served on the Attorney General's office a neutrally-worded, third-person request for discovery. In criminal cases, the defendant has the sole right to initiate discovery, a matter linked to the right against self-incrimination. It made sense to have Entis request discovery. Jangle probably had a prior from his stateside gangbanging days that I would just as soon not let Marielle unearth. With just a little effort, the Attorney General's office could locate Jangle's record. But I was sure Marielle wouldn't make the effort. It's not that she's lazy. It's more like no one at the Litigation Department quite knows what he or she is doing, although heaven help the defense bar if the Attorney General ever hires a career prosecutor.

Compared to Jangle's, Entis's record was clean as a Kosraen after a bath on an *etawi* confession Sunday. No convictions, no arrests. No drunken and disorderly or disturbing the peace charges that are more like island rights of passage than black marks on a criminal record.

A few nagging details kept interrupting my otherwise occupied thoughts. First was that Buster, my common law dog, had disappeared. I call Buster that because we never had a formal agreement to live together, it just developed over time. Buster might disappear for days when a nearby female went into heat, but he always returned to where he knew he would be fed. I don't worry much about Buster getting snatched by some hungry locals in search of barbecue. He's wary of all locals, friendly only to *menwhi*. To his nose, Americans must smell differently.

After missing a few nights, I wondered if Buster was the victim of a Public Safety dragnet. When the boonie dog population gets too large, or if a mutt bites some kid, Public Safety will round up and shoot any stray they find. Police are known to be a wee bit aggressive on the possibility of fresh dog meat. A few years back, some Americans' pets, well-fed ones especially, got knocked off that way, as if it wasn't a dog's life anyway. After the resulting brouhaha, the cops said they wouldn't shoot any dog wearing a collar. I bought a collar for Buster.

I figure Buster is savvy enough to delay the inevitable dog-napping. Still, I miss Buster on those nights he's gone. With his head on my lap, Buster is the closest thing I have to family on-island. In Washington D.C., they say if you want a friend, get a dog. On Pohnpei, it's the opposite.

Another nagging detail was Jasmina, who had turned noticeably formal toward me, although typically efficient. Around her I felt as if I had stuck my foot, zori and all, squarely into my mouth. Jasmina debriefed me coolly when I returned from Jangle's arraignment. I told her Coleman had embarrassed me so completely I felt as if I had appeared in court in my pajamas; and I sleep naked. That kind of line to a local is generally good for a laugh, but I couldn't get a rise out of Jasmina. She was out of the office more often, too. After a day off from work, was all smiles and no information. Jasmina's lunch breaks grew longer. One day, she came in with a brand new boombox. She set it on some file cabinets and kept the volume low when I was in.

On a rare morning when I got to the office before Jasmina, I found her cousin, Freddy Solomon, waiting outside. Freddy is from the Marshall Islands, on Jasmina's mother's side of the family. I call him "Freddy the Freeloader" because he frequently hits me up for a beer when he sees me at the Ox & Palm, or for small loans, usually on those Fridays that aren't paydays. Freddy is an ass-kisser nonpareil, and I generally have to keep myself from gagging when he asks a favor. I once defended Freddy on a malicious mischief charge. He paid my fee with a box of used videotapes. About half of them worked.

"I have to ask you for one small favor, my good friend and Defender, Mr. Drake Burnham. You see my family wants all of us back together in the same place. They will give me one very good job cleaning at the Surfway Store at the US base on Kwajalein. It's a nice job with plenty money in an air-con building."

"That's great, Freddy. I think you should do it."

"They will also give one nice place to stay on Ebeye."

"I didn't know there were any nice places on Ebeye."

"The family also has one very good job for Jasmina, also on Ebeye. So I must ask. Can I take Jasmina back to the Marshall Islands?"

"Jasmina hasn't said anything to me about moving back to the Marshalls. I thought she liked it here."

"I did not tell her yet, because I want to ask your permission first."

"Why ask me?"

"We all see Jasmina is acting different. She is never home when we need her. She has some new, very expensive clothes. I think she moved the flower from her right ear and put it on her left ear. She was open. Now she is close. I think you will marry her."

"Marry her? Me?"

At that moment, my would-be bride-to-be walked into the office, saw Freddy, and began to shout in Marshallese, as if she knew precisely why her cousin was at my desk. Freddy scurried into the outer office to shout back. Soon enough the two were in a pitched battle, a crescendo of Marshallese, of which I know barely a word. Then Jasmina began chucking things at Freddy, starting with pencils and working her way up through pens. By the time I got to Jasmina's desk, she had grabbed the boombox and was swinging it at Freddy like a sledgehammer. When I wrested the boombox away from Jasmina she turned to swipe a stapler from her desk and had it in hand ready to fly. Discretion being the better part of valor, Freddy retreated, scampering to the office door while continuing to fling verbal brickbats at Jasmina. He slammed the door behind him.

"Jasmina," I pulled the stapler from her hand. "What the heck was that about?"

"That Freddy. He makes me so angry. Sometimes I really hate him."

"What for?"

"Ever since he saw my new boombox, Freddy wants it. He is always coming to our place asking for it. I brought it to the office so he would not take it. Now he knows it's here."

"Is that why you think he came? Freddy told me he wanted to take you back to the Marshall Islands."

"Oh Freddy always says that. He always says 'keep the family together.' But I don't want to go back. I want to stay on Pohnpei. Maybe I can start a new family here."

I had Typhoon Jasmina promise not to throw office supplies at any visitor, no matter how provoked. She did, but stewed through the rest of the day. At closing time, I noticed Jasmina sported a fresh hibiscus blossom behind her ear. Freddy was wrong. The flower was tucked behind her right ear. Jasmina was still available.

At home that evening, I got a phone call from Valentin Onan, the Pohnpei Justice Ombudsman. The call was a surprise, since Onan and I do not run in the same circles. He's from Madolinimh and has family and clan connections to both traditional and elected leaders on the main island and on Mokil Atoll. If Pohnpei has a Tammany Hall, Valentin would be known as "Mister Fifty," for the 50-pound bags of rice he delivers to assure a family's vote for the correct slate of candidates. His appointment and tenure as Justice Ombudsman are seen as a quid pro quo, a reward for pre-election work.

Onan's influence was whispered to be critical to the appointment of Judge Coleman to the bench on the Trust Territory High Court, and later to the Supreme Court. In many ways they are inseparable. Valentin is Coleman's designated drinking buddy, the one who can drive when Maximum Max reaches maximum alcohol intake.

On other islands, justice ombudsmen are busy as translators, clerks and marshals all rolled into one, pinch hitters for any Supreme Court job that needs filling, short of actually trying a case. But the Supreme Court staff on Pohnpei is bursting with bailiffs and translators, so that Valentin rarely appears in either courtroom or file room. On occasion, Onan might be assigned to mediate a contested collections case, or oversee a judicial sale of assets in aid of judgment, but most of the time he sits in the office and plays Reversi on an office computer. This lack of responsibility makes Valentin's job something of a sinecure, steady pay for occasional work. Some ex-pats grumble the title "Pohnpei JO" really means "Pohnpei jack off." But featherbedding is so common in government jobs that to single out Onan for abuse is unfair. Valentin is a nice enough guy, who gets belligerent only when falling down drunk. His only other vice, if you could call it that, was a tendency to ESL-malapropisms, what I call "Onan-isms."

Valentin told me he was buying at the Sans Souci, the bar at Daosokele. I told him I'd be there in twenty minutes. Daosokele is close to a tidal estuary, past the hospital and just before the circumference road makes a big S curve to cross the Green River Bridge. The San Souci parking area is hidden from the road by a stand of bamboo, and the bar itself is on the water, down a dark, winding path through the jungle. The path doubles back to a spot from which you can clearly see the bridge. The San Souci – locals call it the "Sand Sushi" – was once a pretty swanky place. The owners had sunk a lot of money into it, hoping to draw on the ex-pat and tourist trade en route to the Coral Reef Hotel. Bugs drawn to the electric lights from nearby mangrove swamps plague the bar. The owners had installed two enormous ultra-violet bug zappers, but the sheer mass of electrocuted insect protein shorted them out, a pair of matching techno white elephants overwhelmed by the fecund island. With prices too high for locals and an atmosphere to buggy for most *menwhi*, bartender Sneaky Pete Caleb often has the place to himself. That makes it a good place to meet someone on the sly. From the water's edge you can clearly see anyone approaching on the bridge, while the jungle assures they can't see you. Al Frost had recommended it as a prime spot for a romantic liaison.

A single car sat in the lot, not Valentin's, and I wondered if I had beaten Onan there. I stumbled down the path toward the light and music from the bar, stubbing my toes en route. Valentin was behind the bar, the picture of a contented island barkeep, perusing a three-month old copy of the Pacific Daily News as if it were scripture. Sneaky Pete was nowhere to be seen. But wherever the regular bartender was, Valentin had the volume up on Caleb's music, slack-string reggae, a cross between Hawaiian and Jamaican, a style known as "Jawaiian." Valentin asked if I was thirsty, fished a cold Budweiser from a cooler behind the bar, cracked the top, and then wrapped the can in a paper napkin.

"You've made me very happy, Valentin." I took a slug from the can. "Now what's up?"

Onan nodded to a table on the lower level of the bar, close to the water. Seated at the table was Judge Coleman. I walked over. Coleman's chair faced upriver, toward the Green River Bridge, his back to the bar.

"Sit down, Burnham." Maximum Max was used to giving orders.

I sat across the table from him. "Good evening, Judge."

"Val? Bring me another cold one, dim the electric lights, and turn down that damn jungle music."

Coleman looked as if he was on his way, but by no means had arrived at the same condition he was at the Bench and Bar Banquet. When Valentin turned off the Jawaiian, I could hear someone pounding *sakau* nearby, maybe on the other side of the river. The sound carried clearly and I wondered if rain was due.

"I guess I should have seen through Valentin's invitation," I said as Onan brought a new beer to Judge Coleman, and a kerosene lantern to the table.

"Sorry for the mystery." Coleman took the beer Valentin offered, then turned to me and smiled. It may have been the first time he'd ever smiled at me. "I thought we might continue our chat from the Bench and Bar Banquet. You disappeared rather abruptly that night."

"I didn't know you wanted me to stick around."

"I did," said Coleman. Then he frowned, "By the way, how did you get here tonight? Taxi?"

"I drove."

"Good, good." Coleman eased his face into another smile. "I'll bet Al Frost never told you that he and I were drinking buddies when he first came down to Micro."

"He didn't, Judge. But I heard you use one of his favorite phrases the other night and I had to wonder."

"Oh we were a dynamic duo in those days, Drake. Do you mind if I call you Drake?"

I didn't, but I knew I didn't have a snowball's chance in Satawal of in turn calling him anything other than "Judge" or "Your Honor."

"Yes, back in Trust Territory times Frost and I rode the circuit together with some of the original TT jurists, like Judge Hansen and Judge Curtis."

"Frost told me that Judge Curtis had a bad habit of cutting in on arguments. He said lawyers called him 'Curtis Interruptus.'"

"Maybe Al would call a judge that. Not me. Attorneys must show the proper respect for the bench." Coleman waxed serious for a moment, then forced another smile. "Yes, Frost and I rode the circuit together, me prosecuting, Al defending. We were at each other's throats in the courtroom, of course, but we were pals everywhere else. We drank beachfront bars from Peleliu to Majuro, chased skirts on Saipan, Yap, Kwajalein. It was one hell of a good time."

Coleman looked away across the river, as if enchanted by reverie. I wondered how much of this was true and how much was embellishing on the memory of a dead opponent. Al had certainly not told me about drinking or chasing dames with Maximum Max Coleman.

"Practice was simpler then. We didn't have to worry about half the crap we face every day now. There's so much more violent crime today. Rarely did we have to deal with anything like murder."

"What about the coconut husker homicide?" I had a laundry list of Frost's favorite war stories to trot out if Coleman continued on this track.

"There were exceptions, of course. But practice was less complex, and a lot more civil. We didn't have to face what we have today."

He stopped for a moment and we listened as across the river a second *sakau* pounder joined the first, the pulpy mass of the pepper root muffling the sharp glint of the basalt stone into a hearty thump. I was surprised that Judge Coleman was speaking to me at all, much less so candidly. I sipped my beer slowly to keep my wits about me.

"This is a fragile society. Opening Micronesia to the world has made the islands uncertain places. Sometimes I wonder if we are standing at the bedside to listen helplessly as a great island society heaves its death rattle. Traditional controls are falling aside. The chiefs have lost most of their power everywhere but Yap, and it's slipping away there, too. But the elected leaders, the ones who went to the States for schooling, to learn about democracy and government and free market economies, they're not quite ready to take up the reins of power. Do you know what I mean, Drake?"

"I think the locals will learn from their mistakes, if we let them make mistakes."

Coleman laughed. "You sound just like Frost, just like Al. You're both confused about our purpose out here. I have a different perspective now, earned by sitting in judgment. I believe – and there are many others, local and ex-pat, who agree with me – that it is our responsibility as Americans to keep things under control until the new leadership can take over and bring this society fully into the twenty-first century."

I've heard this neo-colonialist bullshit before, if not from Judge Coleman. His white man's burden speech was almost touching. Almost. I was ready to disagree more vigorously, but caution kept me from believing that this was an open session of the Pohnpei debating society.

"Sorry, Judge. I disagree. I often think we cause more problems out here than what we're worth."

"You're a lot like Frost. But you're a damn good lawyer, Drake. Better than Al in many ways. Your briefs are tighter, and though your oral arguments tend to melodrama, you're not nearly as bad as Al, who took every evidentiary objection as a chance to make a speech on the Constitution. You've got a good head on your shoulders, Drake. You know when to fish and when to cut bait. And you know when a hole is fished out."

I took another pull on my beer. Across the river, the *sakau* pounders were getting into a rhythm.

"Let's talk about a defendant in my courtroom; on a case you are involved in. Don't worry about your ethical obligations. I'm speaking in a strictly hypothetical sense. We won't discuss the substance of your case.

I swallowed hard. No longer was this a philosophical rambling.

"Certain locals in positions of power have suggested to me in no uncertain terms that this person is a menace to society, any society, but particularly so on a small, isolated island. If not for your professional relationship with this person, you would agree with me, I'm sure. Some have suggested that this certain person is trying to foist some sort of class warfare on-island. He might have a lot of takers here on Pohnpei. Maybe that's why he set up shop here. I don't know that I would go that far, but this person is a divisive force, and must be reckoned with. It's funny if you think about it. Back in the States, that certain person would be nothing but a small time hoodlum, a hooligan, not top of the heap."

Sort of like you, I thought, but kept it to myself. Instead I said, "You're talking about Jangle Elwell."

"Don't be a damn fool, Burnham. I won't confirm that."

"But you just did. Listen, Judge, we cannot talk about an active file in your courtroom unless someone from the Attorney General's office is present."

"Nonsense. No one even knows that we're here. Did you tell anyone that you were coming to Daosokele?"

"No."

"And you didn't know until you arrived that I'm here."

"True."

"And you have no reason to tell anyone about this meeting. I swear, Burnham, if anyone else hears one peep about this rendezvous, I'll hang you. I'll deny ever being here, of course. Valentin and his wife will swear an oath that tonight he and I drank *sakau* at his place. My truck is parked there even now. Think about it. You would accuse a sitting justice of the Supreme Court of improper conduct. And you wouldn't have a shred of evidence."

I wished for a copy of today's Pacific Daily News, and a Polaroid camera.

"Just like your partner," Coleman continued. "No one will believe you, not even your drinking buddies. People will say that things haven't changed at Frost & Burnham. They're still spinning out fantasies and conspiracies. And they'll be right."

I glanced up at the bar. Valentin had his back to us, his eyes on his newspaper, ignoring our conversation. "Looks like you hold all the cards."

"So hear me out. You're a stand-up guy, Drake. You know what's good for the islands. Why don't you do the right thing and lose this case?"

"You want me to take a fall?"

"You have to believe that the island would be a better place if that certain person were locked up for the next twenty years. Don't you agree?"

I hate to admit it, but I hesitated. I thought about Jasmina and the drive-bys and the business card with the threat written on the back. But I didn't answer Coleman's question, not directly. "Why do you need me?"

"Let's face it. Marielle Hargraves may be a ripe papaya of a woman, but she couldn't try her way out of a paper bag. She could screw up the prosecution, big time. And you're just the type who would sit back and let her blow it."

"I'm sorry, but it isn't my job to help Marielle Hargraves."

"It isn't. But you'd take advantage of every mistake to try to get the conviction reversed on appeal. Judge Baxendale and the Chief Justice have always taken a shine to your arguments."

"How do you know there will be a conviction?" I asked reflexively, then regretted the stupid question.

"Make no mistake about it, that certain person will be convicted."

"What if you have a reasonable doubt?"

"Spare the summation, counsel. No matter what kind of job you do, if one iota of evidence connects him with the charge that fellow is going to swing. The question is not whether he is convicted but when. And so the question to you is whether you go down with him. And I think you are too smart to let that happen."

"I won't do it."

"Jesus, Burnham. Don't play hardball with me. There'll be something in it for you. No questions asked on your bill. Top of the list for future conflict assignments."

"What a designated defense attorney? A kept counselor? No thanks, Judge. People would sniff that out quicker than a barracuda strike. Then the only business I'd have would be through you."

"Then what about some of your other clients? I know you have requests for work release pending for Secman James and Daniel Mongospam. Favorable reviews may be in order. And what about your petitions for parole? Get some clients out of jail, free."

"I can't roll on one client to spring another."

"Yes, Drake. You can. I know this is a surprise. So go home, take a few days to think about it. If you ever want to talk to me, just tell Valentin and he'll set up a meeting." Coleman called out, "Val, come on down here."

I got up from the table, leaving the half-empty Budweiser – the first alcohol I'd walked away from in quite a while – just as Valentin came and stood over my shoulder.

Coleman turned to Valentin, "Show our friend to his car."

Onan said nothing as he followed me up the path to the parking lot, so close behind that I could hear him breathing. Across the river, the rhythm of the *sakau* pounders sounded almost like a heartbeat.

CHAPTER EIGHT

Persona non grata: a person not wanted, an undesirable person. In international law and diplomatic usage, a person not acceptable (for reasons peculiar to himself) to a court or government.

The morning after my off-the-record meeting with Judge Coleman, I flipped through our termite-riddled copy of Black's Law Dictionary, fourth edition. The as yet uneaten definition of "persona non grata" figured into my musings on what next to do. As I saw it, I had four choices to respond to Coleman's offer, each with its own particular downside. Funny thing, I couldn't see an upside to any of them.

The first choice – go public with Coleman's backroom blackmail – would be the most satisfying personally and the most devastating professionally. Maximum Max was right about one thing. If I accused him of improper conduct, my island career would be over. Coleman would counterpunch by having me disbarred, professional excommunication, as Al Frost called it. Then some local, probably Valentin Onan, would spearhead a drive to label me "persona non grata," have the national government pull my work permit and resident alien visa, and kick me back to those United States on a one-way ticket that I would have to pay for myself.

The Micronesian government is lately enamored with labeling troublesome Americans "personae non grata." Last year, I had helped Roberta defend such an attempt to ostracize Bosworth Fields, the often-odious editor of the "The Daily Dilemma." We eventually convinced the Supreme Court that self-deportation was simply an attempt to silence unfavorable criticism of the President and certain senior senators in the only private newspaper published on Pohnpei. Fields got to stay, and bartered down my fee from cash to free newspaper advertising. The entire process took less than six weeks, but Bos had to have his bags packed daily, not knowing whether any given morning would be his last on-island. I would just as soon not undergo that ordeal.

The second choice was not an option. I wasn't even tempted to call Valentin to accept Coleman's offer. I wouldn't give Maximum Max the satisfaction of making me an offer I couldn't refuse, no matter who was my client. But what to do? While I couldn't just hand my client over to the gallows, any effort would be futile. It is a tad difficult to defend against a foregone conclusion. Maximum Max threatened to convict Jangle no matter what I did. Even if a conviction was reversed on appeal, Jangle could sit in jail for months, even years.

To make matters worse, the mail had brought a handwritten letter from Secman James, still behind bars in the Kosrae Jail. Coleman had convicted Secman of trafficking marijuana; he'd grown far more than he could possibly smoke himself. Then Coleman convicted him again, for escape, after Secman left jail without permission to attend his father's funeral. Secman is an ace mechanic, and has an open job offer outside if only he could be released on workdays. Secman wrote that his would-be employer was about to give the job to someone else if he could not take it soon. I've twice applied for work release, but Coleman wouldn't even

97

schedule a hearing. Now all I would have to do to get Secman released to work was roll on Jangle. And I couldn't do that.

Nor could I simply carry on and hope for the best, the third choice, but which was more like water torture. I knew I wouldn't get a fair trial for Jangle, and for that matter for any other case I might ever have in front of Coleman, civil or criminal. Doing nothing guaranteed that Jangle would join Secman James and Daniel Mongospam in jail, three clients who couldn't catch a break because of the judge's disdain of their counsel. Maximum Max would make my professional life miserable, and when, not if, but when Jangle was convicted, the Taro Patch Kids would make my personal life hell, too.

The last option – withdraw as Jangle's counsel – depended on the ruling on the pretrial motion to change venue. If Coleman granted the motion, and the case was transferred to Judge Baxendale in Chuuk, then I could carry on. If Coleman denied the motion, I could submit a motion to withdraw as counsel for Jangle. I had good cause; my client had threatened me with personal harm. I would have to submit the evidence in camera, for the judge's eyes only, so that in theory Jangle would not be prejudiced by my withdrawal. And I would pay a price. Frost & Burnham would lose the conflict assignment fees, and Jangle's "referrals" – Charlie Warheit's personal injury case and the Operator's land deal – would walk out as fast as they walked in. But I had gotten by before Jangle Elwell darkened my door. I could get by after.

To withdraw, I'd have to move quickly, while the case was still in the pretrial stages. I couldn't wait for trial. If a stateside defense attorney withdraws at trial it's a pretty good sign the defendant intends to perjure himself.

But Jangle would pay a price as well. He wouldn't get Roberta as counsel; she has a conflict of interest because she represents a co-defendant. Jangle might end up with Dick Harkness, or another member of the private bar, lawyers who couldn't try their way out of a cooking basket, even if they gave a damn about the client. Were Jangle to get a bright-eyed public defender from Guam or Saipan that could help his chances, before anyone other than Maximum Max. No matter who represented him in Coleman's courtroom, Jangle would hang.

Later that week, on a damp day of passing rain squalls that hammered the corrugated steel roof of the Namiki Building like a squadron of demented carpenters, a bailiff brought a "show cause" order charging Jangle with contempt of court. In formal language, the order required Jangle to "show cause" why he should not be held in contempt. In other words, Judge Coleman wanted Jangle to explain why he offended the dignity of the court by being five minutes late for his arraignment.

The contempt case was scheduled for the same day as the hearing on our pretrial motion on the bank robbery case. That was bad. I had hoped that the pretrial hearing would be a low-key discussion among professionals, but Maximum Max clearly wanted to make the day something more. Maybe Coleman was hell bent on a conviction, any conviction, even for contempt. That way he could hold Jangle in jail, until Jangle apologized.

Normally the public defender office defends contempt cases. But I figured I might as well handle it. I was already representing Jangle on the bank robbery case. Why share the misery, and the fees, with anyone, particularly a good friend like Roberta? The charge was for contempt to the court, a criminal charge that Jangle's tardiness was an affront to the dignity of the office, an office held by the same judge who would hang Jangle out to dry. Of course had Jangle come to court late but contrite he might not be facing a contempt charge at all. But then that wouldn't be Jangle; nor would it be Maximum Max. Coleman does not tolerate what he considers contempt. In Trust Territory times, he held a *nahniken,* a paramount chief, in contempt for a nearly inaudible comment that justice in his courtroom smelled like a *benjo,* an accurate, and, yes, contemptuous remark.

I applied only a little gray matter to defending a charge of contempt for not being punctual. Sometimes you're just late. Call it passive-aggressive or rude, but labeling it doesn't change the ultimate fact. The best, really only defense for being late is a rock solid excuse, such as 'I had to take my wife to the hospital,' or 'I was in a multiple car accident that left me crippled for life.' Having only lectured him not to be late instead of asking him why, I thought I'd better speak with Jangle before the contempt hearing. So I called the public defender office and asked Utticus Uzziah to run over to the Taro Patch to arrange a time for me to meet with Jangle to discuss the contempt charge.

Utticus showed up at my office an hour later with a split and bleeding lower lip that would for a while make painful any chewing of betel nut. The public defender office investigator is an active sportsman, and a bit of a brawler when he is in his cups. He could have gotten the lip in a bar fight, or a basketball game. When I asked him what happened, Utticus just shrugged his shoulders.

"Did you talk with Jangle?"

Utticus arched his eyebrows, then scowled. That explained the split lip.

"Is he coming to the office?"

Utticus scowled again and shook his head.

"Was it Jangle who did that to you?"

Utticus shrugged his shoulders again.

"Look, Utticus. I cannot read your mind. So please tell me what happened, and whether I can expect similar treatment."

"That guy. I really hate him. I told Jangle that you wanted him to come to the office and talk."

"What did he say?"

"Jangle said, 'Tell Burnham that cooler the police took, it isn't mine.'"

"I don't care about that now. Did he say anything about why he was late for his arraignment?"

"No. But Jangle told me to say why is the case taking so long to finish."

"Why it's taking so long? I just got the case."

"Then Jangle ask me if I like working for you. I said its okay, that you were my friend and pretty good for a *menwhi*. Then he asked me for some betel nut. When I look in my basket, he punched me, bang, on the mouth."

"Utticus, you didn't mix it up with him?"

"I really want to fight. But Jangle has Chuukese magic, so I wait for one minute. Then two other guys grab me and hold my arms."

"Which ones were they? The guys from Chuuk in the big black truck?"

"No, it wasn't them. I don't know who those guys are. They're Filipinos, I think the guys who played music at the Bench and Bar."

"You mean the band?"

"Yeah, called 'The Operator?' I saw their Casio at the Taro Patch. I think maybe they played at the Blue Magic last week."

"Damn. Now I have one client help another client punch my investigator. Well they're dreadful musicians. How were they as fighters?"

"Very strong. I could not fight them myself. Then Jangle came up in my face and said 'You tell your boss, Mr. Drake Burnham, he better win the case.' Then those two guys push me out on the gravel road."

"Did you come here first?"

"Yes. And now I'll go to Public Safety to report this."

"Utticus, don't report it just yet."

"But our Governor says 'every offense must be reported.'"

"I know what the Governor says. I also know that someone at Public Safety talks to Jangle. Any time the police get a complaint about the Taro Patch Kids, the news gets to them faster than it does to the prosecutor. If they find out you ratted on them, you can expect more, maybe worse."

"But if I don't report it, then I might fight Jangle myself if I see him."

"Don't do it, Utticus. I know a better way. Just let me take care of it."

Utticus frowned. My excuse was for him, but the reasons were also mine. I could add this conflict to a motion to withdraw as counsel for Jangle, if it came to that.

I said to Utticus, "Let's keep this under our hats for now. Okay?"

Utticus arched his eyebrows again, signaling assent. His sister was a secretary at the prosecutor's office and he would probably tell her. But thanks to the leak, better to have the prosecutors know than the police.

A half-hour later, Roberta telephoned during a lull between torrential downpours.

"I'm sorry about Utticus, Roberta. But if a client socked me in the choppers, I'd take the rest of the day off, too."

"Is that what happened to his lip? He wouldn't tell me a thing."

"Looks like client control has taken on a whole new dimension."

"Well don't worry about authorizing Utticus to take a few hours leave. I'll cover for you. I'm calling about something else. Has Marielle Hargraves called you lately?"

"Oh, if only she would."

"I saw the way you looked at her at the arraignment. Right down her ..."

"Just admiring her tattoo. Come on, Roberta. Real men don't date prosecutors."

"Well I just got off the phone with Marielle, and she made Entis another offer."

"After reading the deathless prose of the venue motion?"

"Or maybe looking again at her material for the discovery response. Whatever her reason, Marielle made a better offer if Entis will turn state's evidence on Jangle."

"Has Coleman called you, too?"

"What would the Judge want with me now?"

"Never mind. What's Marielle's offer?"

"She'll drop the grand theft and conspiracy charges if Entis pleads to receiving stolen property."

"Anything on sentencing?"

"Probation only. No jail time."

I whistled. "What if Maximum Max won't bite?"

"Marielle said she'll guarantee it."

"I wonder how she thinks she can swing that."

"I don't know. But probation or suspended imposition of sentence is a must. If you rolled on Jangle, would you want to do time in the same jail as him?"

"Considering what he did to Utticus to send me a message, I don't want to be on the same island as him."

"What's up with your client?"

"I haven't a clue, Ms. Ely. Jangle's sending me a lot of messages lately, too, and none of them are good. You think Entis will go for it?"

"Unlikely, given Taro Patch loyalty, and your own experience on Kosrae."

"More to the point, will you recommend it to Entis?"

"It's a lot better than her last offer. But I don't know about recommending it until Marielle shows us her evidence."

"Has Marielle responded to your discovery request yet?"

"Not a peep. But she doesn't have to until the hearing on the venue motion."

"How long is her offer open?"

"Marielle said she'd call me before it expires."

"She sure changed her tune."

"I don't know about that. I think Entis just got caught up in all this. The only thing he'll tell me is that he didn't do anything. It's clear that Jangle is the one the government's after."

"Among others."

"What do you mean?"

I'd already decided against telling Roberta the whole story. "For one thing, Coleman sent a show cause order for the same time as the hearing on the venue motion."

"Coleman charged Jangle with contempt?"

"For being five minutes late."

"What happened to the stern lecture about honoring the dignity of the court by coming on time?"

"This isn't moot court. Besides, I don't think the word 'tolerance' exists in Coleman's vocabulary."

"Yeah, he's probably even lactose intolerant. Do you have any defense?"

"Sometimes you're just late, Ms. Ely."

"Jangle didn't have a previous engagement?"

"Not as far as I know, and the summons was served on time. Although the copy made it to me at the end of the day, the bailiff served Jangle around noon."

"Are you going to throw yourself on the mercy of the court?"

"If I throw anything, I'll toss some *sakau* in front of the bench."

"What, to turn away Coleman's wrath? That only works with a chief."

"Yeah, but maybe he'll trip on it."

I put aside my notes and paced the tiny back office, stopping at times to gaze out the window at rain shedding from the leaves of the breadfruit tree across the way, or to stare up at my late partner's framed portrait of Clarence Darrow. Now that was a lawyer. Articulate, relentless, possessed by a passion to do right by his clients. Frost was right about one thing; Steve McGarrett wouldn't last ten minutes in a Clarence Darrow cross-examination. Darrow had given up a thriving practice representing railroads to defend labor leaders, anarchists and immigrants, clients no one else would take: Eugene Debs, indicted for conspiracy in the Pullman Strike deaths; Big Bill Haywood, treasurer of the Western Federation of Miners, who was nearly lynched on the put-up prosecution for the murder of the former governor of Idaho; not to mention Leopold and Loeb, the wealthy, intelligent, but deluded nineteen-year-old thrill-killers. Who am I left with? A small-time hood on a small-time island, smack dab in the middle of the Pacific Ocean.

I reached up to unhook the portrait. Al had hung it so that nothing short of a super-typhoon would knock it off the wall, sinking masonry nails into the cinderblock with a sledge hammer, and wiring the frame into place. The dark-haired man in the portrait scowled at the camera, his face frozen for a century in vivid black and white.

"Why am I defending Jangle?" I asked aloud. Not that anyone would hear it. Jasmina had taken the day off yet again. I half-expected Darrow himself to answer. After all, when Al had conferred with the photograph, Jasmina said he was "talking with Clarence." The portrait was mute. So I did what Frost would do to invoke his muse. Al, inspired more by Phillip Marlowe than Clarence Darrow, kept a bottle of hot stuff in the bottom desk drawer. A drinker, Frost had a rummy's nose the shape and color of a ripe mountain apple. Al poured his bourbon neat, but give me the arctic clarity of vodka. So I reached into the bottom drawer for my duty-free bottle of Stoli, poured myself a glass and waited for Clarence to speak.

But Darrow said not a word.

Overhead, a gecko padded after an insect on the drop ceiling, making a tiny drumroll on the plywood.

Darrow said nothing.

I don't know what Darrow's answer would be. But I know what Al would say that Darrow might say. Al would say I wasn't defending Jangle for the money – at fifty per hour, I'd better not be – or for the challenge. Al would say I was defending Jangle because I was asked. I had accepted and was now promised to do the best that I could.

Al would have an answer to each protest. He'd say that I wasn't the first lawyer to be threatened by a client, and that I wouldn't be the last. He'd say that it didn't matter that Jangle was sleeping with my secretary or had punched my investigator, reminding me that I am neither father to Utticus nor husband to Jasmina. And he'd remind me of that latter fact with a knowing chuckle.

The portrait felt heavy in my hands. Clarence Darrow was not a handsome man. His face was deeply lined; his eyes dark, a lank of dark hair fell across his forehead. I poured myself another drink, a short one.

Darrow stayed mute. Al would tell me that it didn't matter to me that Jangle was a rotten apple, an addled egg. It wouldn't matter because he and I both had represented young men that everyone else had given up on but who had somehow turned it around. Al would remind me of Carson Johnnyboy, a frequent client of the Kosrae public defender, who came to the office so regularly that I kept a pleading caption with his name on the hard drive of the office computer. Carson spent more of his adult life in jail than out, but when he turned thirty, he had some sort of epiphany, took a construction job from an Australian contractor building a hotel on island, and managed to save enough money to build a house, start a farm, and even get married. The last time I ran into Carson, he was on his way to church.

Al would say that I could not give in to Coleman, the schemer, the conniver. I don't know what Darrow would call Maximum Max, but I'd heard Frost call him "a fascist terrorist cross-dressed in the robes of justice." Al would say I couldn't judge Jangle, it wasn't my job.

Clarence Darrow said not a word.

A knock on the door interrupted my thoughts. It was a local's knock, one that started softly as a gentle tap and grew increasingly loud.

"Just a minute," I shouted, as I looked for a place to set down the Darrow portrait, then shoved the vodka back into the desk drawer. The knocking stopped. No one was at the door, just the afternoon rain pouring from the eaves of the corrugated roof like three score of evenly spaced waterfalls. I walked to the railing to see if my visitor was down the stairway. From the railing I spotted the black pickup truck shedding rain as it sped away. Whoever knocked left in the truck, and likely left the bulky, brown paper envelope with my name scrawled on it beside the office door. Inside the envelope was a dog collar, Buster's. Jangle had taken the stray dog law into his own hands.

This was much lower than low. I thought about the butcher shops I'd seen in the Philippines and Vietnam that had advertised fresh dog meat with a window display of severed dog's heads. At the thought of Buster's head at the end of a row, I winced. It seemed obvious that Jangle had Buster dog-napped, maybe to feed his houseguests, the ones who tangled with Utticus at the Taro Patch, the ones who couldn't carry a tune, but who could throw a punch with the best of them. And I found myself with a client who threatened me, who killed my dog, who cold-cocked my investigator, and who slept with my secretary.

Maybe I should take up Coleman's offer and roll on Jangle, the bastard.

CHAPTER NINE

The contempt case was up first on the morning calendar, and I sat alone at the defense table. Jangle had never come to the office to discuss the contempt charge. I still had no idea why Jangle was late for his arraignment, much less whether his reason was good enough as an excuse, or sympathetic enough to offer in mitigation.

Roberta Ely sat in the first row behind the bar, ready to come forward to argue for a change of venue motion on the bank robbery case. Our strategizing continued. I would stand first, and likely lose the contempt case. Roberta would argue the venue motion for both defendants, since the issues were the same for both Jangle and Entis. Roberta didn't know that if she lost, that I would then withdraw as Jangle's counsel of record.

My motion to withdraw was buried in my papers. It was a simple motion. Good cause to withdraw as Jangle's lawyer was his threat to injure me, and his actual battery of the investigator, Utticus Uziah. My statement of good cause, and Exhibit A, my business card with Jangle's fighting words written on the back, were sealed in an envelope I would submit to Judge Coleman in camera, and omitted from the copies to serve on the other counsel in the case. Coleman alone would judge my good cause.

At five minutes to nine, Marielle Hargraves swept into the courtroom, her chin pointing appropriately at Pewshen Malek, the steep peak just south of Palikir. (Pewshen Malek, by the way, means "mound of chicken shit" in Pohnpeian.) This was a potential stroke of luck. Were Marielle to prosecute the contempt charge, I could have her disqualified as a percipient witness to the offense, and maybe swing a continuance, that is, if the case were in any courtroom other than Coleman's. Stumbling into court behind Marielle was a middle-aged American, to all appearances hung over, dressed in a frayed Aloha shirt, cargo pants, and zoris. Marielle, by contrast, was loaded for bear, wearing possibly the only evening dress I've seen in Micronesia. It was an ankle length sheath, black as basalt. Coleman would have to be impressed, or distracted.

Marielle's case file was even bigger than what she brought to the arraignment and from a redwell she extracted two packets of documents held together by rusting binder clips. She placed one packet on the defense table in front of me.

"Who's your friend?" I asked Marielle's chest as she leaned to hand the other packet across the bar to Roberta.

"Government witness."

"For the contempt case?"

"No. The bank robbery. He's the branch manager of the bank your clients robbed. He'll testify that he has no problem with us trying the case here."

"Our clients? Our clients didn't rob no bank." I turned to wink at Roberta. Marielle had served two discovery responses – one for Jangle, and one for Entis – for the price of one request. Part of our defense strategy worked.

I was too nervous to do more than glance through the government's discovery response. Compartmentalization has never been a forte, and I was distracted, not by Marielle's formal attire, but by my still absent client.

There was no sign of Jangle when Judge Coleman banged into the courtroom promptly at nine. After the case "In re Contempt of Jangle Elwell" was called, Coleman gestured at me with his pen as if it were a stiletto and said to take the podium.

"Do you see the time, Mr. Burnham?"

I decided to open with my closing statement.

"Time is such an elastic concept here in the islands, Your Honor. Everyone jokes about 'local time.' If the party invitation says three o'clock, don't dare arrive before five. On Kosrae, we had three different times. First is state time, when the air horn at the government offices sounds. Second is Air Mike time, when the island hopper lands. And third is church time, when the village church bell tolls. All three times are different, yet all three times are correct."

"It seems to me that your client should never send to know for whom the bell tolls. But let's get down to brass tacks. Where is Mr. Elwell, counselor?"

"He's my client, sir, not my son."

"Don't crack wise with me, Burnham, or I'll hold you in contempt as well."

"Your Honor, I only suggest that I have no power to direct Jangle to do anything."

"Well, then. Shall we expect Mr. Elwell to breeze in here ten minutes late with yet another snappy comment on his lips?"

"I suggest that Your Honor issue a bench warrant for the immediate arrest of the defendant," Marielle interrupted. "I've taken the liberty of preparing a form bench warrant for just such a likelihood. If I may approach the bench?"

"Please give a copy to opposing counsel first," said Coleman.

Marielle sashayed to the podium to hand me a copy of the one-page warrant. "Counsel?"

"Thank you," I said, then added quietly, "Nice *fasr.*"

I glanced to see Susanna, the court reporter, stifle a giggle at my comment, then mark the tape to erase my comment from the record. Marielle gave me a quizzical look then handed a copy to the bailiff to hand up to Judge Coleman. I examined what Marielle gave me. Everything looked in order, except that she had misspelled Jangle's last name, "Ewell," like the Confederate general at Gettysburg. Frost, the old rebel, would get a kick out of that. In fact, the misspelling was identical to one on a previous court summons, and I wondered if Coleman was feeding forms to the prosecutor, and what was expected in return.

Coleman asked over the bridge of his reading glasses if I had any comment.

"It's up to you, Judge." A misspelled name on an arrest warrant is probably not suspect on an island where just about everyone knows each other, but I wasn't about to point out a potential error.

Maximum Max scrawled his signature on the warrant and handed the paper to the bailiff. "Enter this order and serve it on DSI immediately."

"I have an officer waiting outside, Your Honor," Marielle said.

"Thank you, Miss Hargraves. I'm glad to see the Attorney General's office is prepared this morning. Too bad I can't say the same about all counsel. Let's proceed to the next case. We have the defendants' pretrial motion in 'People versus Jangle Elwell, et al.' Mr. Burnham, you represent the, ahem, absent moving party?"

"One of them, Your Honor. As you know, my client has the right to be here, but is not required to attend a pretrial hearing on an issue of law. But I've said enough. Roberta Ely of the public defenders office will argue the motion."

I kept only half an ear on Ms. Ely's argument. I wrote the motion and left to Roberta whatever emphasis she saw fit. Instead, I looked through the discovery materials. A written response sat atop the stack. It noted the documents attached, gave a list of potential trial witnesses to be called by the government, and indicated the physical evidence held by the government, as well as those few days on which we could examine the physical evidence at the Department of Security and Investigation office. Marielle also proposed a date a week before trial on which all counsel were invited to visit and examine the scene of the bank robbery in Chuuk. The discovery response mentioned no confession, by either Jangle or Entis. That was good. Also missing from the discovery response was any statement of exculpatory evidence, but then few prosecutors willingly volunteers Brady material.

I recognized only one name on the witness list, Winston Sigraht, a Kosraen working for the national Customs Service here on Pohnpei. I know Winston's family, but I have yet to meet him myself. The list of physical evidence included $25,855.00 in U.S. currency, an Igloo ice chest, several gallons of water, and several pounds of reef fish. The documents included a police report on the robbery by the Chuuk

State Police, an affidavit by the manager of the Micronesian National Bank (probably the gent who accompanied Marielle to court), another affidavit by Winston, a third affidavit by a DSI officer seeking arrest warrants for Entis and Jangle, and, of course, Marielle's affidavit of probable cause to charge the pair. I double-checked the figures. The amount of cash listed didn't match the bank manager's affidavit, by thousands of dollars.

By the time I finished skimming through the papers, Roberta was wrapping up her argument.

"Do you have anything to add, Mr. Burnham?"

I glanced up at Coleman from my seat and shook my head.

"Stand at the podium to address the court." Coleman enunciated each word as if he lectured a first-grader.

I walked to the podium and stood next to Roberta. "May it please the Court, no."

"Rather than waste more time by hearing argument from the government, I'll simply deny the defendants' motion."

"But Your Honor, my witness came all the way from Chuuk." Marielle pouted.

"Miss Hargraves," Coleman sighed, "You've won. A memorandum will issue shortly. All counsel, we will recess the contempt case until we get a report from DSI on the arrest of the defendant. You need not stay in the courtroom, but please remain in Palikir in case we need to contact you. We'll call the next case in thirty minutes."

Coleman banged his taro pounder to call recess. Once he'd left the courtroom, Roberta grabbed her copy of the discovery response and walked to the prosecutor's table. I tagged along to eavesdrop.

115

"Marielle, would you mind if we went over to the evidence room this morning?"

Marielle stuffed papers into a redwell and did not look up at Roberta.

"Drake has to wait here on the contempt case anyway, and it would save me a trip back to Palikir."

Marielle glanced up, arched her eyebrows at me, then looked back to Roberta.

"It would be, how did you put it, 'in the interest of efficiency?'"

Marielle tilted her head a couple of jots my way until Roberta caught her drift.

"Drake, would you excuse us for a moment?"

"Oh, sure. I've got to file some papers anyway."

I returned to the defense table and with my back to both, pulled out my motion to withdraw from my papers. I slipped a copy into Roberta's briefcase, then went to file the original. I put a copy in the Attorney General's in-basket at the clerk's office and was back to the courtroom in ten minutes. Roberta and the prosecutor waited at the door.

"Shall we repair to the evidence room?" said Marielle, who then set off to the far end of Palikir like a motorboat speeding from a jetty.

"Repair? I didn't know it was broken," said Roberta trailing in her wake.

I scrambled back into the courtroom to grab a yellow pad, and scurried to catch up with the pair.

"How did you swing this?" I asked when I caught up with Roberta. Marielle was already ten paces ahead.

"I told Marielle that examining the evidence would help me assess her plea bargain proposal to my client alone."

"And Marielle still thinks I'm in the dark about that?"

Roberta nodded.

"Ms. Ely, you're an angel. Listen, we've got to double-check the physical evidence. Marielle listed twenty-five grand in cash, but the bank manager's affidavit said more than $35,000 was stolen."

"Hmm. Let's ask if Utticus can take an inventory."

A thin rain that clung to Palikir like a wet towel kept us all to the covered walkways from the Supreme Court back to the Department of Security and Investigation office. The office door faced the cage in which DSI keeps Reza, a drug-sniffing German shepherd donated by the U.S. Drug Enforcement Administration. Colombia and Micronesia have to be the only places where drug dogs are kept in protective custody. Reza whined as three Americans passed, and I thought of poor Buster.

The evidence room is a dark interior closet off the chief investigator's office. Before the Capitol complex was built at Palikir, when the national government was spread throughout offices in Kolonia, DSI shared the evidence room with Pohnpei Public Safety, a room for which keys were apparently as common as empty beer cans. Evidence – especially marijuana plants and cases of beer – disappeared regularly and chain-of-custody dismissals were de rigueur. Today, though, the chief investigator holds the only key. He was summoned, and we were ushered into the evidence room, where the chief investigator displayed the ingenious features of one piece of the physical evidence.

Roberta was the first to speak. "I have to admit I've never seen a false bottom cooler before."

The cooler appeared in all respects typically Micronesian, a standard size Igloo cooler, the kind Honolulu skycaps call "Samoan Samsonite," bearing bumps and bruises of scores of journeys, binding tape still stretched around the top and sides. A spindled Air Mike luggage tag dangled from a handle. "Jungle Cooler" was written in black magic marker on one side. This was the cooler Jangle denied owning. What made it unique was a razor cut under the lip of the inner rim, detectable only by running a finger inside the rim, and even then barely visible even if one was looking for it. At either end were two small slots into which one could slip a knife blade or the tip of a machete to lift the entire liner up from the outside of the cooler, as the chief investigator demonstrated.

"That's where the customs agent discovered the cash," said Marielle.

"What else was in it?"

"The cooler was filled with ice water and reef fish when it was seized."

"Did anyone claim the fish?" Roberta said.

"We threw it out."

"Why? It's on the list of physical evidence."

"Why not? Your client has no interest in that."

"The issue is not whether my client has an interest, but whether the government does. Ice isn't contraband, at least not the frozen water kind. The reef fish aren't contraband, unless you plan to add a count of illegal fishing. What if Entis claims the legitimate contents as his?"

"Look, the ice melted. The fish began to smell as it went bad."

"Sounds like spoliation of evidence to me," I said. "What I don't get is how the customs agent sniffed it out."

"The fish?" Roberta winked.

"Of course, but also the false bottom cooler."

"He tried to drain the water from the cooler to look beneath the fish, and the drain didn't work." Marielle sounded proud of the customs agent's work. "At first he didn't know why. He just thought the drain was clogged. When he tipped the cooler on edge, the false bottom slipped and he discovered the money."

"Seems pretty tight now." I turned the cooler on its side.

"The ice and cold water probably caused the liner to shrink. Not very much, but enough to allow it to slip."

"And where's the money?"

"In the office safe. We don't leave cash in the evidence room."

Marielle lead us to the Attorney General's office, where Roberta and I cooled our heels for fifteen minutes while she found the one clerk who knew the combination to the office safe. Inside, stuffed in a large ziplock evidence bag, were neat stacks of bills, hundreds and twenties in green and red Micronesian National Bank bands, plus assorted tens, fives, and singles. The bills were all U.S. currency, but they were bills that would have been removed from circulation stateside years before, dirty, crumpled, faded.

"Have you counted it?" Roberta asked.

"It comes to $25,855 exactly," said Marielle.

I whistled and said, "That's a lot of scratch."

"Please," said Marielle. "I made three times my first year out of law school."

"And you got to be making about that now. But where's the rest of the money?"

"This is all that was seized."

"Yeah, but your discovery response listed a total of $35,222.98, which has to include some change. I don't see any coins in there."

Marielle said nothing, as if pondering for the first time why the evidence in the safe might not match her written description of it by about ten grand.

"Marielle, we'll have to arrange for a time for my investigator to come over and re-count the money," said Roberta. "Under guard, of course."

Just then a local secretary crept up to Marielle and quietly told her that Judge Coleman had called us back to the courthouse.

"Sounds like DSI found your client." Marielle pointed her chin back at Pewshen Malek.

Although I expected, even hoped to see Jangle roughed up and handcuffed between two DSI agents, there was no sign of him in the courtroom. Judge Coleman was taking testimony in what sounded like a collections case, with Valentin Onan to one side glowering at the debtor. When Valentin noticed us, he whispered something to the Judge. Coleman continued for a few moments before he interrupted his examination.

"Ladies and gentlemen, an urgent matter has come to my attention. We will take a brief recess. Mr. Onan, show Miss Hargraves, Mrs. Ely, and Mr. Burnham to my chambers in five minutes."

My gut rumbled uneasily.

Maximinus T. Coleman looks considerably smaller and older once he removes his robe. In chambers he sat with a fresh cup of coffee behind an enormous mahogany desk stacked with case files.

"Counsel, I don't mean to make light of this. Apparently, a serious felony has been committed but then I feel as if a very large thorn has been removed from the sole of my zori. Miss Hargraves, I have here the written report of the DSI officer that I sent to arrest Mr. Burnham's client this morning."

"It's Ms., Your Honor."

"Whatever. The DSI report is poorly written. It uses local syntax and has numerous spelling errors and typos. But I can nevertheless draw several conclusions by reading it. First, Miss Hargraves, your caseload has been lightened by one."

Marielle's face lit up as if Coleman had produced a stick, a blindfold, and a piñata, and said she could have first whack. I began to feel queasy.

Coleman continued. "Mrs. Ely, you no longer have a conflict of interest."

My stomach began to do somersaults, as Roberta cocked her head to the side.

Coleman turned to me with an expression halfway between grave concern and a smirk. "And you, Mr. Burnham. You no longer have a client for either case called this morning. Jangle Elwell is dead."

CHAPTER TEN

The office was stuffy when I returned from the morgue, the coffee pot the only thing cold. Jasmina's boombox was no longer atop the filing cabinets in the outer office. She had either left early or not come in at all. I figured Jasmina knew of Jangle's demise. The coconut telegraph – like the grapevine stateside – is swift.

First I had to inform Kosrae. I spoke briefly with Zebedee James at the Kosrae Public Defender office, and asked him to find Jangle's father regarding the untimely passing of his son. Then I switched on the air conditioner and pawed through the in-basket, looking for something to occupy my mind. I ended up preparing two papers for Jangle's case, a suggestion of the death of my client, and a motion to dismiss because my client was dead. Neither task took long, and soon I was at the window waiting to see if a ripe breadfruit would fall from the tree across the way. When the office was cool, I prepared my first and final bill for services rendered on behalf of the late, great Jangle Elwell. That didn't take long either, and before long I paged through the Attorney General's discovery response, served by Marielle that morning in court.

The first document beneath the written response was the affidavit of Charles Throckmorton, manager of the Micronesian National Bank, Chuuk State branch. The affidavit was made out in stilted legalese, ending in the phrase "Further affiant sayeth naught," as if the witness was a contemporary of Chaucer. Throckmorton said when he came to work the morning of June 7, he found the office safe unlocked. He explained that was not unusual, for bank employees frequently left the safe open to save the trouble of unlocking it again when the bank reopened. But on June 7, all the cash was missing from the safe and every teller's drawer, even singles and coins. The only money left untouched was the petty cash box, with less than fifty dollars, locked in his desk. Nothing else was out of place. No other papers were disturbed. An accounting followed, showing a theft of $35,221.98.

I blinked at the figure twice, then compared it to the attorney general's list of physical evidence, $25,855.00, a difference of $9,366.98, too much and too precise to be a simple typo.

"Jangle," I asked aloud. "What did you do with the rest of the money?"

I paged back through my desk calendar. June 7, the day Throckmorton said he came to work was a Saturday. Island banks are closed on Saturdays.

The second document was the report by the Chuuk State Police. As such reports are worldwide, this one was rife with typos, but the language, in frightfully fractured English, seemed more readable than the formal language of Throckmorton's affidavit. Two detectives had been assigned to the case. I knew neither, but our compadres at the Chuuk Public Defender office had to know both. The detectives wrote that they examined the crime scene, and sent a request to messenger over from Pohnpei DSI's fingerprint detection equipment, the only kit in the entire nation. The Chuuk detectives found that a small air conditioner had been removed from a small back window to the bank and placed on the floor inside. Other than the door, the window was the only potential entry to the bank building, which was solid enough to double as a World War II bunker. The detectives considered the window as the potential point of entry, but said that the space was so small that a child would have difficulty squeezing through.

But it might be large enough for Entis Robert, that wisp of a defendant from Pingelap. That might explain the dislocated shoulder. But the air conditioner was found on the floor inside the bank. The detectives didn't say that it was damaged. If Entis had pushed the air con unit through the window from the outside, wouldn't it have been damaged or dented when it fell? If Entis tried to break and enter from outside, it would make more sense for him to pull the air conditioner out and leave it on the ground outside the bank building.

The Chuuk detectives said that they interviewed several, but not all, bank employees and former employees, and planned to interview the rest when the Attorney General's office called from Pohnpei to inform that they had arrested two suspects on Pohnpei, and that DSI would take over the investigation. The detectives then put the case on low priority, cancelled their request for the fingerprint kit, and did nothing further unless specifically instructed.

The third document in the clasp was the report from Winston Sigraht, the Customs agent who discovered the missing money, or some of it, in the cooler. Winston's report was fairly clear and detailed, more of an internal report than something prepared for the bank robbery case. Winston himself is a good sight better than his immediate predecessor, who apparently thought that "FOB" meant "Fell Off Boat."

Winston had been assigned to clear for entry into Pohnpei the SS Gunner's Knot, an FSM Transportation ship making a regular run from Guam to Pohnpei, with a load of Japanese cars and mixed cargo for various merchants, including, naturally, 150 cases of Budweiser, about an hour's worth on a Payday Friday. The Gunner's Knot had called on Chuuk en route, discharging some cargo and picking up new cargo and passengers. Among the Chuuk boarding passengers was one Entis Robert. Agent Sigraht stopped Entis because the manifest showed his shipment, said to consist of frozen meat, was addressed to one Jangle Elwell. Winston knew Jangle from both Kosrae and Pohnpei, and he knew the Gunner's Knot had no refrigeration. He suspected that Entis might be smuggling something, maybe methamphetamine, because frozen meat would not last the thirty-hour trip from Chuuk to Pohnpei. Winston's suspicions were heightened when a Gunner's Knot crewmember reported that Entis sat on or near the cooler the entire length of the passage. Agent Sigraht asked Entis's permission to open the cooler, which contained reef fish, not meat, shad and red snapper in a pool of bloody water. Winston asked Entis of he could drain the water, and when he tried to open the tap, he found it didn't work. When Agent Sigraht tipped the cooler to drain the water over the lip, the lining slipped and he discovered the cash in the false bottom.

Good solid detective work, I thought, and put down the file.

Without a hint of Jasmina and with Utticus no longer at my beck and call, I drove back to Palikir myself to serve and file the suggestion of death and the motion to dismiss, and to submit my final bill. No-Amp Lester pontificated on the gospel radio station, but for once I paid him little attention. When I returned to the office – after a late and liquid lunch at the Ox & Palm – it was nearly quitting time, and there was still no sign of Jasmina. Former partner, former client, former secretary; my compatriots were dropping like flies. I wondered for only a moment what the late Algonquin H. Frost would do in a moment like this. Then I reached into the bottom drawer for the bottle of vodka I'd been saving for *mabuhay*, or for victory, and glanced up at the portrait of Clarence Darrow for a little heart-to-heart.

Jasmina took the next day off as well, but returned to the office, morose and silent, on Wednesday. I missed my happy secretary, but said nothing to try to cheer her. I felt as if I had to step as carefully as a net fisherman on the reef around her. I dared not broach the subject of Jangle, although I knew she knew. Jasmina would grieve in local fashion, with wailing and gnashing of teeth until the brief period of grief was over, and then get on with life. According to the locals, there is time enough to grieve to honor the dead, and then time enough for living. It's sort of like the Irish wake for Judge Coleman I fondly hope to one day attend.

Doctor Perez called the next morning to report that a cousin had come in to identify John Doe Number One and that Jangle's father, Moses Elwell, had agreed to allow an autopsy. Mario mentioned that an extra copy of his draft autopsy report would be delivered shortly, by a method to be determined.

The Supreme Court's audit of my first and final bill for services in the Jangle Elwell case arrived that day, too. Judge Coleman, whose signature looks like an earthquake seismograph, signed the audit. That meant that Maximum Max, and not the Justice Ombudsman, had vetted the bill personally. He'd used a felt-tip pen, and my statement, bleeding red ink, looked as if it suffered stigmata. All the time I submitted for the initial appearance and arraignment was marked down, "COUNSEL NOT PREPARED." Coleman had slashed time I allotted to discovery, but allowed most of the time for the motion to change venue, plus all the

126

time I had submitted for preparing the suggestion of death and motion to dismiss. Still, I hadn't spent that much time on the case altogether, and even after adding my minimal expenses and subtracting the retainer advanced, the resulting sum might be enough for dinner for two at the Coral Reef, without much left over for a tip. And it would be months before a check was cut.

In the meantime, the briefly busy Frost & Burnham practice slipped back into its pre-Jangle sloth. Jasmina turned her attention back to chunky romance novels, and I pulled out a six-month old Sunday crossword puzzle and then volume 3 of the collected works of William Makepeace Thackery. It isn't that I care much for the Victorian novel of manners, but I do like the author's middle name. Activity on all my cases slowed, in one of the inevitable lulls of small town practice. I actually started wishing that Kazuo Olopai would call about Charlie Warheit's personal injury case, although I wouldn't call Kazuo first, lest I appear too eager to settle.

I got half my wish. I was pleasantly surprised to see Kazuo at my door one afternoon, sporting possibly his latest and loudest Aloha shirt. Anticipating a settlement offer, I suspended Al Frost's posted sanction on the door to the office, his inner sanctum, the one that read, "Posted. No trespassing. Prosecutors will be violated."

"*Kaselehlia*, Kazuo. You look very handsome today. And I really like that shirt. Is it new?"

"Good afternoon, Drake." For once, Kazuo did not return a compliment.

"Is this a social or a business call?"

"Business. Can we close the door? I want to talk in private."

"Don't worry. Jasmina is very discreet."

"Please, Drake. In private," Kazuo insisted.

To get her out of the office, I asked Jasmina to go to the State Court for a copy of the docket on a civil case. I closed the inner office door so as not to be disturbed. I rubbed my palms in expectation of a settlement offer.

"I presume you want to talk about Charlie Warheit?"

"Oh. No. You must not have gotten the substitution papers."

"Substitution? I haven't gotten any substitution."

"Charlie Warheit is no longer your case. Dick Harkness served a substitution on my office this morning."

"Heartless? God damn it. When the hell did that happen?"

"Please do not take the Lord's name in vain, Drake. The papers were dated last week. But I was served today. You'll get them soon."

"It's just like Harkness to sit on a substitution. Maybe he thinks he can get me to do some more work on the file. Well I'm protected. I'll file a lien."

"Drake, I want to talk about Jangle Elwell."

"Jangle? What do you want to know?"

"How well did you know Jangle?"

"Not well at all."

"Was he your friend?"

"No. He was a client. You may find this surprising, Kazuo, but very few clients are friends, especially a client who might have whacked my dog."

"I was always surprised that Jangle was your client."

"How come?"

"For one thing, Jangle stoned your place."

"I never said it was Jangle, although I still think it was the Taro Patch Kids. Regardless, Jangle was just my client."

"A long-time client?"

"The bank robbery case is, well it was, the first one I handled for Jangle. I was going to defend him on a contempt charge, but then he turned up dead before Coleman could hold a hearing."

"The Filipino doctor, Perez, he finished the autopsy. He told me Jangle was murdered. I want to know what you know."

"Kazuo, if you are investigating a murder, I assure you that you know a lot more about it than me. Defenders are the last to know anything."

"He was your client."

"And what he told me in the course of that relationship is confidential, protected by the attorney-client privilege."

"Even when the client is dead?"

"Even when the client is dead."

"Is there anything in the case that is not confidential?"

"Court files are public record. Have you looked there?"

"Yes."

"What about the Attorney General's office. They thought they had a great case."

"I already talked with the new attorney general, Miss Marielle Hargraves."

"You mean Ms. Hargraves."

"She cooperated. She told me all about Jangle's case, all about both cases against Jangle, the bank robbery case and the contempt case. I also spoke with Justice Maximinus Coleman. He told me plenty about Jangle Elwell. He let me see the court file, too."

I thought about my motion to withdraw as Jangle's attorney, including the material I submitted for the judge's eyes only. Coleman might have let Kazuo take a gander at that. "Did Coleman show you everything he had in the court file?"

"Justice Coleman let me look at everything in his files. Then we talked about Jangle. You represented Jangle on the contempt case?"

"Yes."

"He was held in contempt for coming late to court?"

"I already call him 'the late, great Jangle Elwell.'"

"Was he paying you for that?"

"For the contempt case? We didn't discuss payment. I figured Jangle would apologize and that would be it. There's no need to discuss fees for something so simple."

"Do you think a contempt case in Judge Coleman's courtroom is simple?"

"That's very astute, Kazuo. Now that you mention it, no. But it just made sense for me to handle the contempt case because I was already defending Jangle on the bank robbery charge."

"Was Jangle paying you on the bank robbery case?"

"Kazuo. If you went to the Supreme Court, you'd know I'll be paid for defending Jangle by the court as a conflict assignment."

"I know plenty about conflict cases, Drake. Every Thursday at the State Court you ask me if there is a new conflict case. What I want to know, was Jangle paying you extra, something more than the conflict case fees."

"No. Whatever gave you that idea?"

"Judge Coleman said he thought Jangle might be one of those people who pays a special bonus to the lawyer for defending them."

"The only bonus I got for representing Jangle was aggravation."

"You say you'll be paid on the bank robbery defense. Have you been paid yet?"

"Nope. Just the retainer."

"So Jangle Elwell owed you money."

"Jangle did not owe me one red cent. The Supreme Court will pay me out of its conflict assignment budget. If anyone owes me money, it's the Supreme Court. Now what does my payment have to do with Jangle's death?"

Kazuo ignored my question. "Was there another relation Jangle had in this office?"

"I don't understand."

"Several witnesses say they saw Jangle rolling through town with your secretary."

"You're not trying to pin anything on Jasmina. If you saw how upset she's been over this, you'd know she isn't involved."

"Please, Drake. I'm just trying to be thorough."

"Are you going to question her? Because I'd like to be around for that."

"Did you know that Jasmina was seen with Jangle?"

"What Jazz does on her own time is up to her. I'm not her father."

"But she was your wife?"

"Jasmina? Jazz is my secretary, not my wife."

"Jasmina's older male relative, Freddy Solomon, came to ask you. He asked your permission to take Jasmina back to the Marshall Islands. Freddy said you refused to let him do that."

"Refused? Permission like that isn't mine to give. I told Freddy that it's up to Jasmina whether or not she goes back to the Marshalls."

"But she's your 'special friend.'"

"She certainly is not. Whoever told you that mistook me for my old law partner."

"Freddy also told me that you asked Jasmina out."

"Kazuo. That was years ago, and only once, and before I even started working here. And Jazz turned me down."

"You just called her 'Jazz,' three times, not her real name, Jasmina."

"So what? A nickname? That's a mighty slender reed on which to hang an inference, counsel. If you ask a question like that in court, my objection would be sustained."

I didn't like Olopai's questions. From experience I know he is better at cross-examination than his appearance lets on.

"Does Jasmina know that Jangle was seeing other women?"

"That's her state of mind, Mr. Olopai. I have no way of knowing that."

"Witnesses saw Jangle rolling through Kolonia with some other women, too."

"It's mighty handy that you have so many witnesses, Mr. Prosecutor. Maybe you'll turn up someone who saw the murder."

"Did you ask Utticus Uziah for help on this case?"

"Yes I did."

"Even though he works for the public defender."

"Part of the agreement on conflict assignments is that I use the public defender office investigator. He knows what he's doing, and it helps keep costs down."

"Utticus is your friend."

"He is."

"You think Utticus had any reason to hurt Jangle Elwell?"

"Of course not."

Kazuo was angling, first to hook Jasmina, then Utticus.

Kazuo took off his glasses for a moment, rubbed his eyes. "Did you know that Jangle Elwell ordered someone in his gang to punch Utticus and push him in the road?"

"It wasn't ... someone in his gang."

Kazuo had me there. He had gotten me angry then nailed me with a misdirection question, clever bastard.

"Who was it then who hit Utticus?"

"I wasn't there. You'll have to ask Utticus."

"Do you think that would give Utticus a reason to want to hurt Jangle Elwell?"

"Utticus is not that kind of guy. And I don't like the implication of your questions. Have you seen Jangle's body Mr. Prosecutor?"

"No. Have you?"

"Yes I have. I went to the morgue the morning I learned Jangle was murdered to see myself. If you saw Jangle's body you'd know Jasmina couldn't do that. Utticus couldn't do that."

"So why did you go to see Jangle's body?"

"A cop said my client was dead. Now I know how cops can lie in court so I went to see myself."

"Did you tell Utticus Uziah not to tell the police that Jangle had punched him?"

Since the best defense is a good offense, I said, "Am I suspected of something?"

"I see a pattern. This is the second time in a month that you have failed to report an offense. The first was when your roof was stoned. Now this with Utticus. Will you answer my question?"

"I will not, until you answer my question."

Kazuo sighed, and pressed his hands together as if in prayer.

"Mr. Burnham. This is not a holding room at Public Safety. This is your office. This is an investigation, not an interrogation."

"But Kazuo, you have me on the horns of a dilemma. You say I'm not a suspect. In my defender's mind, that makes me think I am, though for what reason I do not know. But I do know if I answer your last question you might think you have a case for obstruction of justice. If that's so, we can end the questioning right now."

"So you refuse to answer on the grounds that you might incriminate yourself?"

"What do you think this is, a grand jury?"

"It is also obstruction of justice to interfere with an ongoing investigation. By refusing to answer my questions you are obstructing justice."

"Do you want to arrest me for obstruction? Then cuff me." I swung my hands up, wrists together, and held them in front of Olopai.

"Mr. Burnham. I'm glad you take this seriously. But look at it from my point of view. I am investigating a murder. The victim may owe a man some money. The victim has a relationship with the same man's girlfriend, or former girlfriend. The victim strikes another friend of the same man."

"Jangle had a lot of enemies, but I wasn't one of them."

"Are you leaving Pohnpei to go stateside soon?"

"I have cases on Kosrae and Chuuk that need my attention, but not the States."

"Good. You know our extradition laws." Kazuo stood.

"What's that supposed to mean?"

Kazuo replied from the door. "It means stay on-island. I may want to ask you more questions."

I shouted to the prosecutor as he left the outer office. "Kazuo, I think you've rented too many crummy detective videos to exit with a line like that."

CHAPTER ELEVEN

I'm not quite sure how I was selected to fly Jangle Elwell's body back to Kosrae. Repatriation of deceased clients certainly is not part of the standard Frost & Burnham contract. But the Elwell family apparently has no close relatives on Pohnpei, none save the distant cousin who admitted kinship for the sole purpose of identifying John Doe Number One. No Taro Patch Kid volunteered to return Jangle's remains to his home island. The gang had lain low after Jangle's murder. No second-in-command stepped forward to take Jangle's place. No surprise; Jangle numbered himself among the immortals.

Yes, Jangle was a gang leader, who would not be buried on the island of his passing. The pastor of the Kosraen community on Pohnpei had decided against holding even a memorial service, reasoning that Jangle was both a Mormon and a known criminal who had died before confessing his sins to the entire congregation. Hard to say which the pastor thought was worse.

Having finished the autopsy, Doctor Perez, like Roberta before him, begged me to take what remained of Jangle off his hands.

"My morgue has room for only one. What if John Doe Number Two shows up?"

"Mario, this isn't Guatemala. An unidentified stiff here is as rare as snowfall. You told me it was five years since the last John Doe."

"It could happen."

I finally agreed. Of course this still begged the question of money. No one seemed to have scratch to spare to repatriate a deceased gang leader. True to form, the Kosraen pastor on Pohnpei decided against taking up a collection from his congregation. The Kosrae Liaison Office on Pohnpei has no money to spare for paperclips, much less for the transportation of a corpse. No one was willing to go down to La Brea to pass the hat among the Taro Patch Kids. Finally, Doctor Perez managed to re-budget some money to pay the excess cargo fee, but only if someone - me - would accompany the body to ask for compensation from Jangle's family. I agreed, with misgivings, knowing well the strain an island funeral can put on family finances.

Of course for the funeral of someone wealthy and powerful no expense would be spared. Al Frost used to talk about the funeral of a revered and reviled Senator, for which fully half the national Congress crossed Chuuk lagoon in open boats. Some Senators arrived at the funeral grave and concerned; others green from the rough passage. More pigs were killed for that funeral than in a week at a Hormel packing plant. Naturally, the expense of the Senator's funeral was borne by the national treasury, as the islands' potlatch economy assured that all Compact funds would be spent, if not actually accounted for.

In another minor miracle, Doctor Perez located enough fluid to embalm Jangle's corpse, thereby adding mortuary science to his list of learned responsibilities. Even then, ever-cautious Mario packed the body with ice into the biggest cooler he could find, a monster with rope handles and a split-top lid. One thing was sure. No one who knew would ever use that cooler to store fish.

I had my own reasons to get off-island. I'd sent a letter to the Attorney General's office asking if they would agree to dismiss all charges against my now deceased client. In response, I got a nasty call from Marielle Hargraves who told me not to stick my nose into DSI's investigation of the homicide. Marielle had no reply when I asked how the murder of a local is within the jurisdiction of the national police.

Murder is in the bailiwick of Pohnpei Public Safety, and thanks to Kazuo Olopai, who doesn't want so little as an unsolved traffic ticket on the books, I had a Pohnpei police officer tailing me weekdays during daylight hours. Score it 12-5, not 24-7. Still, I was close to asking Kazuo for round-the-clock surveillance. Although some quiet nights followed Jangle's murder, Taro Patch drive-bys started up again later in the week. The Kids hadn't forgotten me. Rudderless without a leader, they had drifted back to a familiar course, hassle the *haole*. A late night visit by a pair of Taro Patch Kids with nylons pulled over their faces was proof the remaining gang members were insane. No one wears hosiery in that kind of heat.

A swarm descends on Taketik Island to meet every flight: Air Mike ticket agents, Pohnpei police, taxi drivers, hotels touts, locals awaiting friends and family, or folks just bored and looking for something to do. Add to that Mormon missionaries – clean-cut white kids in white shirts and skinny black ties and nametags – plus contract workers in Aloha shirts, or the handful of Japanese or American tourists. The swarm doubles at midday on Mondays when both the eastbound and westbound island hoppers arrive on island at almost the same time.

No special night flights connect Kosrae with Pohnpei. To get to the Island of the Sleeping Lady, I would take the regular Air Mike flight that leaves Pohnpei at noon, en route from Guam to Honolulu. With seven stops across the mid-Pacific, the Air Mike island hopper is the dictionary definition of a milk run. Taking a mid-day flight meant paying mid-day prices, but it didn't have to be a money-losing proposition for Frost & Burnham. The firm still has a couple of cases on Kosrae, and I planned to work them to underwrite a portion of the trip.

I was a little tipsy at the airport, having jumped for beers with Utticus Uziah in the icy darkness of the Harbor View, advertised as the bar with the air conditioner with 10,000 BTUs of cold-cranking power. Utticus had picked up the ice chest-cum-coffin from the hospital, secured it beneath a tarp on the long bed of the public defender office truck, then stopped at my office to drive me out to the airport. We drove in silence down the causeway to Taketik Island past the rusting cranes dredging sand and coral, fighting the endless war against time and tide. Roberta's husband, Spenser Ely, a Hightower Texan and a tree-hugger, despises the dredging, and calls the rusting crane the national bird. I planned to buy Utticus lunch for driving me to the airport, but he wasn't hungry, so we drank instead. I wanted to apologize for getting Utticus into this mess, and a beer or three was a start towards penance.

Sitting in the gloom, I thought if only Jasmina would join us, then the State would have all three of its prime suspects in one place: Jasmina for jealousy, Utticus for revenge, and me for, well, I wasn't quite sure what Kazuo's theory was on me. Maybe money. Because my travel plans came together at the last minute, I drove out to Jasmina's aunt's place the night before to let Jasmina know where I was going, and for how long. When I pulled around the corner near the place, I could have sworn that I saw Judge Coleman's truck speeding away. Although I didn't tell him why, I asked Utticus if he would check on Jasmina while I was gone. He had no problem with that assignment.

Although I couldn't believe it, Kazuo's suspicions seemed strongest about Jasmina. According to him, Jangle was getting some action on the side. Maybe Jasmina knew it. I could say that hell hath no fury like a woman scorned, but that'd be more less p.c. than Coleman calling Marielle "Miss." Let's face it; hell hath no fury like anyone scorned, especially when that anyone is nicknamed "Typhoon."

Mario Perez walked up to me at the airport check in line.

"I came down to wish you a safe flight, Drake. Have you seen yesterday's paper yet?" Mario winked as he held out a copy of the latest Pacific Sunday News. "There's an interesting article on page twenty-seven."

I was about to open the paper, but Mario kept a hand on it.

"Careful. Don't let the ads to fall out. Maybe you should read it after takeoff."

I took the newspaper more gingerly and thumbed open the corner. Inside was a brown envelope that I guessed contained a draft of Mario's report on Jangle's autopsy. I folded the paper and tucked it firmly beneath my arm.

"Say, Mario," I asked. "You mentioned the other day some other people came in to see Jangle's body before me. Who were they?"

"Seemed like everyone was interested in John Doe. You were my fourth or fifth visitor that day." Mario smiled, "I should have started charging admission."

"Were they locals or expats?"

"Locals. You were the only *menwhi* to show any interest," Mario frowned. "Let's see. Pohnpei Public Safety brought the body in, around five. But that was just the start. Someone from the state prosecutor's office came down at eight."

"Attorney or investigator?"

"Cop. You know him? Beefy guy, with a neck like a water buffalo? Said he was investigating a reported homicide. Of course, I was the one who reported it as a possible homicide. All he did was take some notes and leave."

"Who was next?"

"Your colleague, the Pohnpei Justice Ombudsman, Valentin Onan. Judge Coleman sent him. He said there was a criminal case pending against John Doe, but he couldn't identify him."

"What time was that?"

"About an hour after the first visitor, maybe nine o'clock. A half an hour later, a DSI officer showed up."

"With the bench warrant?"

"To arrest a corpse. I had to talk him out of cuffing John Doe and dragging him off to court. I think you were the next one after that."

I was by then the next passenger to check in. I held up the Sunday paper and reached to shake Mario's hand. "Thanks, Dr. Perez. I owe you a San Miguel."

The Air Mike baggage handlers triple bagged the ice chest, probably having heard rumors of what it contained. I dutifully signed a waiver of claims form on the ice chest. Every box on the form was checked off: fragile and unsuitably packed, perishable (I smiled at that one), waiving any and all damage to packaging or contents, subjecting all claims to the Warsaw Convention, although I'm pretty sure Micronesia is not a signatory to that treaty. I waived all claims for outright loss or misdelivery, if for example, the cooler was sent to Honolulu instead of

Kosrae. Stranger things have happened. Once when I lived on Kosrae, we were stiffed on a Payday Friday because the courier bringing the national employees' payroll "forgot" to deplane at Kosrae. The authorities (I don't know if it was Hawaii 5-o) caught up with the courier in Honolulu a week later, after he had gone on a shopping spree at nearly every store in the Ala Moana Shopping Center. Still, I thought it unlikely that anyone would highjack a casket/cooler.

The ticket agent slid my boarding pass down the counter to the state revenue officer for payment of the departure tax. I handed over my ten bucks, and the revenue officer had just stamped my boarding pass when a state police officer, in full uniform, chugged up to the counter to grab the boarding pass before I could take it.

Officer Kiatoa Koht is without a doubt the largest person on the force at Pohnpei Public Safety. He is bigger than Al Frost ever was, and Al sort of resembled Orson Welles near the end. In court, I have to literally look up to Officer Koht even when he is seated in the witness box. Kiatoa was the island-wide wrestling champion in his youth, and his preferred method for subduing criminal suspects is to sit on them, ala Rosie Grier. Officer Koht held my boarding pass in one hand and laid the other on the grip of his pistol. The airport is just about the only place on-island where police officers pack heat, and I was appropriately intimidated.

"Good day, Mr. Burnham. Where you go today."

"Just read the boarding pass, officer."

"I can read that. But I want you to tell me."

"I'm going to Kosrae. Kosrae, where the locals live in bamboo huts and drink milk from contented coconuts."

"You won't stay on the plane and go to Honolulu."

"Of course not. If I wanted to flee justice, I would get off at Majuro, then hop a plane to Tarawa and then to a country with no extradition treaty with Micronesia."

That confused Kiatoa long enough for me to snatch my boarding pass. "I have business in Kosrae. If you need to reach me there, call the public defender office."

As I walked from Officer Koht, I noticed Kazuo Olopai eyeing our encounter from about thirty feet away. Although I could clearly see his eyes, large in the reverse refraction of his glasses, Olopai's face was a blank. He turned and walked away.

I waited next in line at security, a tad annoyed that Dick Harkness's Chinese clients – the ones I'd met at the Bench & Bar Banquet – were whisked around the metal detector without search or delay. When I got to the front of the line, I spoke with Absalom Absalom, an acquaintance from Kosrae who often works security for the Air Mike ground crew.

"How come those Hong Kong guys get the VIP treatment, while I'm left here, a PIV, a Poor Innocent Victim."

"That one is a diplomat, Mr. Drake, People's Republic of China. Besides, you are not a victim. You are our Defender."

"I'm not the Defender any more."

The departure lounge was packed, naturally enough when two planes land at the same time. Over to one side, Aang and his two young heavyweights, sat behind the ropes in the VIP area. Dick Harkness brushed by on the way to his clients. He carried a small paper bag imprinted with the logo of Lucy's, a Kolonia gift shop.

"What's in the bag, Harkness? Your client's jock strap?"

"What? Oh, hello, Drake. This is just some souvenir that Aang picked up. Security wanted to look through it so I had to convince them it's part of his diplomatic pouch. They can't search it. Say listen, I'm awfully sorry about the Charlie Warheit case. I didn't solicit him. He just came to me; said he needed a lawyer. I didn't know you'd done any work on the case. I guess you know how it is with local clients."

"No, I don't know how it is. Why don't you tell me, Dick?"

"You know, Drake, it doesn't have to be a loss. The case is yours if we become partners. I need a cracker-jack litigator like you."

Ever since his late partner, Burt Bayless, had died, Harkness has been shopping for a new one; a barrister to handle courtroom work while Harkness makes the rain fall. I parried yet again. "No thanks, Dick. But be advised I will serve a lien. Flying your clients somewhere?"

"I'm just seeing them off. Let's go talk with them a minute."

Mr. Aang rose to shake my hand when we walked up. "Mr. Burnham, a pleasure to see you again. Harkness, will you check again to see if my associates can get upgraded to business class?"

Harkness set the gift bag down on a bench and walked to a ticket agent.

Aang turned to me. "Mr. Burnham, will you reconsider our offer? Harkness mentioned that your case load was getting lighter."

I couldn't help but notice the way that Aang treated the lawyer he hired, but demurred simply, "I have not reconsidered."

"But you should know that the circumstances have changed. That portion of the collection matter against the local has been resolved. That leaves only the part against the American I mentioned, the one who lives on Chuuk. Surely you have no qualms over suing a fellow colonialist."

"I'm sorry, Mr. Aang. But the answer is still no."

"As you wish. But I hope you understand our offer will not remain open long. The matter I mentioned needs attention."

"Jangle Elwell didn't happen to recommend me to you."

"Elwell? I know no one named Elwell."

Both flights were then called and I said goodbye. A sudden squall brought the rain that had been expected all morning. I guess Aang had a business class seat, for an attractive Air Mike flight attendant walked him to the plane beneath an umbrella. No such treatment was offered to coach-boarding passengers like me, and I waited a few minutes to see if the rain would let up. I was about to sprint across the tarmac when Dick Harkness and Absalom Absalom came up to me, both out of breath, Harkness holding the paper bag from Lucy's.

"Mr. Aang forgot his gift bag," said Harkness. "Can you carry it out to him when you board?"

I took the bag, heavy for its size. Inside was a small, neatly gift-wrapped package and a greeting card. Al Frost used to joke that he could have started his own courier service for all the packages people had asked him to deliver when he flew from island to island.

"What does he have in here?" I said.

"Stone carving, a bust by a local artist. Don't worry, Drake. It's not an antiquity. I was with Aang at Lucy's when he bought it."

I shrugged, stuffed the package in my backpack and sprinted to the plane. Absalom radioed the crew that the last passenger, me, was leaving the terminal. Onboard, the cabin temperature was set low enough to safely store meat, and me and the other well-soaked economy class passengers had to deal with the possibility of contracting pneumonia. I looked around the business class cabin for Aang, but didn't see him. I then asked the flight attendant to page him, but there was no response. Then I figured it out. Aang must have gotten on the westbound plane, headed for Guam, from which he would transfer to a Hong Kong flight. I was on the eastbound flight, which stopped first at Kosrae en route to Honolulu. I still had Aang's package, but there was nothing left for me to do but give it back to Harkness when I returned to Pohnpei.

The captain of the island-hopper was yet another Texan, and he managed to mangle his pronunciation of both the name of the next destination and the traditional island greeting. He even called the flight the "I-Hopper" which made me think they might serve pancakes. The captain then went silent the rest of the hour-long flight, except to point out the turquoise rings of two coral atolls set in the sapphire Pacific, first Mokil, then Pingelap, the latter the home island to Entis Robert, now the sole remaining defendant in the great Micronesian bank robbery case.

Frequent flyers say flights give them time to think. They give me time to brood. Fortunately, I had the draft report of the autopsy of Jangle Elwell to pass the time. Jangle Elwell died of multiple gunshot wounds. Mario counted five bullet wounds, two in the left lung, from which he had retrieved slugs, a through-and-through just below the right ribcage, a wound beneath the waist from which he had retrieved a third slug, and a scoring wound on the left side of the torso. Based on the mass of the slugs he recovered, Mario believed that two weapons were used, but he couldn't be certain. Mario also ruled out the blow to the head as a cause of death, although it did cause substantial injury, perhaps enough to stun the victim. As to water in the lungs, Mario concluded that a reflex reaction brought water into the lungs when Jangle went into the water. He did not drown. Mario noted that he awaited blood results from Honolulu and that he had sent the slugs to a private crime lab there for analysis.

I don't want to sound blasé about gunplay in the islands. Micronesia is one of the few America-infected places where gun violence is rare. Between Al Frost, Roberta, and myself, we've handled murder charges where the weapons are Army knives, a jailhouse shiv, a length of mahogany, nun-chucks, and hunks of coral, although the weapon of choice here is a machete. But among the three of us, we've defended not a single case of murder by a firearm in Micronesia. In fact, the only gunfire you're likely to hear on island is on video.

It was sunny by the time we landed on Kosrae, and the shimmering heat off the tarmac made the lush mountains waver as if in a mirage. But then Kosrae always seems an island less real than most, too beautiful, too peaceful, too friendly for someone like Jangle to call home. I consciously unclenched my neck and shoulder muscles when I stepped from the plane, something I hadn't done since Jangle walked into Roberta's office to see me a few short weeks earlier.

The Customs agent, Melti Tonna, smiled and shook my hand when I walked up. Mel has been on my side ever since the day I got her kid brother sprung from a negligent homicide rap. An unlucky passerby had been struck down by a fifty-pound jackfruit that fell from her brother's tree. I convinced the judge that turning an accident into a crime would only compound the tragedy of the victim's death. Mel waved me through Customs without bothering to inspect my suitcase or the cooler. That was just fine, because I didn't want Mel to discover the case of Victoria Bitter and the box of turkey tails Utticus and I had stashed inside the cooler with Jangle. The beer would not be seized, although I would have to pay a duty for bringing in alcohol to a religiously, if not legislatively dry island. I had a commercial interest in the turkey tails. I planned to sell them to a family of Nauruans who have abandoned their moon-scaped home island for the greener shores of Kosrae. At ninety percent saturated fat, turkey tails are irresistible to the portly Nauruans. But if anyone learned the turkey tails shared space with a stiff, I'd end up feeding them to the pigs.

The Kosrae airport looked like a twin convention when I came out of Customs. Matching pairs of snotty-nosed kids hung from the backs of pickup trucks, clung to the sides of their mothers' voluminous muumuus, or chased each other around the wooden benches of the open air terminal. Hyper-fertile Kosrae has always had an unusually high incidence of twin births. Not that anyone complained. Why settle for one baby when you could have two?

But more than twins mobbed the airport. People claimed every bench; the parking lot was jammed. The Lelu Village Women's Choir was leaving for a concert on Majuro, and it looked as if every other family on-island was there to see them off, to the call of a song, naturally, several of the many Kosrae departure songs. The Lelu Village Women's Choir sang interminable choruses in response. Outside the terminal, makeshift tables were heaped with watermelon wedges and banana pies, pyramids of lime green tangerines. Food in great abundance accompanies any event on Kosrae, itself a feast for the senses. The smell of jet fuel mixed with the salt tang of the ocean and the musky muck around the mangroves. Members of the Lelu Village Women's Choir, dressed in their Sunday best, were adorned with construction paper leis, handmade *mwarmwars* of hibiscus and plumeria blooms, or garlands of ylang-ylang, scented like lilacs on steroids.

Both Zebedee James and Hudson Henry came out from the public defender office to meet the plane, so jointly pleased at my return that they tried simultaneously to shake my hand. But Zebedee reached me first and would not let go, so Hudson had to make do by shaking my wrist. First things first, we hauled the cooler to the far side of the parking lot to retrieve the beer and turkey tails. Then we turned over the cooler to members of the Elwell family, and stood by as they opened the split top lid to acknowledge Jangle. I nodded to their invitation to come to the funeral that would begin that night and run to burial the next day.

Zebedee had arranged for me to stay at the house of the American lawyer who had taken over for me as staff attorney at the Kosrae public defender office, six or seven months after I left. The house was vacant. My successor was off-island, back in the States actually, interviewing for a job on his return. By staying there, I would save the cost of a hotel room, and the house would not be vacant, and a temptation to crimes of opportunity. In that way, locals can be bold. I recall a party in my first year on-island where someone outside swiped a boombox sitting on the kitchen window. And it was playing music at the time. My successor had agreed to let me stay at his place on condition that I deposit a case of Australian beer in his refrigerator, a brand otherwise unavailable on Kosrae. By transporting the beer in the manner I had, I avoided the possibility of pilferage. No one would dare drink beer stashed next to a dead body. And what my successor didn't know wouldn't hurt him.

My Kosrae itinerary was simple: attend Jangle's funeral, talk with some former clients here, set up a status conference on a probate case, maybe get a little fishing in. Zebedee let me borrow the public defender office pickup truck on my assurance that I had not the slightest intention of reporting my use of the truck to his superiors on Pohnpei. It's an ancient Mazda, a relic from my days on Kosrae, reliable, but with a universal joint that gives a clank like someone hitting an empty scuba tank with a monkey wrench if you turn the steering wheel too far. Borrowing the truck was a bargain for me. In a week I would pay at most twenty bucks for gas, while the cheapest rental car started at twice that per day. My first stop after the airport was a local emporium – named in the unfortunate Kosrae habit for the initials of the proprietor – the WTF Market. I bought a box of chicken parts and a fifty-pound bag of rice for the funeral, a jar of instant coffee and a package of Marie biscuits for breakfast, and a bottle of hot stuff in case I needed to buy some information. Then I drove past the site of the old mission school to my successor's Tafunsak village house and took a nap to shake off the effects of my three Budweiser lunch.

CHAPTER TWELVE

Two locals make up the bench of the Kosrae State Court. Both are called throughout Micronesia "The Honorable Judge Presidents." Thanks to Boston missionaries, Kosrae has had a full century of exposure to all things American. Many a Kosraen baby boy is named for a U.S. President. The last census numbered a half-dozen Kennedys spread about the island, and two Nixons, although after Watergate one petitioned to change the spelling to "Nickson." Two Reagans work on Guam. Two Tafunsak villagers are named Clinton. Oddly enough, no one is named "Bush," although I know of a greedy boy in one village named "Saddam." Nor is naming limited to Presidents of recent vintage. I know of four Madisons, three Jeffersons, and a Harrison or two. So it's no surprise that Kosrae's judges are Washington George and Lincoln Abraham.

Unlike my experience with certain jurists on Pohnpei, I get along jim-dandy with the Kosrae judges. The island had a long hiatus between fulltime public defenders when I first arrived, and both judges were glad to clear a backlog of low-level felony cases awaiting a public defender staff attorney. The fact that both judges and I sat in the same informal drinking circles didn't hurt either. Kosrae's local prosecutors are politically inclined, and claim to be *etawi*, sworn to stay on the wagon. Although no prosecutors imbibe with the judges, the issue of

Coleman-like ex parte contact never arose. I simply do not talk shop with the Kosrae judges, other than to regale both with stateside war stories, while the judges in turn, burnish the reputation of my late partner, Algonquin H. Frost. The drinking circles usually convene at the respective judge's house, which has the salutary effect of keeping the Honorable Judge Presidents from driving home under the influence. Kosrae has no fallen guardian angels like Valentin Onan for its jurists.

I drove to Sansrik, across the harbor from Lelu, to visit Judge Abraham. I figured he wasn't alone when I saw a police truck parked on the road near his place. I thought it might be a cop asking for a warrant until I saw two darkened figures sitting in the shadows by the water. The glowing coal of a cigarette hovered before the face of one figure, waxing and waning like a patient firefly. Across the harbor, the lights of Lelu were steady and unwavering in the short, humid distance.

"*Ekewo*, Judge," I called to alert the pair as I walked up, the harborside mud sucking at my zoris.

"Hello, Drake." Judge Abraham stood and switched the cigarette to his other hand to shake mine. "We heard that you returned home to the island today.

He opened a cooler to grab a beer for me and motioned for me to sit on a purloined courthouse folding chair.

"Come and drink beer with us. We only have a few more to pour down. You remember Chief Gerber."

That explained the police truck. Rob Gerber is the Chief of Police on Kosrae, and I shook his hand as if he had just cleaned some fish. The coconut telegraph had lately buzzed about Kosare's zealous new police chief. Lockdowns and tight security at the Kosrae jail are now the norm. Interrogation of suspects is more "diligent" and warrantless searches are on the rise. Zebedee James complained Gerber has switched search incident to arrest into arrest incident to search, a neat trick to get around the warrant clause. Gerber even tried to subpoena me to testify as a witness adverse to my own client at a parole hearing, a subpoena Judge Abraham had quashed. Another time, Zebedee groaned that Gerber had started to cultivate social contacts with Senators, mayors, even the judges. But I told him not to grouse because I had done pretty much the same thing.

I'd heard a little bit about P. Robert Gerber, just enough for me to conclude that he's like most other bits of Yankee flotsam washed up on Micronesian shores, at once under-qualified for the job at hand, yet full of himself, smug in his supposed superiority, not by training or experience, but simply by being American. Think Marielle Hargraves, but without the discreet tattoo or nice legs.

"What brings you back to Kosrae, Drake?" said Judge Abraham.

"Yeah. We thought you had given up on this place years ago," said Gerber.

I answered the judge. "Same old. Check on some clients, visit friends, maybe set up a status conference on the Jackson Palik case."

"Don't bother with your friends in jail, Burnham. Visiting hours are over." Gerber sounded as if he had drunk his share of the cooler's contents. I glanced at him but said nothing.

"Speaking of former clients, Drake, Carterson Micah was just paroled," Judge Abraham said. "Do you remember that case?"

How could I forget the case where Jangle had set up my client to take a fall? I said I remembered it.

"Carterson sure learned his lessons. He went to church every time it was offered and he led the prayers when church groups visited the jail. He turned out ideal, didn't he, Rob?"

"Micah was better than most. I won't say he was 'ideal' though."

"Lighten up, Rob," I said. "Carterson is no longer your responsibility."

"Maybe. But I know that property crime is up 18 percent from last year."

"What does that have to do with Carterson Micah?"

"It's no deterrent when felony-one convicts are released in two years."

"He took a can of corned beef."

"And jewelry. And he burglarized a store to commit the theft."

"Rob, is it true that you once killed a man by sticking your pen in his neck?"

"*Fa!* Enough!" Judge Abraham stood and like Solomon put out a hand to both of us. "You *ahsets* always fight. I deal with fighting enough every day in court. Must I see it again at my own place? This return should be happy for you, Drake. And Rob, I'm sure that Carterson won't be a repeat visitor to the jail. So both of you, stop your fight. Now I have to go visit the Governor."

Judge Abraham walked over to the mangroves to relieve himself. I smiled. It would melt Frost for him to know that judges everywhere were now quoting him.

"So you brought Jangle Elwell back to Kosrae," Gerber said quietly when the Judge was hidden behind the bushes. "Very noble."

"What do you care?"

"I don't."

154

"So why ask?"

"Call me curious. I wonder if you know half of what we know about Jangle Elwell. What was he to you?"

"A client. A particularly difficult client, but nothing more."

"What was he charged with?"

"Bank robbery."

"Bank robbery? That's just the fin above the water. The danger is below the surface. Jangle was mixed up in all kinds of nasty business."

"Such as?"

"I don't want to speak ill of the dead, especially in front of the Judge." Gerber nodded towards the mangroves.

I was surprised at Gerber's diffidence while drunk. Maybe he was one of those who grew less loquacious as he drank. But I was curious about what goods he had on Jangle.

"We're out of beer. Should we get some more?"

"We've got time. Josefina's closes at 2100 hours. But you drive. I've already had a few," Gerber admitted.

"Let's take your truck then. Mine's a little low on gas."

I was more surprised that Gerber agreed. To take a police truck to buy beer was against policy, if not state law, especially if one planned on returning to drink the beer with one of two judges on-island. But I didn't want Gerber to find the bottle of hot stuff I stashed beneath the seat of the truck I drove, not the least of which reason is that I did not have a current Kosrae drinking permit. But Rob seemed amenable to suggestion.

Judge Abraham liked our program, and sweetened the deal with a promise to have his wife prepare some sashimi chasers.

I got behind the wheel of the police cruiser as Gerber slid in on the passenger side. The truck was a rust bucket, the side panels filigreed with rust, and flakes of dun-colored metal cascaded from the fenders when I opened the door. There was nothing special inside, no siren, just a police band radio slung beneath the ashtray and a switch for the dome lights. The hilt of a machete protruded from a shotgun holster. Of course on Kosrae the only legal use for a shotgun (and a small gauge at that) is to hunt pigeons. The engine's no monster; high-speed car chases are rare on an island with twenty-seven miles of paved road. Full throttle wouldn't get us anywhere fast, so why bother. Still, it was more than a wee bit unreal to tool over to Tofol behind the wheel of a police patrol. I felt like Jack Lord, swinging that big, black Mercury all over Oahu. I actually wondered for a moment whether we might see a crime being committed. No, of course not. It was Kosrae. I used to joke that I had to commit a few crimes myself in order to stay busy as the public defender.

"So what's your interest in Jangle," I said.

"Strictly law enforcement. The Governor and prosecutors agree. We want to keep anything like the Taro Patch Kids from even starting on Kosrae."

"You keep tabs on someone on another island? That's outside your jurisdiction. Only the national police can do something like that."

"You think I should rely on a bunch of Pohnpei yahoos at DSI? Those guys couldn't investigate a fender bender. Besides, we didn't 'keep tabs' on Jangle. We just exchange information with other Pacific island law enforcement agencies."

"What, like Hawaii 5-0? There isn't enough crime in Micronesia to merit that."

"You'd be surprised. Take for instance your buddy, Jangle. The Taro Patch Kids were into smuggling, big time. That's probably where they got the money for new trucks, new clothes, junkets to Manila."

"You sound envious. What do you think they were smuggling?"

"Cannabis, to start with."

"Everyone's heard those rumors."

"I've got more than rumors. The Taro Patch Kids put themselves in the middle. They're the guys who can deliver the goods, from the growers here on Kosrae and on Pohnpei to the markets in the Marshall Islands, in the Gilberts, on Nauru."

"Can't they grow their own?"

"Every blade of grass on Kwajalein is numbered, so there's a huge market there. It is a military base, and unfortunately there is always a temptation for enlistees."

"Of which you were once one."

"Yes sir. I served my country on Oahu, Johnston Island, and Kwajalein. But I wasn't involved in the use of any kind of recreational drugs." Gerber interrupted himself to belch. "Hell, I know about officers, and particularly, civilian contract workers who smoked Kosrae cannabis on Kwajalein."

"What's the harm of some bored civilians blowing some grass?"

"Spoken like a dyed-in-the-wool public defender."

"Guilty. I guess you think some goes to Ebeye, too."

"Stands to reason. Same with Tarawa. But what's really interesting is the TPK began exporting to Guam and Saipan. Both those places have their own supplies of boonie weed. But territorial police in Guam say Kosrae cannabis is the best in the Pacific."

"Pohnpeians all say that Kosrae *sakau* is the best."

"Apparently the same is true for cannabis. Call it a blessing, call it a curse. Everything grows better here."

"I'm sure border control is pretty lax between here and the Marshall Islands, but smuggling dope to Guam? A U.S. territory? With U.S. drug laws? That's lunacy."

"How well do you know the Taro Patch Kids?"

"You got a point there. But risk time in a U.S. jail? No thanks."

"Believe it or not, the Taro Patch Kids got sophisticated. Boxes full of Kosrae tangerines, oranges, bananas shipped to Guam might have a layer of cannabis at the bottom."

"And no one would suss that out? Come on, Rob. They've got a drug dog on Pohnpei. There must be a dozen on Guam."

"I think they took a page from Filipino drug smugglers. You know the Taro Patch has a Manila connection. The Syndicate there knows that if you smear a drug shipment with urine from a wild dog, a domestic dog will shy away from it."

"Tell me. Where does one find a wild dog in Micronesia?"

"Details."

"Even then, that assumes there is someone at the other end who knows exactly which box to open to retrieve the goods."

"That's why the Taro Patch Kids are a good match. Think about the gang organization. They recruit from every island. Jangle could have a Kosraen buddy pack the stuff here for a Chuukese buddy working in a hotel kitchen on Guam or Saipan. Same with fruit from Pohnpei. Hell, there are Rasta-nesians on every island now."

"So how come I never heard of an arrest?"

"Haven't had one yet."

"Not one? Sounds like a cop fantasy. Scores of resorts on Guam getting tons of fruit from Pohnpei and Kosrae, and you don't have a single bust. Where's the evidence?"

"I'm working on it. That's just one possible path. I'm investigating other possible couriers, too. Think about all these Chinese fishing boats coming through Micro these days. More boats chase less tuna, so most boats are losing money. It has to be a mighty big temptation to a captain whose long liner is mortgaged up to the gunwales if say someone from the TPK came up and said, 'Here, just take this package along when you sail to Guam with your catch.'"

"Highly unlikely. The risk-reward ratio is all wrong. How can a fishing boat smuggle enough dope to make a profit? Most of these boats are small and all of them are slow. It's not like taking a speedboat full of cocaine from Bimini to Miami. On top of that, a fishing boat in Micronesia is searched more often than a cell in your jailhouse. Where would you hide it?"

"Bottom of the holds, beneath the ice."

"Won't it get wet and rot?"

"Wrap it in plastic, I don't know. Put it in a cooler."

Or a false bottom cooler, I thought but didn't say.

I said instead, "Besides, wouldn't the Taro Patch Kids need money upfront for an offer like that? Isn't it standard to pay half up front, half on delivery?"

"With the threat of an anonymous tip to the authorities if they don't deliver."

"So you think Jangle set this up?"

"He's the one with the connections everywhere. But where did he get the capital? Where did he get the upfront money to tempt a fishing boat captain?"

"Would five grand be enough to carry his dope?"

"Could be. Five thousand dollars is a lot of *yuan* back in China. It's why so many of them are fishing illegally. Boy, if I could just bust one drug smuggler without a fishing permit, we seize the catch and the vessel, and levy the fine."

"But that's only if the captain is stupid enough to fish illegally on the same voyage that he's carrying a load of drugs."

"Any foreign fishing boat that isn't fishing illegally is suspicious to me. It's the perfect cover."

"Nice logic, Rob. So every boat that isn't fishing illegally is suspected of some other crime? Why don't you just arrest the whole lot? You really don't know anything, do you?"

"As I said, I'm working on it. It's very difficult for me, with a force of twenty-three officers, to investigate a criminal enterprise as far-reaching as the Taro Patch Kids."

"Criminal enterprise?' You make it sound like the Mafia."

"That's a damn good comparison. We have so many leads to run down. Taro Patch Kids, long liners, sailing boats. I don't trust any of those cruising sailors, especially singlehanders. No job, no visible means of support. Where do they get the money to live on?"

"Independently wealthy?"

"Doubtful. You should see some of the dregs that cruise through here. Guys like Blue Hesselman."

"I saw Blue at the airport today. He's looking more and more like a lifer. There's always work for a handyman like him. Forget him. Tell me instead why Kosrae Public Safety is interested in all of this?"

"Cannabis plantations on-island are on the rise again. The jungle here is so dense that you can't see anything thirty feet back from the road. Someone could cultivate cannabis on the sly and no one would know."

"But the island is so small. You said so yourself. Everybody knows each other, and gossip is the favorite pastime. No one can keep a secret on Kosrae."

"Cannabis trafficking is increasing, arrests are up twenty percent. And it isn't just one way. More contraband than ever is smuggled into Kosrae."

"Maybe you should give yourself some credit, Rob. Your improved methods might be catching the stuff that used to leak through. Besides, who would smuggle marijuana to an island that grows the best and has an overabundance anyway. Guys were giving away whole 'trees' of pot when I was here."

"It's not marijuana coming back. It's guns, ammunition. Just this month Customs intercepted a cookie tin full of bullets, and a .38 Smith packed in chicken parts. We traced it to a gun shop on Guam that sold pieces by the dozen."

"So check everything coming from Guam, but you're not going to find that kind of hardware coming from Nauru or the Marshalls."

"You forget about the military base on Kwajalein."

"Is that what you're seeing? Military issue?"

"We seized a police special. But no military issue, not yet."

"There's not much of a market for firearms on Kosrae, not for an M-16 anyway. It would be overkill for hunting pigeons."

"One thing I do know is that the Taro Patch Kids are involved in the fruit bat trade from Pohnpei to Saipan and Tinian."

"You have firsthand evidence?"

"No. But I read a DSI report about Taro Patch Kids putting fruit bats in the bottom of a cooler and covering it with oranges or bananas."

"Fitting in a way."

"Also a category four felony here, on Pohnpei, and on Guam."

"But the DSI report was on smuggling from Pohnpei. You're still outside your jurisdiction. You don't have a TPK case here, just rumor."

I pulled the truck off the road in front of Josefina's, a local store constructed out of two empty shipping containers sitting side-by-side.

"The best is yet to come, Burnham. I'll tell on the way back."

Gerber stepped from the truck and skulked to the door in an Australopithecine slouch. I decided to go in with him, and kicked off my *zoris* at the door. When Gerber asked the clerk for a case of Budweiser, I told her quietly in Kosraen to be sure to ask for his drinking permit. I did not want to witness entrapment. The clerk, a pretty young woman, maybe three years out of high school, arched her eyebrows at me, then asked Gerber for his drinking permit. She scrutinized it closely for a moment, frowning. Then she smiled and pushed the cardboard box and permit across the counter to Gerber, and made the one-dollar change for the offered twenty-five.

"What did you say to her in there?" Gerber leaned over the deck to put the beer next to the spare tire. I smiled when we got back in the truck, and then I told a lie to a law enforcement officer, which is probably a category one misdemeanor.

"I said, 'Who is cooking your rice?'"

Gerber laughed and punched me on the shoulder, hard. "I guess all those stories are true. You must have gotten a lot of action in your day."

I knew the stories were false, but I just smiled as I started the truck and wheeled it back in the direction of Sansrik and Judge Abraham's.

"God, some of the local girls are so hot. There are a couple in Malem I'd like to get to know better. Tell me, Drake. What's your secret?"

Gerber reminded me of the guidance counselor at Kosrae High School during my stint as the public defender. Tom Mifflin haled from a mining hellhole called Harlot's Crick, Montana. His counseling was not in the standard books, since he seduced two students and supposedly impregnated a third. The Education Department finally got wise and chased him off island about the time that assorted boyfriends and fathers started sharpening their machetes. The last I heard, Mifflin was counseling again, college students on Guam, and occasionally taking out lovelorn personal ads in the Pacific Daily News.

"Later, Rob. Let's talk about Jangle for now. You were saying there is two-way traffic, marijuana and fruit bats going to Guam, guns and ammo coming back."

"I said the best is yet to come. Guam's warning us of other contraband coming our way. Methamphetamine."

"Alias ice, crank, *shabu*."

"It's already coming from Guam and Saipan to Pohnpei. And I think it's just a matter of time before it shows up here, too."

"I don't get it. Guam and Saipan have meth problems because they're markets for it. But why would anyone want it here?"

"That's my thinking exactly. We don't have enough money on Kosrae to make a methamphetamine trade worth it, although you might have enough on Pohnpei."

"But it's more than money. Ice turns users into something most locals don't want to be, skinny, uptight, up all night. And if Pohnpei is laid back, Kosrae is horizontal." I thought suddenly of the stone-throwing drive-bys by the Taro Patch Kids. Maybe they weren't just drunk but cranked as well.

"I thought the same thing. What drugs are abused on-island: cannabis and *sakau*. Both are soporifics. Users get sleepy, relax, slow down. That's what the locals want, not to be amped up into some hyper, paranoid crook. Then I figured it out. The market isn't here. It's the other end of the island hopper, Hawaii."

"How do you figure?"

"Because I was on the streets of Honolulu dealing with it. When I was with the M.P.'s, we drilled weekly in 'I&I,' identification and interdiction, of methamphetamine. We know most of the Pacific's meth is manufactured in drug labs in the Philippines and Malaysia. Hell, someone could set up a methamphetamine lab here. All they need is a quiet spot with a ready water supply. They can import all the chemicals they need. Anyway, the meth markets started with Guam and Saipan, fat and happy on the tourist trade, relatively relaxed places. Meth then hit Honolulu hard, swimming in tourist money. I ought to know. Did you ever try to arrest a 350-pound Samoan, strong as a WWF wrestler, cranked up on ice?"

"No thanks."

"The route is the connection. A direct route from a Philippines meth lab to the market in Honolulu zips right through Micronesia. That's how the Palau ice problem got started. Couriers coming into Guam directly from Manila were stopped and searched. But if a courier from Manila to Guam stopped a couple of days in Palau, maybe unloads some of his stash there, then came on to Guam. Since he flew from Palau, not Manila, he didn't fit the courier profile."

"Palau to Guam is now known as a drug route."

"As is Guam to Honolulu. So what do the couriers do? Just like they did in Palau, they break up the flight route. If Palau-Guam is a profile route, then stop in Yap. And if Guam to Honolulu is a profile route?"

"Then stop on Chuuk or Pohnpei. So that's why passengers are searched when they leave Guam, to give a heads up to Honolulu."

"And Guam doesn't search passengers heading for Pohnpei, Chuuk, or Kosrae. These couriers know I have no resources here, just my police force, plus the Customs office. You have to know how easy it is to sneak something through Customs here."

"It's not that easy."

"As the meth problem spreads, so do the supply routes. If a mule takes the Guam to Honolulu non-stop, the odds are higher that he or she will be searched. But if you take the island-hopper, then the suspicion is a lot lower. And the suspicion is non-existent if you are a local boy taking your aged auntie on a church choir trip, or taking Papa for treatment at a Honolulu hospital."

"So you think the Taro Patch Kids were doing this?"

"They're the middlemen, Drake. Whatever they learned on cannabis, they parlay on methamphetamine."

"So a Kosraen kid headed stateside for school could be a mule? Jesus, Rob, you've got me thinking like you. And you think Jangle was behind this?"

"Our Pohnpei contacts sure thought so. They think the Pohnpeian guy who was arrested in Palau last week was a Taro Patch Kid. He got caught with a big load of ice he brought in from the Philippines. I think Jangle's the one who sent him to Manila."

"I guess you took Jangle's demise as good news."

"The best. But it's only a temporary setback. Another one like him will step forward. They always do."

CHAPTER THIRTEEN

Hitchhikers on Kosrae don't thumb rides. Instead, they call to the driver from the side of the road, "Have a ride?" No one drives very fast on Kosrae, so stopping is not a problem, just drift to the side and let the hitchhikers hop on the deck. They signal their stop by banging on the truck's side panels. I've picked up more hitchhikers on Kosrae than I would even consider doing anywhere else. In fact, I don't think twice about stopping for someone carrying a machete, which is a tool after all. But I'm reluctant to pick up hitchhikers after dark. Many are drunk by then, itching for trouble. Early in my Kosrae days, I mistakenly gave a ride to an early evening drunk, who then stubbornly refused to get out of my truck. It wasn't until I pulled up in front of the police station that he decided to stumble away from the passenger's side.

I mention this because en route to funeral services, while slowing to pass the state offices in Tofol, a voice called from the side of the road, "Have a ride?"

I slowed enough to see whether I should speed away, but pulled to a stop. Soley Andrew limped toward the truck; hauling six bunches of swamp taro tied to a carrying stick across his shoulders. I threw open the door as Soley heaved his burden onto the deck.

Soley Andrew - possibly the straightest arrow on arrow-straight Kosrae - was certainly not a former client. He was *etawi*; didn't smoke, didn't drink, and probably went to church twice every Sunday. Soley's congenital defects left him mildly retarded and with a permanent limp. Although he managed to graduate (proudly) from Lelu Elementary School and his English was good, high school proved too much for Soley. He went to work as a stocker and maintenance man at Lelu Island Trading Company, helping customers by lugging fifty-pound bags of rice, sometimes two at a time, to waiting cars and trucks. Although he moved slowly, Soley had a powerful build. In the canoe races on Liberation Day, he was nearly unbeatable.

"Thank you, Mister Defender." Soley slammed the passenger door. "I bring some taro for the funeral."

"Lucky for you, Solely. I'm going there myself."

"I know it. You brought the body to the island."

The coconut telegraph was as efficient as always. I had little doubt that if Soley so desired, he could learn not only what I was doing on Kosrae, but also whom I had visited and what I had bought at the WTF Market that afternoon.

"Did you know Jangle very well?" I said.

"Just a little. He was kind to me. Sometimes he brought food – a sandwich or a donut -- to me at work. Sometimes he just came to talk."

I'm sure Soley was the butt of many schoolyard pranks on account of his limp and poor grades. But for Jangle to show a glimmer of kindness to anyone, well.

"Was Jangle in your class at school?"

"No, we were not in school together. I am plenty years older than Jangle. He came to visit me after he came back to Kosrae from the States, but before he left the island again."

"Did he ever give you money?"

"No. He said he wants to be rich like my boss, Yoshiwo Kanka."

So much for the Robin Hood theory. Jangle apparently did not rob from the rich employer and give to the poor employee. "Did Jangle see you at your place?"

"No. Only at my work at LITC. Jangle wanted to know about my work, so I showed him. I showed him the loading dock and the storeroom. I showed him where I help unload the containers and where everything goes."

"Did you show Jangle everything in the storeroom, even the window?"

Soley thought for a moment. "Yes. Once Jangle helped me empty out one box that was up on a shelf at the window. I could not climb up to it because of my legs."

It was clear to me, if not to Soley, that Jangle, the bastard, befriended Soley to case the joint. Posthumous character assassination is not my style, so I didn't let onto Soley about my suspicions. But I had to ask, "Did you ever show Jangle the office?"

Soley thought again for a moment and I waited.

"No. I never show him that. I do not have a key to the office."

It was good that Soley was with me, for I wasn't exactly clear on where was the funeral. Just past Tofol, Soley said to turn on the dirt road along the Innem River and we began driving toward the island's landmark, the Sleeping Lady.

Back when the island was flush with the first generation of U.S. treaty funds, Kosrae's leaders dreamed of pushing the Innem River road over the mountains and down to the deep water port and airport at

Okat, making a highway necklace over the ridges that form the Sleeping Lady's profile. But funding never materialized and the Innem River road snaked up to the first hills for only a mile or so, stringing along a few hardscrabble jungle farms of poorer families, like Jangle's, who couldn't afford to live on Lelu proper. When the road toward the Sleeping Lady veered left, Soley told me to stay right, and soon a crush of cars and trucks showed him to be right.

We rolled to a stop near a teenage boy who nodded to a house up the slope when Soley asked the location of the funeral. The tiny house was illuminated from within by bare incandescent light bulbs, and outside by the warm, yellow glow of half a dozen kerosene lanterns. The house itself was a poor structure on an island where few houses are bound for Architectural Digest. The only nods to upward mobility were the cook shed's corrugated steel roof, and the low walls of cinder blocks around the plywood shack, as if Jangle's family intended to erect the skeleton of a new house around the skin of the old. The cook shed, to one side, was a hive of activity. Funeral-goers had brought baskets of fruit, taro and yams, bags of rice, whole chickens, spare ribs, hot dogs, strings of reef fish, and at least a cord of rust-colored mangrove wood, split and sized for cook fires that billowed smoke like venting volcanoes.

Soley went to the back of the truck and heaved my fifty pound bag of rice onto his shoulder as easily as if it were an empty book bag, then limped toward the cook shed. I locked the doors of the truck – the bottle of hot stuff was still beneath the passenger seat – and grabbed the case of chicken parts from the deck. Samson Nadab, a former client of mine and apparently a distant relative of Jangle, greeted me as I walked toward the house. Samson took the box of chicken parts from me and nodded when I told him about Soley's gift of taro. He hissed to the teenager who gave us such minimal directions, and the boy sauntered to the truck to heave Soley's taro up to the cook shed. It took the teenager two trips to do what Soley could do in one.

At the front, well, only door, Samson re-introduced me to his father, Sam, uncle or great uncle to Jangle, I forget which. At any rate, Sam was the eldest male relative now in the house, and was thus in charge of greeting newcomers to the funeral.

"Good night, Mr. Burnham, and welcome back to Kosrae. I am sure that *Papa* Moses, the father, will want to speak with you. But please take my thank you for returning Jangle to his home."

Sam led me inside. Benches were set up in the front room of the two-room house, facing the back room where Jangle was laid out. Men sat in the front room, some men hunched over Bibles and prayer books. Others leaned toward each other in muted conversation. Older men and those with high status, sat up front, with younger ones like Soley behind. I nodded to two Lelu senators and the mayor sitting in the front row. Jangle might have been a gang-banger, but his family voted. A large doorway opened onto the back room, where Jangle's body was laid out on a bier covered with a cloth as white as plumeria blossoms. In the matching white burial shroud, Jangle looked like a fallen king, improbably handsome on this island of comely people. A group of older women, dressed in their Sunday whites – the designated mourners – sat on folded legs in front of the bier, praying. This group of mourners had probably come off cook shed duty to mourn, and after another group replaced them, they would go to bathe as part of their ritual. By custom, mourning is continuous so that the body will not go unaccompanied from the time it arrives on-island until it is interred, early the next morning.

171

Since funerals give me the heebie-jeebies, I sat on the second to last bench and tried to calculate how long to stay. A few moments after I sat, a thin and sweet girl of thirteen or fourteen brought me a styrofoam cup of coffee, Kosrae-style, thin and painfully sweet. I could feel my fillings swell on the first sip. Moments later, another teenaged beauty brought me a plastic bowl of soup Kosrae, a chowder of fish and pureed breadfruit, which I slurped from the bowl, no spoon provided. I felt as if I intruded for no other *ahsets* attended the funeral. What's more, there were no Filipino construction workers or MDs, no Japanese or Australian volunteers, no other ex-pats of any nation. The locals were an older group, too; no Taro Patch Kid candidates other than the teenager who had given us directions. Between sips of coffee and soup, a few men approached and thanked me for coming. No one chatted for long, or asked me to share a prayer for the departed, thank God. After half an hour, Sam fetched me to meet Jangle's father.

We walked to a jumble of cars and trucks parked haphazardly on the curve of road closest to the house. An elderly man leaned against a truck fender in moonlight bright enough to read by, which is what the man was doing, perusing a Kosraen language New Testament. When he stood up straight he was not that tall, maybe three inches shorter than me, but he stood erect, not stooped. Moses Elwell looked tired. He smiled sadly and shook my hand firmly. The old man's teeth looked straight and even, unmarred by either sweets or betel nut, and his high cheekbones might have shown some Marshallese blood. I thought for a moment he resembled Jasmina, but when he turned to Sam the illusion disappeared. I thought, too, that I could see a few traces of Jangle's features in Moses' face, but I wasn't sure. I was sure that I would not ask this old man from this poor house to reimburse anyone for footing the bill to fly Jangle to Kosrae.

Sam translated as the older man mumbled in Kosraen too swiftly for me to begin to comprehend.

"Moses, thanks you for returning Jangle to his home."

"Please tell *Papa* Moses that I'm glad I could help."

The older man spoke again. Sam translated. "Moses wants to know if you knew the boy well."

"No, sir. I did not." I answered Moses directly. "He was my client for only a short time before he was, well, before he died."

Sam continued. "You are the only *ahset* to come to the funeral so far. Jangle said he had many friends on Pohnpei, but you are the only one to come. He went to school on the mainland. But no friends from the States come to honor his memory."

"Well, it's a long way for someone to come from the States. But I would have thought that some elders from the Kosrae LDS church would have come."

Moses chopped the air with an open hand and spat out a flurry of words. I had gone yet again from being merely tongue-tied to sticking my foot into my mouth.

Sam explained. "The Mormons don't come here any more. They promised to build a new house, but look how far they got. When Jangle stopped attending the Mormon Church on Kosrae, they came to Moses and tell him to repay all the money they spent to send Jangle to school in Salt Lake City. After that, Moses stopped attending the Mormon Church."

Moses peered at me and said something to Sam.

"Moses wants to know if you are a saint."

"Well, my mother thinks so."

"No, no. Moses means a Latter Day Saint."

I could have taken Moses to the truck to show him the bottle of liquor beneath the seat, but said instead, "Catholic."

"Ah. In nominee patrie, et filio, et spiritu santu." Moses spoke letter perfect Latin and made a sign of the cross. The old man, like his son, was full of surprises. At that moment, he looked nothing like Jangle.

I felt uncomfortable and groped for something to say. "I think it must be very difficult for a father to outlive his son."

Sam coughed, and said, "You don't understand, Drake. Moses adopted Jangle."

It was my turn to cough. Then I said, "I meant to say it must be difficult to lose your only son."

Moses stared at me, jutting out his lower jaw. He clamped down on my elbow like a moray eel on a fish and steered me away from the other man. When Sam began to inquire in Kosraen, Moses motioned him away with an abrupt wave. Moses did not loosen his grip on my arm until we were across the road and well down the road from the bustle of the funeral. In the shadow of the jungle, Moses let go of my arm and said, "I want to tell you something."

"You speak English?" I rubbed my elbow.

"I speak enough. Between Boston missionaries and Mormons I learned some. Are you surprised?"

"It's just that if older men here speak another language, it's usually Japanese."

"I can speak a little of that, too."

"And the Latin?"

"A very small joke, Catholic. Mr. Burnham, how long did you stay here?"

"You mean on Kosrae? Almost three years."

"Always the problem. Contract workers come here for two, or four years, and when you begin to figure out the blessed island your contract is finish and you leave." Moses shook his head. "You said before it is hard to lose my only son."

I arched my eyebrows, nodded, and said "*hai*," all at the same time. Facing a polyglot local, I wanted to cover all the bases.

"You did not live on Kosrae long enough to hear all the stories."

"*Papa* Moses, I admit I know very little."

"Do you, Catholic, remember your Scripture?" Moses held up his Bible. "The Book has plenty of stories about fathers and sons. Abraham and Isaac, Isaac and Jacob, David and Absalom."

"Plus the Father and his only begotten Son."

"Of course. Did you know Jangle was born on Christmas Day? It's very strange. That boy was like the devil, but he was born the same day as our Savior."

I said nothing, waiting.

"I hit that boy, every day it seemed like. But still he would not behave. He was trouble, so much trouble, but he look like an angel. We wanted a boy, wanted a son. That's why we adopt him. But our joy on the first day turned every day after. That's why we sent him away to school. Those Mormons always looked so handsome and acted so kind. We thought going away might change Jangle, but it did not."

Moses paused for a moment to look up at the sky. Then he turned to me and said, "When Sam brought you, I was reading about the Prodigal Son. Do you know it?"

175

"But that was a parable of two sons."

"Yes. One stayed to do as he was told. The other ran away."

I had a sudden insight. "Does Jangle have a brother?"

"Ask his mother, she knows." Moses paused again, and then said, "I want you to tell me who killed my son."

"Why me?"

"Because Public Safety doesn't know, and our prosecutors have a different program. The last time he came to Kosrae, Jangle said only the Defender would be able to figure out if anything happened to him. Jangle thought you were very good."

"He had a funny way of showing it."

"I cannot change what Jangle did. I might raise him wrong, but he is my son. I want you to find out who did this to Jangle, and why."

I was reluctant to tell Moses what I had learned about Jangle, that his troublesome boy had grown up to become a gang leader who had punched my friend, seduced my secretary, and cost me many a night's sleep. But my insomnia was not as much; I'm sure by a long shot, as what Jangle caused his father.

Moses continued, "And what did you learn about my son here on the island where he was born."

"That he was suspected of selling Kosrae marijuana to bored soldiers and contract workers on Kwajalein. That he was thought to be smuggling fruit bats to Guam and positioning himself to smuggle *shabu* through Micronesia and into Hawaii."

"Who told you this? That *ahset* police chief?"

I nodded.

"Beware that Chief. He lies to get what he wants. Some people say he is here on a different program. His first wife, from the

Marshall Islands, she blew up like a frightened pufferfish after. Now he is looking for another wife, a younger wife. But I think Gerber is here to poison us, to turn father against son, brother against brother."

"Moses, would it trouble you to know if I learn worse about Jangle?"

"Isn't it enough for a father to want to know why his son is no longer there to take care of him?"

One thing about examining a witness is that you have to know when to stop asking questions, so I did. "Let's go back to the house before we are missed."

We walked slowly back to the row of parked cars. Moses assumed the position he was when I met him, leaning against the fender, his attention on his Bible. I walked back to the house where Sam was again at the door. I told Sam I would like to meet Moses' wife, to express my sorrow.

Gender separation is still the rule on Kosrae, although the number of extra-marital affairs and illegitimate children shows that the rule is observed in the breach. Still, Sam followed protocol by asking his wife to inform Mrs. Elwell that the *ahset* wished to speak to her, then walking down to the cars to inform Moses.

In a few moments, a very large woman in her mid-thirties walked out from the cookhouse, wiping her hands on her apron. If this was Jangle's mother, then she was ten years old when he was adopted. Mrs. Elwell was accompanied by one of the teenage girls who served the food. The girl translated without raising her eyes to mine.

"This is Sepe Moses Elwell," said the girl.

"*Ekewo*, Sepe Moses. I want to tell you that I am very sorry about Jangle."

The girl translated my regards and then Sepe's short thanks to me for coming.

"Moses said you might know where I can find Jangle's brother."

The woman and the girl glanced at each other. "Sepe does not know that."

"Are you sure, *Nina?* Moses said to ask Jangle's mother."

The two spoke a moment in animated Kosraen before the girl turned back to me.

"Sepe said you made a mistake. Sepe is the second wife of Moses. They were married after Jangle left and Moses' first wife died. Sepe said Jangle's mother lives in Chuuk. Her name is Rollo Treadwell."

CHAPTER FOURTEEN

Spending five days on the Island of the Sleeping Lady is too, too long for the uninitiated – Sunday alone can seem like a week – but my dance card filled up. I went fishing with Zebedee James one day, then visited that evening with a few of the *ahsets* remaining on Kosrae from the days I lived there. I even went to Thursday evening services at the Lelu Congregational Church to hear the choir, hitching a ride into town, then walking back along the stretch of low tide sand from the causeway all the way to Tafunsak, a beach walk of several miles not possible on swamp-rimmed Pohnpei. Church services were in Kosraen, although the pastor stared directly at me when he announced in English the subject of his sermon, "A Lesson on Foul Language." He must have overheard me fishing.

Jasmina called me at the public defender's one day. The Operator – my pair of Filipino clients who may have worked with Jangle – had stopped by the office on their way to the airport to leave Pohnpei. They had left a package for me, a small, heavy object wrapped in shredded paper. I figured it had to be an antiquity, something they'd dug up on their leased land in Kitti. I was glad they didn't try to take it off island. I didn't want to rush back to Pohnpei to defend a smuggling antiquities charge. What I really wanted was to stay longer on serene Kosrae. I told Jasmina just to stick the package in a desk drawer. I smiled when she said she'd put it next to my bottle of hot stuff, and that I should talk to Clarence about it when I got back to the office.

Utticus Uziah telephoned me, too, to report that Judge Coleman had again stopped that weekend at Jasmina's auntie's house. When I asked Utticus whether he was sure, the investigator said he snuck up to the door to check, and had seen Coleman's zoris, the ones on which the judge had written "Maximum Max" on the heels, in the pile by the door. I thanked Utticus and asked him to keep his eyes open and his mouth shut.

When Roberta telephoned later that week, I was alone in the Kosrae public defender office, reading a three-week old Pacific Daily News as rain rapped the corrugated steel roof. It was a pleasure to hear from one of the few souls on Pohnpei whom I had reason to believe was still harboring friendly feelings for me.

"If anyone asks, this isn't me."

"Now, Roberta. Have you been up reading thrillers again?"

"I'm serious, Drake. Is anyone else in the office?"

"On a Friday afternoon on Kosrae? Of course not. Everyone's gone home. Actually, it's Hudson's turn to cover the office, but he's picking up his kids from school," I yawned. "I'm doing my best to cope in this busy practice."

"I'm doing my best to see that no one traces this call. I'm not at the office."

"So you're at home."

"Actually, I'm in your office."

"Fine. I'll send you a bill. So what's with all the secrecy?"

"Promise you'll never reveal the source of the information you are about to hear."

"Cross my heart."

"You know how we always complain about those Friday arrest warrants? The ones timed so that arrestees spend the entire weekend in jail before they get a bail hearing? Well, we've heard a rumor from an unconfirmed source at the Pohnpei State prosecutor's office."

"Utticus's sister, of course."

"Don't you dare say a word."

"I won't. I won't. What did you hear?"

"That this morning, Kazuo Olopai asked a State Court judge to issue an arrest warrant in the case of the murder of Jangle Elwell."

"It's about time. Who is it?"

"You."

"What?"

"It's for you, Drake. You are now officially 'wanted.'"

"I can't believe it. What the hell is Kazuo thinking?"

"Somebody's sister typed up the warrant this morning."

"Sounds like a sick joke."

"I'm deadly serious. You have an outstanding arrest warrant here on Pohnpei."

"Wait a minute, Roberta. Am I a suspect? Or is Kazuo trying to keep me from leaving the island by naming me as a material witness."

"I don't know; though I've never heard of Kazuo holding a witness. We can find out if you're charged. I'll send Utticus to take a look. A warrant is a public record."

"Can you send him today?"

"He might not have the time. It's late. It might be Monday morning before we can check. When are you scheduled to return?"

"Tomorrow, mid-day flight."

"I'd miss that flight."

"Why Ms. Ely. Are you advising me to dodge a warrant? Is that ethical?"

"Drake, I asked you not to mention my name. You got to figure out what to do. Does Kazuo know you're off-island?"

"He saw me off at the airport on Monday. He actually sent Officer Koht for a little Q&A about where I was going."

"Does he know when you're scheduled to return?"

"I'm sure I didn't tell him, or Officer Koht. But Jasmina has my itinerary."

"I spoke with Jasmina before sending her on a mission so I could make this call. She said she hasn't talked with anyone from the police or prosecutor's office."

"Kazuo's probably checked with Air Mike already. That explains a Friday warrant. It's not to keep me in jail all weekend, but to arrest me the minute I step off the plane tomorrow."

"Maybe you could go somewhere else?"

"Where? Nauru? The Kosrae-Nauru flight goes only once a month and it's not tomorrow."

"Take the Monday island-hopper to the Marshalls or Honolulu."

"No good, Roberta. The only cash I have now is two ten-buck retainers and the proceeds from selling a case of turkey tails. The only place I can go from here is back to Pohnpei. Besides, what will Kazuo do if I don't step off the plane tomorrow? He knows I'm on Kosrae."

"He'll call the Kosrae prosecutors and police and have them arrest you there. Who's the Chief of Police on Kosrae now?"

"Ugly American named Gerber. He'd only be too happy to haul me in."

"Gerber? Name's familiar for some reason. Do I know him?"

"Doubtful. I met him the first time last week. Ex-military, full of himself."

"What if you could get onto Monday's plane? Say someone ran a little misdirection here, said you were already on-island?"

"Even if I managed to get on a plane to the Marshalls or stateside, I'd be arrested there, too. Both places have solid extradition treaties with Micronesia. I ought to know. And I don't want to sit with a bunch of drunks in the Oahu Correctional Center or in that pesthole on Majuro waiting out extradition proceedings."

"Are there any ships berthed on Kosrae now?"

"Jumping ship won't work. Ship-to-shore radio would haul me back in a minute."

"How about a cruising yacht? You know I had a friend who fancied a yacht in the Greek Islands. She put on her bikini, swam out to it, and asked if they took stowaways."

"I don't know, Roberta. I don't look so hot in a bikini. Besides, the last time I looked, Blue Hesselman was the only yachtie in Lelu Harbor. And he's not going anywhere. Maybe we'd better think about putting some bail money together."

"Don't get on the Saturday flight, Drake. If you do, you'll spend thirty-six hours in jail. You know there isn't a judge on this island who will schedule a bail hearing on a Sunday. When's the next flight from Kosrae after that?"

"Tuesday."

"Change your reservation to Tuesday, and talk with the American prosecutor over there on Kosrae. Maybe he'll agree to house arrest if you show him you're not a flight risk. I'll tell Kazuo that you're returning on Tuesday. That'll give us two more days to figure out something on this end. Maybe we can challenge the arrest warrant before the whole panel of the State Court."

"I've never heard of an appellate panel convening to challenge an arrest warrant before it's even served. No harm, no foul."

"Maybe we can challenge it in the Supreme Court."

"The Supreme Court? Maximum Max? I won't ask Coleman for mercy."

"Just a thought."

"Well thanks for the heads up, nameless stranger. I could make like Bob Woodward and call you 'Deep Throat,' but your husband might protest. Speaking of Coleman, does he know anything?"

"He's off-island for a bit. Appellate cases on Saipan and Palau."

"Well I was told here this week that judges and public defenders are the last to hear anything. I'm glad you had your ear to the rail."

"See you Tuesday."

When Hudson returned to the public defenders office with his eight-year-old son in tow, I put Roberta's plan into motion. I walked to Air Mike, on a Friday afternoon in Tofol possibly the only place open. I asked the clerk to change my return flight to Pohnpei from Saturday to Tuesday, and made sure that she registered the new day on the computer. Instead of printing a new ticket – the Kosrae Air Mike office is low on office supplies in general – the clerk wrote out the new departure day onto an adhesive sticker that she fit neatly onto my old paper ticket. I'd had Air Mike clerks do the same in the past, and I was counting on her doing it again.

Solving the riddle of Jangle's demise was now imperative. I had discovered just about all the clues I could on Kosrae and would have to look elsewhere. Moses Elwell, Jangle's stepfather, told me to ask Jangle's mother, who supposedly lives in Chuuk. So my Plan A, a variation on Roberta's suggestion, involved not only dodging arrest on Pohnpei but getting to Chuuk to locate the next piece of the puzzle. A problem, and a big one, was that the only way to fly to Chuuk from Kosrae was the westbound Air Mike island hopper, a flight that stopped on Pohnpei between Kosrae and Chuuk. Plan A required a lot of luck, and lately in that department, I felt like a snorkeler caught in a rip tide.

The westbound island hopper, seven stops from Honolulu to Guam, normally reaches Kosrae at mid-afternoon on Tuesdays, Thursdays, and Saturdays. I called Air Mike Saturday morning to ask when the flight would arrive, adding I was meeting a passenger. Air Mike regretted to inform me the flight had yet to leave Honolulu, and was presently scheduled for an early evening arrival. I passed the day distracted by the delay, picking up, then dropping several times, a long novel. I could have spent the day with friends, but Plan A called for keeping an exceedingly low profile. The weather was stormy and the electricity flickered on and off throughout the day, as if Public Works was experimenting with unannounced power outages. When I checked again with Air Mike in the late afternoon, the flight was rescheduled to arrive near midnight. I waited until it was full dark, then risked a trip to Raimond's Rendezvous, the only bar in Tafunsak village, one of only two on-island. But warm Budweiser – refrigerators need electricity, too –

and Raimond's musical tastes, soon chased me back to the darkened house.

The storm showed no sign of relenting as midnight approached. It was possible that a night landing in the rain might prove too risky. The pilot could overfly Kosrae and head directly for Pohnpei. That would be bad luck indeed, for Plan A relied considerably on directing attention elsewhere, that everyone, including Roberta, was to believe that I rescheduled to leave Kosrae on Tuesday. If I didn't get on the Saturday flight, I would have to go to Plan B, and Plan B didn't exist. At a quarter past eleven, after locking up Shaw's house, I drove to the airport in the rain, wishing the plane to land.

The weather broke. In a respite in the near constant rain, the Air Mike 727 swooped from the darkness onto the runway like a tern wheeling onto a school of tuna. As the jet taxied to the terminal, I sat in the cab of the public defender office truck and carefully peeled off the adhesive ticket from my flight coupon, transforming my Tuesday ticket back into one for Saturday's flight. I hid the key in the truck's ashtray, left the door unlocked, and hurried to the counter.

At the check-in podium, a different Air Mike clerk than the one at the office raised his head from his arms. He looked as if he awaited the flight all day in basically the same position. "Any luggage to check?"

I had none. I left both my small suitcase and the paper bag from Lucy's that I had volunteered to bring to Mr. Aang, Heartless Harkness's Hong Kong client, on the bed at Shaw Taylor's house, so that anyone looking would think I was still on Kosrae. I carried only my backpack to board.

The clerk scrutinized my ticket and asked for my passport. My heart leaped as he frowned at it for a moment, until he realized that he held my passport upside down.

"The computer is down, so I cannot assign your seat. But there should be plenty room onboard tonight. Take an open seat when you get on."

I paid my departure tax and went immediately to stand in line to board, wanting to be neither first in line nor last. I closed my eyes and yawned regularly, as if bored by the delay. I avoided all eye contact but was ready to give a tired smile if anyone called my name. Security was a breeze.

Air Mike flight attendants rarely check the boarding passes of Kosrae-boarding passengers. The island has only one flight per day, so it really isn't possible to board the wrong flight. Even so, I took the offensive when I reached the flight attendant at the top of the stairs.

"When are we scheduled to arrive in Chuuk?"

"We expect a 2:00 a.m. arrival, Chuuk time."

I chose a window seat more than halfway astern, stowed my backpack and sat. The flight was about half full, the usual mix of locals and outsiders, with hopefully enough passengers that I wouldn't stand out. I closed my eyes and pretended to sleep, but I was a bundle of nerves. I had boarded a flight that would land in the lion's den. But I managed to keep my fidgeting to a minimum whenever someone passed. Before long, a local took the aisle seat on my row. Despite a late start and nasty weather, the flight was smooth and quiet. I actually dozed, and opened my eyes only when the plane bumped down on Pohnpei an hour later. My seatmate deplaned at Pohnpei, grabbing his bag from the overhead bin. I waited for all the Pohnpei passengers to deplane before standing to stretch and yawn. Then I stuffed a blanket and pillow beneath the seat in front of me and placed my "Occupied" airsickness bag on my seat. Actually, the one in my seat pocket was stuffed, probably with betel nut detritus, so I borrowed one from another seat. I strolled to the rear of the plane and smiled sleepily at a flight attendant collecting pillows and folding blankets, working from the rear of the plane forward. When I reached the rear of the cabin, I glanced back to make sure that no one was watching. Then I opened the door to the starboard rear lavatory and stepped in. I did not lock the door, part of Plan A. With the door unlocked, no one would know that I was in the lavatory, particularly a flight attendant making a pre-flight passenger count. I stood at the mirror with my trousers up, but undone, as if I were just finishing up. If anyone came to the door, there might be only mumbled apologies.

I chose the starboard lavatory on purpose. Most people are right-handed, and a righty coming down the aisle is likely to turn right, into the port rear lavatory, across the aisle from where I stood with my pants undone. Plan A worked like a charm. Twice I heard passengers use the port lavatory, but no one even tried the starboard door. I listened for the announcements requesting that passengers take their seats, then heard the muffled thump as the passenger door was closed. When the engines roared to life and the plane began to taxi, I buttoned my trousers, stepped from the lavatory and smiled apologetically to a flight attendant standing in the rear galley. A different man, also a local, sat on the aisle in my row, and made way as I reclaimed my window seat. We taxied to the runway and took off. In an hour we landed at Chuuk.

CHAPTER FIFTEEN

Not long after the Air Mike flight left for Guam the lights began to go out, rolling up the runway like a slow wave on a broad summer beach. Weno Island, Chuuk State, is a dark and quiet place without electricity. I glanced about the terminal before the building lights cut off to see if I recognized anyone. On my last trip to Chuuk I'd gotten three job offers, two marriage proposals, and an offer of citizenship. On this night, though, no familiar face appeared among the sleep-deprived who awaited a flight ten hours late. I saw no one from the public defenders office, and better still, no one from the prosecutor's office. The handful of police officers on airport duty didn't know me, and didn't know that I was on the lam from a Pohnpei arrest warrant. In their eyes I was just another American; dive tramp, missionary, carpetbagger.

The parking lot was still slick from an evening's rain, puddles glinting darkly in the headlights of departing cars and trucks, by then the brightest illumination of a cloudy night. Those few businesses and homes with generators were well lit; Telecom, of course, plus the Seabees HQ halfway up Mount Tonachau, the highest point on Weno, the hill capped with an enormous chunk of basalt stone that in daylight glowers over the runway like a giant carrion bird.

Just outside the terminal, I paused to paw around my backpack for the flashlight when someone approached from behind.

"Mister. Give me one dollar."

I flicked my flashlight into the face of a lone Chuukese teenager, who carried a guitar strapped shoulder to hip like an M-16. My flashlight, the size of a ballpoint pen, gave so little light that the panhandler didn't blink even when I shone it in his face. I told the truth; I had no money to spare. The teenager shrugged and disappeared into the gloom.

I turned the other way and crossed the main road toward the neon glare and diesel generator thrum of the You-Me-Now (Togetherness) Lounge. You-Me's has cold beer, and thanks to recent adventures in stowing away I had a powerful thirst. But I resisted temptation and crossed a second road behind the bar to the Magellan Inn.

No one was at the front desk. A kerosene lantern flickered a jaundiced glow on a figure sprawled on a rattan sofa across the lobby. I rang the bell. The young man, snoring lightly, didn't move. The lantern flamed sputtered, throwing wild shadows about the room. In Chuuk, undiluted kerosene is said to be difficult to find. A moth danced about the lamp for a moment before alighting nearby. I glanced at the dive map of wrecks in Chuuk Lagoon on the wall behind the desk, the grainy World War II photos of Japanese ships under attack by American warplanes that seemed to dive and swoop in the faltering lamplight.

I rang the bell again, hard. The figure on the sofa remained still. I gave him a once over. He was maybe a year or two older than my first encounter of the evening. From the elbow up to beneath the sleeve of his tee shirt his arm was scarred with a row of cigarette burns. I shook his shoulder. "Hey."

No response.

"Hey, get up."

Like many locals, this one had the sleep of the dead.

"Hey. Time to go fishing."

That got him moving, and I retreated a prudent two machete lengths. His eyes snapped open and he bolted upright before he noticed me in the dim lamplight.

"Yes sir. Good night to you. How may I help you?"

"I'd like a room."

"Okay. Stay here." The young man remained on the couch and for a moment I wondered if he would check me in, go for help, or fall back asleep. He shouted instead, "Katrina! Katrina!" followed by a flurry of words in Chuukese, pocked with rolling "R's" which sounded uncomfortably reminiscent of a Taro Patch drive-by.

Coconut oil slick hair appeared from behind the desk, and then the face, neck and shoulders of a young woman, as if she were surfacing from a deep dive. She, too, had apparently been asleep, on the floor behind the desk.

Katrina said yes, then smiled, her fine collection of gold caps gleaming in the low lamplight. "Hello, Mr. Kosrae Defender. It's very nice to meet you again."

It was good to see Katrina again, too. I had been a regular at the Magellan Inn back in my public defender days, when a steady stream of conflict cases brought me to Chuuk. The Magellan is central, cheap, and they always took my personal check in payment. Not every room has air conditioning; which matters very little when electricity is out island-wide. Al Frost had begun the custom of public defender stays at the Magellan, mostly for the string of ladies he tried to entice from You-Me's to his room. But Chuuk is a damn tough place for an outsider to get

191

laid, and Frost, who told war stories, like all stories, with gusto, was reticent about success, professional or otherwise, in Chuuk. For locals, it's a different matter. The cigarette burns on the young man's arm, I'm told, are the local equivalent of love bites from partners.

"No reservation, Mr. Kosrae Defender?"

"No reservation. Do you have Room 16?"

Room 16 was a regular fallback in tight times – like my present budget – the cheapest hotel room on the island, maybe in all of Micronesia, and with good reason. No TV, no air conditioner, and the only window opens into a conference room. Room 16 has a ceiling fan, and a dorm room refrigerator stocked with cans of Japanese fruit juice and a pitcher of boiled drinking water, plus a private bath, though the shower is a plastic dipper in a bucket beneath a leaky tap. The young man slung my backpack over his shoulder and led me up the darkened stairs with a dive flashlight, crooning the chorus from an old blues number. "Room 16 ain't got no view. But the hotplate is brand new."

I didn't stay in bed long after the Micronesian dawn chorus of roosters and barking dogs greeted the new day. The power was back on. The refrigerator hummed, and a bare, low watt bulb shone from Room 16's only fixture, the ceiling fan directly over the bed. I pulled the chain for the fan, but that only roused a musty odor from the corners of the room. I arose instead, and cursing my four hours of nightmare-tainted sleep, climbed the back stairs to the Magellan's rooftop restaurant, where a hint of a fresh breeze stirred the window curtains. I ordered coffee and a cheese omelet with toast, the cheapest breakfast on the menu. The only other patrons were a couple of dive tramps, Australian by accent, doing Micro on the cheap, fighting Foster's hangovers with liberal doses of instant coffee and Tabasco. I took a seat across the room from them by a window facing west to Faichuuk and some of the other islands in Chuuk Lagoon, green Udot's three humps, and the misty gray-green of Tol behind it. From You-Me's across the street, I could hear someone with a coal shovel heaving a heap of Budweiser cans, detritus of a Micronesian Saturday night, into a red and white mound of empties. Beyond You-Me's was the airport. A Caroline Pacific prop plane was being readied for a flight to one of Chuuk's outer islands far beyond the lagoon.

"Hello, Drake. What brings you to the happy islands of Chuuk?"

Justin Benoit took a seat across from me and ordered a cup of coffee as black as his suit. A longtime acquaintance, Father Benoit is a Jesuit who knows more about more different subjects than I could ever dream. He teaches at two local high schools plus the University of Guam extension, and turns out scholarly tomes such as a history of Micronesia, and op-ed pieces for the Pacific Daily News and the Honolulu dailies on subjects like the local teen suicide rate and the islands' version of "black-on-black" crime. The padre is regularly called as an expert witness in Chuuk and Guam to testify about social conditions that contribute to youth crime on both islands.

What's more, his appearance was simply unfair. I was dressed for the topics, in an Aloha shirt and shorts, while Father Benoit wore crisp, Jesuitical black. I might have broken into a sweat if I thought too hard, and the good father looked as cool as if he awaited a January audience with the Pope.

"Business as usual, Father," I said. "And why do you sip coffee at the Magellan instead of counting latecomers to the 7:00 a.m. Mass?"

"It's my turn to fly down to the Mortlock Islands to say Mass. The pilot is waiting for a break in the weather sufficient to get us there and back. It looks as if Pohnpei has sent us yet another typhoon, though early in the season this year."

"Pohnpei has been stormy this year, on a number of fronts. Say, Father, as long as you're waiting, let me run a couple of things by you. Do you know of a family here named 'Treadwell?' I don't know if Treadwell is a middle name or a family name."

"Doesn't sound Chuukese."

"I don't know that it is. But I'm trying to locate a witness named 'Rollo Treadwell.' Maybe one of her relatives was enrolled at Xavier High at some time."

"The name doesn't ring a bell. I teach at Outer Islands High School, too, and Treadwell doesn't sound like an Outer Islands name either. A witness to what, if I may ask?"

"I don't even know that, Father. I had a former client end up murdered on Pohnpei recently. His adopted father suggested that I check with his birth mother."

"Murdered? It wouldn't happen to be Jangle Elwell?"

"How did you know?"

"It's a small country, Drake. News travels fast." Father Benoit shook his head. "What a waste. A priest in our Pohnpei mission told me that Jangle was uncommonly bright. Too bad he turned out as he did."

"Let me ask you something else, then. Do you know the meaning of the phrase 'Who will save the widow's sons?'"

"It's a Freemason's call for help. It likely derives from King Solomon's mason for the first temple in Jerusalem, Hiram Abiff, who was the son of a widow. I don't know about the 'sons' part, though. Do you remember your Rudyard Kipling?"

"Someone paraphrased 'The White Man's Burden' to me recently."

"Ever read 'The Man Who Would Be King?' Kipling's narrator, a Freemason working in India, is obliged to help the pair of ne'er-do-well adventurers out of a jam simply because they show him their Masonic badges thereby invoking the assistance of a fellow Mason."

"I remember the movie. Sean Connery and Michael Caine."

"There's another story, not Kipling's, of a Freemason who is a judge in England. He presides at the trial of young fellow accused of theft who is likely to be hung or transported to Australia for what probably would amount to a life sentence. Very few of those transported to Van Diemen's land ever made their way back to Mother England. Now, Drake, when a defendant stands in the witness box for sentencing, he is allowed to make a statement on his own behalf. What do you call that?"

"Allocution. Although it's rarely eloquent."

"Allocution, of course. In this tale, the defendant's allocution consists of a single question, guessing that the judge is a Mason. The defendant asks, 'Who will save the widow's son?' Now the ball is in the judge's court, so to speak. He has before him a fellow Mason, who has invoked his brotherhood's protection in a most public fashion."

"So what did the judge do?"

"Some level of mercy was in order. Maybe the judge would suspend his sentence, or even let him attempt to prove his innocence before handing him over for transportation or to the hangman."

"We could use a few judges like that here."

"Lawyers always complain about judges. Remember what George Orwell said, switch places and handy dandy, which is the justice and which is the thief?"

"You don't know how right you are, Father. I just wish I'd get a case before a judge who has a sense of mercy in addition to justice."

"How do you know we don't have judges like that here, Drake? You have to look beyond your first impressions to take the measure of any man. Take for example your late partner. Someone who didn't know him well might think he was just some rummy ex-pat living out time on the islands, when in fact Al Frost could be described as 'a lawyer, yet not a scoundrel, a thing that made the people wonder.'"

"I like the phrase. What's it come from?"

"It was said of St. Ives, patron of lawyers, as you should know. Anyway, the phrase 'Who will save the widow's son?' also has a different, but related meaning. Saying it one Freemason to another can mean, 'Don't be so quick to judge. You may find yourself in my shoes someday, wrongfully, or even rightly accused. Don't be so high and mighty.'"

"Riddle me this, Father. How would a local, a Micronesian, learn so much about the Freemasons?"

"Was the person who posed this phrase to you ever a member of the LDS Church? Masonic ritual looms large to Mormons, though the Latter Day Saints will never admit to it."

"If you haven't guessed by now, it was Jangle Elwell who ran the phrase by me. He actually spent a few years in Utah, though he didn't run with a bookish crowd. Rumor has it that he joined a youth gang in Utah, a branch of the Sons of Samoa."

"It's one of the little shames of the LDS Church that their Pacific island converts face old-fashioned American bigotry on the Utah home court."

"Why reverend Father. Are you casting the first stone?"

"Not at all. Take my comments as the observations of an informed outsider, not aspersions cast upon a rival creed."

"And why an American-style gang, the Sons of Samoa?"

"Your question smacks of Yankee conceit, Drake, that America's problems with youth gangs are somehow unique. They're not. An abundance of testosterone in young men and the need to belong to something greater than the self are all-but universal traits. It doesn't matter what the society is. What's disconcerting is how the Taro Patch Kids reach across traditional barriers. Boys from rival clans in Chuuk somehow bond on Pohnpei, when they would be at each other's throats back here. Low islanders work with high islanders; low caste with high caste. Jangle must have had an iron will to keep his gang from spinning apart. It'll be interesting to see what the result of his death will be on the Taro Patch Kids."

We both turned to look out the window when the Caroline Pacific plane coughed and revved its engines. Father Benoit glanced at his watch.

"Do you have time for one last question, Father? What do you know about Chuukese magic?"

"That depends. It's daylight now, so I can say that it is nothing more than silly superstition, rumors that help to explain Chuukese fierceness in battle a century or two ago, and which may perpetuate discrimination against the Chuukese today. But after dark, our local acolytes might give you a different answer."

197

"Thanks for your help, Padre. I could tell you more, a lot more, but I think we are getting close to confidential communications."

"Say no more. So how about it, Drake? Will I see you at Mass the next time you spend a Sunday in Chuuk?"

"Interesting offer, Father. Wouldn't I have to go to confession first?"

"Yes. And the confessions of Westerners are invariably complex," Benoit sighed. "Locals are generally more direct. 'I did it. It was wrong. I'm sorry.' It's refreshing in a way."

A Sunday on Chuuk is only marginally swifter than one on Kosrae. The same rule holds true throughout Micronesia: Sundays are best spent on one's home island. Going diving would be nice, fishing better, but I had no room in the budget for recreation. I actually considered Father Benoit's suggestion that I go to church, if only for something to do. But the Chuukese got that old time religion, and I might bump into someone who knew me, and who knew that an arrest warrant awaited my return to Pohnpei. So I stayed at the Magellan after watching Father Benoit's prop plane roar off to the south. I perused the hotel's miniscule library of German paperbacks, and Japanese manga, then sat in the lounge through half a kung fu video, one flight up from reception. The lounge coffee may be lousy, but for guests it's free.

By noon, the general rain that had drenched Kosrae - a nascent typhoon according to Father Benoit - had reached Chuuk. Fishing would be no fun, even if I could afford someone to take me out. So I decided to make the most of the meteorologically enforced idleness by checking the telephone directory for Treadwell -- no listing -- and then quizzing the hotel staff on what they knew of a 'half-half' from Kosrae named Jangle, or the Taro Patch Kids. No one heard of either. And no one knew a family named "Treadwell" either.

Katrina shook her head. "It doesn't sound Chuukese."

At one o'clock, I walked across the street to the You-Me Now (Togetherness) Lounge for lunch. They serve a fairly decent burger, and it's the one place on Weno that everyone knows skirts prohibition. I ordered the cheapest lunch on the menu, a grilled cheese sandwich that I planned to fortify with sliced pickles, and what the menu specified as "Australian Tea," which is an oil can of Foster's lager poured into a teapot, for sake of appearance only, not outright deception.

You-Me's was almost empty. That same pair of Aussie dive tramps had grabbed a booth, grumbling that the weather had washed out their afternoon dive. A local was slumped over the bar, asleep on his folded arms. His trousers had slipped a bit to show the proverbial plumber's crack, his stern was clearly breached. Even with that unappetizing sight, I still finished my lunch too quickly – all that cheese would soon begin to bind. I then drained the teapot into my mug, and walked to the backroom, located behind the bar but in front of the kitchen. I know which unmarked door leads to You-Me's backroom, having found only the egress the first time I tried to locate it. You see, You-Me's backroom is well known throughout the Western Pacific. The new casino on Tinian, the one proposed for Madolinimh on Pohnpei, even the infamous gambling and booze cruises that used to sail out of Guam into international waters, all want a piece of the wagering pie that runs through You-Me's backroom.

No one knows what genius put a half-dozen video poker machines into You-Me's, but they were moneymakers from Day One. Chinese fishing boat captains spent small fortunes trying to beat the machines, as did assorted odd visitors, Taiwanese diplomats, Japanese salarymen, a few lost American souls, including a defrocked Jesuit, no friend of Father Benoit's, who managed to fritter away parish funds in his trust. You-Me's video poker machines were rumored in the Pacific Daily News to be behind the downfall of not one, but two separate Chuuk State governorships.

You-Me's is Weno's dirty, yet open secret. Everyone knows that You-Me's permits gambling and breaks prohibition. But no one has the juice to turn off the taps or shut down the machines. Every other politician, it seemed, or a politician's family or clan member, had spent a weekend lost in front of the machines, extending himself on credit, until as a gesture of 'good faith,' the management agreed to forgive the debt in exchange for cash in hand and unmentioned future favors.

I'm no gambler. My tastes in cards run strictly to low-wager poker with friends. The flashing lights, the boards covered with brightly colored dollar signs, hold no fascination for me, although I thought they must to the lone American sitting in front of the last machine on the left. I didn't recognize him at first, although his faded Aloha shirt was a little too frayed to have come directly from a department store shelf. He wore shorts, like me, and his zoris looked flattened from long use. From time to time he reached into a large pickle jar for more quarters, dimes, and nickels to feed the machine, but soon all I could see were pennies. The American kept hitting the video machine buttons, as wrapped up in trying to beat a machine as John Henry, or Anatoly Kasparov.

Before I could finish my mug, the American exhausted his accumulated credit on the machine. He sighed and pushed back his chair. When he turned, I recognized him; the guy that Marielle Hargraves dragged to the hearing on the change of venue motion in

Jangle's case. He called to the backroom attendant for another beer. The attendant shook his head. The American began to argue until he noticed me.

"Don't know why I bother to play the fool machines any way, except that drinks are free as long as you do. It doesn't compare in the least with the real thing."

"Like to feel the cards burning in your hands?" I asked.

"Hell, yes, and the looks on the faces of the other guys at the table. This one thinks he has a poker face, but I can see right through him. Or that fool, with the big pile of cash, will try to bluff his way through every other decent hand, until he runs low, and then gets so conservative that he'll bet on nothing but a sure thing."

"Doesn't look as if there's much else to do on a rainy Sunday."

"Got that right, soldier. What am I supposed to do? Go to church with the wife?"

"I suppose you already scuba-ed every wreck in the lagoon?"

"I'm no diver, actually, I'm cautious by nature, or maybe nurture. I'm a banker."

"Banker? I wouldn't have guessed you for a missionary here in You-Me's. I guess I don't think too much of bankers in paradise."

"Yeah? But here I am. I'm Chuck." He held out his hand. "I manage the Micronesian National Bank branch here."

I considered introducing myself as "Jack Lord," but didn't. Micronesia is ultimately a small town. "Drake Burnham."

"Oh, so we're doing last names, too? Well, mine's Throckmorton. What do you think of that? A name like that, you'd expect me to wear a three-piece suit, talk with a Locust Valley lockjaw. You've heard it, guys who talked with their teeth clenched tight."

"That's not so bad. Do you know what the locals on Kosrae call me? '*Fulok ahm.*' That means 'burn ham.' Get it?"

"Hey, I like it. That's a nickname worth having. Me? I prefer to be Chuck, Chuck from Chuuk, although I'm from Boston originally. Or maybe if you prefer, my old nickname from prep school, 'The Rock.'"

"Are you 'The Rock?' Stable, a banker you can depend on?"

"Hell, no. I'm here in the islands, aren't I? Aren't we both? I don't know about you, Drake, but I'm what they call the black sheep of the family. I washed out of prep school and two or three colleges. I worked at my Dad's off and on for a few years, the office gopher at a private bank. So you see, I'm a banker and an SOB, a son of a banker. After I got fed up working for Papa came a little stint in the Navy, a posting to the Philippines and then Guam. I finally finished school on the GI Bill, then moved back to Guam, and then here. That's the nutshell edition. So what's your line, Drake?"

"I'm a lawyer, in private practice."

"Here in Micro?"

"On Pohnpei."

"I thought I recognized you. You were the lawyer whose client never showed up. I thought that judge on Pohnpei was going to rip you a new one."

"I thought so, too. Judges here on Chuuk are generally friendlier than the ones on Pohnpei, or at least that one in particular."

"Been to Pohnpei a few times. Mostly when the bosses want to haul me on the carpet. That time I saw you in court there, a couple weeks back, I just flew in on a Sunday night flight, took care of business; pow, and was out on the afternoon flight back to Chuuk. A day was long enough for me. I don't care too much for Pohnpei."

"You prefer Chuuk's power outages and murders? You prefer petty theft and merchants cutting the kerosene with water?"

"You make it sound a lot worse than it is. Everybody exaggerates the aggravation of living in Chuuk. Locals here are much friendlier, not all nose-in-the-air like on Pohnpei. Just don't get into a beef with anyone. Keep your head down and your nose clean on Payday Friday. Forget the bad press. This place is actually a lot safer than the same sized city stateside. And a lot safer than Beantown."

I nodded, and thought about the slew of homicide cases in Chuuk, the speargun murder I'd helped Roberta with, the knifing at the barbecue pit, the clan fights.

"So Drake. If the judges don't like you, and your clients disappear, then why practice in Pohnpei? I think there's plenty of business here in Chuuk, especially if you play your cards right with your friendly neighborhood bank manager."

"Why stay in Pohnpei? Well, as Willie Sutton answered when they asked why he robbed banks ..."

"'That's where the money is.' I like your style, Drake."

"Pohnpei is the heart of it all, as far as Micronesia is concerned. The national government's there, and that government is still solvent. I'd starve if I tried to practice here." I didn't bother to mention that I was starving already. "What good would it do me to get a judgment against Chuuk State. I'd have to get in line with every other creditor."

"You ever do any collections work?"

I lied, sort of. "Believe me, Chuck. My Papa taught me to grab for every buck that passes by."

"I hear you. Say, listen up, Drake. Besides this pickle jar of pennies, I'm basically tapped out. Buy me a beer today, and I'll see if I can't refer a collection case or two your way, instead of to that shyster, Dick Harkness. The Bank pays its collections lawyers one-third of any sum they collect. Better your pocket than Harkness's right?"

"Sounds good. I can write off the cost of your beer as a business expense."

"That's the spirit."

We walked to the front room and sat side-by-side at the bar to order two more Australian teas. Throckmorton started drinking his almost before it arrived, slurping down big gulps in between glancing at the mirrors behind the liquor bottles above the bar. I figured since I was no longer a lawyer on the bank robbery case, I could ask Throckmorton about it, if I managed to steer the conversation that way.

"So what's it like being a banker in paradise?"

"Simplest job in the world." Chuck wiped his mouth with the back of his wrist. "Loan out at ten, pay interest at two, out the door by four."

"Sounds like a banker's life stateside."

"But its even better here than back in the States. Thanks to the Compact, the U.S. government guarantees all of our deposits, the good old FDIC. Thank God for Franklin Delano Roosevelt. If only my blue-blood father could hear me say that. The FDIC is our failsafe. Take the Micronesian National Bank, for example. Most branches, even Pohnpei's, are so low on deposits that if, God forbid, a bank ever went belly up, the feds would step in and everyone would eventually get their money back. Eventually, but then most locals are used to waiting. But the way I figure it, the feds wouldn't even bother to investigate a bank failure here. The cost of the investigation would be so high that they would probably just pay up and close the books.

"But that's only part of why my job is the best. Take loans for example. I don't have to hire an appraiser to check on collateral, because no one expects a secured loan here in Micro. All the lendee needs is a job with a paycheck, something the bank can garnish. I told the bosses in Pohnpei we should change our motto to 'Got a Job? Get a Loan!' Get it? My bosses said no, the weenies."

In law school, I nearly flunked the Secured Transactions course. But I didn't need to take the course to know that a bank that makes only unsecured loans won't last very long.

"And what happens if the guy you loan money to loses his job?"

"Not my problem. The bank just refers it to Harkness, the shark. I don't even have to try to get the guy to pay his loan. Simplest job in the world, remember? Yeah, it's a good job and a great life out here. Except for that bank robbery. I don't know how much you heard about it. Man, what a hassle."

"What happened?"

"I don't know. But I figure it had to be that little shrimpy guy. He had to come in through the back window by taking out the air conditioner. Then he cleaned out the safe that my staff, the bozos, decided to leave open when they left for the day. That's the only logical explanation. The window's small but it's the only place he could have gotten in."

"Will the FDIC cover the loss?"

"I sure hope so. We reported it, but no word yet."

"So other than the bank robbery, it sounds like you have the banker's life, except you're not sneaking out to play golf."

"Golf's not my thing. Poker. Now that's a man's game."

"A game of chance?"

"'Not the way I play it.' That's W.C. Fields, you know."

"I have to say, I'm a little surprised to see a banker playing video poker."

"What can I say? I love money. I work with it all day. I play with it all night."

I leaned so close our shoulders touched. "You, uh, ever think of using the company's money?"

He laughed as he pulled away. "Mighty tempting isn't it? All that money just sitting there, waiting to be spent. But no, Drake, I've never done that. I'll swear on a stack of Bibles. I keep work and pleasure separate."

I leaned in again. "So, what was your biggest score?"

"I never made squat here. But I cleared fifteen grand one night in Vegas. I got comped all the way to the state line that time. And I made close to twenty-five thousand in a day and half in Macau. You ever been there? It's right across the harbor from Hong Kong. Only six hours from Guam. Hell, it's closer to Chuuk than Hawaii."

Chuck drained the rest of his teapot into his mug. I was beginning to worry that I would have to buy another round. "How about your sorriest day?"

"Come on, counselor. Don't ask about that. You'll jinx me. I don't lose big, but I do seem to lose for long periods of time, just pissing it away. Some days I can't catch a break on anything. Then I just have to fold up my tent and lay low."

"Do you know a sure thing?"

Chuck took a long gulp from the mug and stared past his image in the mirror. "Time was when I thought I had a sure thing, but I know now there's no such creature."

I thought it prudent to change the subject. "Married?"

"You bet. I met Gina when I was in the Navy in the Philippines. She's probably getting back from church about now, busy praying for my immoral soul, or is it immortal? I'm not sure which. Funny thing, though, Gina holds the purse strings. Me, the banker, and I don't get to handle my own money at home. It's just as well, though. Saves me the headache. How about you? Are you married?"

"No, but I've got a couple of local girls on strings just in case."

"Damn, I like your style, Drake." Chuck looked ready to call the bartender to order another round of Australian tea, on me, when he suddenly stood and grabbed the pickle jar of pennies. "Listen, I got to get back to the house before long. Stop by the office this week, and we'll discuss our little arrangement. Maybe if you're not too busy, you can stop by the hacienda for a little supper. Gina makes wonderful lumpia."

"It's a deal."

"You know, I'd invite you over right now, it being a rainy Sunday and all, but you see, my butt is probably already in a sling for coming home smelling like beer and cigarettes, and well, if I brought you home like some wet puppy ...." Chuck trailed off, then tucking the pickle jar beneath his arm like a football, he scooted out the back door. I heard him stumble through the pile of Budweiser empties behind the building.

Catching the reflection in the mirror, I turned to see You-Me's front door swing open. Two of the Hong Kong gamblers, Cho and Lai, if I remembered correctly, the muscle of the outfit, not the brains, strolled into You-Me's as if they owned the place.

CHAPTER SIXTEEN

At eight sharp – busy Monday at last – I telephoned the public defender's office. I had made no headway locating anyone named "Rollo Treadwell," and decided to pick the capacious cerebrum of R.K. Asher, the only local staff attorney among the four main public defender offices. I was told that R.K. and office investigator Semeon Simon had gone to the Supreme Court for a trial call, so I trudged the half mile to the courthouse along Weno's main waterfront road, once the pride of Navy Seabees, now looking more like a stretch of the Ho Chi Minh Trail after a squadron of B-52's had unloaded over it. Potholes big enough to fish in have erupted in the chip seal and workday Weno traffic winds about them – on the road here, off the crumbling berm there – like an eel sliding past stones in a river.

The barn-like courtroom was full, a trial in local eyes being both solid entertainment and cheaper than renting a video. It was cool inside, too, on an already torrid morning. Unfortunately, the AC added white noise to an already acoustically challenged space. Justice Hadley V. Baxendale, the Supreme Court justice based in Chuuk, constantly asked lawyers and witnesses to speak up.

R.K. Asher sat at the well-used and rather beat-up defense table, conferring quietly with his client. His middle name is "Killawatt." He was so dubbed (and misspelled) by his father, Singkichi Asher, the first certified electrician in Chuuk, who had helped the U.S. Navy string Weno Island for electric power right after World War II. R.K., my old public defender cohort, has sat on both sides of the aisle in his legal career. After working his way through law school at the University of the South Pacific in Fiji, R.K. had put in a stint with the Chuuk State prosecutor's office before hooking onto the better karma of a public defender gig. I made my way up behind the bench and hissed to get R.K.'s attention.

"Drake Burnham. I didn't know you were on-island. When did you arrive?"

"Late Saturday night. I didn't call ahead because the trip came up literally at the last minute. Listen, R.K. I need some information. And I may also need to borrow your investigator."

"No problem if Judge Baxendale continues the trial. He should. My client first came to ask for help on Saturday, and the prosecutor won't object. Semeon is supposed to be waiting out in the parking lot. What do you have going?"

"Investigation, for now. Know a family named 'Treadwell?'"

"Which island?"

"I'm guessing it's inside the lagoon."

"'Treadwell.' I don't know that one. It doesn't sound Chuukese. Is it a family name or an adopted name?"

"I don't know that either. All I have is a woman's name 'Rollo Treadwell,' who lives in Chuuk. There's no telephone listing for her."

"That only means she doesn't live on Weno, or doesn't have a telephone if she does. Do you know how old she is?"

"Old enough to have a grown son."

"Old enough to collect social security?"

209

"I don't know. But that's a great idea. I'll check."

I slinked out of the courtroom as the bailiff called the courtroom to order.

Sticking to the shady side of the road as much as I could, I walked to the social security office. The day had started as a scorcher, and got only more oven-like as the sun baked the weekend's rain back into the atmosphere. But when I stepped into the social security office – locals call the building "the ice box" – I went snow blind when the air conditioning befogged my sunglasses.

R.K.'s thought proved dead on. A social security clerk, another young local with a gold-plated smile, had located a file folder labeled "U. Treadwell." Although it had no telephone number, the Treadwell file listed Okarito village as a home address. Unfortunately, Okarito is on the island of Tol, on the far side of Chuuk Lagoon and smack dab in the center of Faichuuk. Even missionaries are unwelcome on Tol. I wasn't sure how they might greet a lawyer, even one working on the side of the angels.

The clerk opened the Treadwell file and pulled out a form labeled "Power of Attorney." Ms. Treadwell had authorized an agent, probably a relative, named "J. Treadwell," to pick up and deposit her social security checks. When I asked if the account was current, the clerk shuffled around the desk – the soles of her zoris never actually broke contact with the floor tiles – and disappeared into a back office. She returned moments later with several annual ledgers for last names beginning with the letter "T." In the current year's ledger, the clerk pointed down the list of monthly disbursements received, in precise, right-hand cursive "J. Treadwell for R. Treadwell." The same precise signatures were listed in last year's ledger, until the clerk located a signature in different handwriting, "Rollo Treadwell." Jackpot!

The clerk frowned as she examined the current ledger. "Will you go see Rollo Treadwell?"

"I hope so."

"When you see her, tell her to come to social security." The clerk pointed to blanks for the last two months. "No one came to pick up her social security checks."

"Did social security try to contact Rollo's agent, the one who signed for her?"

"Let me see." The clerk opened the file folder containing the power of attorney. Written in pencil on the folder itself below the agent's name was a post office box and a four-digit local telephone number, but no village, no place of residence.

"Should we telephone?"

The clerk arched her eyebrows and placed a telephone on the counter in front of me. I punched in the number. The line rang five times before a woman picked up mumbling as if I had awakened her from a well-deserved nap. "MNB."

"I'm sorry. Whom did I reach?"

"Micronesian National Bank."

I arched my eyebrows to the social security clerk. "J. Treadwell, please."

"I am sorry. Jingle does not work here any more."

"Did you say Jangle?"

"No, Jingle. Jingle Treadwell. That's who you ask for."

"Do you know where I can reach Jingle?"

"Who is calling?" The voice went suddenly suspicious.

"I'm calling from the social security office." I glanced at the clerk who smiled back. "J. Treadwell is the agent to pick up checks for someone, and social security has two checks waiting to be picked up."

"I don't think Jingle lives on Weno any more. Are you American?"

"Yes."

"We have one American here. Do you know Mr. Chuck The Rock Morton? He can help you find Jingle. They are friends. But I cannot get Mr. Chuck right now. He is in meeting with some overseas investors, some VIPs."

"Please don't bother Mr. Throckmorton. I have a meeting with him anyway and I can tell him myself," I said before hanging up. I hoped the bank secretary would prove as unreliable as she sounded and relay no message that an American called asking about Jingle Treadwell.

I smiled again at the social security clerk. "If I find either Treadwell, I will tell them to come to the social security office."

She dazzled me with a gold-brilliant smile.

Back at the Supreme Court, I found the Chuuk public defender office investigator, Semeon Simon, leaning on the front fender of the office truck in the inadequate shade of a tangan-tangan tree. With Semeon were a couple of police officers in uniform, and the trio looked to be debating the price of kerosene or the best spot for an afternoon nap. Semeon used to be a cop, and when R.K. left the prosecutor's office, he took Semeon with him to join the public defender staff. Although he had switched sides, Semeon stayed in touch with friends and family on the force. A cousin was a police lieutenant, which came in handy on an occasion when clan members of a murder victim planned to make short work of the accused en route from the public defender office to the courthouse, enlisting some of the police to look the other way. By alerting his cousin, Semeon averted more violence, and perhaps another round of retribution.

Although I still didn't know whether the Chuuk police had been alerted to my Pohnpei arrest warrant, I thought I would be more obvious by trying to get Semeon's attention than to simply hide in plain sight. So I walked up as if I had not a care and shook hands all around as Semeon introduced me to the officers.

"R.K. said you might be able to help me find a witness named 'Rollo Treadwell.' She lives in Okarito village on the island of Tol."

"Tol," sniffed one police officer. "Nothing but trouble there."

"Just rascals and hooligans," grumbled the other officer.

Semeon was more helpful. "Rollo Treadwell?' That doesn't sound Chuukese."

"Jingle Treadwell works at the Micronesian National Bank," the first police officer volunteered. "He went to high school with my youngest brother. This Rollo might be the mother."

"Jingle doesn't work at the bank any more," I said. "He might have left Weno."

"Jingle might have grown up on Tol. But I think he was born in another place."

"Do you know the village called 'Okarito?'" I said.

"I know that place," Semeon spoke up. "When I was on Chuuk public safety, I investigated a clan fight near it. It's on Faichuuk, away on the sunset side of Tol."

"How long would it take to get there?"

"By late afternoon, if we are lucky," Semeon frowned. "High tide is in the afternoon today. That would make the trip faster. But we have to leave soon to make it today. Do you want to radio ahead and tell the village we are coming?"

"No. I don't want to spook the witness," I said. What I meant was I didn't want a radio report to be broadcast saying I was in Chuuk.

"We would have to come back at night," said Semeon. "You know that no American is permitted to stay overnight on that island. Not even a priest."

The police officers and Semeon began an earnest discussion on what was needed for a trip to Tol.

As if on cue, R.K. Asher stepped from the courthouse to tell us that his trial had been continued. R.K. readily assigned the office investigator to help me, and I promised to have Semeon back at his desk by noon the next day, although I couldn't promise that he would be awake. Semeon said one of his cousins had a boat to rent, very cheap, but that we would have to pay upfront. I handed Semeon two twenties – the profits of my sale of turkey tails – for rent, gasoline, and motor oil, sighing at the continuous exodus from my wallet. We agreed to meet at Weno Municipal dock in an hour. R.K. did his part by driving me over to the Chuuk Trading Company – known as the "counterfeiter's clearinghouse" for the vast number of knock-off brand names on the shelves – to buy supplies for the trip.

The Trading Company is right across the main road from the municipal dock, which has its own nickname – "Madison Square Garden" – a full fight card every Payday Friday night. Semeon and his boatman, Innocente, a burly guy shaped like a bowling ball with legs, who had a broken nose and a shy smile, were right on time, waiting in a twenty-foot plywood boat, by looks both homemade and prone to capsize. I handed over the supplies I'd bought for the trip, three bags full. One bag had sea biscuits and drinking water; the second, three cellophane-wrapped take out lunches, consisting of fried reef fish of some unknown genus and species, a scoop of boiled rice, a hunk of purple swamp taro, and a hard-boiled egg. I would be well on the way to "Regina v. Dudley & Stephens" before I touched any of that, but Semeon and Innocente might appreciate a meal. In the third bag I had gifts for the village chief: several cans of Great Wall corned beef, soy sauce, sugar, instant coffee ("Nescafay" brand, made in China), plus some hooks and fishing line, and two pairs of *zoris* big enough to use as oars.

I had my doubts as Innocente fiddled a few minutes with the starter cord to restart the outboard engine. Eventually, he pulled up the choke and gave the cord a few more rips to get it going. We motored swiftly away from a Weno Harbor crowded with Chinese fishing boats all riding high with empty holds, idled by light catches. Weno Harbor twenty years ago was said by Al Frost to resemble a scene from a Michener novel – net fishermen stalked reef fish, Outer Islands traditional sailing canoes came in for plug tobacco and spam at the Chuuk Trading Company. It now looks more like a miniature scale Hong Kong. The net fisherman stopped fishing when cholera began to appear inside the lagoon. Outer Islanders now sail a hundred miles further to Yap for cigarettes instead of to closer Chuuk. Chinese long liners hung with tattered laundry are now berthed haphazardly forming a floating labyrinth. Onboard, fishermen in dirty clothes stared vacantly from the sterns; one hawked up spittle the size and consistency of an under-fried egg as we passed. The clack of mah jong tiles came from several boats. Some of the long liners listed like drunken sailors, and every boat it seemed pissed a steady stream of bilge water, engine oil, and fish guts. On one vessel – from which Innocente steered us well wide – an unhappy sailor with dysentery hung his bare ass from the stern, dripping his own bilge into the lagoon.

Once we were clear of the long liners, Innocente accelerated into the open water of the lagoon, west toward Udot, with Tol beyond that. I was glad to be in the company of two big guys. Semeon has often said that he owes me, no matter how much I tell him he doesn't, that anyone with common sense could have handled the matter. Back in my public defender days, I'd represented Semeon's cousin, Master Simon, on an ADW charge, assault with a deadly weapon. Master had supposedly waved a handgun in a village argument. But Master wasn't charged with possession of a handgun, illegal throughout Micronesia, because what he brandished was a bottle of aftershave shaped like a handgun, something Master had picked up on Guam at his job cleaning out rental cars returned to the airport. Judge Baxendale dismissed the felony charge when I pointed out the facts.

I was glad to have Semeon and Innocente onboard for more than payback. Faichuuk in general and Tol in particular are not renown for friendly relations with Americans. Not to say that they are friendly to anyone else. The entire region once tried to secede from Chuuk State, angry that the lion's share of U.S. treaty funds were spent on Weno. A Faichuuk senator – subject of the treasury-draining funeral – actually got chummy with Communist China before independence. The Peace Corps, which annually placed 300 volunteers in Chuuk in the '60's, had by three decades later pulled out of the western side of Chuuk Lagoon entirely. Tol, fittingly, is the only place in the eastern Caroline Islands where the poison tree grows, the viscous, insoluble sap of which can raise blisters just by brushing by it.

I had never been to Faichuuk. Al Frost, my late law partner, had. As chief public defender, Al had represented one of four teenagers accused of murdering another boy from a nearby village who had trespassed on their land, likely looking for love in all the wrong places. It was, according to Al, a harrowing homicide. The perpetrators had surrounded the interloper, prodding him with the butt ends of their machetes, then the pointy ends, before taking their whacks at him, one at a time. The defense investigation was a fiasco. The two villages were then, and perhaps still are, at war, and no one dared guide Al into the no man's land between. All four boys were convicted of murder, and if they remain alive today, they may possibly be the senior citizens of the Chuuk State jail.

Innocente said it would take at least three hours to reach Tol, plus maybe an hour more to get to the village. It would take much longer to return in the dark. Innocente said we would have to cruise slowly. His homemade boat is not wired; he has no running lights. I was looking at another sleepless night, and I already felt exhausted. I was tired of sitting in direct sunlight without a hint of shade, tired still from my late arrival on Saturday night, tired of running through a list of questions for which I had very few answers. As the outboard engine droned and the low voices of Innocente and Semeon slipped infrequently into conversation, I curled up on a bench as best I could, threw an elbow over my eyes, and tried to sleep.

Instead of sleeping, though, I ended up running through a list of suspects for the murder of Jangle Elwell of whom I could safely cross off only me, myself, and Utticus Ulysses. I didn't do it, and I knew

Utticus didn't bump off Jangle, not for cold-cocking him. Utticus is like one of those Plains Indians who esteem the coup, that it's a greater honor to simply touch one's enemy than to slay him.

At the top of my list of the motivated was Coleman, although I couldn't picture the judge as able to whack a pesky housefly, much less a street smart local half his age and twice as shifty. Valentin Onan ran a close second, especially because he was at the bar at Daosokele when Coleman made me an offer he thought I couldn't refuse. But where would Valentin or Coleman get a gun, much less two different guns? Not from the evidence room. There hadn't been a firearms case in years. More importantly, both the judge and the Justice Ombudsman had too much at risk to their own standing to get caught up in something as sordid as murder.

For the rest of my list, I had to *cherchez la femme.* The mere thought of my secretary as a murder suspect left an empty spot in the pit of my gut. Even though her family nickname is "Typhoon," and Jangle had done plenty to rile her, I knew deep down that Jasmina had not pulled the trigger or triggers.

Innocente's boat, despite appearances, rode well, and the trip was fairly smooth, although the boat bounced in a few spots where deep ocean rollers came in through the passes. Although I felt open and exposed beneath the great extent of tropical sky, I closed my eyes again, and slept. When I awoke, the boat had slowed and the sun was halfway to the horizon. We were west of Udot, behind which Weno had disappeared. Tol's mountain, gray-green in the morning light from across the lagoon, was now jungle green and monstrously large up close.

A channel appeared in the guise of randomly placed bamboo stakes. The stakes led into a mangrove swamp, the tangled roots of which narrowed the channel, while the intertwined branches inexorably closed off the sky. Semeon, seeing I was awake, explained that Innocente's course was for a canal between two parts of Tol; dug at gunpoint by locals and POWs during World War II, as the Japanese Imperial Navy hid smaller ships and submarines from marauding American warplanes. Toward the center of the island, the canal was dug straight from stone, twelve feet up from the high tide line. A village footbridge spans the canal at the crest, on which a lone man stared at us. He had facial tattoos, something out of fashion for five decades, and one cheek was swollen by a large quid of betel nut. Between the tattoos, the cheek full of spittle, and a sullen stare, the man looked like a rabid raccoon, and I flinched as we passed.

Once through the canal, Innocente opened the throttle in the protected waters between the two westward reaching arms of Tol. Okarito village is at the western end of the southern arm, where the mountain slopes down to what appeared an idyllic spot at sunset. Innocente guided the boat at last toward a seawall made of hunks of coral stone from which a sandy beach, fairly narrow at high tide, sloped swiftly into deeper water. Flipped keelside up on the grass above the beach were a few inshore canoes, and a couple of plywood motorboats, much like Innocente's, were anchored in shallow water. Okarito has no village dock or pier. Innocente stopped the engine well short of the sand to glide in close before tossing an anchor aft. Semeon took the bowline ashore and tied off to a rusting metal pole jammed into the seawall.

Okarito village spreads haphazardly along the beach and seawall. At the center of the village is a small church with a smaller steeple. Next to the church, hanging between two posts, is a large, rusting compressed air tank. A couple of cinder block buildings stand nearby, the blocks stained with mildew, perhaps a school or a municipal office. Most houses are built of plywood with corrugated steel roofs; others look wholly traditional, with thatched walls and roof. In the old days, young men gone courting would slide their wooden "love sticks," each one carved with the owner's unique design, through the thatch to alert young women inside of their presence. The young lady would pull on the stick to say, "come on in," or push it away to rebuff the advance.

A group of schoolchildren gathered at the seawall to watch, a few boys smiling and posing, the girls with expressions alternately curious or alarmed, but most simply standing still with arms folded. An older boy strode away from the group to the church and with a length of mahogany, struck the compressed air tank, a makeshift, church bell.

A handful of older men and a group of women of varying ages joined the children at the seawall. Semeon spoke to them from the beach in Chuukese. I understood nothing between "*Ran anim,*" and "Rollo Treadwell." But then the white-haired man at the center of the group waved us ashore with a gesture that looked as if he were brushing away a mosquito. I rolled up my trousers, tossed my zoris ashore, and followed Semeon into the surf, my toes scrunching in the coarse sand. Innocente, who said he would stay with the boat, handed Semeon the bag with the chief's goodies.

"You give these to the chief." Semeon's eyes darted about the village as if he expected an ambush. "I will translate."

I nodded as we scrambled up the seawall. I know the routine with chiefs, but I was glad more than ever to have Semeon running interference. The white-haired chief was dressed in western garb, as were all but the youngest children, though everyone's clothes were tattered and worn through. For a moment, I wished I'd brought some decent tee shirts to give away as well.

"Thank you, Chief," I began as Semeon translated. "You don't know me, but I am an American lawyer working on Pohnpei. I do not want to stay here overnight. I just want to talk with someone who I was told lives in this village. Her name is 'Rollo Treadwell.' I also brought these small gifts for you."

The chief peered into and pawed about the plastic bag, then looked up and said, "No ice cream?"

The adults laughed, and that seemed to break the spell of silence that held the village children. Several laughed and screamed and then the whole group wheeled away like a flock of seagulls toward the school; all save the bell ringer, who waited with his arms folded as before.

"I speak a little broken English," said the chief. "You can land now, but you cannot stay the night. You won't find who you came for. That woman lived at the other side of the village, in the blue house. This boy will show you the way. Next time you come from Weno on the same day, bring some ice cream for all these children. Many of them do not know what ice cream tastes like."

The Okarito bell ringer led us away from the village center; past homes that seemed to gain in dilapidation the further we walked from the boat landing. Near the western end of the village, I spotted a plywood house painted blue, the yard bordered by a low stick fence. I nudged Semeon, who nodded, his eyes still searching the jungle farms behind the village. I saw nothing other than a row of banana trees, dead leaves and branches heaped about their roots, and an occasional scalloped-trunk papaya tree heavy with fruit high near the leaves.

Semeon, I'm sure, was looking past the farms to see if danger lurked behind the bananas.

Up close, the blue house looked fairly prosperous by local standards. Unlike other houses we passed, it sat on a cement pad, and the louvered glass windows were protected behind both rat and insect screens. The corrugated steel roof sloped into gutters made of white PVC pipe cut lengthwise. The gutters drained into a round cement cistern with a faucet to one side. The roof sagged a bit in the middle. Perhaps termites had started on the rafters.

Beyond the cistern was a traditional cookshed, open on three sides, with a thatched roof except for directly over the hearth, which was protected by a small piece of corrugated steel. A few coals smoked on the hearth, and a half cord of rust red mangrove wood stood to one side. The yard in front of the house was swept clean of leaves and twigs. An overturned canoe, also painted blue, sat beneath one overhanging eave of the cookshed, and fresh green palm fronds formed a proscenium arch over the keel.

Beyond the cookshed was an unmarked concrete grave, the stone a cement cross on which was draped a *mwarmwar* of fresh plumeria blossoms. No jungle creepers or plants had yet secured a hold on the gravestone, showing that it was a relatively recent addition to the village, and that someone was taking particularly good care of it. The bell ringer proved that he did have the power of speech, and told Semeon in Chuukese that we had reached a dead end.

"Drake," said Semeon. "This boy says this is the grave of Rollo Treadwell. She died last month."

Jangle hadn't lied when he said he had come to Chuuk for a funeral; it was his mother's.

A ball of ice formed in my stomach, unmelted by the heat of a tropic afternoon. All my actions of the past few days – stowing away on Air Mike, keeping a low profile in Chuuk, abandoning all efforts to clear my name save this one – had come up short. I may as well have surrendered on Pohnpei. I could have stayed stowed away all the way to Guam. I may as well have radioed ahead to learn of the death of Rollo Treadwell.

I could think of nothing to do or say other than to make Father Benoit proud. I made a sign of the cross and said a prayer for the soul of Rollo Treadwell.

"I am really sorry, Drake," said Semeon. "If you want, stay here. It's safe at this place. I'll go tell Innocente to bring the boat over so we can go back."

I watched Semeon and the bell ringer walk back to the village. Then I half-sat, half-collapsed onto a bamboo bench under the eaves of the cookshed and watched the sun inch lower, setting the lagoon waves asparkle. Off in the distance, miles away, I could see the thin white line where breakers curl relentlessly onto the outer reef. I scanned the horizon for the fisherman's telltale signs of terns and gulls diving into frothy seas. But I saw none. Maybe those longliners had emptied the ocean. Maybe Coleman was right, and my hole was fished out.

Because he came directly from the sun, I couldn't make out the approaching figure until he was only a few yards away. I could tell he was local, a tall young man, dressed in dripping trousers that frayed to a stop at mid-calf and a soaking wet tee shirt. In one hand he had a fishing chain on which he'd strung a dozen reef fish. His snorkel and mask hung from a fishing spear propped on the opposite shoulder. Feeling as if I had trespassed, I suddenly wished that Semeon had stayed. As the young man came out of the sun and I could finally see his face, the ice ball in my stomach exploded into a hundred jagged icicles, plunging into all of my joints. I stumbled to my feet and stared for coming at me, out of the sun, his fishing spear now raised, was Jangle Elwell.

CHAPTER SEVENTEEN

As the figure approached, I could do nothing but stare, wondering what potent Chuukese magic had conjured up my worst client, here and now, living and breathing, the body I had seen laid on a slab in the Pohnpei morgue and on a bier on Kosrae. The figure continued directly toward me, with fishing spears now raised.

"You are trespassing." The figure strode by me and slipped the fishing spears into place in the rafters of the cookshed. "The fence marks my family's land. You are inside the fence and you are not invited."

From the rafters, the figure grabbed a machete – the blade shiny with whetstone marks – and pointed it at me. As visions of Al Frost's failed Faichuuk murder investigation danced in my head, I couldn't help but stare at him. He brushed by me to a banana tree at forest's edge and lopped off a large leaf by letting the blade fall of its own weight against the stalk. He placed his string of fish on the banana leaf near the catchment.

"Besides, it's illegal for an American to stay the night on this island, and the sun is now setting." He pointed west to the sun with the machete before putting it back in the rafters. I said nothing, still trying to sort out what he said and what all this meant.

The figure placed a plastic pail beneath a faucet on one side of the catchment. Back in the cookshed, he grabbed a knife and cradled it easily in his right hand before gesturing again at me. I thought about my case of the knife fight at the barbecue pit, and wondered if the figure wanted to play mumbly-peg on my face.

"If you want to buy some love potions, that woman is now gone. You'll have to go somewhere else."

I continued to stare as he began to clean his catch, dropping cleaned fish into the bucket and fish guts onto the banana leaf.

"Well?"

Second by second, I saw just how this one differed from Jangle. The differences were subtle, hard to discern without staring directly at him, which is precisely what I was doing. I saw that his arms and shoulders were more heavily muscled than Jangle's. When he stepped into the sun, his eyes had none of the predatory gleam. This was not Jangle Elwell, unless he had undergone something that had softened his eyes and hardened his body.

"You're not Jangle Elwell."

"No. I am Jingle Treadwell."

"Jingle?"

"My brother and I were born on Christmas Day."

"Your brother and you?"

"Have you never seen twins before? Maybe you should go to Kosrae. They have plenty twins there."

"My God. Jangle Elwell had a twin brother. Would you stand still for a second so I can see you better?"

Jingle cleaned another fish first and plopped the entrails onto the banana leaf before standing and turning to the sun. He was a hair shorter than his twin, and he held the knife in his right hand. I knew that Jangle was a southpaw. Jingle plainly worked outside more than his brother. His skin was darker, and his shoulders were developed, probably from swimming, paddling that canoe, maybe climbing coconut palm trees when he was a boy. In comparison, Jangle had looked soft; probably by letting others do the work for him. Were this "Tom Sawyer," Jingle would be whitewashing the fence, while Jangle would shake down neighborhood boys for their lunch money.

Both were handsome devils, no question. Jingle's still wet hair was thick and glossy as his brother's. The shape of the face was similar, too. But the eyes were different. Jingle avoided my gaze, where Jangle would have stared right back.

"Jangle and Jingle, born on Christmas Day."

"Jingle and Jangle. I was born first." Jingle returned to his task, squatting next to the catchment to slice out the viscera of his catch in three swift slices, then rinsing off the cleaned fish in the pail.

"You know that your brother is dead."

Jingle placed his hand against the catchment and shut his eyes.

"Do you know how he died?" I asked.

Jingle turned and opened dry eyes to stare at me. "My brother was murdered."

I suddenly wished that Semeon and Innocente were with me, instead of dealing with Innocente's balking outboard motor, or flirting with village hausfraus, or whatever the heck they were doing. Jingle's eyes turned hard, as if he, like everyone else, suspected that I was the one who had killed Jangle.

I spoke quietly. "I'm Drake Burnham. I'm investigating your brother's murder."

"What are you? Police?" Jingle picked up another fish to clean.

"Worse. I'm a lawyer."

227

"Jangle told me lawyers would come if he died. So Mr. Lawyer, do you represent the people who killed my brother, or the government that tried to put him in jail?" Jingle hacked at the guts of a red snapper.

"Neither."

"Well then, Mr. Lawyer, why do you come around here – a place forbidden to you – to ask about my dead brother?" He dropped another cleaned fish into the bucket.

"Moses Elwell, Jangle's adopted father, your uncle, asked me."

"That's no reason to me." Jingle kept his eyes on his fish.

"Then because Jangle is my client."

"He was your client, but now my brother is dead."

"Yes. Jangle is dead, and maybe you can tell me how it happened. I'm down to my last straws, and I don't know where else to go."

"Why should I tell you anything?"

"Because I am accused of murdering your brother."

Jingle turned to size me up. "You didn't kill Jangle. But why should I help?"

I know what Steve McGarrett would do in a spot like this. He'd say, "Book him, Dan-O." And if Jingle protested, he'd throw down a slew of charges against him. But I don't have a badge or a lieutenant handy, or that big black Mercury to speed away from the scene.

And I know what Al Frost would do in a spot like this. So I bluffed. "Then tell me because I'm asking, and I'm asking politely. But if you don't tell me, I'll go back to Weno and ask Judge Baxendale for a subpoena to order you to talk, and I'll come back with a posse of police officers to make sure you do. You don't want me to. I don't want to either, but I can. I can get an order directing you to tell everyone. On the other hand, if you tell me what you know, here and now, in confidence, then I cannot tell anyone what you tell me, unless you say I can tell someone else. So Jingle Treadwell, it's up to you."

A minute passed. A lizard rustled through the thatch over my head, and the sun crept another inch lower. Jingle grabbed the machete, walked to a young palm, and sliced off a green frond. Back in the cookshed he began to restring his catch onto the frond, which he then hung in the thin smoke above the wood fire. He returned to the catchment, rinsed his hands and smoothed back his still damp hair. He glanced at me for a moment, then turned and gazed at the water.

"I wasn't sure I had a father when I was a boy, but I knew I had a brother. A small place like Okarito, this village, has plenty of boys, but not too many men. I like this place. It's quiet. Everyone knows me. I can grow what I need to eat and fish for the rest. I know a secret fishing spot I can only reach at high tide."

"You went there today?"

"Yes. Okarito is a hard place to earn any money, but you don't need money here, not like Weno or Pohnpei. When I was a little boy, most of the men, guys who are the age I am now, they went to Weno to work for the Navy or the Trust Territory. Now most men my age go to Guam or Saipan, any place where they can work for money. So you see, it's not unusual for a boy growing up in Okarito to have no father around. Mother used to say a man needs two feet to survive. Put one foot on an island with jobs, like Weno or Pohnpei or Guam. But keep your other foot on your home island.

"Although this is a small place, there are always plenty of children. When I was a boy, there was always someone around, friends, boys my age, to play with or share chores, go fish, go swim, climb trees. I knew that I had a brother somewhere, a brother who I could tell where was the best spot to fish, and where does the cold spring come out of the mountain. I knew I had a brother, but not where he was. Mother said I had a brother who lived on Kosrae, who was adopted by a rich family there. But I didn't know where Kosrae was. It might have been on the other side of the world."

"Have you ever been to Kosrae?"

"I was born on Kosrae, but I don't remember my time there. Mother used to talk about Kosrae. She said there was plenty of food and not too many people. I thought how lucky my brother was to live on such an island, especially when I was hungry and tired of eating just fish and coconut and breadfruit here on Tol. When I went to the College of Micronesia on Pohnpei, I finally met some Kosraen students. They were kind to me."

Jingle picked up the banana leaf and walked toward the beach. I followed, wanting him to continue talking, but not wanting to prompt him too much. In the shallows, we both watched a small stingray, no bigger than a dinner plate, being hectored toward the beach by a pair of juvenile sharks. Jingle tossed the banana leaf and fish guts into the shallows and squatted to rinse his hands. The sharks abandoned the ray and zipped to feed on what Jingle had discarded.

"Mother told me plenty about Kosrae," Jingle said as we returned to the cookshed. "Her father, my grandfather, was sent to Kosrae by the Japanese during World War II, to help build an airstrip. After the War, the Americans sent Grandfather back here to Chuuk. But Grandfather always liked Kosrae. Mother told me her father said Kosrae was rich like a high island, friendly like an outer island. He thought the missionary teachers on Kosrae, the ones who came from

Boston, were very good. He still liked everything American, even after they sent him back to Chuuk."

Jingle unhooked a soot-blackened kettle from the rafters of the cookshed, filled it at the catchment and placed it on the single-burner kerosene stove. "Do you want some coffee? I always like to drink something hot after spearfishing."

I nodded, and Jingle rummaged about a shelf to find a jar of instant coffee crystals and a Mason jar half-filled with sugar and crawling with ants. He then went to a corner where a bunch of bananas hung. He pulled off a half-dozen thumb-sized fruit and set them on a plate.

"When Mother was old enough for school, Grandfather sent her to board at the Mission School on Kosrae. She said the school was in a village very much like this, where she could sit to watch the sun set in the ocean. Mother learned her English at the Mission School, and she taught me. Mother stayed on Kosrae even after the Mission School closed. She went to the high school on Kosrae, another boarding school. And Kosrae is where my brother and I were born. We were born on Kosrae, but I do not remember that island. Mother brought me back here to Chuuk when I was very young."

"But she brought only you, and not Jangle. You said your brother was adopted. Did your mother ever tell you why?"

"Yes. You might not be able to tell it from my skin, but our father, the father to me and Jangle, wasn't a local. Mother said she met a handsome American, a Navy sailor who played a guitar and who liked to listen to jazz music. He especially liked music by Django Reinhardt. Maybe that's where my brother's name came from. You know about his left hand? Birth defect. My father told Mother he would come back for her, and that he would take us all to live in the States. But he never came back. The Navy told her that he was killed in an accident, and that was before Jangle and I were even born.

"Mother said giving Jangle for adoption was the hardest thing she ever did. Almost all her life she was living at different schools, first at the Mission School, then at the high school. She was lucky if she could come back to Chuuk to visit her mother and father once a year, some years not at all. When Mother graduated she had no place to stay on Kosrae, no money to return to Chuuk. She had two babies. So she gave up one of her babies to a couple on Kosrae who could have no children of their own."

"Moses Elwell."

"Yes. Mother said Nina Elwell told her she was doubly blessed to have two children, and some women could have no children at all. Mother wanted to help because they wanted to have children and couldn't. They said they would buy her tickets to return to Chuuk. Moses said a light-skinned baby, the child of an American, would be accepted on Kosrae better than he would on Chuuk, where he might get beat up. Mother believed Moses because she thought what he said was true, and because she was young and thought she could have more babies.

"Grandfather wanted Mother to be strong, stronger than steel, but he didn't know how strong she had to be. Mother said that when she let Jangle be adopted that God played a trick on her. By giving up one of her babies, she lost the chance to ever have any more babies. When Mother came back to Chuuk, she had no more children. And so she learned from an old woman here on Tol – a widow who lived alone apart from the village – how to make love potions. That's why I asked you if you want to buy a love potion when I first saw you here. Mother sold love potions to people, some locals, some Americans, people who were sick with love for someone they could not have. I think she did that because what happened to her and the handsome American, my father."

"You grew up here, with your mother, while your twin brother lived on Kosrae?"

"Yes. I stayed here in Okarito until I was ready for high school. Then I went and boarded at Xavier High School, on Weno. I used my grandfather's name, not Mother's so other students wouldn't tease me. No one else from my village went to Xavier, just me. I was frightened at first, but Mother told me about how my brother was alone, too, and that he was much further away from his home. She meant Jangle was on Kosrae, but she didn't know how right she was. When I went alone to attend high school on Weno, twenty miles across Chuuk Lagoon, my brother was thousands of miles away going to school in America. When I thought about my brother alone without his first family, or his second family, I wasn't so scared for myself."

"Did you have a class with Father Benoit?"

"Yes. But I don't know if he will remember me. He is a very smart man, and I was a very quiet student. Everyone knows about Father Benoit, and the other priests in black. Xavier High School is a very good school, very difficult, but much better for learning than Chuuk High School. One boy from Tol my age was killed at Chuuk High School in a clan fight. I was a good student. Not the best. My best marks were in English, thanks to Mother's teaching. When I graduated from Xavier I went to the College of Micronesia on Pohnpei. Some of the other students at Xavier went to University of Hawaii or University of Guam, but I thought I should stay in Micronesia."

The kettle atop the kerosene stove began to whistle, and Jingle turned off the burner. He scooped instant coffee and sugar into two mugs and poured steaming water into both. He handed me a mug that read "Stolen from ABC Store, Honolulu, Hawaii," then put out the plate of bananas. Jingle peeled a banana the size of a butcher's thumb and finished it in two bites.

"Jangle gave me that cup. I never went to Hawaii. Someday, maybe." Jingle stirred his coffee and passed me the spoon. "Don't worry about our water here. It's all rainwater, not from the stream."

"I saw your catchment and gutters when I came. It looks very clean." I took a small sip of coffee, trying not to burn my tongue. "Did you meet your brother when you were at College of Micronesia?"

"Yes. I had already finished my first year at COM. Jangle came to Pohnpei when I was in my second year. I was so surprised when I met him that I couldn't speak. I was in shock. And then when I did speak, it was in Chuukese, and Jangle could not understand me. So we, my twin and I, always spoke English, our second language.

"Mother used to say when Jangle and I were babies we wanted to stay together, it was very hard to pull us apart. When I met Jangle, I knew why. Jangle looks like me, he sounds like me, he walks like me. We could wear the same clothes. Our names are close, Jingle and Jangle. Not everything was the same. Jangle was taller, by just a little, but I am older and stronger. Plus, his clothes were new, and I was still wearing some old stuff, all I could afford on Chuuk. And you know, his hand was different. He used his left hand and I use my right."

"You look almost exactly like Jangle. You could fool most people, especially at a big school like College of Micronesia."

"We did that. It started with girls. I was shy and very quiet around girls. Jangle was always better at meeting them. I think he wasn't shy because he went to the States and knew how to meet people. At college, Jangle would talk to the girls and friends to set up meetings. Then I would go meet the girls, usually at night. I dressed in Jangle's clothes and wore his aftershave. Most of them did not tell the difference."

"I'm not surprised. You strike me as the love-stick-through-the-thatch type, but not Jangle."

"Later, we tried switching places during the day, and that worked, too. No one could tell the difference between us. It felt like we were drunk with being able to do it, to fool people into believing that I was Jangle. Jangle asked me to do other things for him, too. I'm a better student, and since I was a year ahead of Jangle, I already took most of the courses. I wrote some papers for him. That's how I pay him back for helping me meet girls. I even went to some classes for Jangle so the instructor would think I was him. I don't think we could have done that at Xavier. The Jesuit priests are too smart. But at COM, there are many students, and the instructors, especially the Americans, don't look too closely at the students, at least not the boys."

"Did Jangle ever take your place?"

Jingle was quiet for a moment, then said, "Only once. And that was after."

"What about Jangle's friends? Did you meet them at College of Micronesia?"

"The Taro Patch Kids? I knew them, but I didn't like them. I think they're a bunch of crooks. They remind me of a bad clan here on Tol, always fighting, always making trouble. When I met Jangle, the

Taro Patch Kids said they wanted me to run with them. Small stuff at first, driving overspeed, stoning *menwhi* houses, stealing small things from stores. But I said no, I would not do that. When they started to bother me, Jangle told them to leave me alone."

"Did you finish school?"

"Yes. I graduated after three years at College of Micronesia with an Associate Degree in Business Accounting. Mother was very proud. She wanted to come from Chuuk for graduation but she couldn't afford to fly. I told her she should take the ship, but she said no, that it would remind her of leaving Kosrae. I think it was an excuse. I think Mother was afraid to come to Pohnpei to meet Jangle. I told her I met Jangle. But she didn't tell anyone else about her other son."

"What about Jangle? Did he graduate?"

"He did not. I told Jangle I will help him study, help him with his papers. But Jangle wasn't interested in school. Even before I graduated, Jangle stopped attending his classes. He left the Kosraen family he was supposed to stay with on Pohnpei and started to live at La Brea, the Taro Patch, where the troublemakers stay. When I asked him why he was leaving school, Jangle said that he needed to make a lot of money and be rich like the Americans. He said he had a program on how he could do it.

"I never saw Jangle smoking marijuana, but I know many of his friends did. I think that's where he got the idea. Some students from the Marshall Islands were smoking marijuana all the time. You know them. They said it was very hard to grow *maru* on their home islands, but there's plenty on Pohnpei. Jangle wanted to sell Pohnpei marijuana in the Marshalls. That part was easy, because he just sent some on a ship to Ebeye and Majuro. But he thought he could make more money by

236

selling Pohnpei marijuana on Guam and Saipan. Jangle told me once he met a fishing boat captain who would take some to Saipan, but he needed some money first before he would do anything. Jangle had the money. After that, Jangle learned about *shabu* and he wanted to sell it, too."

"Did you say anything to Jangle about his program?"

"I told him he will be thrown in jail for it. He said he sold in the States and he never got caught even though the police there are much better than in Micronesia. I told him everything in his program was illegal. Jangle told me to mind my own business, and then I was a Chuukese baby and that I should go back to my village. I told Jangle Mother wanted to see him. Jangle then said he had something to say to Mother, but that she would not like it, and neither would I. We argued about that and then we fought. After, I left him and left Pohnpei. I left my brother who I did not see for all my life except for two years, because he insulted our mother."

"Did you see Jangle after you left Pohnpei?"

"Yes. Jangle came here, to Chuuk. I sent him a letter telling him that Mother had died, and he came. I was surprised to see him, but he said he wanted to see where his mother was buried. So he came to Chuuk, and came out here to Okarito. We went back to Weno together after he visited Mother's grave. And when he left Chuuk, Jangle took my cooler. He really liked my cooler."

"Before he was killed, Jangle told me the cooler wasn't his. So it was yours," I said. "But back up a little, back to Pohnpei. After you graduated from COM, you came back to Chuuk?"

"Yes. I got a job at the Micronesian National Bank, here in Chuuk, assistant manager. Our first manager, Mr. Royston, was good.

237

He wanted to hire locals to handle most of the jobs at the bank, not just tellers and clerks, but managers, too. He wasn't a bank employee. He was in the Peace Corps, a small business adviser, so he was independent. The bank president and board on Pohnpei, though, they wanted someone who they could tell what to do. Mr. Royston was very honest, and he told the bank president that they could not continue to make bad loans and they should make out only secured loans. But the bank president wouldn't listen to him. When Mr. Royston left, the board passed a resolution saying no more Peace Corps, and for the Chuuk branch, they hired Mr. Throckmorton."

"I've met him."

"I trusted Mr. Throckmorton at first because he is friendly and he came from Boston like my father. But Mr. Throckmorton is not a good man, not like Mr. Royston."

"I'd be surprised if any board would put Throckmorton in charge of the corner bar, much less a bank."

"I'm sad to say this because at one time I thought Mr. Throckmorton was my friend. But I learned he wasn't good. First, he hid away all the books in his office so that no one could see them. He spent weeks inside his office, alone, copying down what was in the books, or so he said. As part of my job, I had to see the books to make the new entries. When I asked Mr. Throckmorton to show me the books, he brought out copies that he wrote out. I said keeping double books is not done to generally accepted accounting principles. But that was the way he learned. He said the books balanced."

"So you thought he was cooking the books?"

"But I had no proof. No one copied the entries before, and no one could tell if anything was different. Mr. Throckmorton said don't worry, a failsafe was in place."

"I think Throckmorton has a few other problems as well."

"He drinks too much."

"And there's all the time that he spends in the backroom at You-Me's."

Jingle paused for a moment. "Mr. Burnham, before I say anything else, let me ask you one question again. If I say something to you that is confidential, then it is true that no one can force you to tell them what I told you?"

"Yes. It's called the attorney-client privilege. But there's more to it. Not only can no one force me to say what you told me in confidence, I cannot voluntarily tell anyone what you told me. It's only when you authorize me to say something that is confidential that I can do so."

"Do you have a paper that says what you say you are, an attorney?"

I had not been carded since the day I left Kosrae, and that was for my drinking permit. I pulled out my wallet and handed Jingle my dog-eared Pohnpei bar card.

"Is this like what the priests at Xavier said about confession? That they cannot tell anyone what they heard?"

"It's similar, but then I have no power to absolve you of anything, though you might be able to help me out of a jam."

"Then what I am saying is confidential." Jingle put his hands up to the rafters of the cookshed. The sun had just set and the clouds in the western sky were slowly draining their purples and reds. Behind us, in

239

the jungle, I heard the call of a wild bird that sounded vaguely like a dove.

"I learned I have one bad habit, maybe the worst thing there is about me. It is worse than not being married, and living alone, with no Mother left to care for, and no brother left to pray for. I learned I like to gamble. I might even be addicted to it. Mr. Throckmorton showed me how. We started playing on those machines at You-Me's, and I even won some money at first. It wasn't very much, just enough to buy Mother a new kerosene stove, this one, and some new clothes. But I didn't have to work for that money. I just risked a little bit and got paid a lot. I like the way gambling makes me feel, both excited and calm at the same time. Do you understand that?"

"I've heard people talk about gambling the way you do. I think maybe your brother liked to gamble, too. Not with machines or at a casino, but the way he tried to turn a little bit of money into a lot."

"You may be right. But my feeling goes deeper. I said I felt like I might be addicted to gambling. You know, I tried things at Xavier and College of Micronesia. I know that I don't like the way *maru* makes me feel confused, or the way that too much beer or hot stuff makes me feel angry. *Sakau* is okay, and betel nut, too. But nothing I took ever made me feel the way I did when I was gambling. The feeling I got playing the machines was just the start. I liked it even more when I was playing with people. Mr. Throckmorton used to talk with me about it, like the way you feel you can almost tell what someone is thinking. I found out I like gambling a lot."

"But you lost money, too. You had to. Nobody wins every time."

"I started losing quickly. It began at You-Me's, of course. I lost a thousand dollars in one night. I didn't have a thousand dollars and I did not know what to do. Mr. Throckmorton told me not to worry about it, that he would take care of it. And he did. After that, I tried to stay away from You-Me's. But Mr. Throckmorton said I owed him for his getting me out of trouble at You-Me's. He also said he liked me, and I began to worry. But he just wanted me to go with him to what he called 'bank conferences,' where we met the big shots, even the guy from California who was so rich that he bought his own bank on Saipan. I thought Jangle will like that, to own a bank instead of the bank owning you. After the conferences, Mr. Throckmorton took me to the gambling boats on Guam and we went to the casinos on Tinian. I gave in to the temptation. I gambled, won some, lost some more.

"One time, Mr. Throckmorton took me to a private game on Guam. I think he brought me to be, how do you call it, a small bird for the others. I lost so much money, more than I could earn in a year. The others in the private game on Guam were some gangsters from Hong Kong. When I said I had no money to pay, they showed me a gun and said they would kill me if I didn't find a way to pay them back. Mr. Throckmorton came to my side and said to them that they would not kill me because then they would guarantee that they would not get their money at all. Then they said they would kill my family. They knew my name. They knew I live in Chuuk. I was afraid, afraid for Mother here on Tol, afraid for my brother on Pohnpei. Then they gave me some papers to sign, a promise to pay them back."

"When we left Guam, Mr. Throckmorton told me not to worry, that he knew how to pay back the gangsters. He told me later, when he was drunk, how he paid off the thousand dollars that I owed to You-

Me's, back when I first started gambling. He said the bank loaned You-Me's manager one thousand dollars to buy a small fishing boat with an outboard motor. That is what Mr. Throckmorton put on the books. I told him I didn't remember the loan, but he said 'Maybe not. But you signed the papers.' He showed me the papers and what looked like my signature. But there was no boat. There was no outboard motor. There was no person with the name he wrote in the books. It was all just a story to pay You-Me's the money I lost gambling."

"Wait a minute. Throckmorton forged your signature on a phony loan?"

"Yes. He did it to cover my debt."

"But you could have taken out a loan yourself to cover it, pay it back over time."

"But I didn't know what Mr. Throckmorton did until much later. I thought all he did was loan me the money himself. He comes from a rich family in Boston."

"I don't know why you're still calling him 'Mister.'"

"When I lost all that money in the private game on Guam, Mr. Throckmorton said he had a plan to pay off both our debts to the Hong Kong gangsters."

"Both your debts?"

"Yes. Mr. Throckmorton owed them money, too. Part of the way he paid the vig, you know, the interest on the debt, was to bring pigeons to gambling games. That's why he brought me to Guam. Not because he liked me, but so that he could keep paying the Hong Kong gangsters."

"What was his plan?"

"He called it the 'Dillinger Plan.' But I can't say any more right now. The sun has set, and you must leave Tol. Here come your friends to take you."

In the bad-timing department, Semeon and Innocente had arrived by boat. I could hear Semeon calling my name over the growl of the outboard engine as they approached, Semeon sounding as if he half-expected to find me bloodied and beaten in a banana grove, instead of talking, openly and calmly, with the only person I knew who could shed some light on the murder of Jangle Elwell.

"Jingle," I turned back to him. "I need you to come with us, back to Weno, maybe even to Pohnpei."

"What? Are you crazy?"

"I know we only just met, but you're the only one who can help me out."

"Who will take care of this house and the gravesite now that Mother is gone?"

"I can't answer that. But I think your chief is a good man, and nothing bad will happen to your place."

"My chief knows I owe people here some money. He won't let me go."

"But you must. If you don't come, I'll be in a lot of trouble."

"Why should I help you?"

"Because you couldn't help your brother. Because someone is accused of committing a crime that you know he did not commit. And that someone is me."

I heard the boat engine cough to a halt, and what must have been Semeon splashing into the water. "Drake? Mr. Burnham?"

"I'm here, in the cookshed. It's okay, Semeon."

Semeon huffed his way to the cookshed to stand in the door. "Drake?"

"Semeon, meet Jingle Treadwell, the son of the woman we came to see. He might be able to help, and I'm trying to convince him to come back with us to Weno."

Jingle looked up at Semeon, who met his gaze. They spoke briefly in Chuukese. Then Semeon turned back to me and said, "Jingle wants to know if there is someplace on Innocente's boat where we can put his fish. He thinks he can sell them on Weno."

The tide was out in the early evening and we had to wait until nearly midnight before leaving Okarito. Semeon admitted to nerves. We were in the village after dark without permission from the chief. Jingle told him not to worry, that the chief knew about the tides, and that we wouldn't be in trouble so long as I, the lone American, didn't spend the entire night. Innocente continued to fiddle with the outboard engine, with a flashlight after dark, but he eventually announced that he had resolved the problem, or so he thought.

Jingle had quieted once Semeon and Innocente appeared, but he played the good host, offering coffee and some smoked fish and rice. Jingle struck me as moody, and I wanted to keep him talking. So I asked him general questions, about how many banana trees he had, and whether he planted the plantain that makes you piss bright yellow. I asked him if he tapped *tuba*, but in a way that didn't sound like I wanted some local coconut brandy (even though I did). Jangle said he did tap *tuba*, but said he hadn't done so lately. I asked him about his papayas, and he replied with the pride of an Iowa farmboy asked about his blue

244

ribbon sweet corn. I even asked Jingle to show me around the house, and he guided me through the musty interior with a kerosene lantern.

At a quarter to twelve, Innocente judged the tide high enough to risk departure. Returning from Tol, at night, without running lights and with a balking engine, would take much longer than coming over in the day. Returning by the canal in the dark was out of the question. Jingle said the villages along the canal were the least friendly on unfriendly Tol, so Innocente took us instead well to the south. Weno's glow was visible until about two a.m., but then Public Works shut down the power, and the island on the horizon went dark in phases. We slowed prudently, on a moonless night in waters the boatman did not know well. Innocente spent the night at the tiller, the throttle turned low, while Semeon and Jingle took turns at the bow shining a dive flashlight forward and warning Innocente to turn one way or the other to avoid unexpected coral heads.

Dawn found us well south, heading in the direction of Fafan instead of Weno. Innocente corrected his course and sped up, joining the daily flotilla of commuter boats heading from other lagoon islands to Weno. We berthed at the municipal dock just after nine o'clock, and were at the public defender's office by ten.

I telephoned Air Mike first, and reserved two seats on the following night's flight to Pohnpei. I then called Roberta Ely.

"Drake! Everyone thinks you're hiding out in the jungle some place on Kosrae. The police found your suitcase at Shaw's house, when you were a no-show for your flight. Kazuo thought you'd skipped off to Hawaii. Spenser guessed France. I thought it was Canada, or some other country with no extradition treaty with Micronesia. By the way, where the heck are you?"

"Chuuk."

"Chuuk? How in God's name did you get there?"

"It's a long story, Roberta, and a longer explanation. I'll tell all some day, once everything calms down. But listen, I'm coming back to Pohnpei tomorrow night.

"You're going to fight it here?"

"*Mabuhay*, Ms. Ely."

"What's that supposed to mean?"

"It's a little something I picked up from Dr. Perez. It means 'to life,' and I'm not running from it. Can you do me a couple of favors? First, call Kazuo Olopai to tell him I called you but don't say from where. Let Kazuo know I'll surrender at Public Safety on Thursday."

"For your information, though, the arrest warrant is to charge you with murder, not hold you as a material witness. Somebody here mentioned that his sister was preparing an Information charging someone you know very well with murder. Somebody's sister also typed up an all points bulletin for nationwide distribution to be on the lookout for someone I happen to know."

"No need to be so indirect any more."

"Sorry. Force of habit."

"Can you also knock out some subpoenas for me? I'll fax you the list from here. The date doesn't matter, but I want to get the witnesses under order. Can you have Utticus serve them, as he would say, 'as soonest possible?'"

"No problem. We can always adjust the dates later. What else?"

"Ask Utticus to meet tomorrow's night flight from Chuuk. Tell him not to park, just to keep circling the parking lot until he sees me. I'd just as soon not spend a night in a jail cell, after spending last night in an open boat."

"I look forward to a complete explanation once you've been exonerated. Anything else?"

"Well, that depends. I'd prefer not to spend my one free phone call to ring up Jasmina and tell her to transfer sufficient funds to cover some rubbery checks. How's my credit rating at the Bank of Roberta and Spenser Ely?"

"Rated AAA. How much do you need?"

"Enough to cover a couple of nights at the Magellan here, and for a couple of tickets on Air Mike from Chuuk to Pohnpei."

"Two tickets? Why, Drake Burnham. You didn't go and elope. And after all the nice girls I've introduced you to. Who is she?"

"He's neither a she nor a bride-to-be. But that does raise my last favor. Can you put a witness on ice for a few days? He has to be kept out of the public eye, at least until we schedule a hearing on my case."

"We can put him up in the spare bedroom to start. Congress is between sessions, so Spenser can babysit him. It's no sweat, as long as you trust him."

"Roberta, you will sweat once you see him."

CHAPTER EIGHTEEN

"Mr. Drake Burnham. You are under arrest for the murder of Jangle Elwell." Officer Kiatoa Koht, the Two-Ton Tillie of Pohnpei Public Safety, paused as if he wasn't quite sure how to advise me of my rights in English.

"Go on." Kazuo Olopai, the chief Pohnpei prosecutor, stood by, I guess to make sure Officer Koht didn't make too many mistakes.

"You have the right to remain silent. Anything you say can and will be used against you in court." Kiatoa paused again. "I'm sorry, Mr. Prosecutor. I don't know about the second one."

"Tell him he has the right to an attorney."

"Even if he is a lawyer?"

"Just, just read him what's on the paper."

"Mr. Burnham. You have the right to an attorney and to have your attorney present during questioning." Officer Koht paused again, this time longer. "I'm not sure about this next one."

"You mean if he cannot afford an attorney? I'm not sure of that one either." It was Olopai's turn to pause. "Drake, let me ask you. You're a foreign national, not a Micronesian citizen. Does that mean you do, or do not, have the right to free assistance of counsel."

I scratched my head. "Well, Kazuo. It's still an undecided area. Although I'm a foreign national, I am a legal resident. If I were in your

248

place I'd advise me I do have the right to free assistance of counsel. I'm goddamn sure I could use it."

"Drake, please don't take the Lord's Name in vain. Okay, Officer, tell him."

"Mr. Burnham. If you would like to have the assistance of a counselor, someone from the Public Defender's office will be assigned to help you. Okay, Drake. Now you have to come inside here."

"Officer, don't forget to ask Mr. Burnham if he understands his rights."

"Oh yeah. Mr. Burnham, do you understand the rights I just read?"

I nodded, although I was tempted to say no, if only to gauge their reactions.

Officer Koht smiled at the prosecutor. "Can I handcuff him now?"

"What do you normally do?"

"Usually, he is handcuffed."

"Which handcuffs do you have?"

"Only these plastic ones." Koht held up a pair of chicken chokers, the plastic handcuffs they call zip-ties down in Gitmo. The cuffs cinch up tight and tend to cut off circulation.

"No, don't use those," said Olopai. "They'll hurt his wrists."

"So what?"

"So what? Officer Koht, what does the Chief of Police always tell you about how to treat someone who is arrested for an offense?"

"I don't know. 'Book him, Dan-O?'"

"No. Your Chief says, 'You treat someone who is arrested like he is the king,' and I happen to agree with him. Now where are the other handcuffs?"

"I cannot find the steel handcuffs. I think maybe they are lost."

"Never mind. We won't handcuff him. What's next when you arrest someone?"

Officer Koht paged through the thin file folder. "Inventory his privates."

"You mean his personals. His personal effects."

"Yes, his private effects. Mr. Burnham, can you please take everything out of your pockets?"

I pulled out the pockets of my trousers and held them with my fingertips to show there was nothing inside. I considered asking either if they had ever kissed a rabbit, but said instead, "I brought nothing today, knowing I'd be arrested. I left my wallet and keys at home."

"What's next, Officer?" Kazuo did not sound amused.

"Suicide prevention." Officer Koht paged forward through the file. "Mr. Burnham, give me your shoelaces."

"I'm wearing zoris."

"Okay, check. No shoelaces. Give me your belt."

"But my pants will fall down."

"So what?"

"We don't want that to happen, Officer Koht. Never mind the suicide list. This is Mr. Drake Burnham, not a local teenager. What's next?"

"Ask the person if he wants to make a statement."

"So, ask him."

"Mr. Burnham, do you want to make a statement?"

250

"No thank you."

"Okay, Drake," Kiatoa's hand was surprisingly gentle on my shoulder. "Come inside, this way."

And so I was ushered behind the desk and into the Pohnpei jail. Sure, I've been inside the big house before, hundreds of times, here in the islands and back in the States, and with no sweat. I'd visited the Pohnpei slammer dozens of times without ever thinking about it, mostly to speak with clients, but also a few times with Al Frost to document a class action to address the somewhat less-than-habitable conditions at the jail. Now, at least in theory, there should be clean bedding and enough water to shower and flush at the same time. But not once did I ever think of what it would be like to be inside as an arrestee, a perp, a suspect. Not until now.

As it was, I had little to worry about. It seemed the other jailees knew all about my arrest. The trusties had decided to assign me my own room, well, my own cell, the best of a mostly sorry lot, but the one with a window and a view down to the ballfield at the Spanish Wall, that is if I stood on the edge of the bunk, leaned right and twisted my head to the left. I figured the cell they gave me was almost as good as Room 16 at the Magellan, but for the fact that there I could check out. As I was checking out the features of my cell, one of the trusties came by to give me the skinny on the other prisoners; who was crazy (about that one the trustie screwed his index finger into his temple and said he was "off-island"), which ones were snitches, and who could be trusted.

Maybe my luck had turned, or maybe it was payback for earlier kindness. It's not just representing some guys inside. At island feasts or parties like the Bench and Bar Banquet, guests are given a "take out" bag – a cardboard box or palm frond basket of extra food to take home to eat at one's leisure. Since I'm generally given far more food than I can eat by myself, I'd gotten in the habit of stopping by the jail to donate my extras for those inside, generally after telling the desk sergeant in no uncertain terms to make sure the prisoners get the food. Like Al Frost used to say, in the islands you're considered wealthy by what you can give away, not what you have. I hoped they appreciated it. Jailees have a pretty bland diet, mackerel and rice mostly; or maybe a few plantains or some grated coconut thrown in for variety's sake.

Of course I learned the reason for the trusties' largesse. I soon had potential clients lined up to meet me in the privacy of my own cell, each with questions about the possibility of parole or work release, or for assistance with assorted matters, like divorce petitions or collection suits pending outside while they, or rather we, were locked up. In a single day, I became a jailhouse lawyer, as busy as I had been in months.

So occupied, my first day in jail as a murder suspect passed quickly, even quicker when Roberta Ely stopped by with two bits of good news, about as good as one could expect while incarcerated, short of receiving a form release rubber-stamped "paroled." First, even though Kazuo Olopai had gotten a judge to sign two search warrants – one for my house, one for my office – Kazuo had told Roberta that he wouldn't search either place without me, or without someone representing me, actually being there. Kazuo, God bless him, wanted to invade neither my attorney-client privileged files nor my personal privacy. Second, Judge Omishima had put my bail hearing on Friday morning's calendar. To top it all that evening, to welcome the newest prisoner (i.e., me), the cook made the best of what he could find, a fish curry so tasty that I couldn't quite believe the mackerel came from a can.

Roberta stood up for me at the bail hearing before Judge Omishima in the Pohnpei State Court at nine the next morning. I had asked her to represent me so I could keep my mouth shut. I wanted no questions on why I went to Chuuk from Kosrae, or how. All I hoped for was that the judge would order a reasonable bail for my release. 'Justice rushed is justice crushed' is a catchphrase for Judge Omishima and I wondered whether I would have to spend a weekend in the lockup.

"Drake, you owe us big time," Roberta whispered to me. "When I first saw him, I couldn't believe who you asked us to keep hidden."

"Tell me about it, Ms. Ely. When I first saw him I said to myself 'it's the dead man walking the green mile to the monster's ball.' The resemblance would be even better if your guest were to wear some of his brother's clothes."

"Oh, once he's dressed for court he'll fool a lot of people."

"Tell me how he's been?"

"Nervous. He's worried about being here on Pohnpei. But he's spending a lot of time reading, just paging his way through our library. Once in a while he'll ask Spenser the meaning of a certain word. And what a prince. Jingle is polite, quiet, helpful, and he's really handy. He and Spenser are going through the job jar for things to fix around the apartment. At the rate he's going we'll have nothing left to repair."

"Hopefully he won't have to stay with you for too long."

"Are you kidding? As of today, neither of us wants him to leave. And that leads me to item two, Mr. Burnham. Your subpoena list had a few surprises."

"I figure my best shot for dismissal is to raise questions on all potential suspects."

"I agree that you have to subpoena Dr. Perez for his autopsy report, but to call Jasmina? I never would even think to subpoena my own secretary. And Valentin Onan? I had no idea that J-O was so unpopular. The trial counselors in my office said they would have stood in line in the sun at noon to serve that one. Utticus practically sprinted out the door with it. What are you up to?"

"In good time, Ms. Ely. In good time."

Kazuo Olopai stood for the state at my bail hearing. He argued bail should be denied because of the grave nature of the offense and because I had apparently tried to evade justice by going to Chuuk. Roberta countered that I was a long-term resident, the owner of a valuable business (I stifled a smirk at that one), who had surrendered voluntarily upon returning to Pohnpei. She argued the prosecutor's office was well aware I was off-island when it sought my arrest warrant, and that the chief prosecutor himself was at the airport on the day I left Pohnpei. Roberta also said I needed to be released so that I could take an active role in my own defense. Finally, Roberta gestured to the gallery and said she could produce character witnesses on my behalf. She suggested I be released on my own recognizance.

Judge Omishima gave no indication of how he might rule. He sat impassive as a silver-haired frog awaiting an errant fly. I thought Omishima would split the baby, and ask me to post something for bail. My hopes of staying out of jail over the weekend fell when the Judge called a recess to consider the arguments, but rose again when he asked everyone to remain in the courtroom.

It didn't take long for the Judge to make up his mind.

"I have looked in our book of laws and listened carefully to both sides. For plenty of reasons, including that this is the defendant's first time offense, I have decided to release Mr. Burnham on conditions, and without asking him to post any money for bail. The conditions are: first, Mr. Burnham surrenders his passport to the Probation Officer. Second, he is not allowed to go to the airport or the seaport, except to prepare for his defense or to conduct the necessary parts of his business, but only upon him giving one-day's notice to the prosecutor's office. Third, all the assets of his business, the law firm of Frost & Burnham, will be held as security for his good behavior and may be forfeited along with his foreign business permit if Mr. Burnham violates any of the conditions for his release. Finally, Mr. Burnham is not allowed to consume, possess, or manufacture any alcoholic drink while he is released under these conditions."

Roberta stood. "Your Honor, the charges against Mr. Burnham do not mention alcohol, and there is no indication that alcohol played any role in the commission of this offense. I ask the Court to reconsider the last condition as unreasonable."

I could have gagged Ms. Ely were she within reach. She had hit a triple and was trying to stretch it into an inside-the-park home run.

"Thank you, Counsel. You are correct. I will not impose the last condition."

Safe!

Now it was Kazuo's turn to object. "Your Honor, the charge against this defendant is the most serious offense in our book of laws. The State has a very strong case, and the defendant may want to flee justice. Strong measures are needed."

"Mr. Olopai. I know the serious nature of the charge. But you make the defendant sound like a dive tramp, just passing through the islands. This is Mr. Drake Burnham. He has been here for several years and he runs an important business for our people. I'm sure that the American woman lawyer, Mrs. Ely, could bring plenty of people, both locals and *menwhi*, who could talk about Mr. Burnham's good character. For now, I am satisfied that Mr. Burnham will appear for pretrial and trial. I have made my decision. You should go tell the airlines, shipping companies, and sailing captains that the defendant is restricted to the island."

I didn't even have to ask who will save the widow's son.

The good jurist then set pretrial hearing dates and scheduled a trial for a month from the day. If my motion to dismiss went as easily as the bail hearing, I would be, well, could be, home free.

After the hearing adjourned, Kazuo stepped to the defense table to ask if he and some police officers could stop by the office that afternoon with the search warrants. I asked to see the warrants, and they looked airtight. I guess Kazuo has learned the lessons that Al Frost, Roberta and I have taught him over the years.

"I still have to cull out the confidential papers from my files. Hopefully it won't take too long. Why don't you come by after four o'clock?"

Kazuo grumbled, but agreed. I figured he would have a hard time rounding up any cop focused on doing the job late on a Friday afternoon.

"I'm still trying to figure out your strategy." Roberta shook her head after Kazuo left. "Your methods are madness – running away to Chuuk, then turning yourself in."

"Tell you what, Ms. Ely. Buy us some lunch and help me separate the confidential material in my files, I'll tell you as much as I can."

The air in the office was stale, as if no one had been there since I left Pohnpei ten days earlier. Jasmina wasn't in, and her boombox was gone as well. The mildew stains on the back wall had grown a wee bit closer. The linoleum beneath the air conditioner had peeled back a few millimeters more. The fax machine was on, but there were no faxes waiting. No surprise there. I could go a month during lean times without an incoming fax.

With two lawyers examining the files, the task of cleaning them out wasn't so bad. We pulled all confidential file material and made a list of what we pulled as we went to make a log of documents withheld on grounds of privilege. Over take out lunch, Roberta asked about my plans for the defense.

"I figure my best shot is on a motion to dismiss."

"No preliminary examination? You won't ask Kazuo to put up or shut up?"

"No. The State's case has to be on circumstantial evidence, but it could hold together, especially in front of a local judge who doesn't want to make waves by dismissing serious charges against a troublesome American. I need to put on evidence, not just throw stones at the State's case. Besides, if I ask for a preliminary exam, that will just give Kazuo a chance to try his case twice, figure out the holes on the first run and patch them up for trial."

"Will my mystery guest testify?"

"He has to, although I haven't asked him directly. I don't see a dismissal on a point of law. I can't count on Kazuo making a mistake, and so far he's been very careful. The arrest was spotless. His search warrants look clean. But if Jingle testifies, he'll need separate counsel. I can't represent him, obvious conflict of interest."

"What will Jingle testify about?"

"The bank robbery, and what he knows about the murder."

"Well if he testifies about the bank robbery then I have a conflict, too. Entis is still up on the bank charge."

"You'd think that Marielle would have dropped it by now."

"She hasn't. Entis, by the way, is now saying a little bit more. He was working with a cousin on Chuuk. When the job stopped Entis had no way to get back to Pohnpei. Said he knew Jangle from COM, and was surprised to see him on Chuuk. Jangle bought his ticket to Pohnpei, paid him twenty bucks down and promised him another fifty to sit on the cooler on the way back. Seventy dollars is a lot of money to a local kid, and Entis didn't see anything wrong with it. And Drake, I'm really glad that Entis wasn't on your subpoena list."

"Ms. Ely. You know that even if I did subpoena my own secretary I wouldn't ask you to subpoena your client. It's just as well that you don't represent Jingle, Roberta. You'd probably convince him to hold his tongue. I think I'll have to convince the national public defender office to fly R.K. Asher over from Chuuk to represent your mystery guest. R.K.'s sharp, and he and Jingle can confer in Chuukese. Besides, Jingle is more likely to trust someone from his home island."

"How will you convince the national office to foot the bill?"

"I'll do a little seahorse trading, maybe tell your boss that I'll spare him the cost of my defense by representing myself."

"Drake, you're not even going to consider that."

"I have to, Roberta. I've got no choice. I've got it all planned out in my head already."

"I just hope you know what you're doing. As for your plans, like the old saying goes, 'do you know how to make God laugh?'"

"How?"

"'Tell Her your plans.'"

"Ms. Ely, I do believe that Kazuo Olopai would be first in line to discuss the gender of your deity, followed by Father Benoit, and then a few pastors on Kosrae."

"And then the Vatican," Roberta laughed. "And the Southern Baptist Convention."

Kazuo was at the office door precisely at four o'clock. A coke oven morning had given way to a blissfully rainy afternoon, and Kazuo was huddled from the rain beneath the eaves of the Namiki Building. He clutched a brown envelope in one hand.

"Got your search warrants in there, Kazuo? But no help? You won't accomplish a lot coming all by yourself."

"I don't know if you or Roberta were served with this order yet, so I brought two copies. I feel terrible about this, Drake, just terrible. It looks like I'm off the case."

"Off my case?"

"When I got back to the office after lunch this afternoon, Marielle Hargraves and two guys from the Department of Security and Investigation were waiting for me. They took everything, Drake. My whole case file, my witness lists, my Brady material. They took it all, even my notes. Marielle told me they had the right to do it."

Poor Kazuo sounded heartbroken that he wouldn't be prosecuting me for a murder I didn't commit. I put my hand on his shoulder. I felt sorry for him, almost.

"She also served me with a subpoena and said she would call me as a witness," Kazuo continued.

"A witness? To what?"

Kazuo handed me the envelope, addressed to him, with a return address of the Supreme Court. "Maybe you'd better read the order."

I opened the envelope and handed a copy to Roberta. It was a one-pager, a writ of prohibition from the Supreme Court, addressed to Judge Zacharias Omishima, Pohnpei State Court. It read:

> A criminal charge having been filed in the Supreme Court by the Attorney General's Office accusing Drake Burnham, a citizen of the United States, with the murder of Jangle Elwell. Because the defendant is a foreign national, not a Micronesian citizen, original jurisdiction for this case is proper only in the Supreme Court, not the Pohnpei State Court. The Pohnpei State Court is directed to suspend all action on this matter until the Supreme Court has had the chance to review and if necessary to bring Mr. Burnham to trial for the charges against him.
>
> Honorable Maximinus T. Coleman

I was back in the Supreme Court, charged with murder, to be tried in the courtroom of Maximum Max.

I handed the order to Roberta. "Looks like Coleman's gunning for me. What should I do?"

"Duck, Drake."

CHAPTER NINETEEN

Coleman was quick to fire across my bow, sending an order for a hearing to show cause why my pretrial release should not be revoked. The order and notice arrived just after Kazuo and Roberta had left my office, and a few moments before I had planned to leave for the Ox & Palm, where, thanks to Roberta, I could still enjoy a cold one.

And so I spent my first Saturday of (relative) freedom in the office briefing the issue, a brief I hoped I wouldn't have to argue before an appellate panel of the Supreme Court. My point was simple. Judge Omishima had exercised his discretion in deciding to release me from jail before trial. I had violated no condition Judge Omishima had set. Both Coleman and Omishima are trial court judges, although in different courts. Coleman therefore could not overrule another trial-level judge's exercise of discretion. As I said, it was a simple argument, but I had a hard time finding any case to cite as precedent. I talked my way into a Saturday research session at the State Court law library, but found nothing of help. Then again I know of prison law libraries stateside in better shape than Pohnpei's. So I slept on it, then dragged myself back to the office on Sunday to reread the motion to be sure I had it right.

When I left the office Saturday evening, I noticed two beefy locals in a blue four-door sedan following me home. When the car rolled past my place, I turned quickly to see a national government license plate on the rear bumper. The Department of Security and Investigation had taken over tailing me from Pohnpei Public Safety. At least then I wouldn't have to suffer through any Taro Patch Kid drive-by's, I hoped.

Sunday did not live up to its name. It stayed gray and cool – cool, that is, for Micronesia – without a hint of Old Sol other than the inescapable heat. Back in the office, I reviewed and revised my brief until I was satisfied, sketched out a few trial notes, then pulled down the portrait of Clarence Darrow for that long-delayed tête-à-tête. I opened the bottom desk drawer, groped for the bottle of vodka and found first a lumpy package in a dirty plastic bag. I pulled it out, along with the bottle of vodka, and placed them side-by-side atop the desk. Both made hefty thunks as I set them down.

I stared at the package for a moment until I remembered Jasmina's telephone call when I was on Kosrae. This could only be the package my Filipino clients, the two guys in the band called "The Operator," had dropped off. The package looked to be wrapped in miles of shredded newspaper. I began to unwrap it, figuring it could only be an antiquity; something the pair had dug up on that plot of land in Kitti that they'd leased. I'd warned them against trying to take any antiquity they found off-island, and they had delivered it to me instead. It could have been a taro pounder from the shape, possibly carved from basalt from its heft, heavy in my hands relative to size. I continued to unwind the newspaper, thinking that I could deliver it to the director of antiquities at the Department of Local Culture. There would be no reward, of course, except for the goodwill that might generate a referral later on. But as I continued to unwrap, it dawned on me that I would not turn over this particular piece to the director of antiquities. It wasn't a taro pounder, or an antiquity at all. It was a handgun.

It was a two-dollar pistol, to be more precise, a small caliber piece of junk whose action probably skewed off center and was no good for anything other than sticking in some poor sucker's ribs; a Saturday Night special, with a jet black barrel and a shiny metal grip, all the better to show finger and palm prints. I checked to make sure the safety was on, and like I remember Steve McGarrett doing, picked the pistol up by sliding a pencil into the barrel. Then I walked to the coffee machine and grabbed a paper towel to release the clip. Empty. I sniffed the barrel and smelled oiled metal and gunpowder. I turned the pencil to examine the barrel and grip. Japanese military issues are marked with kanji figures, and this could be a discard from World War II. Then again I've seen Yakuza knock-offs with similar figures for sale in Guam pawnshops. No kanji, no maker's marks, in fact, nothing to identify the gun. I pushed the clip back in against the back of my wrist, glanced up at Clarence Darrow and wondered what to do.

Every law school ethics exam has this question: a client comes into your office and leaves a smoking gun. Given both the attorney-client privilege and an attorney's obligations as an officer of the court, what must you do? Do you know if a crime likely to result in death or serious bodily injury has been committed? Do you know whether a crime likely to result in death or serious bodily injury is about to be committed? Did your client confess when he dropped the gun on your desk?

But what if you suspect one client used the gun to murder another? What must you do?

And what if you are accused of murdering your client?

What then must you do?

In Micronesia, possession of a handgun is a category three felony. Over in Palau – where they've had assassinations and assorted gun violence – it's a category one felony, with a mandatory minimum fifteen-year prison sentence. Possession of just about any firearm here in the islands is illegal, except for some small-bore pigeon poppers, something this dime store piece most assuredly was not. Simply being found with a handgun would be enough for any judge, much less Coleman, to revoke my pretrial release. If anyone found out about it, I'd be thrown right back into the Pohnpei lockup.

But there was more to it, a lot more. Handguns are as rare as hens' teeth here in the islands, and I had one, like some pulp fiction detective, stashed in the bottom drawer of my desk. And I stood accused of murdering my client, Jangle Elwell, who had been whacked by someone using a handgun. It all became very clear to me. I knew who the killers were, even without the eyewitness account of Jingle Treadwell.

It had to be The Operator, the Filipino muscle Jangle had imported, brought on island to help the Taro Patch Kids step up into the wide world of meth, smuggling it through Micro to Hawaii, and maybe even manufacturing it in a jungle lab. That would explain why the Operator needed a remote shack with good water, not to practice guitar, but to manufacture meth, a jungle lab right here on Pohnpei. Only Jangle and The Operator had some kind of falling out, and The Operator rubbed Jangle out. That's why they skipped the island so fast, after leasing land in Kitti and applying for foreign investment permits. They had to leave. Those two were smarter than they looked. Had they tried to leave the island with the gun in their baggage, for sure they would have been busted at the airport. So to hide the gun, and to cover their tracks, they conveniently left the weapon with me. If I got caught with the gun, I was ready made to take the fall. If I got rid of the gun, to protect myself, they would go scot-free.

But how could I prove that The Operator left me the gun? If I went public with a handgun in my possession, my next stop would be a short stay at the Pohnpei jail, a swift and certain conviction at trial, followed by a much longer stay at the Pohnpei jail. No one would believe how the pistol even came to me. The Filipinos were off-island, probably forever. Jasmina would have to testify about them dropping it off, and I would then have to testify – something I loathed even contemplating – about how I found the damn thing. And no one, least of all Maximum Max Coleman, would believe it.

But the strangest thing was that I had Judge Coleman to thank for my finding the handgun first. Roberta and I were so busy pulling confidential papers out of my case files that I didn't even bother to check my drawers, desk drawers that is. Had Coleman not snatched the case when he did, then Kazuo Olopai and Pohnpei Public Safety probably would have found the gun while searching my office. I had come within an afternoon of having a murder weapon found in my desk, and I had the officious Coleman to thank. But all that still begged the question of what to do with the damn thing.

I glanced again at Clarence Darrow. The face scowled back at me. I think I know what Darrow's advice would be. Come clean and let the chips fall where they may. I know what Algonquin H. Frost's advice would be. Trust the process and things will turn out right. Ditching the gun, evidence of a crime, would violate the canons of ethics, and such moves generally come back to bite one. I could guess what Father

Benoit's advice would be. Trust the people involved, knowing there are judges who do the right thing. But I couldn't risk trust, process, or sympathy. I had to get rid of the gun.

I had to move quickly, knowing full well that Marielle Hargraves was about to serve me with a search warrant. My first thought on getting rid of the pistol was obvious. I live on an island in the middle of the South Pacific. All I would have to do would be to drop the damn thing, kerplunk, in the middle of Big Blue. If it went overboard outside the reef, there isn't a treasure hunter anywhere who could recover it, not even the guys who located the wreck of the Titanic. But there was one problem with dropping the gun overboard. Under the conditions of my pretrial release, I was barred from going to the seaport except on twenty-four hours notice to the prosecutor, and I didn't have a moment to spare. I could probably arrange for a fishing expedition, but that would be hard to do on a rainy Sunday. I thought of other options – burying it in the backyard, dropping it into a volcano, except that anyone would see where I buried the piece, and the volcano that formed Pohnpei went extinct several million years ago. I thought about trekking into the jungle and heaving the gun off the trail. But someone could find it that way, too, and I didn't want some young kid finding the piece in the forest and shooting himself or somebody else. That would be just my kind of luck.

I put the pistol into a redrope file folder, a sturdy, new one, along with a yellow pad and a couple of pens. I closed up the office, locked it up good, and got in my truck to drive away. Sure enough, the blue sedan with the government plates and the two muscular locals pulled out to follow me, out of Kolonia, past the rusting wreck of the World War II Japanese tank by the side of the road, past the Pohnpei

Hospital, then to the Green River Bridge at Daosokele, the site of Jangle's murder. I stopped the truck at mid-span and got out. I could see the two DSI guys back at the curve of the road, just within sight. I reached back into the truck for the redrope folder, opened it, and placed it carefully on the curb, out of sight of the two guys tailing me in the car. I took out the yellow pad and pen and started scribbling some notes. If anyone asked, I was investigating my case. If the DSI agents asked, then everything in the redrope file folder was confidential, and no they cannot look into it, not even with a search warrant. But the DSI guys stayed back at the curve in the road, just watching me.

Soon enough, I put the pad back into the redrope folder, picked up a few stones from the curb and started tossing them idly into the river, up close at first, then a little further, then further still. I bent over to pick up some more stones to toss, sometimes pausing between throws as if thinking. The third time I bent down to pick up stones, I reached into the redwell, grabbed the pistol and chucked it as far as I could. It made a nice plop where it landed in the middle of the river. I bent again and tossed a few more stones for good measure, just making sure the bad boys in the blue sedan thought nothing of my little exercise, then I got in the truck, turned around on the far side of the bridge and drove home, resisting the temptation to wave at the DSI guys as I passed them.

That night, for the first time that I can remember on island, I prayed for rain. I prayed for a deluge that would swell the Green River and lift the gun downstream and into a deep hole in the reef, never to be seen again.

CHAPTER TWENTY

"May it please the court." Marielle Hargraves stood to deliver the opening statement in my trial for murder. She looked smashing in a sleeveless summer dress, short enough to show off her legs but just long enough not to be daring on an island where some muumuus are considered scandalous. And her perfume smelled like springtime somewhere else, a place more temperate and less fecund. I'm sure Judge Coleman caught a whiff, given how he lingered during the pretrial conference to cover procedures. I did, too, although I tried to focus on Marielle's determination to send me up the river for ten to twenty-five.

"The government charges the defendant, Drake Burnham, with murder in the second degree, of one Jangle Moses Elwell, in violation of Title II F.S.M. Code section 911. Jurisdiction is proper in this the Supreme Court because the defendant, a U.S. citizen, is a foreign national. The government will submit evidence to prove all the elements of the offense beyond reasonable doubt."

Marielle, as is her habit, brought about half the law library with her. The prosecutor's table was crammed with casebooks, a tabbed exhibit file, several notepads, a black vinyl three-ring binder that I guessed was her trial book, plus a treatise on evidence with little yellow post-it notes marking at least a dozen pages. Slouched behind Marielle's library rampart was Anton Gedankenlos, the Attorney General. The AG, who preferred to be called by his initials, AG, had worked his way through a stateside law school – the first local to get a U.S. degree – and, after a short stint prosecuting on his home island, had been bitten by the bug of politics. After he came in close second in a re-election bid for Senator from Chuuk, AG was tabbed by the President to be the Attorney General. On the morning of my trial, however, he looked more like a schoolboy dragged to a violin recital when he could be playing ball outside. Every so often, AG the AG would turn to either of two Department of Security and Investigation agents sitting in the first row behind the bar, instructing them on some ministerial task. One or the other agent would then scurry from the courtroom and return ten or fifteen minutes later to whisper urgently to AG the AG, as if he monitored the Final Four by proxy.

Marielle continued. "The defendant is an attorney in private practice here on Pohnpei. He scrapes by, mostly off goodwill amassed in the practice by his former partner, the late Algonquin H. Frost, and by taking conflict case assignments for criminal defense matters in the state and supreme courts. The government will submit into evidence the books of Frost & Burnham, which will amply demonstrate the sorry state of the firm's financial affairs. It's not lucrative. In fact, the defendant lives pretty much hand-to-mouth."

Ouch. That stung.

"The defense of Jangle Elwell was one such conflict assignment the defendant actively sought and took. Mr. Elwell was charged with bank robbery. As the Court may be aware, Mr. Elwell and the defendant had a contentious relationship. In fact, on the date of Mr.

Elwell's murder, the defendant filed a motion to withdraw as counsel for Mr. Elwell. The government contends the basis for their contentious relationship provides a motive for the defendant to commit the offense. The evidence will show that any of the following scenarios contributed, although any one would be sufficient to convict the defendant of Mr. Elwell's murder."

The prosecution didn't have to prove motive to prove murder, but it sounded like Marielle wanted to show it to improve her odds at sentencing. Of course, she wouldn't have to show much to convince Maximum Max to throw the book at me.

Also at the prosecutor's table, sitting shoulders erect, and straight back, paying rapt attention to the unmemorable Ms. Hargraves, was Kazuo Olopai. He wore, for the first time that I could remember, a neutrally toned and colored Aloha shirt. Kazuo would testify, but about what I did not know. At the pretrial conference, I had asked Coleman for a pro forma order excluding all witnesses from the courtroom before they testified, so as not to be influenced by argument or the testimony of other witnesses. Valentin Onan left, as did Uttiucs Uziah, plus a young local who seemed familiar but whom I could not quite place. Pietro, the bailiff, looked only too pleased to escort my secretary, Jasmina, to a vacant office to be used as a witness waiting room. Marielle, though, explained that as well as being a witness, Kazuo Olopai was a critical member of the prosecution team, thus exempting him from the general rule banning witnesses from trial. Of the legal talent at the prosecutor's table, I was most concerned about the one without a law degree, Kazuo.

On the other side of the aisle, I sat alone at the defense table, with a couple of ballpoint pens and two yellow legal pads - one blank, one filled with notes for assorted witnesses. Roberta Ely had telephoned early that morning to say she had a trial call in state court, but she would send her husband. She would come to provide moral support and counsel from behind the bar as soon as she could.

Marielle pressed on. "In the first scenario, the defendant was jealous because Mr. Elwell was involved in a romantic relationship with the defendant's secretary, Jasmina Solomon, for whom the defendant holds a strong affection. Challenged by the presence of a younger, more virile male, the defendant acted rashly and killed Mr. Elwell."

A younger, more virile male? That was punching below the belt. I'll bet Maximum Max didn't care for the age implication either.

"Second, the defendant was assisted in his defense of Mr. Elwell's bank robbery case by an investigator named Uttiucs Uziah, a friend of the defendant. In the course of that investigation, Mr. Elwell struck Mr. Uziah in the face. The defendant, Mr. Burnham, on learning that Mr. Uziah had been battered, told Mr. Uziah not to report to the police that he'd been assaulted, saying that he, that is, Mr. Burnham, 'would take care of it.' This took place just a few days before the victim was murdered. The defendant 'took care of it' by taking matters into his own hands, and killing Mr. Elwell.

"Finally, the defendant and Mr. Elwell argued repeatedly over money. Although the defendant was to be paid through the court for taking the conflict case assignment to defend the victim on the bank robbery charge, the defendant also represented Mr. Elwell for the defense of another, unrelated criminal charge. Examination of the Frost & Burnham books will demonstrate that the defendant was not paid for that second defense.

"But there is more to the money trail than the defendant's representation of the victim in criminal matters. Being a man of some influence, though in his own petty way, Jangle Elwell regularly referred other cases to the defendant, including a potentially lucrative personal injury case, a land case, perhaps others. Because of their contentious relationship, Mr. Elwell pulled the cases he referred to the defendant – one way gangs control their lawyers. As a result of Mr. Elwell's actions – pulling case files and not paying for a criminal defense – the defendant was desperate for money. He confronted Mr. Elwell and killed him.

"The defendant's subsequent conduct also suggests his involvement in his late client's death. Upon learning that a Pohnpei state judge had signed a warrant for his arrest, the defendant acted in a manner consistent with culpability. He fled; although his finances were in such disarray that the defendant only made it as far as Chuuk."

The gallery was full, hardly a free seat anywhere, it being the first murder trial in the Supreme Court in a half a dozen years. There was, of course, the "Matlock" crew of local retirees who attend every trial they can – older men wearing sun-faded baseball caps and banlon shirts that look like rejects from the half-off bins at the Guam Ben Franklin store. Old women in muumuus sat quietly, as if in church, hands folded in their laps, a few fanning themselves with scraps of paper. But there were also a few younger guys, too, although they had the look of the chronic unemployed, not Taro Patch Kids. Coleman wouldn't mind. He's enough of a ham to play to the quite crowded courtroom.

Bosworth Fields, editor of "The Daily Dilemma," sat front and center, reporter's notepad at the ready. For Bosworth's sake, I hoped he was stringing for the Associated Press. An American, on trial for murder in paradise, had to be worth some copy somewhere. I smiled only when I noticed Spenser Ely on the aisle in the third row, at that point my only supporter.

"To conclude, I respectfully request that the Court pay attention to all the evidence and listen carefully to all the witnesses." Marielle wrapped up her opening statement. "The government has no eyewitness to the murder of Jangle Elwell. The evidence against the defendant is circumstantial and involves a degree of inference. But the government believes its case is sound, and has every confidence that the Court will find the defendant, Drake Burnham, guilty of murder in the second degree."

I was impressed. Marielle had made it through an entire opening statement without stumbling once. Of course, her case was a load of crap. Such an overly detailed opening statement normally leaves a lot of room to argue prosecutorial overreaching, and I'd like to hold her feet to the fire to prove what she said she would. But those tactics work best with an objective judge and a stateside jury. I had neither. Even had I pulled a hanging judge stateside, I could still count on the jury, twelve men, good and true. But here in the islands, I would have to rely instead on one man, dirty, and dishonest. Coleman would be both judge and jury, thanks to the morons who thought a jury system would never work in Micronesia.

I could think of only a couple of advantages of being tried for murder in Coleman's courtroom. I already had Coleman's driver/ enforcer/drinking buddy, Valentin Onan, under subpoena. Under the rules then, Maximum Max couldn't speak with Valentin about his testimony. I know that Coleman doesn't play by the rules. But with a subpoena, Coleman couldn't simply ignore his ethical obligations.

The second advantage of appearing in Coleman's courtroom was, well, I hadn't figured that one out yet. Needless to say, the downside was considerable.

Coleman chuckled and shook his head when I stood to say that I would reserve the time to make my opening statement at the beginning of the defense case-in-chief. But then Maximum Max had questioned my every strategic decision before trial. He had asked if I had been smoking *pakalolo* when, in order to invoke my right to a speedy trial, I waived pretrial motions and decided against requesting discovery from the government. Not asking for discovery was a tough call. Until the morning trial began, I had no idea of the identity of Marielle's witnesses and no chance to review in advance any documents she planned to submit into evidence. But then by not initiating discovery, I had no obligation to reveal the identity of Jingle Treadwell, the ace up my sleeve, or rather, hiding out at Roberta's.

Coleman raised the biggest stink when I said I would represent myself at trial. I told him on the record I was aware of the old admonition that he who undertakes to provide his own defense has a fool for a lawyer. Maximum Max's countered that my counsel was bold, but that my client looked uncertain.

The government called Utticus Uziah as the first witness. Utticus, dressed in his Sunday best – 'black and white with tie' as locals say – frowned as he glanced my way en route to the witness box, teetering uncomfortably in black leather boots.

"Please state your full name." Marielle was all business once he was sworn in.

"Utticus Ulysses Uziah."

I didn't know his middle name is Ulysses. I'd have to change my nickname for him.

"Do you have a job, Mr. Uziah?" Marielle continued.

"Office investigator, Pohnpei public defender office."

"How long have you worked for the public defender?"

"I think it is about five years now."

"Do you know a man named Drake Burnham?"

"Yes."

"Is Drake Burnham in the courtroom today?"

"Yes."

"Where is he?"

Utticus, in deferential local fashion, merely nodded and arched his eyebrows toward the defense table.

"That's not sufficient," Coleman interrupted. "The witness is ordered to point his finger at Mr. Burnham."

Utticus glanced passively at the judge, then pointed at me, square in the chest.

"May the record reflect that the witness has identified the defendant," said Marielle.

Like a flatworm avoiding electric shocks in a high school biology experiment, Ms. Hargraves demonstrated a basic capacity for learning. Once in state court, early in her prosecutorial tenure, a defendant had been dismissed because Marielle had failed to identify him by testimony. But she didn't make the same mistake in my case, not with Coleman helping her out.

"Do you consider Mr. Burnham a friend?"

"He is okay for a *menwhi*, an American."

"You don't like Americans?"

"No."

"Why not?" Marielle tilted her head.

"You're too pushy."

"Very well," Marielle pouted, as if she expected an apology on behalf of 300 million Americans. "Have you ever helped Mr. Burnham on any of his cases?"

"Yes."

"Even though you work for the public defender and he doesn't?"

"Objection. Lack of foundation." I had to break up Hargraves' rhythm.

"Overruled. Please answer the question, Mr. Uziah." Max Coleman gave early notice that he would pay me no favors. But that was nothing new.

"Yes," Utticus continued. "When Drake, Mr. Burnham, has a conflict case assignment, I am allowed to help him out. But not on his private cases."

"Did Mr. Burnham ask you to help him out on his defense of Jangle Elwell to the charge of bank robbery?"

"Yes. That was a conflict case, so I could help him."

I stood up. "Your Honor, the prosecutor is skirting hazardous ground here. May we approach the bench?"

Coleman nodded. I could smell Marielle's perfume at the sidebar, but tried to ignore it by thinking about baseball.

"I'll have to object if the prosecutor asks about my instructions to Utticus on Jangle's defense. Any instructions I gave are absolutely privileged as work product."

Marielle rolled her eyes and leaned forward as if to give Coleman a peek at her tattoo. "Your Honor, I have no intention of invading Mr. Burnham's privilege on specific instructions. My questioning here lays foundation for other testimony."

"Mr. Burnham, I have noted your concern, and Miss Hargraves has said she does not seek your work product. I will disregard any inadvertent disclosure. Let's go off the record for a moment."

I heard the loud click as Susanna, the court reporter, turned off the tape recorder.

"No invited error, Burnham. You won't get off that easily." Coleman gave a frigid smile, then shooed us back to our tables.

Marielle continued. "On July 18 of this year, did Mr. Burnham instruct you to contact Jangle Elwell regarding an appearance in court?"

"Objection."

"Overruled."

"With all due respect, Your Honor. You haven't even heard my objection."

"Isn't it work product? Could it be anything else? If the defense objection is work product, the objection is overruled. Such a ministerial instruction is entitled to no protection as work product. Answer the question, Mr. Uziah."

"Drake, I mean, Mr. Burnham told me to go to the Taro Patch to ask Mr. Jangle to come to his office," Utticus said.

"What happened at the Taro Patch?" Marielle asked.

"Someone punched me."

"Where?"

"I just told you. In the Taro Patch."

"No, I mean, where on your body?"

"On the mouth."

"In the customs and traditions of this island, Pohnpei, is it insulting for someone to be struck in the face, as you were?"

"It is very insulting. It also hurts."

"Who punched you?"

"Jangle. Jangle Elwell."

"Why did Jangle punch you?"

"I don't know," Utticus paused, and then unwittingly drove a coffin nail. "I think he was mad at Drake for something."

"Did you tell Mr. Burnham that his client had punched you in the mouth?"

"Yes."

"Did you tell Public Safety that Mr. Elwell had punched you in the mouth?"

"No."

"Why not?"

Utticus looked at me and sighed. "Because Drake told me not to report it to the police. He said that he would take care of it."

"No further questions," Marielle finished.

"Does the defense have any questions?"

"Subject to the witness being recalled, I have no questions at this time," I said. I could think of nothing that would lessen the sting of Utticus's testimony.

The next witness on the prosecution's hit parade was Daniel Warheit, the young local who had left the courtroom just before trial began, the one I couldn't quite place. Daniel, of course, was the older brother of Charlie Warheit, my on-again-off-again, once-in-a-decade personal injury client. Daniel, whose testimony had to be translated from Pohnpeian, testified that he knew Jangle Elwell, and that it was Jangle who recommended that he bring his brother's case against Public Works to my office. Later, Daniel said, Jangle advised him to tell his brother to take the case to another lawyer. Marielle asked Daniel if he knew why Jangle would change his mind, Daniel echoed what Utticus had said, only without the pregnant pause.

"I don't know. But it seemed like Jangle was angry with Mr. Drake Burnham."

I had no questions for Daniel Warheit and Coleman announced a lunch recess of two hours, so that those who had come to the courthouse from town would have time enough to drive over the hill to Kolonia restaurants. I stayed close to court to eat at the Palikir canteen. Dysentery Mary left me alone with a cup of coffee, a tuna sandwich, and my thoughts. I couldn't help but notice how the canteen chatter faded when I ducked inside. Maybe they were talking about me.

CHAPTER TWENTY-ONE

The government called Mario Perez right after lunch, Marielle explaining she called the witness out of order to accommodate Doctor Perez's schedule. Mario wore a white lab coat with his name embroidered above the chest pocket, the image of a busy M.D. who had interrupted important work to come to testify. After a few preliminary questions, Marielle asked Perez about the morning that Jangle's body was brought to the morgue.

"What was the condition of the body brought in?"

"Condition? DOA, dead on arrival, that was obvious."

"Could you identify the body when it was first brought in?"

"No. It wasn't until some time later that the body was ID-ed."

"Did you begin a post-mortem?"

"I conducted a preliminary post-mortem, but I came to no firm conclusion. For that I needed to conduct an autopsy, but to autopsy any remains I need authority from a relative. As long as the body was unidentified, I could not proceed with an autopsy."

"Did anyone come to see the body before it was identified?"

"Yes. Several people came that morning."

"Was one of those people the defendant, Mr. Burnham?"

"Yes."

"What was the defendant's reaction upon seeing the body?"

"Calm, professional; he took it all in. I was actually a little surprised at that. Given the shape of the remains, I had warned Drake, as I did everyone who came that morning, that they were liable to lose their breakfast on seeing the corpse."

"You call the defendant, 'Drake.' Are you two friends?"

"Drake Burnham is a good friend."

"The body was eventually identified, correct?"

"Yes, by a cousin within the week."

"And who did the cousin say the body was?"

"Jangle Elwell, or as Mr. Burnham would call him, 'The Late, Great Jangle Elwell.' You know Drake's always making up nicknames. He calls me 'Mario Speedwagon.' You should hear his nicknames for some other people here in court."

Coleman coughed to interrupt the witness, then gestured to the prosecutor.

"Did you prepare a certificate of death?" Marielle pressed on.

"I did."

Marielle handed Mario a copy of the certificate of death, which she moved into evidence. I saw no reason to object since she easily could get the original.

Marielle continued. "Dr. Perez, are you board-certified in forensic pathology?"

"No, I'm not."

"But how could you autopsy ..." Marielle sounded stumped.

"I'm not certified in pathology. But as Chief of Staff of the only hospital on an isolated island, I'm often called into areas I would refer to a specialist were I in Manila, or Honolulu, or even Guam. We just don't have the staff to operate differently."

Marielle looked grateful for the line Mario tossed. "Did you then autopsy the until then unidentified dead body?"

"Well, I couldn't very well autopsy a live body."

"And what did you conclude?"

"In a nutshell, not only was he really dead, he's really quite sincerely dead."

Coleman coughed again, and said, "Dr. Perez, your reputation for levity is well-known. But this is a trial for murder, and a person whom you call your 'good friend' is charged. That fact alone should command your undivided attention."

"Oh, it does, Your Honor. It does." Mario sounded contrite, but then added, "It's just that I have a hard time taking this put-up prosecution seriously. Drake Burnham is no murderer. In fact ..."

"That's enough, Doctor Perez." Coleman smacked down the taro pounder to cut him off. "I will disregard your last comments as personal opinion. Susanna, please mark the tape to delete the witness's last two sentences. Now, Doctor, limit your responses to the questions asked, if you please."

It was my turn to show gratitude, and I beamed at Mario.

Hargraves pressed on. "Did you prepare a report of the autopsy?"

"Yes, as required by law and sound practice, I prepared an autopsy report."

Marielle held up a sheaf of paper. "Your Honor, may I approach the witness with what has been marked as the Government's Exhibit B?"

"Please give copies to the defendant and the bailiff. You know the drill."

Marielle gave me a glimmer of eye contact as she handed me a copy. I thanked her, then winked and whispered, "Nice *kom.*"

Susanna shrugged off a giggle and marked the tape for another deletion by inserting a shred of paper in the reel.

Marielle, though, ignored my flirting and handed a second copy to the bailiff who passed it up to the bench. I scanned my copy quickly. Mario had snuck me a copy of his draft report when I left for Kosrae, but this was his final version. His findings could be different, bolstered by information he may have received in the interim. I paged through it to see how the final report differed from the version I had reviewed.

"Mr. Burnham?" Coleman sounded impatient.

"Your Honor, if I could have just a few moments to review this document."

"Do I discern you haven't seen this document before? Madam Prosecutor, did you produce a copy to the defendant before trial?"

"No, Your Honor," Marielle sounded smug as a pig-tailed schoolgirl at a spelling bee. "The defendant did not request discovery, so I had no obligation to provide any evidence to review before trial."

"Well, Mr. Burnham. Had your esteemed counsel decided to ask for discovery, you would have had ample time to review the report before now. It seems as if your lawyer has made a mistake. At any rate, you have been asked if this document appears authentic, not to write a book report. Please proceed, Miss Hargraves."

"Thank you, Your Honor. And it's 'Ms.'"

Marielle handed the original autopsy report to Dr. Perez. "Is this the report that you prepared on the autopsy of Jangle Elwell?"

My man Mario took his time to review the report, making a show that he took seriously his chastisement. That gave me more time to peruse my copy. Mario finally turned to the page with his signature and said yes.

"Dr. Perez, in your final autopsy report, did you identify a cause of death?"

"Yes. Jangle Elwell died from multiple gunshot wounds."

"Did you identify the firearm used to shoot Mr. Elwell?"

"No."

"Do you know if anyone else did?"

"Yes, a crime lab referred by Honolulu PD identified the slugs."

"What did the Honolulu crime lab conclude?"

"Objection. Hearsay." I hadn't expected this.

Coleman sustained my objection, but gave Marielle a gimme by saying that if the prosecution had a copy, he would admit the crime lab's report in as evidence.

"Do you have a copy of the report made by the crime lab?"

Mario opened his folder. "Actually, I have the original, signed in blue ink."

"Please read into the record the crime lab's conclusion regarding the weapons used to shoot Jangle Elwell."

"Pohnpei Hospital, Mario Perez, M.D., asked to determine the firearm that discharged several slugs in a homicide. We conclude that two different weapons fired the five slugs sent for identification. Two slugs are more massive, heavier, which are consistent with a pellet weight used for a large bore handgun, a .38 caliber police special. The other three slugs are relatively less massive, consistent with pellets fired from a smaller bore handgun, a .22 caliber pistol."

"So two different weapons were fired at Jangle Elwell?"

"That's not entirely correct. Two different weapons were fired into the victim. He got a 'special delivery' from a police special and a Saturday Night Special."

"Do you have experience treating gunshot wounds of the type like Mr. Elwell's?"

"I worked for ten years in the emergency rooms at Manila General. I would have liked very much to have never treated another gunshot victim."

"Can you draw a distinction between the types of weapons fired into Jangle?"

"Obviously, the heavier caliber slug is likely to do more damage. But where on a body an injury takes place is much more important than the weight of a particular slug. A .22 in the chest can cause a much more serious wound than a .38 in the leg."

"Would anyone be able to tell the difference between the weapons used?"

"Before the fact, during, or after? Let me put it this way. Have you ever fired a handgun Ms. Hargraves?"

"Daddy had a pistol," Marielle defaulted to pouting mode. "But I wasn't allowed."

"Then let me explain. If you heard a Saturday Night Special being fired, you might not even think it was a gun. It sounds like a string of firecrackers. A police special is louder. It sounds like what people think a gun should sound like, in part because Hollywood frequently uses the sound of .38 being fired for movie sound effects."

"Did you determine which weapon was the cause of death?"

"Based on the information available to me, I cannot definitively determine which weapon, the .38 caliber or the smaller handgun, fired the bullet that caused Jangle Elwell's death. Both slugs caused severe injuries. Both contributed."

At that, the prosecutor, having identified the body and cause of death, finished her examination of Dr. Perez.

Roberta Ely had arrived during Mario's direct examination and took the interruption as a chance to catch my attention. "Drake. Cicero Atticus came back to the office after lunch and told me he saw Valentin Onan getting on today's flight for Guam."

"Onan left the island? I have him under subpoena."

Coleman interrupted. "Mr. Burnham, the witness is waiting, and I have little patience with counsel gossiping with persons in the gallery during trial."

"I apologize, Your Honor. But Ms. Ely has just informed me of some difficulty regarding one of my witnesses, despite being subpoenaed. As for consulting with persons in the gallery, what's sauce for the gander is sauce for the goose. I'd like the record to reflect that the Attorney General has at several times through the day turned to speak with persons in the gallery, and he has yet to be admonished."

"Mr. Burnham," Coleman grabbed his taro pounder and waved it at me. "I will not permit *ad hominem* attacks on opposing counsel. The Attorney General is a busy man, with important matters on his mind."

"Important matters? I'm the one on trial."

Coleman glared.

Instead of glaring back, I tried to focus on the witness at hand, instead of the one disappearing over the horizon. I turned to Mario.

"Doctor Perez, you testified that I came to the hospital to see Jangle Elwell's body the morning it was brought in?"

"That's correct."

"When did I come to visit?"

"I was just starting lunch, so it must have been around noon."

"Did anyone else come to see Jangle's body before I did?"

"Yes, several people. First was a police investigator from Public Safety to investigate a possible homicide. There was also a Department of Security and Investigation agent who wanted to arrest the dead body and bring it here to the Supreme Court. That was funny. Gives a whole new meaning to 'habeas corpus,' you know, 'produce the body?' I had to talk that guy out of handcuffing and hauling the corpse off to jail."

"Anybody else come?"

"Yes. The Justice Ombudsman, Valentin Onan."

"Did Mr. Onan say why he wanted to look at the body of Jangle Elwell?"

Marielle practically sang her hearsay objection, just as I planned.

"Your Honor," I said. "I've just received information that the declarant, Valentin Onan, despite being under subpoena, has today left the island. If Mr. Onan is unavailable to testify, his statement cannot be considered hearsay."

At that point Coleman flushed, but sustained the objection anyway.

I turned back to Mario. "Did Mr. Onan do anything at the hospital that morning?"

"No. He just came in and told me that the victim was a drug user and drug smuggler. Then he left, saying he would report it to the Supreme Court."

"Did Mr. Onan, the Pohnpei Justice Ombudsman, come to the hospital before the DSI agent or after?"

"He came about a half an hour before the DSI officer, but after the police."

"You testified on direct examination that you were surprised at my calm reaction upon seeing the body of Jangle Elwell in the morgue. Did anyone else who came to see Jangle that morning express surprise, shock?"

"No. Each person who came in was pretty calm about it, except for the DSI agent who wanted to arrest the body. He was getting hot under the collar."

"What about the cousin who ID-ed the body for you later?"

"He was calm about it, too, although it was a while later and the word was out."

"Dr. Perez, you testified that Jangle Elwell died from multiple gunshot wounds. Did Mr. Elwell have any other injuries that you could discern?"

"Certainly. Mr. Elwell had several deep lacerations and a large contusion on the side of his head, trauma consistent with someone using a heavy object to strike a blow to the head."

"Do you know what that object was?"

"Not in particular, but I believe that Mr. Elwell was struck with some sort of blunt instrument." Mario almost winked at me on that one. "I found bits of plastic in the scalp, which lead me to conclude that the object was something in a rigid plastic casing, a musical instrument, perhaps, or a tape deck."

"Was Mr. Elwell's head injury sufficient to be a cause of death?"

"In some cases it could have been. The trauma caused by the blow to the head was substantial; the injury to the surrounding tissue was severe. But the intervening gunshot wounds were of a different degree entirely. I could have treated the victim for the blow to the head, and he might have had a good chance of surviving. But there would be very little I could do for a patient with sucking chest wounds."

"So the blow to the head did not contribute to the victim's death?"

"No. I necessarily focused on the massive wounds to the trunk caused by bullets being fired into the body. Jangle Elwell expired from multiple gunshot wounds."

"Do you know which injury came first?"

"The amount of blood pooled in the cranial cavity is consistent with the blow to the head occurring first. Mr. Elwell's heart was pumping blood after he was struck in the head. If he had been shot first, causing the heart to stop beating, then the amount of blood pooled near the head wound would have been considerably less."

The prosecution next called Jasmina. I had seen very little of my secretary in the past few weeks. First she was running with Jangle; then I was running from the law. Her face looked more than a little careworn, as if she had aged a year in the course of a few weeks. I smiled when I saw her lug to the witness box the boombox that Jangle had given her, though in the cardboard box. Judge Coleman frowned when he noticed it.

"Why in God's name did you bring that thing to my court?"

"Your Honor, please don't take the Lord's Name..." Kazuo Olopai stood at the prosecutor's table until Marielle pulled him down by a sleeve. AG the AG just chuckled.

Jasmina answered the Judge. "The subpoena said to bring my new boombox."

Coleman glared at me, then Marielle. "Who subpoenaed a witness to bring a ghetto blaster to my court?"

"Mr. Drake Burnham." Jasmina pointed right at me, the second time in one day that a witness had identified me in court.

"Don't you dare bring that thing to the witness stand," said Maximum Max. "This is the Supreme Court, not the Blue Magic Night Club."

"But someone might steal it." Jasmina kept a hand on the box.

"Then give it to the bailiff to put in the evidence room for safekeeping until you're done testifying." Coleman turned to me. "I don't know what kind of stunt you hope to pull, Burnham. But I will brook no misdirection in my court."

When things calmed down, Jasmina was sworn in. She had never testified at a trial before, and Marielle actually handled her gently, a trait that I did not think Ms. Hargraves possessed. She walked Jasmina briefly through her personal and employment history. Jasmina's mother lives on Ebeye, in the Marshall Islands. Her father, who had passed on, was Pohnpeian, and he had gone to the Marshalls as a young man to help build the American missile base on Kwajalein. Although Jasmina was raised on Pohnpei, her mother insisted that she receive some education in the Marshalls, and she had gone to high school on Arno. Coleman's eyes perked up at that tidbit. All of this was interesting in an abstract way, but I knew it all anyway, and it seemed to have little bearing on the case. I let it go without objection.

Eventually, though, the prosecutor got around to asking Jasmina to authenticate the business books and records of Frost & Burnham. As I expected, Marielle had snatched them all the day after I chucked the handgun the Operator left me into the Green River. Marielle had showed up at my office at nine with a search warrant signed by Maximum Max and a posse of no fewer than four DSI agents. Roberta and I had already done most of the work separating the confidential material from the everyday stuff in anticipation of Kazuo Olopai's search warrant from the state court. But Marielle insisted on taking everything – my notes, copies of letters to and from clients, file memoranda – everything protected from discovery by the attorney-client privilege and the work product doctrine. I was ready to go down swinging on that one. Marielle stood her ground, and the DSI agents, one of whom looked to be itching to cuff a *menwhi*, backed her up.

It took a call to the Attorney General to untangle the standoff. I asked AG the AG if he remembered anything from his law school courses in legal ethics, and reminded him of my duty to protect client secrets. I threatened to take the matter directly to the appeals panel of the Supreme Court, and that not only would I win, the panel might say that the illegal search so tainted the prosecution of the criminal case that the charges against me would have to be dismissed. AG the AG just sighed and asked me to put Ms. Hargraves on the line. I could hear him mumble, although I couldn't quite catch what he said. Marielle then handed the phone to the lead DSI agent and he walked away with a blistered ear. Marielle walked away that morning with a Bekins box of my account books and non-privileged papers.

At trial, things were much calmer. Jasmina authenticated the firm's records. At Marielle's prompting, Jasmina said except for Jangle's contempt charge, nearly every other file had some entry for money received or payment in kind or a promise to pay.

"You testified before that you used to work for Algonquin Frost?" said Marielle.

"Yes, for six years." Jasmina made a sign of the cross. "May God rest his soul."

"And you now work for the defendant?"

"I think so." Jasmina twisted a frown at me in question.

"Did you have a strictly employer-employee relationship with Mr. Frost?"

Jasmina squirmed in the witness box before answering. "No."

"Did you date Mr. Frost?"

"Yes. Maybe one or three months. But it was a long time ago."

"Have you dated anyone else you work with?"

"No."

Good girl, I thought. We might be able to get out of this one yet.

"Has Mr. Burnham ever loaned you any money?"

"Yes, but I always pay him back. One time, when one auntie was sick in the Marshall Islands, Mr. Burnham bought me a plane ticket. I paid him back. It took a long time because I had to pay him ten or five dollars at a time. But I paid him."

"Does the defendant ever tell you that you don't have to pay him back?"

"No, well, yes. But only for small amounts. Like he will give me five dollars for coffee, but coffee only costs one dollar. Mr. Burnham always tells me to get something for myself when he does that, and he doesn't ask for his change back."

"But I thought Mr. Burnham was always looking for money. Don't the business records you identified for me earlier say that the firm is losing money?"

I considered objecting, but knowing I would be overruled, I let it slide.

"Mr. Burnham always asks Clarence 'where is the next dollar coming from?'"

"Asks Clarence?"

"Yes. Clarence Darrow. Mr. Frost had a picture on his wall."

Marielle paused as if deciding whether to inquire further about the mysterious Mr. Darrow. Instead, she went on a different tangent. "Did you know a person named Jangle Elwell?"

"Yes, but I only knew Jangle for a few weeks, just before he was killed."

"Did you date Mr. Elwell?"

Jasmina looked directly at me, her eyes a pair of squalls. "Yes."

"Did the defendant know that you were dating Mr. Elwell?"

"You mean did Mr. Burnham know? Yes, I think so."

"How did the defendant feel about your dating one of his clients?"

"Objection. The witness has no way to know another person's state of mind."

"Sustained," said Coleman. "You may rephrase the question, Miss Hargraves."

It was my turn to be surprised. Coleman had ruled in my favor.

Marielle took the chance to rephrase her question in the form of a dig. "Did the defendant ever say anything to you about your dating Mr. Elwell, one of his few clients?"

"Yes. Mr. Burnham told me to keep the office confidences secret, but I think he was concerned about more than that."

"What do you mean by saying you 'think he was concerned about more?'"

"It wasn't so much what he told me, but the way he said it, like he was scared or bothered that I was dating Jangle."

"What makes you say that?"

"Mr. Burnham is always asking who I am dating, when we go out, how long am I seeing this one or that one. He is acting like the American father to me."

"The 'American father?'"

"Yes. You know, like in the video. The American father always wants to know who his daughter is dating. The American father says 'you be home by ten o'clock.' Sometimes, Drake, I mean, Mr. Burnham, he talks to me like that."

"Is that why he disapproved of your going out with Mr. Elwell?"

"That's part of it. But I also think Mr. Burnham was jealous."

"Why do you say that?"

"Because I think that Mr. Burnham would like to date me himself. Before he was Mr. Frost's partner, when he was still working at the public defender office, Drake asked my cousin to ask me if I would meet him for a drink."

"That makes you think the defendant likes you in more than a fatherly way?"

"Yes."

"Does the defendant have a nickname for you?"

"Yes. He calls me 'Jazz.'"

"As in 'All That Jazz?'"

"Objection." This was going south faster than the Guam-to-Sydney Qantas flight. "Mischaracterization and lack of foundation."

"Overruled. The witness will answer the question."

Damn, Maximum Max would let in anything that smacked of sex.

Jasmina frowned, "I don't understand that question."

"Never mind. I'll withdraw the question." Marielle smiled at me over her shoulder, smiled like the feral cat that ate the last Micronesian canary on the endangered species list.

"Do you think your boss is in love with you?" Marielle was right back at it with hammer and tongs.

"Yes. But you know, it is not such a bad thing to have your boss in love with you." Jasmina nodded to the Attorney General, whom, were it possible for him to blush, would be glowing. He sunk a bit more behind the casebooks on the prosecutor's table.

Marielle stopped to review her notes, and closed her examination of Jasmina on that nadir.

I began my cross by trying to defuse the last, and what I considered to be the biggest bombshell.

"How long have we known each other, Jasmina?"

"I think it must be about three years."

"When I asked your cousin to ask you to meet me for a drink, did we ever have that drink?"

"No."

"Why not?"

"Because I did not want to."

"Did you tell your cousin to tell me?"

"Yes."

"Did you tell your cousin to tell me the reason why you would not meet me for a drink three years ago?"

"Yes. I told her to tell you that I do not date Americans."

"And ever since then, have you ever broken that rule?"

"No."

"Have any other Americans asked you for a date?"

"Yes, other Americans have asked. But they did not follow the custom like you did, Drake." Jasmina blessed me with a rare smile.

I paused to phrase the next question correctly, thinking that if Jasmina denied it, or didn't follow my meaning, that I would have to recall Utticus Uziah to tell whose zoris he saw on the stoop outside Jasmina's aunt's house when I was on Kosrae.

"My next question is a yes-or-no question. Please answer me; yes or no. Is there an American in the courtroom today, other than myself, who has asked you for a date?"

Jasmina scanned the entire courtroom, her eyes passing quickly over Spenser Ely, Bosworth Fields, and a couple of Congressional staff attorneys who stood in the back. Jasmina continued to turn until she reached the bench, her gaze lingered briefly on Judge Coleman. She caught my meaning and arched her eyebrows, "Yes."

"Watch out, Mr. Burnham." Coleman had his spectacles down on the bridge of his nose. "Continuing along this line of questioning is irrelevant."

"I think I've made my point, Your Honor." I turned back to Jasmina. "After I asked your cousin that one time, did we meet for a drink?"

"No."

"Have we ever met for a drink?"

"No."

"After that one time three years ago, did I ever ask you for a date?"

"No."

"Have you ever come to my place?"

"Only for office business."

"Have I ever come to your auntie's place, where you live?"

"Only for office business."

"Now let's talk about nicknames. What nickname do I call you?"

"Jazz."

"And what is the first syllable of your name?"

"Jas."

"Does anyone else call you by any other nicknames?"

Jasmina squirmed, then answered. "Yes. My cousin, Freddy, started calling me one very mean name. Now all my family calls me that."

"What does your family call you?"

"Typhoon." She practically spat it out.

"Do you know why they call you 'Typhoon?'"

"They say it is because of my temper."

"How long did you go out with Jangle Elwell?"

"Two or three weeks."

"You said you felt strongly about Jangle. Did Jangle feel strongly about you?" I felt like I had no choice but to jump right in, as if leaping into a jungle pool.

"Yes," Jasmina's eyes flashed. "Jangle said he was going to marry me."

Damn, didn't see that one coming. "But was Jangle seeing anyone else while he was dating you?"

"Yes." Jasmina bit her lip. "It was that Chuukese girl who lives in Sokehs, and one Kosraen girl at the College of Micronesia, and maybe two other women from Pohnpei. And also that American who was in the Peace Corps and stayed on."

Jackpot! I had hoped to uncover one other jealous lover. Jasmina named five, and those were just the ones she knew about. That Jangle really got around.

"Where were you the night that Jangle died?"

"At my cousin, Freddy's place in Kolonia. We watched videos."

"Is that the cousin that you sometimes argue with?"

"Freddy always wants to take my boombox, and he wants me to move back to the Marshall Islands with him. Freddy is off-island, now. He is on Kwajalein about a job."

"Did you see Jangle on the night he died?"

"No. Jangle said he had some important business to take care of that night."

"Did he say what the business was?"

"Jangle never told me what his business is."

"Do you know whether he was supposed to meet someone?"

"No. Jangle never told me about what he did or where he was going."

I switched gears, ready to shift back depending on the answer. "Have you ever fired a gun?"

"I've never even seen a real gun."

I switched back to the subject at hand, Jangle. "Did Jangle give you any gifts?"

"Yes. He gave me a new dress from Honolulu, and another one from Guam. He also gave me a boombox."

"Is that the one your cousin, Freddy, wants to borrow?"

"Yes."

"Is it the same boombox that you gave to the bailiff this morning?"

"Yes."

"Can you show us the boombox, please?"

Jasmina waved over the bailiff with a gesture that would do European royalty proud. She lifted the boombox out of the cardboard package, and held it up for all to see, and admire. It was a late-model radio-cassette-CD player, with a karaoke microphone, made in Japan. I was gratified to see that the plastic casing all the way around the boombox was intact. Jasmina did not hit Jangle with the boombox, as I had feared.

"Thank you, Jasmina. I'm glad that it wasn't you who struck Jangle Elwell in the head. Now I'm certain, but I knew it all along."

CHAPTER TWENTY-TWO

My trial for murder resumed at 10:30 on a rainy Tuesday morning after Judge Coleman finished off a brief civil calendar. The gallery was even more crowded than on the first day and Maximum Max spent a few minutes directing spectators to empty seats like a ballpark usher expecting a tip. Considering that I was charged with murdering my client, I felt confident. Day One had ended with the prosecution barely laying a glove on me, and I was sure the prosecutor had nothing up her sleeveless blouse. But Tuesday morning began on a sour note. Marielle subpoenaed Telecom to produce my office phone records. When I questioned the relevance, she argued that the log showed a call from my office to the Kosrae public defender office - where I said I could be reached - on the day the court had issued a warrant for my arrest. She suggested that someone had tipped me off. I had no answer for this, because it was true.

The government called Kazuo Olopai as the next witness. I was on my feet to object before Kazuo was on his.

"Mr. Olopai is not a percipient witness," I said. "He has no firsthand knowledge of the facts of this case, only what he has learned from others. His testimony is likely to be nothing more than his own speculation as to who killed Jangle Elwell. If you permit Mr. Olopai to testify, you allow the prosecution to pass off rhetoric as evidence and give Ms. Hargraves two chances to make her closing statement."

Coleman rubbed his hands before speaking.

"But Mr. Burnham haven't I given you the same opportunity? Every objection, every question in your cross-examination of government witnesses, each time you open your mouth is an opportunity to make your own closing statement. Since you represent yourself, it may be difficult to discern what is evidence and what is rhetoric. I've already given you considerable leeway, and I intend to offer the prosecutor the same courtesy. I will allow Mr. Olopai to testify. There is no jury, and I've sat on the bench long enough to know when to consider a witness's testimony, and when to disregard it. If I find any testimony objectionable, I will not consider it in my deliberations."

Coleman made that little 'disregard the objectionable' speech as if he had practiced it in front of a bathroom mirror. I knew it was nothing more than CYA; some coverage in case of appeal. Any judge on an appellate panel would have to defer to Coleman's discretion and Maximum Max said he was going to exercise it. It was a nice little rhetorical trap, and I had walked right into it.

Kazuo, who returned to form by wearing yet another flashy Aloha shirt, gave me barely a glance as he walked to the witness stand. I felt he was still unhappy about the turn of events that snatched his dream case from him, but that he would put his best face forward. Marielle began by asking if Kazuo knew me well.

"How long have you known the defendant?"

"It must be four or five years now. Drake was defending a conflict case here on Pohnpei when he was still the public defender on Kosrae."

"Do you consider the defendant to be a friend?"

"Well," Kazuo paused. "Yes, though we are adversaries at work, we are friendly. I used to respect Mr. Burnham. Maybe I still do."

Marielle and Kazuo then launched into a lengthy discussion regarding Kazuo's investigation into the homicide of Jangle Elwell, and concluded by asking that the Pohnpei State prosecutor be permitted to testify as an expert on the subject. I objected, of course, and my objection was overruled, of course.

"In your investigation, did you determine a motive for the defendant to kill the victim?" Marielle asked Kazuo.

"I had three theories. First was based on Mr. Burnham's friendship with Utticus Uziah. Mr. Uziah, as you know, testified that when he was working for the defendant, Jangle Elwell hit him in the face. When Utticus told him what happened, Mr. Burnham advised him not to report the offense to the police; that 'he would take care of it.' Now Mr. Burnham has an unfortunate habit of not reporting criminal offenses he learned about. One time he told me some of Jangle's friends had thrown stones at his house, but he didn't report it to the police. Later, Mr. Burnham said Jangle had stolen and killed his dog. Mr. Burnham did not report that to the police either."

"How many times has the defendant failed to report a crime?" Marielle asked.

"Objection." I was back on my feet. "The question calls for speculation by the witness. It's not in his knowledge. It's not in anyone's knowledge."

"Your Honor, the question is valid. It tends to show the defendant's propensity to take matters into his own hands."

"That's crazy," I continued. "Asking how many times someone didn't do something has no bearing on whether he did do something."

"Overruled," said Coleman. "As stated before, the court will disregard the objectionable. Please answer the question Mr. Olopai."

Kazuo's 'I don't know' calmed the kerfuffle.

Marielle shuffled through a few pages of her legal pad and turned to Kazuo. "What did you infer from learning about the incident between Mr. Uziah and the victim."

"I inferred from the incident involving Mr. Uziah that Mr. Burnham 'would take care of it' by confronting Mr. Elwell directly. Perhaps then the two argued, resulting in the death of Mr. Elwell. But sitting here at trial, I've had the chance to hear more of the evidence. Mr. Burnham might have tried to protect his client, Jangle Elwell, who was already charged with bank robbery and contempt of court."

"Your Honor," Marielle interrupted her own witness. "I move to strike the last portion of the witness's testimony as non-responsive."

I stumbled back to my feet. "Mr. Olopai is called by Madam Prosecutrix, and is qualified as an expert on her motion. If Ms. Hargraves doesn't like Kazuo's opinion, then she has no one but herself to blame but herself for asking for it."

"The day has just begun and already you're both snippy." Coleman said, and glancing at his wristwatch, found a way to rule against me. "In the interest of saving time, I admonish the witness to limit his answers to the questions asked."

Marielle turned back to Kazuo. "Did your investigation determine any other motives for the defendant to kill Jangle Elwell?"

"Yes. My second theory is based on Mr. Burnham's jealousy over the victim's personal relationship with Mr. Burnham's secretary,

Jasmina Solomon. I believe that the defendant was in love with her for a long time. In fact, I was told by Jasmina's cousin, Freddy Solomon, that Mr. Burnham recently planned to ask Jasmina to marry him."

"Objection. Hearsay. I move to strike the witness's last statement."

"Overruled," Coleman sighed. "Mr. Burnham, your cross of Jasmina Solomon yesterday afternoon established that Freddy Solomon is off-island, out of the country, and out of reach of subpoena. So I will permit the witness to testify about what Mr. Solomon told him. Go on."

Kazuo continued. "Freddy Solomon said Mr. Burnham intended to marry Jasmina Solomon. When Mr. Elwell began dating Ms. Solomon, Mr. Burnham was enraged with jealousy, which, as you know, is one of our seven deadly sins. Mr. Burnham and Mr. Elwell argued over Jasmina, and the victim was killed."

Marielle let that one sink in, and for a moment the only sound was the steady beat of rain on the courthouse roof. She prompted Kazuo. "You had three theories?"

"Yes. I also know Mr. Burnham needs money. The Frost & Burnham law firm finances are in a sorry state, and even in the good times, Drake doesn't make a lot of money. The defendant has to make very strong efforts to collect his fees, like when he defended Jangle Elwell in a charge of contempt of court. But Mr. Elwell also fed cases to Mr. Burnham, including a personal injury case I defended for Pohnpei state. I was ready to settle that case, which would make money for him. But Jangle convinced that person to take his case away from Drake and go to another lawyer. Drake also told me Jangle had sent him a land case, but that it didn't 'pan out.' I inferred that Mr. Burnham, concerned about his finances, argued with Mr. Elwell, and that the victim was then killed."

"Do you think any one motive was primary?" Marielle asked.

"No. But why after I asked Mr. Burnham did he run away to Chuuk? And I still don't know how he got from Kosrae to Chuuk without stopping on Pohnpei."

"Have you considered whether a combination of these motives may have compelled the defendant to act?" Marielle led Kazuo like a *nina* leading a child to school. Knowing how Coleman would rule, I did not object.

"Yes, and I believe this is the strongest inference," Kazuo answered. "Perhaps Mr. Burnham met the victim to discuss finances. Maybe Drake and the victim argued about money, about Utticus Uziah and about Jasmina. Then the victim was killed."

It was nearly noon when I began to cross-examine Kazuo. "Mr. Olopai, did you actually see Jangle strike Utticus Uziah?"

"No."

"Did you hear me tell Utticus not to report his scuffle with Jangle to the police?"

"No."

"Then how did you learn about it?"

"By speaking with Mr. Uziah."

"Were you there four years ago when I asked Jasmina's cousin to ask Jasmina if she would meet me for a drink?"

"No."

"How did you learn about that incident?"

"By talking with Ms. Solomon."

"Did you hear Jangle Elwell tell Charlie Warheit he should take his personal injury case from my office and take it to Dick Harkness?"

"No."

"So how did you learn about that?"

"By speaking with Mr. Harkness."

"Did you examine my account books and business records to form your own opinion regarding the profitability of Frost & Burnham?"

"No. Ms. Hargraves and the Attorney General's office grabbed this case before I looked at any of your business records."

"Then how did you learn that the Frost & Burnham finances are 'in a sorry state,' to use your words, words that echo Ms. Hargraves's opening statement."

"By speaking with Ms. Hargraves."

"Do you have any firsthand knowledge regarding the profitability of my firm?"

"Just what I see, like, that many times you come to the State Court on Thursday mornings to try to get conflict assignments."

"And you therefore assume that I need these cases to get by, you assume that the firm is not profitable?"

"Yes, although I prefer to say 'infer' instead of 'assume.'"

"Is the term 'infer' something that you discussed with Ms. Hargraves as well?"

"Objection," Marielle chimed in, correctly for once. "Argumentative."

"Sustained," Coleman ruled glaring at me.

I returned to Kazuo. "In fact, your entire testimony today, every word, is nothing more than speculation, hypothesis, theory, conjecture, concocted in discussions with Ms. Hargraves?"

"Objection. Argumentative." Marielle was on her feet again. "Your Honor, defense counsel sounds as if he is reading from a thesaurus."

"Sustained." Coleman emphasized the second syllable.

No surprise there, so I turned back to Kazuo. "Mr. Olopai, have I ever made up a nickname for you?"

"Yes." Kazuo puckered up as if he had bitten an under-ripe soursop. "You call me 'Skipjack,' that's American for Katsuo, the big-eye tuna, because of my first name and because my eyeglasses."

I stopped there, not exactly having devastated the witness, but I thought having made my points. Despite Coleman's letting in everything but the kitchen sink, I actually felt pretty confident. All the prosecution had done was to attribute to me some possible motives, and some pretty flimsy ones at that. So far it was the slimmest murder case that I'd ever been involved in. I've gotten a more thoroughly investigated traffic citation; of course that was in Singapore.

Coleman asked the prosecutor whom she would call after the lunch recess as the next witness.

"After he arrives on the island-hopper from Kosrae, the government will call the Kosrae Chief of Police, P. Robert Gerber."

I spent my lunch hour at the Palikir canteen pondering what the hell Rob Gerber would have to say about the murder of Jangle Elwell, other than he was in favor of it. Marielle had not subpoenaed Gerber, so his name came as a surprise, a lot like the one I hoped to spring by calling Jingle Treadwell. There was a delay when trial resumed as we waited for the witness to come to Palikir from the airport and the noon flight from Kosrae. Marielle filled time between testimony by moving various documents into evidence – without my objection – like a pro. For the second time in my trial, I admitted some grudging respect for the fair Ms. Hargraves. She must have boned up on criminal procedure at some point. Finally, one of the DSI agents leaned forward to whisper to AG the AG, who turned to whisper to Marielle. She stood to call P. Robert Gerber.

The Kosrae Chief of Police stood in the back row of the gallery and came forward slowly, his upper back curved into his trademark ascent-of-man slouch. The morning's rain had slowed to a steady drizzle, and even chicken shit mountain was invisible behind a gloomy shroud of clouds. Susanna swore in Gerber and Marielle introduced him to the court.

"Are you involved in law enforcement?" she began.

"Affirmative. I'm the Chief of Police for the State of Kosrae."

"And how long have you worked on Kosrae?"

"Twenty-three months now, although I've lived on Kosrae longer than that."

"Have you had other law enforcement experience?"

"I have nearly two decades in law enforcement, both in the United States and here in Micronesia. I began with the military police while serving my country in the U.S. Army, on the mainland and in Hawaii. I was promoted to corporal and served one term of base security on Johnston Island. After I earned my stripes and was promoted to staff sergeant, I served in base security for two years on Kwajalein. After that stint, I received an honorable discharge from the military and went back to the mainland. I worked as a deputy investigator for the Los Angeles County Sheriff's Department for almost seven years, but I wanted to return to the islands. I accepted a position as security consultant to Air Marshall Islands, and I worked in Majuro for three years. Then two years ago, I applied for and was given the position of Chief of Police on Kosrae."

"Chief Gerber, you must have had a considerable amount of law enforcement training in your twenty years on the job."

"Not only have I been trained, I have put on training sessions for my police force on Kosrae, for the air marshals on Air Marshall Islands, as well as for other enlisted personnel on Johnston Island and on Kwajalein. I have been trained and have given training in all phases of criminal law enforcement, including investigation, arrest, search and seizure, interrogation, incarceration, and so forth."

"Have you ever heard of a man named Jangle Elwell?"

"Affirmative. I don't think there's anyone in the law enforcement community here who doesn't know about Jangle Elwell."

"Had you heard about Mr. Elwell's death?"

"Yes."

"Were you asked to assist in the investigation of Jangle Elwell's murder?"

"Not initially, as the offense took place outside of my jurisdiction. But three weeks ago Sunday, I received a telephone call from my local counterpart on the Pohnpei police, informing me that an arrest warrant had issued for a suspect in the murder of Jangle Elwell, and that Pohnpei Public Safety was informed and believed the suspect was then on the island of Kosrae."

"Did you learn the identity of the suspect?"

"Affirmative. It was Drake Burnham, the defendant in this case."

"Had you seen the defendant on Kosrae at that time?"

"As a matter of fact, I had. I actually had a couple of beers with him." Gerber nodded in my direction. "He's a pretty cool cucumber, if you ask me."

"Did Pohnpei ask you to arrest the defendant, or hold him for extradition?"

"Negative. Pohnpei Public Safety initially inquired whether Mr. Burnham was still on-island. As I understood it, Mr. Burnham was scheduled to return to Pohnpei on the Saturday flight, but that Pohnpei Public Safety couldn't find him. They weren't sure whether he was on Kosrae, Pohnpei, or had left to go somewhere else. We were asked to assure that he didn't board a Honolulu or Nauru-bound flight, and to keep an eye on fishing boats, freighters, and cruising sailors. So we looked into that. It being a Sunday on Kosrae, it didn't take very long. Air Mike confirmed that Mr. Burnham had a return reservation to Pohnpei on Tuesday's flight. No ship was in the harbor or scheduled to arrive for at least a week. After questioning the only cruising sailor then on-island, we concluded he wasn't going anywhere soon."

"Did you locate the defendant on Kosrae?"

"Negative. I knew that Mr. Burnham was staying at the house of another American, Shaw Taylor, who is the current public defender on Kosrae, and who was then off-island. When we could not locate the defendant anywhere on island, I proceeded to the house where Mr. Burnham was staying. I was concerned he may have had an accident or was injured in some way because no one answered my knocks. However, the door was unlocked, and I was able to step inside."

I pinched myself. Shaw's door was locked, I knew it. No way would I leave an *ahset's* door unlocked, not even the public defender's.

Marielle continued. "Were you accompanied by any other police officers when you went to this house?"

"Negative. It being Sunday morning, I decided to investigate by myself. Most of my officers were at church."

"Was the defendant inside the house?"

"No. But in one bedroom I found a suitcase and a small paper bag. When I picked up the suitcase to ascertain whether it belonged to Mr. Burnham, the bed bounced and the paper bag fell onto the floor. Inside the bag was a gift-wrapped package. The gift-wrapping tore open when the bag fell from the bed and I could see that it contained a small box. I could also see the contents of the box. Because the box appeared to contain contraband, I decided to open it further. I did so, and discovered the contraband."

"And what was the contraband?"

"A snub-nosed .38 caliber Colt police special revolver."

I felt as if I had been punched square in the gut. All my breath left me, my muscles went limp as a rubber chicken, and a lump the size of Sokehs Rock filled my throat. Marielle's next question was drowned by the blood roaring in my ears. The impossible had happened. Gerber had put a .38 special – the same caliber weapon used to kill Jangle Elwell – into my hands.

I looked up. Marielle had paused in her questioning and was paging through her trial book. Gerber stared at me; Coleman, too, the judge with a half-grin creasing his face. Voices in the gallery murmured a slow rumble that grew behind me like distant thunder. Coleman let the rumble pass and then called the courtroom to order without resorting to the taro pounder. In another moment, Marielle was standing before me at the defense table. She held a ziplock evidence bag inside of which was a pistol.

"Counsel?"

I nodded. There was nothing else that I could do at that moment. Marielle showed the weapon to Gerber, who identified it as the weapon he had taken from the bedroom in Shaw Taylor's Kosrae house. Marielle then stopped.

"Any cross-examination by the defense?" Coleman asked.

I said nothing. My mind was blank.

"Mr. Burnham. Will you be questioning Chief Gerber?"

I slouched deeper into my chair, daring not to even make eye contact with Coleman.

"Mr. Burnham, the witness is waiting."

I stood, cleared my throat, and managed to choke out. "In light of the surprise nature of this witness's testimony, I hereby request that the trial be recessed until tomorrow morning to prepare for cross-examination."

Then it was Coleman's turn to surprise me.

"Granted. We are in recess until 10:00 a.m."

CHAPTER TWENTY-THREE

After Coleman left the courtroom, I collapsed into my chair, feeling as if I had neither bone nor muscle left in my body. Pulling out Gerber to link me to one of the murder weapons laid me flat, and it was Marielle Hargraves – whom couldn't litigate her way out of a lunch bag – who had sandbagged me. I was incapable of any thought beyond my spending the next two decades in the Pohnpei jail. My notes meant nothing; all strategy and tactics drew a blank, leading to one irreducible conclusion. Although I felt like I would at any moment, I couldn't even muster up the energy to weep.

Marielle left the courtroom without giving me a glance. I could hear others in the gallery whispering, then speaking more loudly as they left the courtroom. Out of the corner of my eye, I saw Mario Perez still in his white lab coat, walking towards the wide double doors and shaking his head. My grand strategy of playing to the cheap seats had gone down the tubes. Coleman was against me. Hargraves was against me. And now, the public had to be against me, too.

When the gallery was almost empty, Roberta and Spenser Ely whispered to me from the first row behind the defense table.

"Drake, Drake," Roberta whispered. "Come on, snap out of it."

"They may have given you a body blow, boy," Spenser said, a little East Texas twang coming through. "But you can take it and prove them wrong."

I didn't stir. My mind was spinning through all of Kubler-Ross's stages of grief, all save acceptance.

"Come on, son," said Spenser. "We know you didn't do it. Proving that you didn't is just harder than you thought, that's all."

"It's still just circumstantial, Drake. There's no direct evidence against you."

I sat stone still and stared at the pad on the table in front of me.

"Drake," said Roberta. "You got to attack this Gerber. His name sounds so familiar to me, especially since he claims to be an ex-LA County sheriff. I do know his cock-and-bull story about the package falling off the bed and coming open is completely unbelievable. He made a warrantless search when he could have just gone to a judge and asked for a warrant. You know he cuts corners, you just have to show it."

I said nothing, but turned slowly in my chair.

"You have got to get back in the game, Burnham," Spenser said. "Or these old boys are going to eat your lunch, today, and every day for the next twenty years."

I turned and stood, grasping the bar to steady my quivering knees. I gazed about the empty courtroom, then focused in on the only allies I had left, Roberta and Spenser.

"You're right. You're both right. Right as rain," I said, my voice gaining strength as I reasoned through the surprise. "Gerber doesn't have a corroborating witness. No other cop was with him. He said he went into the house alone. And that package was so well wrapped, like an origami paper folder had wrapped it. It wouldn't just fall open. Ahh Coleman will let it in, though. It won't matter in the end."

"But you have to put it on the record for an appeal," said Roberta. "It's fruit of a poisonous tree. Gerber made an illegal search. All evidence developed from that search is inadmissible."

"Let me think." I grabbed a pad and scribbled some notes. "Roberta, I need you to subpoena Absalom Absalom. He was there at the airport when Dick Harkness found out that his Chinese client, Aang, had left that gift-wrapped package when he boarded the plane. Absalom can testify he and Harkness asked me to take the package to Aang on the plane. I don't know where he lives, but he works at Air Mike."

"We'll find him," said Roberta. "If Utticus doesn't know where he lives, Cicero or Atticus will. What else?"

"Let's see," I turned my chair and sat facing Roberta and Spenser across the bar. "When I met him on Kosrae, Gerber said public safety was holding some firearms smuggled onto the island. We could subpoena the desk sergeant to produce records of all weapons seized in the last six months."

"Maybe that will turn up a .38," Roberta smiled. "While I'm at it, we could subpoena the time cards for officers on duty the day that Gerber said he found the gun."

"Good thought," I said. "I'll have to ask the court reporter if I can listen to Gerber's testimony on tape. Spenser, can you go over to the Attorney General's office and tell Hargraves that I'll listen to this afternoon's proceedings? Marielle has the right to be there, and she'll probably want to, considering what her witness had to say."

"Can do, Drake."

"Speaking of witnesses, how's Jingle?"

"R.K. Asher flew in from Chuuk on Sunday night, and met with Jingle all day, yesterday," said Roberta. "And he came to pick him up again this morning. He said Jingle will be ready when you are."

"Good. Well, that's one thing that I can be certain of. I just hope that Jingle will knock the zoris off everyone in the courtroom, and better than Gerber did today."

Sleep is a precious commodity when in trial. There's always so much to do and so little time. When trying a case, I have so much on my mind that any sleep I manage to snatch is anxious, irritable. And the night after Gerber testified was no exception. I had stayed at the courthouse until at least ten o'clock, listening carefully to Gerber's taped testimony, taking notes for the next day's cross-examination of the witness who put a murder weapon in my hands. Poor Susanna, the court reporter, stayed with me the entire time; playing the tape, rewinding, and playing portions again whenever I asked. Marielle stayed for the first two hours, then left a senior DSI investigator to monitor me. That was just as well. I didn't want to tip my hand too much on just what I had planned for Gerber come the dawn.

I finished with a pad full of notes that I had to condense into a meaningful outline to question Gerber. I went back to the office, and found a note from Roberta taped to a foil-wrapped supper. She had faxed a records subpoena to Kosrae for the evidence list and time cards. Kosrae Public Safety would fax a reply in the morning and send the originals demanded on the next flight. Roberta also noted that Utticus had found and subpoenaed Absalom Absalom, who would be in court at nine. Then she mentioned that she was following up on a few leads of her own, but that she wouldn't tell me in case she was wrong, or if the leads had dried up. I ate my dinner over my notes, then went home to toss and turn a few hours of fitful sleep. True to form, I didn't sleep long, and greeted the sunrise sitting outside behind the house in the *nahs*.

I was at the Supreme Court by half past nine, tired but ready to do battle with Gerber. Roberta and Spenser showed up fifteen minutes later. Both were all smiles as Roberta handed me a fax. I smiled, too. When trial resumed promptly at ten, I went to work on Gerber.

"The incidence of reported property crime on Kosrae is up, is it not?" I began.

"Affirmative. Reported property crime is up eighteen percent in the last year alone. It was also up a similar percentage the year before." Gerber leaned back in his chair, as if confident in his command of facts and figures on local crime.

"And typically, who are the victims of property crimes on Kosrae?"

"Well, it could be anyone. Locals certainly suffer property offenses more frequently, but Americans are far from immune. Since *ahsets* generally have more material possessions to begin with, they're disproportionately the targets of such crimes."

"Do you advise people on how to avoid or prevent property crimes?"

"Of course. We have radio spots in both English and Kosraen, advising people to latch their windows and lock their doors whenever they leave the house."

"Is locking the door enough? Couldn't a determined sneak thief slip a machete in between the door and the frame and pop the lock?"

"Well, sure. But property offenses are typically crimes of opportunity. If a door is locked, most burglars will move on to another, easier target."

"In light of that, don't you think it unusual that Shaw Taylor's house would be unlocked, as you say it was on the Sunday morning you found the package?"

"I wouldn't say unusual, no. Maybe imprudent."

"Imprudent, but on whose part?"

"Objection. Mischaracterization." Marielle seemed determined to embellish her newly won reputation for competence.

"I'll withdraw the question." I spoke, perhaps imprudently, before Judge Coleman could rule on the objection. "Speaking of crime statistics, has the number of false arrests on Kosrae increased over the past, say, two years?"

I expected an objection that my question was argumentative, but Marielle said nothing. Of course, my question was argumentative, but it was a no-risk venture for me. Gerber could have no good answer for it. If false arrests were up, it reflected poorly on his department. If he said false arrests were down or flat, it was a tacit admission that false arrests took place.

Gerber leaned forward to grumble. "I don't keep track of that."

I moved on to question the search and seizure. "How long did it take you to drive from Tofol to Shaw Taylor's house?"

"Probably twenty minutes. Maybe fifteen on a Sunday morning."

"And where was that bag with the gift-wrapped package when you entered Shaw Taylor's house."

"I believe I testified it was on the bed next to a suitcase." Gerber paused, then smiled and added, "Your suitcase as a matter of fact."

"Are you sure the bag with the gift-wrapped package wasn't sitting on the floor next to the bed? Because if it was there, the bag couldn't very well fall off the bed and partially open, could it?"

"Negative. It was on the bed when I entered the bedroom. It fell to the floor when the bed bounced as I examined the luggage tag on your suitcase."

"What kind of bed does Mr. Taylor own? Mattress and box springs?"

"No. It looked to be your basic college dorm room futon."

"Pretty smart for the tropics, huh? Something light, easy to air out every so often."

"I guess so."

"Not a lot of bounce on a futon, is there."

"I really wouldn't know. Maybe you should ask Mrs. Taylor." Gerber grinned as if anticipating a chuckle from the gallery. A smile danced at the corners of Judge Coleman's lips and he abruptly coughed to hide it. The gallery remained quiet.

I pressed on. "How many police officers are there on Kosrae?"

"Twenty-three. Four shifts of four patrol officers each, four desk sergeants, who also serve as jailers, and two investigators, plus myself."

"So on any given shift, there will be a minimum of four patrol officers on duty."

"That's correct, though with illness or family obligations the numbers may vary."

"But four patrol officers are not the maximum for any given shift."

"Affirmative, sir. We run double shifts on Payday Fridays, and around Liberation Day and New Year's. Investigators are also on telephone stand-by, twenty-four seven."

"When you say that on that Sunday morning when you searched Mr. Taylor's house, you believed most of your officers were at church, it would have been more accurate to say that most of your off-duty police officers were at church."

Gerber hesitated, then said. "That's correct."

"And it being a Sunday morning, wasn't it likely Mr. Taylor's local neighbors were also at church."

"I have no way of knowing that."

"You have a police band radio in your vehicle?"

"I do. All police vehicles now do. Improving communication among police patrols was one of my priorities when I came on to Kosrae as Chief of Police."

"So you can always call for back up."

"Of course."

"Is a lot of crime committed on Sunday mornings on Kosrae?"

"I haven't broken down incidents into days or times." Gerber shifted in his seat. It was my second time to question his vaunted, but far from comprehensive statistical analyses.

"Reason with me, then," I continued. "Between church services on the most religious island in the South Pacific, and the hangovers suffered by the rest, is there a lot of crime committed, or even reported on Sunday mornings on Kosrae?"

"Likely not," Gerber admitted.

"So even though you had a minimum of four patrol officers on duty, plus two investigators on call, any of whom you could have called to assist you, on a Sunday morning when they were unlikely to be busy on other calls, you still decided to enter Shaw Taylor's house alone. There's no one else who can corroborate your testimony."

"I don't know if six officers were available. It was a Sunday morning and many could be at church."

"But we can always check the time clock and records to determine exactly how many officers were on duty that morning, couldn't we? And we could check the radio log to see if there was a sudden spike in offenses reported that morning, couldn't we?"

Gerber looked to the prosecutor's table. Marielle had her head down scribbling notes and AG the AG had turned back to one of his DSI agents. Gerber glanced up at the bench, where Coleman doled out mercy like Mr. Bumble ladled out extra bowls of gruel.

"All right Mr. Burnham," Coleman said. "You made your point."

"I have a question pending, Your Honor," I turned to Gerber. "And no response from the witness. We could check both those records, couldn't we Mr. Gerber?"

"Yeah, you could check them if you want."

"Judge Abraham and Judge George were both on-island on Kosrae that Sunday?"

"Yes, I believe they were."

"But you didn't apply to either judge for a search warrant, did you?"

"I determined that no search warrant was necessary. The bag contained contraband." Gerber stressed the final word.

"But you testified yesterday that you were informed from Pohnpei that an arrest warrant had issued."

321

"Affirmative."

"And that a suspect, thought to be on Kosrae, was wanted for murder."

"Affirmative."

"And that you could not locate the suspect elsewhere on-island."

"Affirmative. I couldn't find you."

"But you 'determined,' by yourself, that no search warrant was needed to search the last known locale of a person wanted for a category-one felony despite the fact that you could have called a patrol officer or an investigator to secure the house, while you could go to either of two judges whom you knew to be on-island, to ask for a warrant."

Gerber paused, then grumbled, "Affirmative."

"Oh, by the way, was there anything else in the bag that contained the gift-wrapped package that you determined you could search without a warrant?"

"No; wait a minute. Yes, affirmative. There was a greeting card in an envelope."

"Did you open the envelope as well?"

"I did. There was a greeting card with a message written in some oriental language."

"Did you bring the greeting card with you?"

"I determined that it wasn't necessary."

"Your Honor," I turned to Judge Coleman. "I request an order that the witness produce the greeting card and envelope. That may give a better indication of who the package belonged to, better than the witness's speculation."

Coleman sighed. "So ordered. Chief Gerber, call your police force and have them courier the greeting card and envelope you found here to Pohnpei on the next flight. You can do it during our recess, which we will take now."

Judge Coleman may have given the witness time to regroup, but I had another round in my chamber, so to speak. P. Robert Gerber looked more confident when court was back in session. He may have thought I had him on the ropes before. But Roberta, bless her heart, had come up with the coup de grace, by making a phone call to a former colleague who made a call to a friend at the Los Angeles Times archives. Roberta had given me a copy of a clean fax she had gotten in reply.

"I knew I recognized his name from somewhere," she whispered.

I started on it by attacking Gerber's credibility. "Earlier this morning you said you don't keep track of false arrests by Kosrae Public Safety."

"That's correct."

"What about you personally? Have you ever been accused of false arrest?"

"I don't know what you're driving at, Burnham." Gerber growled.

"I agree," Coleman piped in. "Mr. Burnham, you had better be able to demonstrate the relevance of this line of questioning fairly quickly."

"Objection," Marielle called too late. "Relevance."

"I am permitted to question the credibility and reliability of this witness, Your Honor. If the Court requires documentation to impeach Mr. Gerber beforehand, I'll need time to serve a subpoena outside the country, which can take several days at a minimum."

I had Coleman there. Maximum Max wanted to move the case along, but he had to give me time to subpoena documents to question a surprise witness.

"Alright, then. I will permit you to continue on this line for no more than twelve questions."

"Mr. Gerber," I turned back to the man-ape in the witness box. "Have you ever been accused of false arrest?"

Gerber set his jaw to parallel the straight line of his eyebrows. "I don't recall."

"Let me refresh your recollection. Didn't you, while serving on Kwajalein, bust to the brig a tourist who mistakenly deplaned on Kwaj Rock, thinking it was Kosrae?"

"I don't remember the details."

"And when you were a security consultant to Air Marshall Islands, didn't you commandeer a Marshall Islands frigate to chase down and haul-to a Portuguese purse seiner thinking it was a Soviet spy trawler monitoring Kwajalein?"

"The Soviets had spy trawlers all around Kwaj," Gerber protested. "That was a legitimate security concern."

"What was the month and year in which you commandeered the frigate?"

"November 1993."

"And when did the Soviet Union collapse?"

"1991."

"Defense counsel should note that it's six questions so far," Coleman rumbled.

I startled Gerber with a hammer blow. "Have you ever been convicted of a felony?"

"I beg your pardon."

"It's a simple question. Have you ever been convicted of a felony?"

"I don't know what you're fishing for, Burnham, but no. Never. I have not been convicted of a felony."

"Not at any time?"

"Not ever."

"And you testified on direct examination that you left the Los Angeles County Sheriff's Department because you missed the islands. But that isn't entirely true, is it?"

"It is true. I left the LA County Sheriff and went directly to work in the Marshall Islands."

"Did you leave the Los Angeles County Sheriff's Department voluntarily, or were you fired?"

"I can state categorically that I left voluntarily."

"And you said just now that you were not convicted of a felony."

"That's one hundred percent true."

"Have you ever been accused of a felony?"

"Objection." Marielle struggled to stand a little lopsided. I glanced beneath the prosecutor's table to see she had one shoe on and one shoe off. It took Marielle a moment to figure out both the grounds for her objection and the location of her other shoe. "Relevance."

"Your Honor, this all goes to the credibility of this witness. The Court needs to determine whether it can rely upon the truthfulness of Mr. Gerber's testimony."

Coleman sustained the objection. "You are well past your allotted questions and you're again getting close to character assassination, Mr. Burnham. And in that regard at least, you have demonstrated your aim is true."

I stared at Coleman – the bastard. Maximum Max stared right back for a long moment, until he looked away.

I turned back to Gerber to attack his credibility in a different way. "What does the letter 'P' in your name stand for?"

"It's a family name. I never use it. I've been 'Rob' since I was a kid."

"But what does it stand for?"

"It doesn't matter."

"What does the letter 'P' in your name stand for?"

"Oh, what the hell. Prescott. It stands for 'Prescott.'"

"And Prescott Robert Gerber, you worked at the Los Angeles County Sheriff's Department for how many years?"

"Seven."

"You must have testified in court dozens of times, Prescott Gerber."

"It was probably more than a hundred."

"Has the accuracy of your testimony while working for the Los Angeles County Sheriff's Department ever been questioned, Prescott R. Gerber?"

"I don't know what you're driving at."

"Your Honor, I'd like to approach the witness with a document in an attempt to refresh his recollection."

Coleman told me to show the prosecutor the document first. It was the fax that Roberta had received from her buddy at the Los Angles Times, a page 18 clipping reporting on a plea bargain in a case from seven years ago. Marielle scanned the copy quickly and whispered "*merde.*"

I showed Gerber the clipping. "Are you the Prescott R. Gerber referred to in this newspaper clipping?"

It was Gerber's turn to jump to his feet. "You son of a bitch. Where the hell did you come up with this?"

"Mr. Gerber I'm not here to answer your questions. Are you the former Los Angeles County Sheriff's Department deputy investigator Prescott R. Gerber who is the subject of this newspaper clipping?"

"You bastard. You murdering bastard. You whack one of your clients and then come waving some trumped up charges at me. To hell with you." Gerber waved the copy of the newspaper clipping at me. "To hell with you."

"You still have yet to answer my question. Are you the Prescott R. Gerber who pleaded guilty to obstruction of justice in order to cop a plea on a charge of perjury?"

"The newspaper clipping is wrong; dead wrong. I didn't plead guilty." Gerber fell back into his chair. "My lawyer, that bastard of a lawyer. You're all bastards, every last one of you. My lawyer convinced me to plead nolo contendere to obstruction of justice. Then the District Attorney would drop the perjury charge and I would get probation instead of jail time."

"I have no further questions. Thank you, Mr. Gerber."

"'Thank you?' You ruin me, probably cost me my job, and that's all you say?"

Coleman, of all people, came to my rescue. "The witness is dismissed. Mr. Gerber, the bailiff will escort you from the courtroom."

Pietro walked on my side of the aisle, between Gerber and me, and held Gerber's arm tightly as he walked him from the witness box. Gerber's eyes shot daggers at me as he passed. Coleman called a recess.

CHAPTER TWENTY-FOUR

It was ten in the morning on the fourth day of trial, the moment I'd been waiting for. The prosecution had closed its case Wednesday afternoon, after I had (hopefully) devastated its surprise witness, Prescott Robert Gerber, in cross-examination. The remainder of the government case against me was testimony by several police officers and DSI agents on the chain of custody of the physical evidence, my business books and records, and that gun that Gerber had tried to put in my hands. Marielle Hargraves rested about halfway through the afternoon.

I had begun the defense case with a simple opening statement emphasizing credibility. My first witness was Absalom Absalom, the Kosrean who worked security for Air Mike at the Pohnpei airport. Absalom testified consistently with what I had remembered, that he had seen Mr. Aang with the paper bag containing a gift-wrapped package, which he did not search due to diplomatic immunity. Absalom said he and Dick Harkness noticed that Mr. Aang had left the package in the departure lounge, and had asked me to hand the bag to Aang on board the plane. As the kicker, Absalom testified that after I agreed and boarded the plane, he had checked the passenger manifests only to see that Aang was on the westbound airplane for Guam, while I was on the one flying east to Kosrae. That, I hoped, explained how through a good deed I came into possession of a handgun that may have killed my client.

I thought the courtroom had been packed for the first three days of trial, but it was standing room only on the fourth. Spectators wedged in behind the tiers of chairs in the gallery and still more stood outside and peered through the louvers like village children peeking in the windows of an expat's house on movie night. The gallery crowd was more than bored locals and courthouse junkies. Staff attorneys from Congress and Attorney General's office and office workers from elsewhere in Palikir stole a few minutes to check on what was happening. I even saw a few Senators. I don't mind a crowd. I had nearly lost it with Gerber's Tuesday testimony, and I could only hope I had brought public sentiment back to the realm of doubt with my cross-examination. I wanted to swing it all the way on my fourth day. The number of people packed into the courthouse raised the room temperature to that of a sweat lodge, and I resorted frequently, ala Clarence Darrow, to a handkerchief to mop my brow. Too bad I couldn't cultivate that trade wind-cooled Steve McGarrett look.

For the second defense witness, I would – like Perry Mason – spring a surprise whose testimony would cast the scales from everyone's eyes. Judge Coleman settled into his chair at ten, cleared his throat and told me to call my next witness.

"The defense calls," I paused for effect. "Mr. Jingle Treadwell."

No one stirred, although heads turned to gaze about the gallery and back to the double doors at the rear of the courtroom.

"Mr. Jingle Treadwell," I repeated, louder than at first.

No one stood. No papers rustled. Those heads that had swung back to the doors pivoted back to me.

"Mr. Jingle Treadwell?" I suddenly felt like the announcer calling for the Family Von Trapp in "The Sound of Music" after they had flown the coop to Switzerland. Then I turned to Roberta and Spenser Ely, seated in the first row behind the bar, to ask where the hell was Jingle.

"Beats me," said Spenser. "R.K. picked him up at dawn."

Daybreak was four hours earlier. My "Sound of Music" image was interrupted by one of Reddy and Jingle mangled in a horrible auto accident on their way to court.

"Mr. Burnham, where, pray tell, is your next witness?" Judge Coleman sounded the very model of decorum.

"Frankly, Your Honor, I don't know. I do know my witness met with his attorney this morning, and they had agreed with me to be here in court at ten."

"Oh, we have been down this road before. I warned you not to play games. I warned you repeatedly that this trial would proceed in an orderly fashion. Yet again you have chosen to ignore both the spirit and letter of my orders."

"With all due respect, sir, I'm the one with my butt on the line," I said. "And I'm the one who has the right to compulsory process of witnesses."

"Your Honor, if I may," Marielle Hargraves, who that morning sat only with Kazuo Olopai at the prosecutor's table, arose to address the court. "I've reviewed the file. The defendant has no witness by that name under subpoena."

"Well, Mr. Burnham?"

"While it's true I didn't subpoena Mr. Treadwell, I do have an agreement with him and his attorney." My strategic decision to keep Jingle a surprise was looking more like strategic error.

"Your constitutional rights," Coleman enunciated each syllable as if lecturing a second-grader, "aren't worth a plugged nickel if you make no effort to protect them."

"Judge, you could issue a bench warrant that would have the same force and effect as a subpoena. That is if the Court would indulge me just this one time."

"Indulge you? I've doled out more indulgences than a Renaissance Pope. The way you've run your defense makes me feel as if I have done nothing but indulge you. No more. There are consequences to playing games. I am therefore ready to hold you in contempt."

Coleman grabbed his taro pounder gavel and raised it.

At that moment, the double doors at the rear of the courtroom swung open. Five men entered. First was R.K. Asher, like the U.S. Cavalry appearing in the nick of time. Next to R.K. was Jingle, dressed like he had just come back from a Honolulu haberdashery and looking for all the world like his deceased brother, Jangle. Behind them were two sweating Americans, looking uncomfortably overdressed in suits and ties. Bringing up the rear was AG the AG.

Jingle strode briskly up the aisle; his face forward, his features tense. He looked nervous, but then it couldn't be easy to walk into a crowded room and just at the sight of you have grown men blanche, women flush, and children hide. The gallery hushed as Jingle passed. Coleman gaped at him like a Napoleon wrasse and Marielle stared wide-eyed, without blinking, like a moray eel. The courtroom was dead silent by the time R.K. and Jingle reached the bar. I glanced back at Roberta and Spenser who beamed at me.

The gallery gave a collective gasp then rumbled with whispered comment.

"Impossible."

"How can this be?"

"He looks just like ..."

Jasmina Solomon stood and peered at Jingle closely, then spoke, her voice cleaving cleanly through the whispers like a *tohk* through a ripe breadfruit. "That one is not Jangle Elwell."

All at once, a roar of voices like breakers on the reef washed through the courtroom. Judge Coleman, who had raised the taro pounder to pronounce me in contempt of court, banged it down several times to call the courtroom to order.

R.K. Asher grasped my extended hand firmly and whispered, "Sorry for the delay, Drake. But you've always liked a dramatic entry."

"Where were you?"

"We've already had a productive morning at the U.S. Embassy, with these two gentlemen from the FDIC, and our own Attorney General. It's all arranged, Drake. Jingle has full spectrum immunity in exchange for his testimony to the FDIC, and here. Ask him anything."

"What took so long?"

"It's a long story. First, I was delayed coming from Chuuk. Air Mike has some new security measures in place ever since they found out someone had stowed away on a night flight. Plus, our negotiations with the FDIC took longer than expected."

AG the AG, who had taken his seat, began to whisper loudly to Marielle Hargraves. Judge Coleman, who looked as if he had to wire his mouth shut after gaping at Jingle, piped up, "Will everyone but me know just what the hell is going on here?"

"Your Honor, I am R.K. Asher, Chuuk public defender office," R.K. stepped to the podium. "I am the attorney for the next witness, Jingle Treadwell. On behalf of my client, I apologize for us being late. Our delay was due to my need to protect my client, and the need of the Micronesian and US governments to obtain evidence that may help solve several serious crimes. Mr. Treadwell may be asked to testify on several different subjects, any of which could be in a manner that he might tend to incriminate himself. But we have negotiated for immunity for Mr. Treadwell. Mr. Anton Gedankanlos, our own Attorney General, negotiated for the Micronesian national government."

"It's true, Judge." AG the AG spoke on the record for the first time at trial.

"Mr. Treadwell is also given immunity from prosecution by the government of the United States, as these two gentlemen will confirm," Asher continued. "We finished negotiating this morning at the U.S. Embassy. It took longer than we expect, and the Ambassador had to say OK. While I will remain in court to assure my client's rights, please understand the immunity given to Mr. Treadwell allows him to testify on all subjects."

"I'm sure I don't know why the United States of America would be interested in this case, but so be it," said Coleman. He pointed a pen at R.K. "I expect you to keep your mouth shut during your client's testimony. I have little patience with those who speak in my courtroom without being recognized, and there have been too many voices raised already today. If anyone else speaks out of turn, I will hold him in contempt."

I called Jingle Treadwell a fourth time, and he was seated and sworn in. I wanted to ease Jingle into his testimony with simple questions at first. We had a lot to cover. Since the ever-perceptive Jasmina had already let the cat out of the bag, I began by asking Jingle to identify himself and his family.

"Jangle Elwell is, or was, my twin brother."

"Where were you two born?"

"On Kosrae, on Christmas Day, twenty-seven years ago. Our mother, who just passed to God in May, was Chuukese. She attended the mission school on Kosrae. The father of Jangle and myself was an American. I never met him. Mother said that the father had died in an accident before we were born."

"Did you and Jangle grow up together?"

"No. Jangle was adopted by a Kosraen family when we were both very small. After, Mother took me back to Chuuk and raised me there herself. Mother never married anyone again, and she never had another baby."

"Did you ever visit your brother while you were growing up?"

"Never. To me it was like Jangle disappeared, just like the father. I grew up in Faichuuk and went to high school on Weno. I never left Chuuk until I went to college. Jangle grew up on Kosrae. He went to the mainland for high school. It was later, when we both went to college where we met again. That was on Pohnpei, at COM, College of Micronesia." Jingle shook his head, and gave a glimmer of a smile. "I was really surprised to meet my own brother, my twin. We looked so much like each other."

"Did your resemblance fool anyone?"

335

"Everyone. We fooled everyone because we looked alike and no one knew that we were twins. Jangle let me borrow his clothes. He had plenty coming back from the States. They were a little tight in the shoulders, but I could fit them okay. We fooled everyone; the registrar, the instructors, even some other students."

"When you were attending college together here on Pohnpei, did you learn about Jangle's reputation?" I changed gears, hoping that Jingle would stay with me.

"Yes, and I am sad to say it, because my brother's reputation was bad. He was my brother, but he was no good. I grew up in Faichuuk, the place where people say rascals come from, but Jangle was the bad one. I did not like the people he stayed with, the Taro Patch Kids. I think they made a bad influence on his life. But I think living in the States made Jangle's eyes too big for things he could not have."

"Do you know if Jangle was involved in any crimes when you were both at the College of Micronesia?"

"Yes he was. I'm very sorry to say it. But those things were mostly 'small birds.' I don't know if Jangle did all of that, but some of the Taro Patch Kids would steal things and try to sell them. They also sold *maru*, I mean, marijuana, to other students. Those things were wrong, and I did not do them."

"Did you graduate from the College of Micronesia?"

"Yes. I graduated with honors. My degree was Accounting."

"What about Jangle?"

"He did not finish school. Jangle thought that college was boring. He said he wanted to make a lot of money and college was not helping him."

"Let's come back to your brother in a minute," I said, and stepped from behind the podium to get a better look at Jingle. "What did you do after you graduated?"

"I went back to Chuuk, my home island. I got a job, assistant bank manager at the Chuuk State branch of the Micronesian National Bank."

"What were your responsibilities there?"

"It changed. When I began I was learning and I had very little responsibility," Jingle opened his hands slightly, and leaned forward, as if eager to explain. "But I learned and then I was supervising our tellers, and then checking their cash counts each day. I also began with some small loans, and later big loans. When I learned more, I helped with some customers' -- excuse me, I mean the clients' questions. We always tried to call our customers, 'clients.' It makes them feel more important."

"How long did you work at the bank?"

"More than four years."

"Are you still working there?"

"No," Jingle looked down and closed his hands. "I was fired a week or ten days after the bank was robbed."

"Who fired you?"

"Our bank manager and vice, Mr. Charles Throckmorton; I mean vice-president," Jingle looked up again, but then put his eyes down. "He said I abandoned my job."

"Did you?"

Jingle brought his head up and fixed me with a gaze that could stop a shark. "If I did that, then I had good reasons."

"What were your good reasons?"

Jingle folded his hands together and sighed. "Mr. Throckmorton likes to gamble. He likes it very much. But I think he loses plenty of money. Mr. Throckmorton likes to gamble so much that he got me involved in gambling, too. I found my weakness. Everyone has a weakness, and gambling is mine. And I lost a lot of money when I gambled. I lost more money than I could make in one whole year. If I saved every dollar I earned at my job and spent no money, I would still not have enough money to cover what I lost when I was gambling."

"But what about Throckmorton? Did he win or did he lose?"

"I think Mr. Throckmorton lost even more than I did. He was gambling much longer than I was. But Mr. Throckmorton could cover his losses from his job. I do not think that he actually took money from the bank, but he would loan money from the bank to the people he owed money to from gambling. Mr. Throckmorton would make them a loan for what he owed them, but he would never ask them to pay back the money. Then he would write it off on the books of the bank as a bad loan."

A ripple of whispers radiated through the gallery, as if the locals' suspicions of bankers' shenanigans had been confirmed.

"Is this what you told to the men from the United States government who you came with today?" I walked past the defense table and gestured up the aisle.

Jingle arched his eyebrows to where the two Americans sat. "Yes, to the inspectors from the FDIC."

"You said you lost more money than you could make in a year? How were you going to pay it back?"

"When I started losing money I just thought it was just a short, unlucky time, and that I would win some more money and pay everyone back. But then I began to think that I would never make the money back. I started trying too hard, staying with hands that I should have folded. Mr. Throckmorton knew everyone involved in the gambling. He went to You-Me-Now Togetherness Bar on Weno. He knew the people who ran the gambling cruise on Guam. And when he went to the casino on Tinian, they treat him like he was an old friend. So Mr. Throckmorton told me he knew how to help me. He started by doing for me the same thing he did for himself, making a false loan to cover one of my gambling debts. I did not know he did this until later."

I let Jingle's answer dangle for a moment. The gallery whispers grew louder, and Coleman impatiently called for order.

I turned again to Jingle. "Was it enough to cover all of your gambling losses?"

"No. My biggest loss was to some gamblers from Hong Kong who ran a crooked card game on Guam. After the game, I owed them $6,000, and when their interest was added to that, I ended up owing them more than $10,000. The interest has to be paid every week, or they will send someone to cut your face or break your arms, maybe do something bad to your family. Mr. Throckmorton called that interest the 'vig.' He said they will send some very strong guys to collect it. The vig is illegal. But what they said I owed them I could not make in one whole year of working."

"Could your mother or brother help you?"

"No. I would not ask my brother. I know where his money comes from," Jingle shook his head. "And Mother, I did not ask her because she has no money, and anyway she was very sick. She asked me to bring my brother to see her before she dies. I sent a message to Jangle saying that our Mother is very sick and she wants you to come to see her.

339

Jangle came from Pohnpei and stayed for a while in Chuuk. Sometimes he stayed in our village; sometimes he stayed with some people on Weno. I think he was looking for some angle he could run. Then our Mother died and we buried her."

I paused for a moment to let Jingle gather his thoughts. "What happened next? Did Jangle go back to Pohnpei?"

"Not right away. Not until after the bank where I worked was robbed."

"What do you know about the bank robbery at the MNB?"

"Plenty. The plan to rob the bank was first brought up by Mr. Throckmorton."

"That's a lie!" Someone shouted from the gallery. I turned to see Throckmorton on his feet in the rear of the courtroom. "Can't you see he's lying to keep himself from going to prison?"

"Order! Order in the court." Judge Coleman groped about for his taro pounder. "What do you people think this is, open mike night at the Blue Magic? Another outburst like that from anyone, and I mean anyone, and there will be serious circumstances."

Throckmorton sat. From the defense table I could hear him grumble to a neighbor.

I noticed the Americans who had entered the courtroom with R.K. Asher lean forward to whisper to him. R.K. nodded. Then one of them stood and walked to the courtroom doors to stand and wait. He pulled a sheaf of papers from his jacket pocket, rolled them into a tube, and patted his left palm, glancing now and then at Throckmorton.

I turned back to Jingle. "Is what you just said a lie?"

"No. It's all true, God's truth. Mr. Charles Throckmorton came up with the plan to rob the bank to pay off both of our gambling debts. Mr. Throckmorton owed money to those Hong Kong gamblers, too, plenty of money, maybe more than what I owed. I think it was more than he could pay by using his old program of loaning money to people he owed money to, people who would never repay those loans. Mr. Throckmorton called his program 'the Dillinger plan.'"

"Why call it 'Dillinger?'"

"How much American history do you remember, Mr. Burnham? John Dillinger was the big bank robber of the 1930's, Public Enemy Number One. But many people in America loved John Dillinger. Why was that? It was because John Dillinger was robbing the banks who were robbing the people. The banks were taking away the people's land and their homes to pay debts that they could not pay. But what Mr. Throckmorton said was that Dillinger was also working in secret with some bankers he robbed. If the bank had a big loss, a bad loan, or something that the bank could not cover, a manager might ask Dillinger to come and rob the bank. Dillinger could take whatever cash he found at the bank, maybe only one or three thousand dollars, and the manager would guarantee that Dillinger would be safe. No one would shoot at him; no one would run to the police. He would get away. The bank manager would then tell the police that John Dillinger robbed the bank and took ten thousand dollars. But Dillinger only took maybe one thousand dollars. The bank manager would say Dillinger took more to cover the big loss or the bad loans. The bank manager could blame Dillinger for a loss that was due to the bank manager making a bad loan. That's why John Dillinger was a successful bank robber."

"This 1930's conspiracy theory is fascinating, although as Miss Hargraves should have noted by now, it consists of speculation and hearsay," Coleman folded his arms across his chest and leaned back in his chair.

"I move to strike the last testimony as speculative and hearsay," Marielle's objection echoed Coleman's comment. AG the AG glared at her and whispered urgently when she took her seat.

"Overruled," said Coleman. "But I question the relevance of this narrative."

"Patience, Your Honor," I said. "Mr. Treadwell's testimony may have more twists than a mangrove root. But it will explain much, perhaps everything."

I turned and nodded to Jingle. "Go on."

"Mr. Throckmorton came up with the 'Dillinger' plan, we could arrange with someone to rob the Micronesian National Bank, and the bank robber could take all the cash he found there. But before the bank was going to be robbed, Mr. Throckmorton would take cash equal to all the amounts we both owed to the Hong Kong gamblers. He would then fly to Guam and pay off our debts. After the robbery, Mr. Throckmorton would report all the money was missing, including the money that he took before the bank was robbed."

"He's lying, Judge." Throckmorton was back on his feet.

"Order," Coleman glared at Throckmorton. "I've warned you, sir, to keep quiet. One more word from you, a whisper, and you will be in contempt."

"Hey, I have the right to be here," Throckmorton insisted, and held up a sheet of paper. "In fact, I was subpoenaed to come to court today."

"Who subpoenaed this man?" Coleman's eyes blazed from me to Marielle and back. I admitted it was me.

"Is this another stunt, Mr. Burnham? I will not have this courtroom turned into a three-ring circus."

"Judge, I'd be a goddamn fool to interrupt my own witness."

Kazuo Olopai jumped to his feet. "Drake, do not take the Lord's name in vain."

A chuckle reverberated through the gallery.

"Order." Coleman banged his taro pounder until it was the only sound left in the courtroom. He pointed it at Throckmorton. "You sir, have been warned. Mr. Burnham, continue your examination, pronto."

"Mr. Treadwell," I nodded to Jingle. "You were saying?"

"It would so be easy to rob the bank. The MNB does not have good security. Some clerks leave the vault unlocked at night so they won't have to open it in the morning."

"Did the plan call for a daylight robbery, like Dillinger?"

"No. An island is not like the States. You cannot rob a bank on an island and drive to another state. Where would a bank robber go on an island? Mr. Throckmorton had it all figured out. He wanted a burglary, maybe through the small back window to the bank. He wanted it on a Friday, after dark, when there was a night flight to Guam, but not on a payday Friday when more people would be out. Mr. Throckmorton planned it very carefully. The only thing he didn't have was someone to do the job. Mr. Throckmorton asked me if there was someone I trusted. I am very sad to say I thought of my brother, Jangle. He was on-island to visit our Mother, and stayed for her funeral because she died."

"So you told Throckmorton about your brother?"

343

"Mr. Throckmorton asked me if I trusted Jangle. I said to him, I trust him like I trust my brother."

"Did Throckmorton know that Jangle was your twin brother?"

"No. Mr. Throckmorton said he did not want to know anything about the person who would rob the bank. He wanted to have, I think he called it 'plausible deniability.'"

"It's all lies." Throckmorton was on his feet again in the back row. "He's the one who robbed the bank. I had nothing to do with it."

"Order! Bailiff, remand that man to custody for contempt." Coleman was all action when courtroom decorum was at stake. "Clap him in irons."

Pietro and one of the DSI agents rushed to the back of the courtroom to corral Throckmorton. When all three walked by, the American waiting by the door handed the bank manager the rolled-up papers.

In the meantime, the other American, sitting behind Reddy Asher, stood. "Your Honor, if I may be recognized?"

"Who the hell are you?" Coleman said.

"My name is Russell Johnson, and my colleague near the door is Roy Hinkley. We're attorneys and investigators for the Federal Deposit Insurance Corporation in Washington DC. We humbly ask that the Court hold the man you just ordered arrested, Charles Throckmorton, as a material witness to our investigation."

"Very well. So ordered. Mr. Johnson, Mr. Hinkley, welcome to Micronesia. Now sit down and shut up." Coleman turned to glare at me. "Continue, Mr. Burnham."

I said to Jingle, "You were saying that Throckmorton wanted 'deniability?'"

"Yes. Throckmorton wanted to know when the job would be done, so he could take the money out just before then. He wanted it to happen after the close of business on a Friday, but not a Payday Friday. He wanted to have an idea of how the bank was to be robbed. But Throckmorton didn't want to know who would do the job. He said the least that each person knows the better."

"So you told Jangle?"

"Yes, I am very sorry to say. I asked Jangle if he would rob the bank. Jangle laughed when I asked him. He said it was like a gift from heaven. Then Jangle said he was having some 'cash flow' problems, too. He said one of the Taro Patch Kids was arrested in Palau coming from the Philippines with *shabu* and that he had to pay some Filipinos $15,000, which was money he didn't have. He asked me how much money there was in the bank. I told him I didn't know, that it depended on how much cash was taken out the week before, like whether there would be a holiday where people would want money, or the first of the month when social security checks would come out."

"How much money could there be?"

"Maybe $25,000. Maybe less."

"What was Jangle's reaction?"

"He said it was perfect. If there was that much money, we could both pay what we owed, me to the gamblers, Jangle to the Manila Syndicate."

"Did Jangle mention whether the Syndicate sent someone to collect?"

"He told me that the Syndicate had sent two guys to set up a drug lab on Pohnpei, that they wanted to see if they could make *shabu* in the jungle on the other side of the island. But Jangle said he thought the two guys were also on-island to make sure he paid for the missing shipment, the one that got stopped in Palau."

"Did Jangle call those two guys 'The Operator?'"

"Not then, but later."

"What happened with the bank robbery?"

"Jangle wanted to know all about the plan, and all about the bank. I could tell Jangle everything I knew about the bank, but I needed to ask Mr. Throckmorton what were the plans for the bank robbery. Mr. Throckmorton began to get very angry with me. He said I ask too many questions and I would know the whole plan before too long. Jangle was getting angry, too. He said he was the one taking all the risks and he wanted to know what he was getting into. I was stuck in the middle, and it got so bad I began to wish that it would not happen, that the bank would not be robbed. But one morning, I saw those Hong Kong gamblers in Mr. Throckmorton's office. He was whiter than any American when they left his office and I knew it would happen soon. After they left, Mr. Throckmorton said, 'we do it this Friday.'"

"Were you ready?"

"I was very frightened when Mr. Throckmorton said that, but all I had to do was tell Jangle. Mr. Throckmorton said he sent a request for extra cash to the Bank of Guam branch in Chuuk to make sure there was plenty in the branch. I told Jangle. He thought the timing was perfect and he went to buy a ticket for that Friday's night flight back to Pohnpei. On that Friday, Jangle told me to say I had a baseball game at lunchtime, but to meet him instead. Jangle told me there is a change of plans because he did not trust Throckmorton. Jangle said he thought that Throckmorton was going to take all the money and leave us only pennies. I didn't say anything because I knew that's what Throckmorton was going to do. Jangle said he would take the money first, before Mr. Throckmorton, and we would split it. Jangle told me to meet him later one half hour before the night flight left for Pohnpei. I am sad to say I agreed because I needed the money."

"What happened at your lunch with Jangle the day of the robbery?"

"We switch off our clothes, just like at College of Micronesia. We would switch clothes to make Mr. Throckmorton think Jangle is Jingle. So we changed our clothes. When we met later, Jangle just laughed and said everyone at the bank thought that Jangle was me; the tellers, the customers, I mean the clients, and, Mr. Throckmorton."

"What about your hand? Jangle had a birth defect; you don't."

"Jangle wrapped some bandages around his hand so that no one could see that it was different from mine," Jingle held up his left hand and mimicked wrapping it in gauze. "Jangle said if anyone asked he would say he cut it playing baseball."

"What happened next?"

Jangle told me that Mr. Throckmorton said loud enough for everyone to hear, 'Don't forget to lock the safe when you leave.' That was Mr. Throckmorton's signal. Jangle said he just nodded."

"That was Throckmorton's signal for what?"

"To leave the safe open. At the end of the day, when the tellers are finished and have counted up all their money, it should go back in the safe. It's my job to make sure the cash boxes are put in the safe, all of them, even the petty cash box from my desk. Jangle did my job on that Friday, maybe better than I do it. But instead of putting the money in the safe, Jangle put all the money into a gym bag he left at my desk. At the end of the day, Jangle and Mr. Throckmorton left the building

347

together. Jangle said Throckmorton told him he would come back after dark. Mr. Throckmorton had a ticket on the night flight to Guam and he told Jangle he would take the money to Guam and pay off our debts."

"Wouldn't Mr. Throckmorton have to declare the money he was bringing into the United States when he landed at Guam?"

"Yes, but it didn't matter. Mr. Throckmorton is a bank manager. He could carry that much cash to deposit in Guam. It wasn't the first time he would do that.

"Did Throckmorton tell Jangle anything else?"

"Jangle told me that Mr. Throckmorton said he loosened the air conditioner in the back window at the bank. The robber should pull the air conditioner out when the night flight left. The sound of the jet engine would cover any sound. Jangle said he told Mr. Throckmorton that it was arranged. Jangle was laughing inside when he said it, because Jangle already had all the money. It was in the gym bag he carried when they left."

"Did you meet Jangle before he left for Pohnpei?"

"Yes. I asked Jangle, where is the money? He said, 'don't worry, brother. The money is going to Pohnpei.' Going to Pohnpei, I said. You're crazy to take that money with you. What if your bag is lost? Jangle just laughed. 'Who said it was in my check baggage?' I said, you can't carry that on with you. The police will search you. Jangle said 'You're so right. Good thing the money is going another way.' That's when he told me about my cooler. He was so proud of the way he changed my cooler, cutting out the inside and taking out the insulation. Jangle said he would buy me a new cooler with rope handles and a scale for measuring fish on the lid. Jangle put the money in that, and gave it to someone he trusted to take it by ship to Pohnpei."

"But FSM Customs searched Jangle's friend and found the money when he got to Pohnpei," I said. "Jangle never got the money back."

"I never got my share of the money either. I was angry at Jangle for sending the money away to Pohnpei. Mr. Throckmorton was going to pay off the Hong Kong gamblers with that money. Jangle said, 'we are in the same canoe, brother. If I don't pay the Manila Syndicate they will kill me. Why don't you tell that to Throckmorton, because he double-crossed us first.' Jangle said he didn't get enough money to pay what he owed to the Syndicate and what I owed to the gamblers. He said Mr. Throckmorton must have taken some money first."

"Did you believe Jangle?"

"At first I did, because I didn't think that my own brother would double-cross me. But when I met Mr. Throckmorton later, he said the one who robbed the bank took everything, even the coins."

I had to make a statement of fact in the guise of a question, and hoped that Marielle would not object. "But in the bank robbery case, the government had no coins to use in evidence."

Marielle gazed at the ceiling, and said nothing.

"That's true," Jingle answered. "Jangle said he left all the coins at the bank, because he didn't want the gym bag to jingle when he left the bank that day."

"But the affidavit by Mr. Throckmorton said all the money was taken, even the coins." I thought of Throckmorton's pickle jar.

Marielle roused herself to object. "Lack of foundation, Your Honor."

"Overruled," Coleman waved her off. "The Court will take notice of the affidavit, Miss Hargraves. You yourself brought the affidavit to my attention."

Coleman ruled in my favor? Things were getting better all the time. But I turned back to Jingle.

"Jangle said he is leaving, and we both heard the night flight landing. Jangle went over to the airport. I went with him and asked can I get on that flight, but I had no money. I think it turned out best I missed the flight, because Mr. Throckmorton would have called the police on me if I didn't meet him later that night. He was very angry when we met, because there was no money left at the bank when he got there. The air conditioner was taken out of the back window and no money was left inside. Mr. Throckmorton said the bank robber I found had double-crossed us and that the money we needed to pay the Hong Kong gamblers was gone. He canceled his flight to Guam, and said he called to try to explain that he couldn't make our payment. He said to me he would go to You-Me's and try to win enough gambling to pay the vig.

"Mr. Throckmorton knew what he was doing. He let the tellers find out about the bank robbery on Monday morning, and he acted like he was in shock when he went into the bank building. He reported it to the police, showed them the air conditioner, and told them the robbers must have come in through the back window. But that window was very small. Only the smallest guy could fit into it. Lucky for me, I am too big for that, or maybe the police would question me."

"What did you do, Jingle?"

"I did not know what to do. I thought that if the police came to ask me questions that I would tell them the truth, so I went back to my village on the other side of the lagoon, to think about what to do. When

I was absent from work for three days, the bank fired me. But the police never came to ask me anything. So I decided to come to Pohnpei to take the money from my brother and give it back to the bank, to the MNB. I asked my village chief if he could give me some money to go to Pohnpei. But all the money my chief could get was just enough for me to take the next ship, not fly on Air Mike. So I sailed to Pohnpei."

"You said Jangle sent the money to Pohnpei with someone that he trusted. Did you meet that someone?"

"Yes. His name is Entis Robert, from Pingelap. He's a very small guy from a very small island. Jangle told Entis to go move the air conditioner from back window to the bank, which I think he did."

"Do you think that Entis Robert would be small enough to crawl through the back window of the bank?"

"I don't know. It would be a very tight fit for anyone."

"Do you think that Jangle was hedging his bet? That if the police thought the bank was robbed through the back window that Jangle wouldn't be a suspect because he was too big to fit, but that he had someone ready-made to take the fall for him?"

"Objection." Marielle didn't bother to get to her feet. "Leading question."

"Overruled," Coleman leaned toward the witness box. "I'll have the witness finish his story."

Jingle answered my question, but looked up at Maximum Max. "I thought my brother would double-cross anyone."

I let that one sink in for a moment, then asked Jingle when he got to Pohnpei.

"I came on the ship in the week before Jangle was killed. I stayed with some Chuukese people in Sokehs. That was a good spot

351

because I wanted to be near to the Taro Patch, and Jangle, but not any place where other people could see me. The Chuukese people I stayed with told me the bad news, that Jangle was arrested for robbing the bank in Chuuk, and that the money was found in his cooler. I went right away to go see Jangle. He was already out from jail on bail. Jangle told me the police took all the money, so he couldn't pay the Manila Syndicate or the Hong Kong gamblers. I asked if he had any more money, like maybe he could sell that new truck. I even said I would go with him to the bank to convince them to use the truck as collateral for a loan. Jangle was really laughing. He said 'I was just arrested for robbing a bank. Who will loan money to a bank robber?' Jangle told me not to worry. He will find a way to get us both out of trouble."

The courtroom had grown very quiet. I could see Judge Coleman, the bailiff and clerks, the Attorney General, by now even Marielle, paying close attention to Jingle's testimony. I could sense the quiet attention of everyone in the gallery. It was time to keep the questions simple, and let Jingle tell the story. I asked what happened.

"One night, one of Jangle's friends came to where I was staying in Sokehs and told me that Jangle wanted to see me right away. He was at Daosokele. So I borrowed some money from the good Chuukese people and took a taxi out to the Sand Sushi bar. Jangle's truck, the big, black one, was the only one in the parking lot. I went down to the bar. It's a long walk in the dark, and I saw Jangle, all alone down by the river, sitting at a table with one kerosene lantern. He was looking at the bridge and drinking *sakau*. That was funny, because I never saw Jangle drinking *sakau* before. Jangle asked me if I wanted some, but I said no. I asked him what we were going to do. If I didn't give the Hong Kong gamblers the money they would kill me.

"Jangle said, 'the same is true for me. If I don't give the Syndicate fifteen thousand dollars, they will kill me. But don't worry, brother. Our troubles will soon be over. The gamblers and the Syndicate are coming here to the Sand Sushi tonight.' I almost screamed at Jangle when he said that. They will kill us both, I said. 'No,' Jangle said. 'They will not kill us. They just want to scare us to give them money.' I asked Jangle what should we tell them. Jangle said, 'We won't say anything. I will. Tell me, brother. Do the Hong Kong gamblers know that you have a twin brother? Do they know anything about me?' I said no. Jangle said, 'And the Syndicate does not know I have a twin brother. How would they know? I use a Kosrae name. You use a Chuuk name. Only Mother knows we are twins and she is in heaven. Go hide behind the bar. I'll tell the Hong Kong people I am you. The Syndicate will think I am me. That way only one of us will be in trouble, and it might as well be me.'"

"So Jangle would try to fool others that he was you?"

"Yes. I was afraid, but I thought there might be a chance of it working. I crouch down behind the bar out of sight, but in a spot where I could see out to Jangle's table through a crack. Jangle 'offed' the electricity and the whole bar went dark except for the kerosene lantern on Jangle's table. After a while I heard car doors slam, and then another car came and I heard more car doors. It was a clear night, and the moon was bright enough for anyone to see the way on the path to the bar. I heard some voices in a language I don't know, then I heard some other voices I knew were speaking Chinese. Then I could see who had come when they went to Jangle's table. First was two Filipino guys, and then I saw the three Hong Kong gamblers."

"Did you recognize any of them? Had you seen any of them before?"

"Yes. I could see one of the Chinese guys was Mr. Aang. I remember him from a crooked card game on Guam. He was also at the casino on Tinian, and he knew Mr. Throckmorton. I saw the two big guys, the ones who came to Mr. Throckmorton's office the week before, the day the bank was robbed. I did not recognize the other two guys, but after what happened I will never forget their faces."

"What happened?"

"Jangle said welcome to Daosokele and asked if they want some *sakau*. No one answered him. But then one of the Filipinos said 'Where is our money? We waited long enough.' Then one of the Hong Kong guys said to the Filipinos 'Your money? This guy owes us ten thousand dollars.' The Filipinos said back to the Hong Kong guys, 'He owes us fifteen thousand dollars.' I think Jangle was trying to get them to fight each other, then maybe he could get away. It looked like it was going to work when one of the Filipinos pulled a gun out of his pants. Then one of the Hong Kong guys did the same thing. But then they both turn the guns on Jangle.

"Jangle said, 'Now don't be too quick. If someone shoots me then no one gets the money.' Jangle said, 'Here's the problem. You say I owe you ten thousand, and you say I owe you fifteen thousand. But I don't have twenty-five. But maybe I know where the money is, enough money to pay all of you.' The Filipinos asked where. Jangle said in the evidence room at DSI in Palikir. How are we supposed to get it out from there, they said. 'Maybe you could break in,' Jangle said. 'That's what they said I did.' Then one Filipino guy said 'You are so good at breaking in, why don't you go get it for us?' But the Hong Kong guy said 'Wait. Do you have enough money to pay the vig?' Jangle said he did, but it wasn't here, but it was nearby. He said he would drive and go get it. Then one of the Hong Kong guys said 'No. We all go together.' Jangle said the money was up at the bridge, and he pointed to the Green River bridge."

"Did Jangle really have any money hidden up there?"

"I don't think so. I think he wanted to get those guys away from the bar, and from me. Jangle turned off the lantern, and they all left the bar. I waited behind the bar until I heard the car doors close and the cars start before coming out. I went down from the bar to the level by the river. I could see the bridge very clearly. That's where it happened."

"Where what happened?"

Jingle pushed his hands through his hair, and looked straight at me. "Where they killed my brother. I saw my own brother, my twin brother being murdered."

"Jingle, I'm sorry. But I have to ask what you saw."

Jingle clenched his jaw, and continued. "I could see the bridge clearly, and the two cars stopped on it. Jangle must have been in the car with the Filipinos in front, and the Hong Kong car was behind. Both cars stopped and everyone got out except the older Hong Kong guy, Mr. Aang. Jangle went and leaned over the bridge, like he was grabbing for something. Then he straightened up and said 'It's gone. Maybe it fell in the river. I'll go swim for it.' And then Jangle stood up on the barrier to the bridge like he was going to go jump in."

"Why did he do that?"

"I don't know. Maybe Jangle thought he could get away from them. But then the one Hong Kong guy started talking to Jangle and he got off the barrier. I saw one of the Filipinos go open the trunk of his car and pull out a Casio keyboard. I thought, wait, are they going to play music? But then I saw him swing the keyboard like a baseball bat and hit Jangle in the head. When that happened it was like I could feel it and I almost shouted to my brother. Jangle fell, but then he stood up like he was going to get on the barrier to the bridge again. But he was holding his head. Then someone started shooting, I don't know who started, but I heard a gun, a very loud bang, then a small sound like pop, pop, pop, and then another loud bang. I looked and one of the Hong Kong guys was shooting and so was one of the Filipinos. I shouted no, and I felt like the bullets were hitting me. Then I saw Jangle falling and both of them were still shooting him. I could not believe it, but I saw those two – one Hong Kong guy and one of the Filipinos – murder my brother. Then the Filipinos picked up Jangle and dropped him in the river. I tried to see my brother in the water, to see if he was still alive, but I could not see him."

"What did you do then, Jingle?"

"I looked up to make sure that no one on the bridge saw me. I saw the Filipinos and the Hong Kong guys get into their cars and turn and drive away very fast. I went back to the river to see if I could find Jangle's body, but I could not see anything. Then I waited in the dark for a long time, two hours maybe. I was in shock because of what I saw. I thought maybe someone heard the shooting and would call the police. But no police ever came. Before I knew it, I could see the light coming from the east and I knew the day was coming. I decided to leave. I went to Jangle's truck, the new, black one. I found the keys in the ashtray. I drove back to the Taro Patch and left the truck and walked from there to Sokehs. I wish I could have walked all the way back to Chuuk."

"But you did go back to Chuuk."

356

"Yes. I had my return ticket on any FSM Transportation ship. So I took the Kaselehlia and said goodbye to Pohnpei and goodbye to my brother."

"You never went to the police?"

"No. I was afraid. I thought that if I stayed quiet then those Hong Kong guys would think they killed me by killing Jangle, and I didn't want the Filipino guys to see me and think I was Jangle. So I did not tell anyone."

I thanked Jingle and sat down. Roberta leaned over the railing to pat me on the back. The crowded courtroom was silent. Senators and clerks had stopped to listen, and even the Palikir maintenance crew gathered outside beneath the eaves. The only sound was a soft rain, and the urgent whispering at the prosecutor's table between AG the AG and Marielle Hargraves. Marielle's face ripened into an angry red. Her lips were pulled thin and tight when the Attorney General himself rose to say that the government would not cross-examine Jingle Treadwell.

Judge Coleman then dismissed my surprise witness. Jingle stood carefully and stepped from the witness box slowly, like a boxer pummeled for twelve rounds. R.K. shook Jingle's hand gently when he came by the defense table, then put an arm about his shoulder and walked him from the courtroom.

It was only when the double doors swung shut behind the pair that the murmur started, first low and under breath, then gradually louder. Each person in the courtroom turned to a neighbor, left and right, in front and behind, and whispered about what they had just heard. It was then that I knew I had the gallery. They might have been downright hostile to me at the end of the government's case. But their sentiments had swung around on the testimony of just one witness.

Maximum Max wouldn't dare rule against me today. He'd have a riot on his hands. Coleman, I thought sagely, let the rumble of voices grow and then recede like a surging wave over the reef before calling for order. He asked me to call my next witness. "The defense rests."

CHAPTER TWENTY-FIVE

"In one sense, the government's case was dead on." I began my closing argument to Judge Coleman on Friday morning in a packed courtroom.

"Jangle Elwell was murdered for money. But it wasn't me who killed Jangle Elwell, and it wasn't for the pittance he may have owed for what little I had done to defend a contempt of court charge. No. Jangle was murdered for considerably more money, fifteen grand, the amount for which he was in hock to the Manila Syndicate, plus the ten thousand dollars that his twin brother owed to some Hong Kong gamblers."

Maximum Max must have been feeling generous. He had given me a half hour for my closing argument, twice the fifteen-minutes he usually cedes to defense counsel. Marielle Hargraves had elected to give the government's closing last, so I was at the podium first.

"The government did well to prove that fact of death, the corpus delecti," - I nodded to Kazuo Olopai who scribbled a note to himself about the Latin term I'd used - "as well as the cause of Jangle's death. Mario Perez testified that Jangle suffered fatal gunshot wounds from two different handguns. Jangle got the double special, and not the one on the menu at Joyful Lunch. The weapons used, based on the slugs Doctor Perez recovered from Jangle's body, were a .38 caliber police special, and a small caliber Saturday Night Special."

After Jingle testified, I had to consider what to do if the government offered to dismiss outright, but Marielle and the Attorney General said nothing. AG the AG may have leaned that way, and perhaps I would have accepted an offer, if only to keep Judge Coleman out of the decision. But I wanted an acquittal. More than a reasonable doubt, I wanted no doubt whatsoever. Without it, I could still be deemed persona non grata, destined like OJ to wander the earth in search of the real killers. I had come this far, and it would be singularly satisfying to have Maximum Max pronounce a judgment of acquittal.

"But the government's attempts to hang a motive on me do not hold water," I continued. "And their attempt to link me to one possible murder weapon can only be seen as a tissue of lies.

"Take the so-called first motivation, the suggestion that I had a motive to kill Jangle Elwell because he struck Utticus Uziah. Mr. Uziah is a grown man, a former DSI trainee who can certainly take care of himself. I am not his protector, not his guardian angel, and not his father." That last one got a chuckle from the local *papas* in the gallery. "In fact, there is nothing to this so-called first motivation other than a prosecutor's speculation that I might have acted this way.

"Second was the imagined motivation that I had an argument with Jangle over my fees for representing him. The Court well knows that I was to be, and actually was paid by the Supreme Court out of its conflict case fund for representing Jangle on the bank robbery charge. Your Honor reviewed the bill I submitted on that conflict case. The Court knows were I to submit a bill for defending Jangle on the contempt charge, I would be paid out of that same fund. That leaves the question of whether Jangle controlled me by dangling case referrals.

Note that the prosecution's witness on this point, Daniel Warheit, did not testify that he told me that Jangle told him to bring his brother's case to me, then to take it away. No evidence was admitted to show that I knew about Jangle's behind-the-curtains manipulation. I knew nothing of it, and I cannot be motivated to act by something for which I had no knowledge. Again, the second motivation is nothing more than a prosecutor's speculation.

"Third is the speculated motivation that I was insanely jealous over Jangle's attentions to my secretary, Jasmina Solomon. Let's examine this in more detail. The government's case is based on the supposition that I am in love with Jasmina because I asked her out, once, and several years ago, long before I became her employer. Nothing more. If that is the case, then there are many more who have the same motivation. I am neither the first, nor will I be the last, to ask out Jasmina Solomon. The government cast its net wide on that one, and must attribute the same motivation to any of a number of people, some of whom may be in this courtroom today."

I stopped to fix Judge Coleman with an unblinking stare. After a long moment, or maybe just four seconds, he looked away.

"Next is the imagined speculation that I am in love with my secretary because I made up a nickname for her. But Jasmina herself testified that the source of that nickname, 'Jazz,' is the first syllable of her name, 'Jasmina.' And other witnesses have testified to my unfortunate tendency to make up nicknames for others as well. Utticus Uzziah knows I call him 'Double-U.' Kazuo Olopai testified that I nicknamed him 'Katsuo' for the big-eye tuna. Doctor Perez said I nicknamed him 'Mario Speedwagon.' But the government does not suggest that by nicknaming them, I am in love with Dr. Perez or Kazuo Olopai. So that speculation falls by the wayside as well."

I paused again to glance at my notes. Next was a proffer of evidence on Valentin Onan. Judge Coleman had asked counsel about rebuttal witnesses in a sidebar first thing that morning. I asked the Judge to have Susanna record the sidebar for the record. Maximum Max shrugged, then motioned his assent to the court reporter.

Marielle said she had no rebuttal witnesses, but reserved her right to call some if I called anyone to rebut portions of the government's case. I told the Judge that I had planned to call Valentin Onan, but could not because the Justice Ombudsman had removed himself from the island while under subpoena. I said I had no choice but to make an offer of proof about Valentin's early morning visit to the Pohnpei morgue. I then said I would recall Utticus Uziah to testify about whose zoris he saw outside Jasmina's house when I was on Kosrae. Maximum Max rumbled like an awakening volcano, but said it would not be necessary for me to call either witness. Call me foolish, but I took the judge at his word. As we left the sidebar, Marielle asked me what Coleman meant by it. I just shook my head.

I continued with my closing statement. "And that brings me next to Rob Gerber, or Prescott R. Gerber, as his name appeared on the payroll of the Los Angeles County Sheriff's Department. As its surprise witness, the government trots out an accomplished liar. Mr. Gerber just couldn't help himself to embellish upon the story of how he found a weapon on Kosrae. But beyond lying, Gerber's search itself was illegal. His seizure of the weapon was illegal. His testimony must be disregarded and the physical evidence he identified, the handgun, cannot be considered.

"Not only does his testimony derive wholly from the illegal search and seizure, and is therefore the fruit of a poisonous tree; Gerber's testimony is inherently unreliable. He has shown himself to be a liar. Gerber has lied in circumstances similar to this to try to force a conviction. Not only has Mr. Gerber lied in court, he was actually prosecuted for perjury, and he copped a plea to obstruction of justice to avoid conviction for perjury. Gerber's testimony cannot be considered credible, even if you accept at face value his story of bouncing futons and gift-wrapped boxes that magically open themselves. So the prosecution's case is shown to be speculation and conjecture, when it is not an outright lie. The government did not prove a sufficient motivation, and did not link me with a weapon that may have been used to commit the crime.

"The Court must consider the uncontradicted testimony of the only eyewitness to the murder of Jangle Elwell, his twin brother, Jingle Treadwell. Jingle's testimony is particularly important, for it explains not only what happened to Jangle, but why.

"We can guess, as many have, that the Taro Patch Kids, led by Jangle Elwell, were already into smuggling, selling marijuana, and assorted petty crime. But Jangle wanted to move up to the big time. Jangle wanted to position the Taro Patch Kids as middlemen between those who manufacture methamphetamine in the Philippines, and the lucrative markets for 'ice' in Hawaii. Jangle began by getting a few shipments through Micronesia, probably by some gang members. But Jangle lost a shipment when one of his couriers was busted with ice, trying to come through Palau. The Manila Syndicate, unhappy about the loss, sent a couple of enforcers to Pohnpei to collect from the Taro Patch Kids for the lost shipment.

"Say what you will about the man, Jangle was an ace at negotiation. He managed to convince the enforcers, who came to Pohnpei posing as a band called 'The Operator,' to help him out in various ways, shaking down some of Jangle's own past-due accounts, and assisting in Jangle's assault on Utticus Uziah. Jangle almost had the enforcers sold on the next idea, that they could build their own meth lab, here on Pohnpei, making ice in the jungle. Why not? There's enough land and plenty of people who are willing to put up with some hardcore industrial pollution in exchange for say, a used pickup truck. But that experiment didn't fly. Jangle still owed the Syndicate, and the enforcers had itchy fingers.

"In the meantime – trouble coming in pairs – Jangle's brother, Jingle Treadwell, was in hock, too, for a smaller but, to a local, still considerable amount of money, the ten thousand dollars that he owed to some Hong Kong gamblers who had played him, not like a piano, but a Casio keyboard. These heavies knew the oldest game in poker; never give a sucker an even break. The gamblers were here on Pohnpei to set up a casino, and to collect on various accounts, mostly from those who extended themselves on credit on the poker machines at the You-Me's over on Chuuk. There they turned the screws on Jingle's boss, Mr. Charles Throckmorton, who had gambling losses of his own. Unlike Jingle, Throckmorton, as vice president of the Micronesian National Bank, was in a position to do something about it. Throckmorton had already set up a series of phony loans to pay down his debts, relying on a plausible inference, the reputation of Chuuk as the wastrel state. He would arrange to loan money to his creditors but he never asked them to repay the loans. The bank could then conceivably write off the bad debts.

"Throckmorton could take that stunt only so far. Soon his superiors would look into why his bad loans were far worse and far more numerous than at any other branch. So Throckmorton cooked the books, and when that wasn't enough, he hatched a scheme to pay off his biggest gambling debts and clean out all of the bad loans that he did not, or could not declare as such. Throckmorton came up with a plan. He would loot the bank he managed, and leave slim pickings for a local who would break and enter, making it look like the local took far more cash than he actually did. Throckmorton would then fly to Guam to meet with the Hong Kong heavies and pay off his, and one would hope, Jingle's debts. Although Throckmorton would have to declare that he was carrying more than ten thousand dollars in cash when he entered Guam, no one would think twice about it because he managed a bank.

"But Throckmorton had counted on the help of a trusting local. He instead saddled up with a person more devious than he. Jangle Elwell beat Throckmorton to the punch, taking the money from the bank before Throckmorton had the chance. Jangle, dressed up like his twin brother, Jingle Treadwell, took all of the money the afternoon before the evening Throckmorton planned to take the money. Jangle double-crossed Throckmorton, who thought he had not and would never meet his co-conspirator. Jangle was also doubly protected in his double cross. Throckmorton didn't know who he was and thought that whoever would rob the bank would go in through the tiny back window.

"Jangle might have gotten away with it. He spirited the money out of Chuuk in a manner unlikely to raise suspicions. He had already borrowed and modified his brother's, Jingle's, cooler, changed the markings to read "Jungle Cooler," hid the stolen money inside the lining, and then sent the package under guard to Pohnpei by alternate means.

You see Jangle knew he was likely to be searched. He couldn't carry the money himself. But two things went wrong, one because Jangle was in a hurry, and two, something Jangle did not predict.

"First, Jangle hurried. He had to get both the money and himself off of Chuuk before Throckmorton discovered the double-cross. Jangle didn't remove the distinctive MNB paper bands from the stacks of money he took from the bank. When the cash was found, anyone could tell that it was from the Micronesian National Bank. Jangle couldn't predict the other mistake, that his courier would be intercepted by a Kosraen Customs inspector here on Pohnpei, who knew that the courier, Entis Robert, was not Jangle. The Customs Inspector, Winston Sigraht, knew that a little shrimp of a guy from Pingelap, was not the tall, handsome Jangle Elwell from Kosrae. Sigraht's suspicions led to the discovery of the money.

"After all that, though, Jangle was still confident. He had someone in line ahead of him to take the fall. He had followed Throckmorton's plan far enough to place the blame on someone else. Jangle had sent Entis Robert to remove the air conditioner from the small back window at the Chuuk branch of the Micronesian National Bank, and Entis might be small enough to squeeze inside through that opening. And Entis was the one caught with the cash in his possession. Even if busted, there would be nothing hard to tie Jangle to the crime.

"But that still left Jangle in hock to the Syndicate. He might have tried to talk his way into a little more time. And according to Jingle, Jangle told the Syndicate where the money was. But at some point, Jangle decided that the jig was up. And that is when Jangle did the most unexpected thing. He gave up himself to save his brother. He ran the misdirection play one last time – as he did at College of

Micronesia and again at the MNB -- convincing the Hong Kong gamblers that he, Jangle, was his brother, Jingle, all the while keeping the enforcers from the Syndicate convinced that he was Jangle. It must have been a masterful performance.

"One thing is certain from the testimony of Jingle Treadwell, Jangle's twin brother. I did not kill Jangle Elwell. Jingle has testified without contradiction, and at grave peril to himself, that Jangle was killed when he was shot, by Hong Kong gamblers who believed Jangle Elwell was Jingle Treadwell, and by enforcers from the Manila Syndicate who knew Jangle Elwell was indeed Jangle Elwell, a Micronesian original. Doctor Perez testified that Jangle died from multiple gunshot wounds. The elements of the offense are established, but someone other than the defendant committed the offense. It was the Hong Kong gamblers who killed Jangle, thinking he was his twin brother. It was the Manila Syndicate who killed Jangle, knowing who he was. Twin brothers, twin debts, but only one death."

I paused a long moment to let it sink in.

"I therefore respectfully request that Your Honor render a verdict of not guilty of the crime with which I am charged, second degree murder, and that the Court then enter a judgment of acquittal."

I had Coleman painted into a corner. He could not in good conscience convict me. If he did, the conviction would be overturned on appeal. The vast weight of evidence stood for acquittal, and the direct, uncontradicted, eyewitness testimony of Jingle Treadwell smashed through the web of inference and circumstance that the prosecution had strung together. Even if Coleman had a notion to convict me, he'd face a riot. The gallery was with me. I could feel it.

Over at the prosecution table, Marielle Hargraves and the Attorney General were locked in a silent debate that seemed to be as much angry gestures and glares as words. Finally, Marielle slumped down into her chair, crossed her arms, and frowned. AG the AG stood and said only the third sentence he made on the record at trial. "The government will not make a closing argument."

"I find the defendant, Drake Burnham," Coleman spoke and then paused. His face contorted briefly. Finally he spat out, "Not guilty."

CHAPTER TWENTY-SIX

A sandy beach on Lenger Island, a lagoon island north of Kolonia, was the wedding site. A mercifully brief civil ceremony ensued, Judge Zacharias Omishima presiding. The Judge, being an island boy, couldn't help but sprinkle in references to the Almighty. It was a small ceremony, only forty or so people attending, and most of those were related to the bride. A few distant cousins who happened to live on Pohnpei represented the groom's family. The weather cooperated. The sun was out and the trade winds piled breakers in a sweet thunder onto the barrier reef north of the island.

Roberta and Spenser Ely attended, of course, as special guests of the groom. On behalf of her client, Entis Robert, Ms. Ely had convinced the national government to dismiss the charges of bank robbery, burglary, and receiving stolen property on condition that he plead no contest in Chuuk State Court to a charge of causing malicious mischief, by removing but not taking an air conditioner from the window at the Micronesian National Bank branch. Entis got no jail time, only probation. In exchange, Entis made strong oaths that he would return either to his home island of Pingelap or to studies at the College of Micronesia and that he would no longer associate with that group formerly known as the Taro Patch Kids. That latter condition was simple for Entis to do because the gang fell apart once Jangle was gone and the drama of the trial for his murder was over. The bad apples – the captain of the drive-bys, for example – were eventually jailed on smaller charges unrelated to the Taro Patch mainline. The rest just faded back to jobs, school, or their home islands.

Valentin Onan was back on Pohnpei within a week after the trial, with some cockamamie excuse as to why he had skipped the island after being served with a subpoena. I accepted his apology, but not his explanation. Judge Coleman made a show of 'disciplining' the Justice Ombudsman, docking him a week's take-home pay, after disbursements about a buck-fifty. Coleman was civil to me for a month or so, but then drifted back to form, suggesting at one point that he detected some smugness in my tone of voice, an attitude to which I feel entitled, frankly.

Charles "The Rock" Throckmorton cooled his heels in the DSI holding cell while the FDIC investigators pursued his extradition back to the States. Throckmorton did not oppose extradition, and I learned he later pleaded guilty in federal court to a variety of charges because he wanted to avoid re-extradition back to Micronesia to face charges of bank robbery, conspiracy to commit bank robbery, attempted grand theft, fraud, obstruction of justice, and perjury, plus a lingering charge of contempt of court. I thought Marielle was piling it on.

Requests were filed in the Philippines to extradite on charges of murder the two members of the band called "The Operator," but no one seriously thought that the pair would ever be located. An investigation based on the passports they presented showed one's would-be name to be that of a ten-year-old who lived in a Malakal highrise. The boy said someone had swapped his passport for an afternoon at a video game parlor. The other name was traced to a Baguio grave of someone who had died fifteen years ago. AG the AG assured me that even though they

370

would not find the two to extradite, each would probably end up badly. And I never managed to bill the pair for services rendered.

Extradition requests were also filed in the People's Republic of China for the two heavies involved in the shooting of brother Jangle. No such request was filed for Mr. Aang, immune from prosecution as a diplomat. But he was declared a persona non grata, not only in Micronesia, but in Guam, Saipan, and Tinian as well. The Tinian casino was soon sold to a Nevada consortium.

The bride looked splendid. She wore a simple, brightly colored muumuu, and a tiara of fresh flowers. The two-dozen *mwarmwars* around her neck gave her the look of a particularly comely Kentucky Derby winner. (I felt like offering her a seabiscuit.) A single, flawless hibiscus bloom was tucked behind her right ear. Jasmina beamed a high wattage smile throughout her day. The groom was quite spiffy. He wore his Sunday black pants and an immaculate white shirt, and sported several garlands of ylang-ylang. Jingle, too, smiled happily. He had a new job, on Pohnpei, but with generous leave that would permit the pair to travel to his home village in Chuuk and her family in the Marshall Islands as needed. And he was about to be married.

And me? I gave away the bride, Jasmina. And I couldn't be happier.

* * * * *

Ruul, Yap, Federated States of Micronesia

Oakland, California

Paris, France

San Francisco, California

371

GLOSSARY

ahset – white person (Kosrae)

benjo – toilet (Japan)

ekewo – good evening (Kosrae)

etawi – faithful (Kosrae)

fal – enough (Kosrae)

hai – yes (Japan)

haole – white person [pejorative] (Hawaiʻi)

kaselehlia – greetings, aloha (Pohnpei)

lava lava – sarong (Samoa)

GLOSSARY

mabuhay – long life (Philippines)

mwarmwar – lei (Kosrae)

maru – marijuana (Japan)

menlau – thank you (Pohnpei)

nahs – cook shed (Pohnpei)

nice fasr – "Hey good looking" (Kosrae)

nice kom – "Hey beautiful" (Kosrae)

Nina – mother (Kosrae)

pakalolo – marijuana (Hawai'i)

Papa – father (Kosrae)

sakau – kava (Pohnpei)

GLOSSARY

seppuku – ritual suicide (Japan)

shabu – methamphetamine (Philippines)

tohk – wooden cleaver (Kosrae)

tuba – palm wine (Philippines)

uhm – earth oven (Kosrae)

zoris – sandals, flip flops (Japan)